Praise for Cocoon

"The twists and absurdities of Chinese history circle each other across time. In the most personal way, *Cocoon* charts a pathway through individual and collective memory, through the most hidden fissures and bonds between young people and their parents. With exquisite, precise, and lyrical language, the novel sets the benchmark for younger authors seeking to write about history and individuals, proving once again that Zhang Yueran's writing surpasses and distinguishes itself from that of her contemporaries."
YAN LIANKE

"An irresistible siren-song of a novel by one of our most original voices … A grandfather lies in a coma, his brain destroyed by a nail, and two friends reach across time and the gaps between them to unravel the mystery of that nail, a mystery that has haunted and tormented both their families. A transcendent novel that suggests that family secrets and family crimes are the nation from which none of us can ever fully escape."
JUNOT DÍAZ

"We in the West know so little about what's really going on in China below the surface of public events, but now there is big news: the advent of Zhang Yueran, one of the finest young writers of her generation. *Cocoon* is a deft, brilliant piece of writing in two voices—a clarion call. Her novel should find a huge and sympathetic audience in the English language."
JAY PARINI, author of *Borges and Me*

"History, the most problematic of China's intergenerational connections. The shadows of a chaotic, confusing past, still just within reach, resonating in a bleak contemporary China. A new generation trying to reckon with a communal past shrouded in secrecy and shame. In this captivating novel Zhang Yueran suggests that the new Chinese society cannot

be at peace with itself until it breaks out of the ideological straitjacket of the past."
PAUL FRENCH, author of *Midnight in Peking*

"Zhang Yueran is one of the most exciting new Chinese writers. Her work is original and thought-provoking, and her writing style is of a mature, well-rounded nature. The world needs an engagement with China more than ever at the moment that goes beyond the stereotypes and well-trodden genres, to develop genuine links and understanding."
FRANCES WEIGHTMAN, Director of The Leeds Centre for New Chinese Writing

"This novel on the ghosts of the Cultural Revolution reveals a talented young Chinese writer in Zhang Yueran."
Transfuge

"A great and beautiful novel, from one of the promising pens of contemporary China."
Image, Demain le monde

"With finesse, and mastery of the two-voiced storytelling technique, Zhang Yueran unlocks, pries open, explores the intricate depths of broken couples, of imploded families, and of scarred generations who inherit the abuses of their ancestors."
Libération

"With mastery of the art of suspense, Zhang Yueran skilfully brings together the pieces of a scattered puzzle."
Télérama

"This book is a raging fire."
Le Nouveau Magazine Littéraire

"Without ever falling into pathos, Zhang Yueran paints an incisive portrait of a generation scarred by decisions made in the dark hours of history."
Le Courrier Suisse

COCOON

Zhang Yueran

COCOON

Translated from the Chinese
by Jeremy Tiang

WORLD EDITIONS
New York, London, Amsterdam

Published in the USA in 2022 by World Editions LLC, New York
Published in the UK in 2022 by World Editions Ltd., London

World Editions
New York/London/Amsterdam

Printed by Lake Book, USA
World Editions is committed to a sustainable future. Papers used by
World Editions meet the FSC standards of certification.

This book is a work of fiction. Any resemblance to actual persons,
living or dead, or actual events is purely coincidental.

Library of Congress Cataloging in Publication Data is available

ISBN 978-1-64286-105-1

First published as 茧 in China in 2016 by People's Literature Publishing
House, Beijing. This translation has been slightly abridged from the
original, in agreement with the author.

This book has been selected to receive financial assistance from English
PEN's PEN Translates programme, supported by Arts Council England.
English pen exists to promote literature and our understanding of it,
to uphold writers' freedoms around the world, to campaign against the
persecution and imprisonment of writers for stating their views, and to
promote the friendly cooperation of writers and the free exchange of ideas.
www.englishpen.org

Twitter: @WorldEdBooks
Facebook: @WorldEditionsInternationalPublishing
Instagram: @WorldEdBooks
YouTube: World Editions
www.worldeditions.org

Translator's Note

Zhang Yueran has long been a leading voice of China's "post-'80s" generation (that is, born after 1980). While her earlier work—such as *The Promise Bird*, a fantasy about a blind woman going in search of her lost memories—has been compared to "a magical bottled garden," Cocoon takes place in a more realistic vein, looking through millennial eyes at the Cultural Revolution. This decade-long trauma has had no shortage of literary exploration; the entire genre of "scar literature" is dedicated to excavating this world, usually by those who lived through it. But what of writers such as Zhang who were born a few years after the catastrophe ended, and who grew up amid its detritus?

Zhang's cohort was destined by the one-child policy of 1980 to be a generation of only children—and indeed, the absence of siblings in Cocoon contributes to the younger characters' sense of alienation. These "little emperors" grew up at a time of plenty, the sole recipients of their parents' resources and attention. After such a rapid change in circumstances, it must have been hard to comprehend what these parents had lived through. All the adults in Cocoon are damaged in one way or another, while their society charges ahead, trying and failing to outrun its past.

This generation gap is perhaps the greatest in recent memory, and it is in this in-between space that Zhang situates herself, portraying both the violent ideological terror of the past and the alienated, sterile prosperity that her generation has grown up in. How can young people process the strife and suffering of those who went before them, when the country as a whole has not done so? Like strands of a cocoon unraveling, Zhang lays bare the many layers of her generation's coming of age.

Jeremy Tiang

"My poor child, the best thing I can send you is a little misfortune."

—William Makepeace Thackeray,
The Rose and the Ring

Li Jiaqi

I came back last month and didn't tell a soul. The night I arrived, the Central Gardens streetlights were busted, and all I could see were the inky shapes of trees, naked branches thrashing in the wind. Moonlight made the protruding goose-egg pebbles on the path gleam faintly. I'd forgotten the cluster of jagged rocks near the artificial lake, jutting unevenly as if the night were baring its teeth. From this distance, the white mansion on the opposite shore could have been a lone island.

The doorbell was broken, but the door was unlocked. Inside, I followed the noise to the far end of the first floor. Two men at a round table were playing a finger-guessing game, while others swayed and sang in a dialect I didn't understand. A man and woman sat entwined around each other. Empty beer bottles lay scattered across the floor. On an electric hotplate in the center of the table, a pot of greasy red liquid roiled.

It took some effort to explain who I was. Once she

understood, a woman dashed out and rapped energetically at a door across the passageway. The girl who emerged was Mei, Grandpa's home aide. She was dressed, but the man behind her was still fumbling with his belt buckle. The visitors hastily scattered, leaving Mei biting her lip and swiping viciously at the table. Of course she was put out, having never set eyes on me, or even knowing the old man had a granddaughter. It seemed faintly ridiculous that this grand old house, a symbol of lifelong glory, had become a playground for the help. Grandpa would never know. Since his lung cancer diagnosis six months ago, he'd been bedridden and confined to his room. No one visited. He hated being disturbed, and had cut ties with the outside world a few years back.

Two days later, I told Mei her services were no longer required. I didn't like that she seemed more the owner of this place than I did. Before leaving, she came to say goodbye to Grandpa, and actually shed some tears. Perhaps she really was fond of him—more than I was, that's for sure. Grandpa had gotten used to her care, but now that he was frail and nearing the end, he still chose me.

It had been so many years he no longer recognized me, but as soon as I said my name, he instantly trusted me, and didn't object when I fired Mei. Blood ties are a form of violence, the way they yoke together people who feel nothing for each other.

Jiaqi! Jiaqi! he called out of the blue, as if to keep from forgetting the name. I spent a lot of time in this room, those first few days. Sitting there staring at him, imagining the conversations we could have had. About the tragedy of our family, how he became the person he is now, how I grew into my current self. I went over what I would say to him, rehearsing the cruelty of my tone, honing every word like a pencil till its point was sharp enough to strike a fatal blow.

As it turned out, we didn't exchange a single word. Instead, the fatal blow was this cold snap. A few days after

Mei's departure, Grandpa caught a chill and started a high fever. I gave him medicine, and his temperature came down after a couple of days, but his mind never recovered. His eyes were clouded, and he didn't seem to understand a word I said. The illness had arrived just in time to save him from shame and hurt. As if a bell jar had been placed over him, leaving him detached but still in possession of thought and determination. He never lost control of his bladder and bowels, and always held it in until I placed the bedpan under him. In order to test his willpower, I once stayed away for more than ten hours, yet he managed not to soil himself. The discipline cultivated by several decades at the operating table.

Now I stay away from the room, other than feeding him or helping him relieve himself. I don't want to face him, though he probably sees me as no more than a fuzzy shape. He seems equally unwilling to look at me, and keeps his eyes down ... Both afraid we might accidentally glimpse the person caught between us. Giving him a sponge bath, I always go over his shoulder and look at the hot, crumpled sheet beneath him. He's gotten so scrawny the towel rucks his skin. Like wiping bones. He turns his head and stares at the floor. This must be humiliating. He once had the power to decide countless lives, but now someone has to lift his arms and scrub his armpits. Honestly, for an old man, he's quite free of nasty odors. Sheer force of will—he doesn't allow himself to stink.

A couple of days ago, we got our only visitors so far: two kids climbed the fence and snuck into the yard. I was on the couch, reading one of Grandpa's hardcover classics, which are mostly for show—they look like they've never been opened. I chose *Wuthering Heights*. Then I happened to look up and there they were, faces pressed to the window. A boy and girl, maybe ten years old. Though there was no resemblance, for some reason I was reminded of you and me all those years ago. After a moment of confusion, I jumped up and pulled the door open.

The boy told me their Chinese teacher had set them an essay: "An Admirable Person." They were both children of professors at the Medical University, and having grown up hearing about Grandpa, they were here to interview him. I said his health was too poor. The girl batted her eyes and said, How about we interview you, then? You're his grand-daughter, aren't you? I said I didn't know anything about him, but they refused to believe that, and kept pestering. I told them to make something up. They looked at me, wide-eyed. Okay, they said, but if our teacher comes asking, you have to back us up. Fine, I said, and they left satisfied. An admirable person needs to be surrounded by many touching stories, whether or not they are true.

When Grandpa was appointed a fellow, it caused a stir through the whole university, including the attached elementary school. Unfortunately I'd already transferred out by then, and no one in my new school knew that the most famous heart surgeon in China, whose story took up two whole pages in the evening paper, was my grandfather. Some mysterious force had pulled me away, preventing me from sharing in his glory. Sometimes I wonder: if I hadn't left, but instead spent my entire life in his halo, would I be a different person now?

The night before last, I was in the living room watching a documentary about Chinese soldiers who'd stayed in Myanmar and ended up teaching Mandarin or opening dry goods stores. The camera lingered on their elderly faces. In a foreign land, even their aging was tentative, and not one wrinkle dared to be too prominent. Their bodies were still sturdy, but some had been deaf or senile for years, as if their senses were deliberately shutting down so this unfamiliar place could feel more like home. Unwilling to take part in the civil war and see their fellow countrymen killing each other, they'd refused to return after defeating the Japanese, sending their lives off track. No longer at the whims of the era. At peace, yet also useless. If a pawn chooses not to cross the board, what further use is it?

The presenter interviewed a veteran's granddaughter who'd taken over her grandfather's business, and now owned his shop. I stared at her tanned face. That could have been me, if Grandpa had stayed. Maybe he'd have opened a clinic there, and cobbled together a living with the help of the local Chinese community. Then my father would have arrived, then me—I'd have grown up and maybe fallen in love with a Myanmarese boy. We'd have run through the rain to hear Aung San Suu Kyi speak in the square, then hugged and cheered when we heard on TV that newspapers would no longer be censored. This life that wasn't mine would have, like a dandelion, puffed into blossom wherever the wind took it. Without the encumbrance of roots, it would have grown in its own manner. That would have been purer, at least. This ancient country was under a thick layer of dust, and leaving would feel like being cleansed. I was drawn to this freedom, even if it came streaked with suffering.

Unfortunately, Grandpa hadn't had the courage to desert, and the impoverished soil of Myanmar didn't arouse his ambition. Peixuan thinks he never had any kind of ambition anyway. When she was interviewed for the documentary, she said: Grandpa once told me he just went with the flow; he studied hard at school, and did his best as a doctor. He joined the army at the right time, then entered the Party at the right time. He made sure to put his feet in the right place. The times were changing so quickly, one false step and you'd find yourself no longer on solid ground, plummeting into the abyss. Going with the flow was actually very difficult. Like a signal operator patiently adjusting the frequency, one needed sensitive ears and a still heart to correctly tune in to the era.

Peixuan mailed me the documentary that's playing on the TV now. While I waited for you this afternoon, I played it on a loop, watching it over and over, though my attention kept drifting. When I have the chance, I'll tell her I like the section about the soldiers most. I enjoy looking back at the first half of Grandpa's life, imagining what would have happened if he'd just stopped at a particular point—what that would have done to our family's destiny.

Since getting back to Southern Courtyard, I haven't been anywhere except the supermarket. Oh, and the drugstore once—I needed something to help me sleep. Otherwise, I've been here, watching a dying man. Grandpa lost consciousness this morning. I couldn't wake him. It was still dark, and the pressure in the room was low. I stood by his bed, feeling death hover like a flock of bats.

I got my thick coat from my suitcase. The heater doesn't do enough, maybe because the room is so big. I've tried to make peace with the cold seeping through the walls, but I can't stand it any longer. I went into the bathroom without turning on the light—the thin, stark fluorescent bulb made me feel even colder. I washed my face at the sink and thought about what would happen after tomorrow. Once he was dead, I would change all the lights in the house. The leaky pipe below the sink dribbled hot water over my feet in the dark, the temperature of blood.

Downstairs I fried a couple of eggs and made toast, and took my time eating. Then I got the ladder from the storeroom and pulled down the curtains in every room. The living room seemed transformed. I stood in the doorway, squinting at the large, bare windows. Daylight illuminated every mote of accumulated dust, stirring up secrets.

This afternoon, his body seemed to have shrunk under the heavy goose-down quilt. It was still gloomy outside, and death continued circling the room, refusing to descend. I felt a constriction in my chest, a throbbing at my temples. Slipping on my coat, I fled from the house and wandered aimlessly around campus. The disused elementary school, the veranda behind the library, the desolate bleachers at the sports field—none of these places reminded me of you.

Then I got to the western side of Southern Courtyard. The old buildings there had been torn down, replaced by brand-new high-rise blocks with gleaming security gates. When I tried to get around them, I realized with a start that your building was still there, huddled against the boundary wall and hidden by the taller newcomers.

After so many years, I didn't think you'd still be in the same place, but went to apartment 102 anyway and pressed the buzzer. Someone answered, Come in. I hesitated a moment, then pulled open the door. It was very dim inside and something was bubbling on the stove, filling the air with steam. A man was slumped on the couch with his eyes shut. Even through the gloom and foggy air, after more than a decade, I recognized you. Cheng Gong, I said quietly. You slowly opened your eyes, as if you'd dozed off from waiting so long for me. For a split second, I felt we must have arranged to meet and I'd forgotten. But you didn't know who I was. Even after I told you, you remained detached. With some effort, I asked about the deserted school and our friends from the old days. Then the small talk was done and we lapsed into silence. I couldn't think of a reason to stay any longer.

You walked me to the door. I said goodbye, you said take care. When I looked around again, the door was shut. It was very quiet in the corridor. I didn't want to go back out into the daylight, where we would be torn apart again. Icy wind rattled the security gate, like someone sighing in the dark. Thoughts flared up, embers fanned into flame. I felt I knew why I'd come. Screwing up my courage, I pressed the doorbell again and asked you to come to the white mansion tonight.

Back here, I felt very calm. I got the DVD from the drawer and put it into the machine. Then I made some tea, pulled two chairs together, and waited for you. The light faded outside, and the man in the bed mumbled to himself for a while before sinking deeper into dreams. He was struggling to breathe. The foul air of his rotten lungs filled the house. Suddenly the light brightened and a gust of wind flung the window open. When I went to close it, I realized it was snowing. Would you still come? I waited anyway.

I somehow knew it would have to unfold this way. Soon it was completely dark, and the snowstorm was getting heavier. The road was no longer visible. I stared into the blurry whiteness until I felt I was going blind. Finally, a small black dot appeared, a sprouting seed breaking through the earth.

You didn't ask me anything, just followed me up the stairs to this room. Seemingly unsurprised to find him lying in bed, you took a few steps forward and studied his face, as if you were weighing up his whole life. But maybe that was too complex a calculation to make. You seemed dazed, until I pulled a chair over and you sank into it.

As you can see, he's about to die. My grandpa. I ought to call the hospital and have them send an ambulance over. They'd work through the night to save him, perhaps prolong his life by a few days, then prepare for the funeral—a grand send-off for Director Li Jisheng. There I'd stand, the only family member. Everyone would weep as they eulogized him, then slowly shuffle past his casket. People I didn't know would tell me what a great man my grandfather had been, how noble, how wise, how widely respected. The provincial governor or city mayor would warmly take my hand and offer their condolences, a Steadicam following them like a loyal dog to capture the appreciation on my face. So well planned, I'd have nothing to do but make sure I had a sufficient supply of tears.

And I think I *would* be able to cry. Not for him, but for the things that will depart with him. Yet I haven't been able to make myself call the hospital. One phone call, and his death will be an official matter, no longer anything to do with me. He'll be surrounded by nurses and doctors, his students and colleagues, visiting officials, the media, a surge of people laying claim to his final moments, giving his imminent death the scale it ought to have, commensurate to the importance of his life. The sinking of an enormous ship. I have no right to stand in the way of a great man's glorious death, but I only have this little bit of time remaining to me and can't bear to hand it over. All these years I haven't asked him for a thing—not his concern or affection or regard. All I want, at this moment, is to claim his death for myself. I have been waiting for this moment, for a nonexistent voice to tell me it's all over.

When I saw you this afternoon, I could feel all this between us. Perhaps you've already learned the secret. Perhaps, with the passage of time, it seeped into the texture of your life. No matter what form it takes, I believe it is still present, and like me, you can't ignore it. Let's talk about it, for the first and final time. We'll talk till dawn if we have to, and after that, everything about the secret will be left behind in this night.

Great swathes of snow are coming down now. As if God were flinging back at humanity every letter we've ever sent him, ripped into tiny pieces.

Cheng Gong

Yes, let's talk, although I can't stay long. As soon as the snow dies down, I need to get to the train station. I'm going far from here. Actually, I ought to have left this afternoon. When you showed up at my door, I thought you were the water delivery guy. If he'd come any earlier, we might have missed each other.

This afternoon, when I was done packing, I went to the kitchen for a glass of water. The dispenser was empty so I called the water place. Half an hour later, there was still no sign of them. I would have cancelled the order, but I'd run out of cash the last time round and still owed the delivery guy. Best to tie up loose ends before leaving. Getting thirstier, I found a battered kettle in a cupboard, filled it, and put it on the stove to boil. The pale blue flame flickered and the kettle hissed. Waiting on the couch, I dozed off and dreamed of Dabin and Zifeng, looking the same as when we were teenagers, sprinting through the nighttime alleyways, drunk and merry. Even our acne was glowing. We ran all the way to the neon-lit main road, where a lot of people our age held beer bottles and walked towards the nearby square. We jumped into a red jeep, cheering and whistling, leaning out the windows as it sped ahead. It felt like a carnival.

When you buzzed, I thought it must be the delivery guy and called out that the door was unlocked. My eyes stayed shut as I tried to cling to the dream. Like the end of a movie, the jeep was in the distance, the buildings and streets were shrinking away, and I could no longer hear the cheers and laughter. The curtain came down and everything was taken away, leaving me alone in the dark, an empty bowl. After a while, I felt a chilly breeze. The door was open but I heard no footsteps, nothing but silence.

I opened my eyes. You were in the doorway. I didn't know how long you'd been there. Had you seen me laughing from the dream, then my sadness when I woke, when I was at my most vulnerable? You said my name in a soft, raspy voice, as if you hadn't spoken for a long time. The sky was dark—about to snow. The boiling water rumbled. I looked carefully but didn't know who you were, yet I felt this stranger standing in the gloom had a deep connection to my life. The thought chilled my spine. I frantically flicked through the Rolodex of my mind. You told me you were Li Jiaqi.

Your breath came white from your mouth. The wind had tangled your curly hair, and your knees were trembling under your coat. All these things told me you were actually there, and this wasn't just a continuation of the dream. I hadn't seen you in eighteen years, no wonder I couldn't recognize you. You weren't wearing makeup, and your pale face looked a little swollen, but it was clear you'd grown into a beauty like we'd all known you would—though you had the numb expression of someone who's been in the big city too long. You asked if you looked how I'd imagined. I smiled and admitted I'd never imagined you grown up. As far as I was concerned, you and everything to do with you had been placed into a sealed folder. Maybe this is hurtful to hear, but I had truly never hoped to meet you again.

I went to the kitchen and turned off the stove. Half the water had boiled away, filling the room with fog. You sat and watched anxiously as I made tea.

"Are you still living with your grandma and aunt?" you asked.

I told you Granny was dead, but yes, I was still with Auntie.

"And she never married?"

"No."

It was a difficult conversation. Every time we fell into silence, I felt something squeezing at my heart, and I wanted to end this encounter as quickly as possible. You seemed to sense this, and searched for something else to talk about. The tea cooled, the fog dissipated. You stood to leave. I'd only just closed the door and sighed in relief when the bell rang again. You said I should come to the white mansion later and walked away before I could respond.

I hadn't planned to show up—I didn't think we had any need to meet again. I sat on the couch and smoked cigarette after cigarette as it got dark. Then someone tapped on the door: the water delivery boy. He wore a filthy gray wool hat and looked harried.

"I had to make a delivery on the west side," he said. "I got lost."

I sent him away, buttoned my coat, and left with my suitcase. It was dark, and snow was beginning to fall. I waited for a long time outside Southern Courtyard until a taxi finally came along, but the driver said his shift was ending. It was freezing cold—I kept stamping my feet and blowing into my hands. The door of the little restaurant behind me swung open and the owner came out, on her way to get cigarettes for a customer. She called out a warm greeting when she saw me—I'd spent a lot of time over the summer drinking there.

"Going somewhere?" she asked.

I nodded.

"Are you in a hurry? You won't get a taxi in this snow."

I stared at the channel of light from the street lamp, and the snowflakes churning within it, as if struggling in an ocean of misery.

I remembered an afternoon many years ago, when it was snowing as hard as this, and you were about to leave. Your mom had put in the transfer paperwork at the school. As you were leaving the office, you bumped into Dabin and told him you wanted to see me, that I should come see you at your grandpa's house that evening.

It would be hard for us to meet in the future—this might be my last chance to tell you everything. And yet, as I made my way over to you, I found my footsteps lagging. Finally, I stopped outside Kangkang Convenience Store, where we used to go all the time, then I turned around and went home. Later, I heard you waited a very long time for me, and it was almost dinner when your mom took you away. I've always been sorry about that. I don't know why I did what I did. Maybe because everything seemed out of my hands, and the only thing I could choose was how to end this friendship. After that day, any connection we had was sealed and archived.

Dabin got hold of your new address and wrote you a card for your birthday, but I refused to add my name. Then he was sad because you didn't reply or send him a card back. No one heard from you. You'd vanished cleanly from our lives, like my hopes. I thought this was your way of telling me you agreed with my decision—since you were never coming back, there was no point staying in touch. We'd once been so close, but the friendship we'd thought was indestructible was in fact utterly fragile. It had been wrong from the beginning, a tree growing in the middle of a road, doomed to be cut down sooner or later.

"If you go up ahead," the restaurant owner now said to me, "you might be able to get a cab at the corner."

I thanked her and plunged on into the blizzard.

There were no taxis in sight, so I kept walking. Along the way, I passed where Kangkang Convenience Store had once been. It was now Dongdong Fast Food. The bicycle shelter next to it had been torn down and the steep slope flattened also. With the snow covering these changes, I had a confused sense that I'd gone back to that evening when I was eleven. You were leaving, and I was coming to see you. This time, I didn't pause when I reached Kangkang, but carried on, and finally completed the journey I'd abandoned all those years ago.

Li Jiaqi

It gets so quiet around here at night. At least during the day I hear children shrieking as they play on the frozen lake. On sunny afternoons, girls in wedding dresses shrug off their coats and pose in front of the house, shivering. Perhaps because it's winter and the seaside is too cold, and warmer climes too far away, they end up at this campus for their wedding photos. This place must provide an ideal backdrop: snow-white exterior, semi-circular balcony, arched windows with iron filigree work—a cut-price image of happiness. It's not like happiness is real, anyway, so this version is no more fake than anything else.

We always called this the white mansion. In an industrial city like this, everything ought to be gray from pollution—houses, sky, air. Our entire childhood was gray. The white mansion clearly didn't belong here. Seen through the greenery of the park, it looked like a mirage.

But do you know, the night you and I crept in, I secretly promised myself I'd get married here. How old were we? Ten or eleven? This place was still the union center then. It was Saturday. The security guard had left his post for a moment, and we snuck in to watch the grown-ups' social dance. There was our pretty music teacher, for once in high heels and a flared skirt, a man's hand at her waist. Perfume and sweat battled each other. A disco ball cast specks of light on the wall. We climbed up to the second floor and found a window. High in the damp night sky was the moon. Wisps of cloud moved away, uncovering its perfect roundness. We shuffled back and forth until it was in the center of the window. We stared at it, feeling as if all had been revealed to us. Then the clouds came back, and the world was once again uncertain. That's when I decided I would come back here as a bride, but I didn't tell you even though I was sure you'd be my groom.

It was many years later that I learned the white mansion

only dates back to the 1950s. A famous educator was appointed the head of this Medical University, and the government built it for him to live in. He refused—it was too luxurious. Even so, during the Cultural Revolution, he got accused of receiving special treatment anyway, and ended up here for his struggle session. One night, after he'd been locked up for many days, he went to one of the second-story rooms—maybe even the one where we'd stood—and cut his wrists with a razor he'd smuggled in. He probably never imagined the place where he committed suicide would one day feature in many wedding photos, just as I never expected I'd end up living here. I could have a wedding every day if I wanted.

I almost got married last year, to a man named Tang Hui. He was above me at university, and though we'd known each other quite a while, we met too late—after the major events of my life had already happened. He knew that, but wanted to try anyway. He's a good person. But it didn't work and I left him. For a while, I was living with one friend after another, a shadowy existence. Then Peixuan came back this summer, and I moved in with her for a couple of months.

You remember my cousin Peixuan, don't you? The pretty one, the flag raiser. She's been in the States for some time—got her PhD last year, and now she's teaching at Ohio State University. She was back for the summer and asked to see me. That's how I found out Grandpa was living in the white mansion. It was too much of a tourist spot, she grumbled, and attracted too many visitors. Sometimes people knocked on the door and asked for a photograph with the former fellow.

"Grandpa's like some rare animal in a cage," said Peixuan furiously. She comes back every summer, and always gets a few new bits and pieces for the house. The oven and coffee machine are hers—she can't live without these things. They go back into the cupboard when she leaves, though—Grandpa's too used to living with just a kettle and a pot. They get on well, though, despite their different life-styles.

I didn't see Peixuan for a very long time after moving away, though we stayed in touch, mostly thanks to her efforts. She sent me a letter from the States with her address there, and wrote from time to time, letting me know if she'd moved. When I went to Beijing for college, she asked my mom for the phone number of my dorm, and called to get my email address. She kept me updated about what she was doing—moving to a different school for her masters, then continuing with her PhD. Every message ended with the same words: When you have time, I hope you'll go home to visit Grandpa and Grandma. I never replied, except once after college, to inform her I'd be staying on in Beijing for work.

As far as Peixuan was concerned, I was a member of Grandpa's family, and therefore she had a duty to keep me from drifting away. Our only real contact in all this time was five years ago, when she phoned me late at night from the States, crying so hard I could barely understand her. Grandma was dead, she said. She was coming back for the funeral—would I go too? But I refused. After that, her emails went back to just the facts: she'd finished her PhD, now she was teaching. Same closing line as before, minus *and Grandma*. Then this summer, she emailed to say she was coming back to Beijing for a while.

We met at a café in the city center. She had a gym-honed body and her skin was as pale as ever, almost inhuman. I was shocked to see how prominent the scar on her face was—I hadn't seen her since her injury. I'd heard she'd had a fall. It was hard to believe—I'd always been the one getting scraped knees and lacerated arms. Remember how she was always scared of heights? When we were playing and she came to make us come home, all we had to do was climb the wall around Dead Man's Tower, and there was no way she could follow.

The scar extended a full five centimeters, from the right side of her mouth down to her jawbone. It dozed when she was silent, then as soon as she started speaking, it came to life and wiggled like a centipede. I felt for her. She'd always been so certain of her path, this must have been the only thing in her life that hadn't gone to plan.

Peixuan told me a TV station was producing a documentary about Grandpa's life, and she was back in the country to help with the research, contacting and interviewing people who knew him. She hoped that, as his other granddaughter, I would take part too.

"Just talk a little about living with him as a child. Nothing difficult."

"I don't remember anything," I said.

"You must! Think about it."

"Nope. Nothing."

"Is this about your dad? That wasn't all Grandpa's fault ..."

"No, that's not why."

"He wasn't perfect, but ..."

"I have to go."

She sighed and signaled for the bill.

Afterwards, she kept phoning. I'd just broken up with some guy I hadn't been seeing for long, and needed to move out of his house urgently. When I told Peixuan I was looking for a place, she suggested I share the service apartment she'd rented for a couple of months. I said yes because I needed somewhere to be, but also there were things I needed to tell her.

Peixuan was surprised when I turned up with just a couple of suitcases, but I've gotten used to this nomadic life. Everything I own—hair straighteners, iron, speakers—are the smallest possible model. All my perfume comes in testers, and I try to choose items that serve many functions: multi-tools that open wine and beer bottles, as well as tin cans; chargers that fit my phone, laptop, and camera; lotion for both face and body. Like a dieting woman, I try to take up as little space as possible.

Of course, Peixuan doesn't understand. She lives alone in a big house in Ohio. She doesn't even have her parents living with her—they're in California, and her dad hasn't been well. He had a stroke two years ago, so he hasn't been back to see Grandpa.

The day after I moved in, she brought up the documentary again.

"Just say a few words on camera, that's all."

I was beginning to realize it didn't actually matter what I said, the important thing was that I appeared. Grandma and Dad were dead, while my uncle and aunt couldn't travel. That left me and Peixuan as his only family members. Peixuan didn't tell the producers I hadn't spoken to Grandpa in years.

"Isn't one granddaughter enough?"

She stared at me. "But you're his favorite."

I laughed. "Impossible. He never got on with Dad."

"Sure, but he likes you. Don't you know that? It's because you look just like your mother."

"Can we stop talking about it?"

She actually did stop, though Grandpa remained between us. I remember during the three years I lived with them both, we each had our own mugs, marked with our names written on bandages on the handles, to prevent the spread of hepatitis. I once used Peixuan's, hoping to give her my cold.

In Peixuan's open-plan kitchen, the tiled wall by the sink had several towels hanging from hooks, each marked *dishes*, *table*, *hands* and so on. The thing is, she hadn't used labels or Post-its, but the same narrow bandages as on the mugs, reeking of antiseptic. Anyone who's ever worked in a hospital probably has a houseful of these—your aunt must too—though likely few found as many uses for them as in Grandpa's household.

Peixuan had also adopted Grandpa's near-fascist regime, though she called it "discipline." As soon as she woke up, she jumped right out of bed, and if we'd said we'd watch half an hour of television, she'd ruthlessly turn it off after thirty minutes, even if the program wasn't over. She wore a retainer, though her teeth were straight as mahjong tiles.

One day, she came home from the supermarket with two bottles of wine and said we could have a little evening drink. I was happy that we'd finally found a common interest, but then she carefully wiped the glasses, put them side by side on the table, and poured exactly three centimeters of wine into each, like measuring cough syrup. Turns out we had very different understandings of "a little drink." I waited till she'd gone to bed, and went to pour myself some more.

I woke up at noon with a headache, and found her in the living room answering emails.

"I guess you don't remember what happened last night," she said, still typing.

"I got drunk?"

"I found you passed out on the floor in the middle of the night. Your glass was shattered."

"Sorry. I'm not a good drinker." I reached up to rub my temples and noticed a large bruise on one forearm.

"Oh, I'd say you're an excellent drinker. You finished the bottle, opened the second one, and drained that as well."

"I did?" A hazy memory arose: searching everywhere for a bottle opener.

She looked worried. "Are you an alcoholic, too?" That word, *too*, forcing me to think of Dad.

"Might be."

"Why not do something about it? There are rehab clinics in the States, there must be some here."

"I like having some bad habits, so I don't hate myself too much." I didn't add: *and it makes me feel closer to Dad.* It's one of the few things I inherited from him.

She never bought wine again. Every time I went for a night out after that, she watched with fury as I blow-dried my hair and put on makeup. Her anger was complicated—sometimes she seemed like a mother with an unruly daughter, other times like a little girl whose mom was going on a date she didn't approve of. Peixuan doesn't believe in makeup, and hates parties. She's always complaining that Americans spend too much time on meaningless socializing, which is making them stupider and stupider. Living with me probably made her realize that things aren't much better in China. Maybe the whole world is becoming more foolish.

Each time I washed my face, I saw in the mirror our bras hanging from the bathtub rail, shoulder to shoulder. Mine were half-moons in cheap lace or faux satin, peach or pale pink, with bows in front and rhinestones that would fall off after a few washes. Hers were all white cotton, full cups with thick bands, so similar-looking she must have bought them in bulk.

"Such flashy bras—I guess they're for men to look at?" she said glumly once, while I was changing.

"For men? Don't you look at yourself in the mirror?"

But she rarely did—probably because of her scar. This kept her in a state of ignorance. Sometimes I thought her expression was the same as when we were little, except that now she'd lost her luster. I remembered how every Monday morning she'd walk to the flagpole with the flag in her arms, skin pale and dazzling, slender figure full of a young woman's vigor. I thought every boy in the school must be in love with her.

One evening we began talking more openly. Nothing that would have been out of place between most cousins, but I felt I was crossing a line.

I asked if she had a boyfriend. She said no.

"A fuckbuddy, then?"

"I don't need one," she said, blushing. "My life is very full."

The right man hadn't shown up yet, she said, but he was out there. Someone from a good family with an excellent education and a respectable job, with eyes only for her. She would wait patiently for him.

"And you?" she asked awkwardly.

"Yours hasn't shown up yet, mine has already gone. Now, I think men are all about the same, neither good nor bad. I'd be fine with any of them."

"Your worldview is problematic."

"I have no worldview. I'm just getting through life one day at a time."

Over the next two weeks, Peixuan was busy with endless production meetings, getting ready for the shoot. I'd wake up at noon and, finding her gone, make myself something to eat, then sit at the computer to work on my manuscript, look for jobs online, and email out my cv. She'd usually come back around dinner time, as I was getting ready to go out. It was summer, and friends would ask me out to bars every few days. I always said yes, no matter who called. Peixuan would be sound asleep by the time I returned. We barely saw each other despite living under the same roof, which was just as well. I've always done this, adjusted my body clock to avoid people I don't get on with.

One rainy night, I came home after twelve, soaking wet. She was still awake, arranging neatly folded clothes into her suitcase. My heart grew heavy. Was the shoot over? Now I'd have to find somewhere else to stay—an exhausting thought. But no, she said, she was just going to Yunnan and Myanmar for a few days with the production team.

"Yunnan? Since when is this a travelogue?"

"Did you know Grandpa was in the expeditionary army? Qilu University moved to Chengdu during the Anti-Japanese War. He joined up there, and was deployed to Yunnan and Myanmar. I found him in a photograph with General Sun Li-jen and the rest of his company."

I'd had no idea about any of this, of course. I didn't even know who General Sun Li-jen was.

Peixuan handed me a book about the expeditionary

army that had been sitting on the table for a few days now. I flicked through and put it down. She grabbed it back and swiftly found the right page: a young soldier in a blurry photograph, from a distant time and place. It could have been anyone.

"He was a medic, then when British troops came over to help, he served as an interpreter too." Peixuan was flipping through the book again.

"Okay, whatever. I'm still not going to be in your documentary."

"You think I'm telling you this to persuade you?" she said frostily, closing the book. "I thought you ought to know, that's all. Whether or not you admit it, Grandpa is the glory of our family. I wanted to share this glory with you. If you accept that, it will enrich you and give you strength."

What, like the holy spirit? It wasn't glory she wanted to share with me, but faith. Her belief in Grandpa was religious. Hence the proselytizing, though she must have known I was a lost cause. She looked at me like I was a lost lamb.

"Peixuan, you're the one who's lost," I murmured, shaking my head.

I suddenly remembered the day you and I were on the wall around Dead Man's Tower, and she came to summon me home. I refused, instead describing the corpses inside in vivid detail. She blanched, started trembling, and walked away. Then she turned back and said very distinctly, "Li Jiaqi, your life is going to end up a tragedy." Her voice was weird, as if these weren't her words, and she was just passing on a prophecy.

"You mean *your* life, right?" I snarled back.

It seems we cursed each other. All these years later, my life is definitely tragic. And isn't Peixuan's too?

She's living for Grandpa and the rest of the clan. They've bound her like that retainer she wears, molding her into shape. Even as an adult, she doesn't dare take it off in case any gaps appear. No gaps between her teeth. No freedom.

"Peixuan." I broke the silence. "Don't you think family glory is ridiculous?"

"Don't." She slowly stood up. "You may not understand, but there's no need to be hurtful." Her scar was quivering.

I looked away. Before I could think of a response, I heard her door slam.

Alone on the sofa, sitting in dangerous silence, I imagined myself charging into her room and saying, "Peixuan, let me tell you something."

Perhaps she'd expect violence, but with me and my shadow filling the doorway, she'd have no escape. Curling up, she'd stare in terror. I'd open my pocket, and the truth would escape like a vicious dog barking wildly, lunging at her and shredding her glorious armor, gouging out her heart, licking away her sugarlike faith with a slobbery tongue. Just like that, she'd lose the thing most precious to her. I'd watch her destruction calmly, telling myself I hadn't done anything. It wasn't me ruining her, but the truth—all I'd done was unleash it.

Was that really how it was? I felt dazed. I'd seen how many people the truth had hurt. I was passive. All I'd done was accept it. But now I held something in the palm of my hand: the power to harness the truth. I could hurt Peixuan, I could pretend not to see the harm I was doing, cloak it in righteousness, maybe even persuade myself it was my duty.

My emotions abruptly diminished. All I wanted was to be kinder. Peixuan's faith in family glory might be delusional, but it sustained her. There was no virtue in this belief, but it purified her heart and made *her* virtuous.

If Peixuan were an ordinary friend, or even a stranger, it would be easier to treat her with kindness. We're born kind, but it slips away as we age. Remember how fervently we searched for the truth when we were kids?

I sat and stared through the window of Peixuan's twelfth-floor apartment. Lightning sliced through the stormy sky.

A bolt of light reached for me and tenderly stroked my hair. I can't explain it, but in that moment I decided to keep these past events firmly in my pocket; I missed you enormously.

Peixuan's trip took longer than she'd planned. She phoned to say she had to head back to the States—her college needed her back urgently—so she'd bought a ticket, and was leaving via Hong Kong. She wouldn't be back in Beijing, but I could stay in the apartment for another month—she'd already paid the rent.

"I hope you find a job soon, and quit drinking." She was at the China-Myanmar border, where the strong wind made her voice sound like a passing flock of pigeons.

"You take care too." I hung up.

I actually did start going to bars less often, found a job in a bookstore, and moved into a small apartment with a friend. In the autumn, Mom came to stay with me for a few days. The stove wasn't working, so we sat in my tiny room eating takeout. She shoveled rice into her mouth, not saying a word. I knew she was disappointed. She'd always wanted me to marry young, buy a house, and let her move in. She'd been living with my aunt all this time and was tired of having to depend on others. Soon after she went back to Jinan, she called me at two in the morning to say she didn't know what was going on with Grandpa. I was surprised—she hadn't mentioned him for years. He was living in the house that the university had given him, she said, and they wouldn't take it back even if he was gone, right? He'd like it if I came back to take care of him—maybe he'd even leave me the house. I said forget it, I wasn't going back. But the idea had bewitched her, and she kept calling every few days. Eventually I forgot her original plan, and only heard her repeated plea, Come back, come back. I remembered my childhood and missed Southern Courtyard. Last week, I dreamed I was in a train that swayed from side to side. A red matryoshka doll rolled towards my feet. I picked it up and a woman's voice said shrilly, Open it. Inside was a smaller doll, and inside that an even smaller one. I tore open doll after doll, faster and faster, sweat dripping into my eyes. I couldn't stop. Half-doll shells tumbled around my feet. The voice said, Open it, open it. My pillow was soaked when I woke up. I had the same dream again, like a summons. I knew I had to come back. Grandpa might soon be dead.

Cheng Gong

My aunt doesn't know I'm leaving. She's probably in bed right now, listening for movement outside. Her nerves have been weak for a couple of years, and she spends more time trying to fall asleep than actually sleeping. If I get home late, she'll still be awake, straining in the dark to hear the door. Only when I'm safely inside is she able to drop off. She'll think I've gone out for a drink, as usual. She doesn't care if I drink, not even if I get smashed. Maybe she likes it that way. A man who gets drunk every night probably won't find love easily. Drunkards don't need much sex, so they lose the ability to love. I'll probably age quickly, catch up with her, and we'll leave this world together. That's for my own good. She doesn't want me to be alone.

She'll stay up all night waiting, maybe doze a little at dawn, but then she'll jerk awake, check the lock, try calling me, and pace around the room when I don't answer. That's when she'll realize I'm not coming home. When sunlight first spills into the room, I can imagine how scared she'll be. Everything familiar will become strange. I know how that feels.

This is the first time I'm leaving Jinan to live somewhere else. Many years ago, Auntie had her fortune told—apparently she needs to spend the rest of her life at home, because traveling is dangerous for her. She decided that my birth numbers are close enough to hers that the same thing must apply to me. We've shared this fortune for some years, and I really am getting more and more like her. Now I'm scared of leaving too. A strange superstition. I believed I had to stay here, as if I were waiting for something.

Granny was admitted to hospital this May with a persistent fever and weight loss. They diagnosed late-stage liver cancer—the doctors said she had less than three months left. Her mind wasn't clear. She insisted that Auntie and I wanted to hurt her and refused to be discharged. The hospital's always full to bursting, but because of Granddad's stature and because Auntie still works there, she managed to get herself a room in the side ward, the same building where Granddad was. It's practically a retirement home these days—just old people waiting to die. The nurses are legendarily nasty—she'll have suffered there. She brought her jewelry and savings book with her, so Auntie and I couldn't get at them, then stayed awake at night because she was afraid they'd get stolen.

"Don't touch anything at home," she said, "I'll be out in a day or two." We watched her get weaker, fading before our eyes.

They put her in intensive care in June. She was still lucid when we went to see her, and asked to remove her oxygen mask. "Do you think your father is waiting for me on the other side?" she asked Auntie, who hesitated. Granny shook her head. "I don't want to be alone anymore."

She was gone a couple of days after that. The funeral was poorly attended—after everything that had happened, no one in Southern Courtyard wanted anything to do with her. It was raining heavily when Auntie and I got the bus back with her ashes. We took shelter by the post office. The rain didn't look like it was stopping anytime soon. Auntie burst into tears. Cheng Gong, she said, I'm an orphan now, please be nice to me.

We buried Granny's ashes on a hill outside the city, all alone, no family around her. We couldn't send them to her ancestral home because Auntie only knew she'd come from Cao County, but not which village. She hadn't been back since leaving at seventeen. On the way back, Auntie said, We have an ancestral grave here now, we can finally call this city home.

When a dictator dies, they leave behind a terrifying void. Resistance had become our whole lives, and we didn't know how to do anything else. Freedom had fallen from the skies, and we could only hold it like some complicated object we had no idea how to handle. For the next week, Auntie and I carefully went on living like usual. She went to work, I bought groceries, and at dinnertime we sat across from each other at the dilapidated table. The overhead light flickered like a twitching eyelid. Auntie overcooked the food, as usual. The greasy plastic tablecloth still stank of Granny's drool. I could still see her sitting between us, gnawing on a rib. On Sunday, at my suggestion, we bought a water dispenser and the juicer that Auntie had wanted for a long time. That was the sum of it, the new life we'd hoped for.

I didn't know what I was sticking around for, and decided to tell Auntie a friend had found me a job in Shanghai. When I got home that evening, all the lights were on, and she was sitting in the living room. I headed to my room, but she called my name and told me she had something to say.

"I don't know why ..." She began sobbing. "Ever since your granny died, I haven't been able to sleep at night. My mind keeps turning. All those things that happened, they're like a play. Sometimes I'm in the audience, sometimes I'm on stage ... Do you know, I have a strange feeling" —she kept her face lowered, shaking her head—"Your grandfather is still alive."

"No one could survive in that condition for forty-two years." I surprised myself by knowing exactly how many years it had been. We hadn't spoken about him for a long time. It's been almost two decades since he was spirited away from his hospital room in the middle of the night.

"What if it's a miracle? Your granny asked about him in the ICU. She must have sensed something. People know more when they're about to die."

"You're just guessing. You have no proof."

"I do," she said. "When I was making the arrangements to have your granny cremated, I had to produce documents to show I was family. They wouldn't do it otherwise. So what do you think they did with your grandfather's body? Buried it? Dumped it? That's illegal. The only thing they could have done is snuck it back."

"They kidnapped him—that's illegal too, isn't it? Why risk bringing him back?"

"Our building is mostly empty. If they brought him to our door at night, no one would see."

"So you've been hoping one day you'll open the door, and he'll be there."

"Not me, but that's what your granny was waiting for," said Auntie. "I understand now—that's why she refused to move away."

"Yeah, right. She couldn't wait for him to die."

"We don't always know what we want. I'd thought all along that I would leave here, find somewhere bigger, with a room of my own. But now ... I feel like I should stay. Your grandfather's story isn't done yet." She was crying again.

"That's enough."

She'd hit on a truth: our waiting hadn't ended just because Granny was dead. We were waiting for something else, though I wasn't sure if it was Granddad's return. Like Auntie, I didn't believe it was all over. Not that there were any mysteries left to unravel—we knew everything there was to know—but something was hanging over our emotions.

We didn't say any more. Auntie kept weeping as I pulled a dish of fried peanuts towards me and devoured them by the handful.

Since then, Auntie's been scared to be alone. I even have to keep her company while she's cooking. She doesn't let me go out at night—I have to sit with her on the couch, watching some boring TV serial and eating watermelon. She'll be sweating nonstop, knitting a thick cardigan. She needs to do something with her hands to feel less anxious. I think she's going through the change, and she's burning up all the desire left in her body. Like a furnace about to be decommissioned getting hotter as it uses the last of its coal. Menopause hit her right after Granny's death, as if to slot her into the "old woman" role that had now opened up. She's also inherited Granny's traits—she's becoming twisted, domineering, suspicious of everyone. Of course no one can help ageing, but this seems particularly cruel. She might still be a virgin. A lifetime's worth of blood, shed in vain.

Li Jiaqi

Is it cold in here? A few drinks will warm us up. I'm not great at holding my liquor, I'll get drunk in no time. Don't worry, I won't talk nonsense. My mind actually gets clearer. Alcohol helps me remember. You know what I mean? A lamp shining into a dark, dusty corner.

Sometimes I wonder how Peixuan and I come from the same family, yet took such different things from it.

Honestly, that probably started the generation before. Her father, my uncle, treated Grandpa like a god, as if everything he said was infallible. Grandpa claimed he never forced his children to do anything, but his opinions held the same authority as the prescriptions he wrote his patients. Dad, the family rebel, pushed back.

From a young age, I'd sensed the tension between them. Whenever they were together, the air thickened as if something was about to blow up. They almost never spoke, and when they did, it was through Grandma. Grandma would say stuff to Dad and finish with, "That's what your father thinks." I thought there was bad blood between them because Dad married Mom. Later, I would discover it was the other way round—Dad chose to marry her out of defiance.

When my parents met, Mom was still a country maiden with rosy cheeks. No one in her family had left Eighteenth Mile Village for generations. If he hadn't been sent down to the countryside, Dad would never have met her. That is to say, if not for the policy of "sending Educated Youths to the farming villages," I wouldn't exist. Knowing I was only born as the result of a political slogan has always made me feel my life was a bit random. Really, though, I should feel fortunate—in this country, as the result of another slogan, many more children never got to be born.

They used to say "the wide earth and heavens hold great possibilities," but Dad didn't find any great possibilities in the village. Instead, he started courting Mom. He didn't get on with Grandpa anyway, and had decided to stay on in the countryside to escape his family. Mom came from a large landowning family, so it wasn't a problem for them to feed Dad, and his labor wasn't needed in the fields. Besides, Mom was the most beautiful girl in the whole village—a quiet beauty, like clear spring water flowing through a ravine. Dad was smitten right away. He liked pretty women, a truth I couldn't accept for a very long time, because it made him seem shallow. Mom was good at farm work, adept at rearing pigs and feeding chickens. A shame these skills didn't help her when she moved to the city—all she brought was her beauty, which was valid everywhere, unlike her hukou residence permit. Because of her all-conquering looks, it was easy for people to forget she was a semi-literate country girl. It was also easy to ignore the isolation she endured, the sense of never fitting in. When I finally realized how lonely she was, she'd been in the city more than two decades, and had stopped being beautiful a long time before.

Dad's talk of staying in the countryside forever was just him throwing a tantrum. Like all young city people, he quickly found the hardship and tedium of the farming village intolerable. When he got a job offer from the city, he went back at once. Not long after that, he mentioned to his father that he wanted to marry my mom. That was the first his family knew of her existence.

Grandpa had wanted Dad to marry his colleague Professor Lin's daughter. Miss Lin was a music student and a very fine violinist, as well as an admirer of my dad. She made sure to give him tickets whenever her orchestra held a concert. According to Mom, this love rival of hers was short and fat with swarthy skin, and wore thick glasses. As a child, I often wondered how I'd have turned out if Dad had married Miss Lin instead. On one hand, I'd have been short, dark, and myopic. On the other, if I'd inherited her talent for the violin, I could have devastated everyone with my rendition of the tragic *Butterfly Lovers* at the New Year talent show, rather than performing a skit with you and Dabin that wasn't even funny.

Grandpa told Dad he would come to regret marrying Mom. Dad replied that his regret was his own business, and Grandpa shouldn't interfere. One morning, during a light snowfall, he brought her to the registry office, just like that. No wedding ceremony, no nuptial chamber, no bride price. For the time being, they stayed at a friend's apartment. A simple place, no more than ten meters square, Mom's first home in the city. A week later, her mother and brother got the long-distance bus to Jinan with a couple of live chickens and a bag of New Year pastries, hoping to visit their in-laws. Dad prevented this, and so the two families never met.

My parents were happy for a while. After all, their marriage had been built by smashing a series of obstacles, and Dad treasured it. As for Mom, no longer rearing animals or harvesting wheat beneath the scorching sun, city life seemed fresh and exciting. Dad taught her to ride his broken-down Gold Lion 28-inch bicycle. One Sunday afternoon, she wobbled through the streets to a department store, where she bought her first-ever jar of cold cream. The rosiness of her cheeks had faded by then, though in photographs of the time, she's still a stunner. Soon after that, Dad pulled some strings to find her a job as a nanny in a local nursery. She liked this work, which allowed her to sing, dance, and play games with her little charges. Later, as they napped, she'd quietly tip their leftover food into her lunchbox and bring it home for dinner.

At the time, Dad was working as a driver at the Grain Administration. Each morning, he would cycle to the garage, where he'd change into his uniform, pull on his white gloves, start his truck with the Liberation plates, and drive his cargo of flour and rice through the city. When he had free time in the afternoons, he'd pick Mom up and take her for a drive. This was 1976, when trucks like this were rare, probably no more than twenty in the whole of Jinan. Mom would stand at the alleyway entrance watching Dad approach, then she'd jump on board as passersby watched enviously. Perhaps she believed she was the luckiest woman in the world. Sometimes work went on so late he didn't have time to get back to the garage at the end of the day, so he came straight home. On these nights, Mom would joyfully rush to the vehicle with a sack and broom, and by the faint glow of the streetlights, she'd sweep the fallen rice into the sack. Then she'd run back and show off her spoils, telling Dad this would feed us for a week. He'd smile, maybe finding her adorable. Back then, her frugality was still something he admired.

Mom told me all this when Dad asked her for a divorce. There were a few days when she was sunk in memory, no longer a coarse, simple country woman. Sorrow made her transcend her usual level of comprehension, transforming her into a woman who knew what love meant. I'd never liked her so much as during that time, nor been so willing to do as she said. I've always liked people who understand love.

The first year of his marriage, Dad hardly saw his father. Then one day, my uncle came to visit out of the blue, saying Grandpa wanted to see him. Dad reluctantly went back home. Grandpa told him the government was bringing back university entrance exams, and Dad should take them. Dad retorted that he was very happy with how his life was going, and didn't need anyone else telling him what to do. Later, Grandma visited Mom for the first and only time. Mom did as she asked and helped persuade Dad, something she regretted for the rest of her days. With her limited knowledge, she'd had no idea that going to college could cause such a big change in someone's life.

It's hard to say how much Dad was influenced by her to take the exam. Maybe he'd wanted to all along, and had only refused to spite his father. He didn't want to become a doctor like Grandpa, but enrolled in the literature department. He'd initially thought of going to a university in Beijing, but ultimately stayed in Jinan—they'd have had nowhere to live in the capital, and he wouldn't have known how to find Mom another job. Already she was holding him back.

Dad lived in the dorms, and only came home at weekends. From Monday to Saturday, he read Tolstoy, discussed poetry and philosophy with his teachers and classmates, and watched films in the small university hall. On Sundays, he'd bring his dirty laundry home, carry fifty pounds of flour back from the grain store, move their charcoal supply into a temporary rain shelter, clear out the blocked stove. Mom made him dumplings, the only way she knew to show affection. This was my dad's week, a romantic body with a pragmatic tail.

He wrote poetry back then. It was published in journals, and his female classmates would read it to themselves in private. Whenever he walked through campus, he was followed by several pairs of eyes. As a child, I found his verses in some old magazines at home. I didn't understand them, but thought they were pretty, romantic in a way that had nothing to do with Mom. Or at least, I found it hard to connect these emotions with her. Dad even set up a poetry society with some classmates, and became its president. They'd often get together to talk about poetry, and he spent even fewer weekends at home. The society became very influential, and the founding members would go on to become prominent poets. All except my dad, though they all said he was the most talented of the lot.

Why did my father stop writing poetry? That's a puzzle. Many years later, I met his classmate Yin Zheng, who told me that he and Dad stayed on at the university after graduating, teaching as they worked towards their master's degrees. In his first year of postgraduate studies, Dad abruptly stopped composing poetry—the ability simply deserted him. It was a dark time for him. The other major event in his life that year was my birth, but who can say if these two things were connected?

My parents' relationship was already beginning to cool. The three of us moved into faculty accommodation, so at least we had a home of our own, but Dad was almost never there—he preferred to stay in his office. Maybe he thought his inability to write poetry had something to do with Mom, or maybe he wanted to get through this difficult time on his own.

One of Dad's classmates was in the same situation, having married a village girl whilst in the countryside. This man returned to the city for his studies, divorced his bride not long after graduation, and got together with a woman from his college. My father didn't get divorced or fall in love with any of his students, though apparently he had his share of admirers. I guess his determination to make the marriage work wasn't because of his feelings for Mom, but resolute defiance of Grandpa.

Trying to narrow the widening gap between himself and Mom, Dad sent her to night school and encouraged her to enroll in self-study exams. She did this in fits and starts for many years, but didn't pass a single one. Finally she had me and stopped trying, which must have been a relief. She thought I was her lucky star and would bring her good fortune. Nothing could be further from the truth. After I started school, Mom would flip through my textbooks, but even after so many years, she still had nightmares about exams. She also had bad dreams about losing children—so as not to distract my dad from his studies, she'd had two abortions. I often thought either of those babies would probably have been a better child than me.

As far back as I can remember, I've always known my father didn't love my mother. They only lived together because they were married. I thought marriage must be like our school uniform—it never fit properly, but you still had to wear it. As I got older, I learned to look at Mom through Dad's eyes, and saw what an irredeemable bumpkin she was. Sometimes she forgot to brush her teeth, and she never dried her face with a towel after washing it. She was unable to remember what different containers were for, and would serve orange soda in a bowl or roast pork in a washbasin. She never turned on the lights, seeming to require less illumination than city folk. Her idea of meals was different too—she'd often shovel down her food standing at the stove, then wash her plate with an air of relief. She could be stingy, saving up the polystyrene netting that apples came in and using it to wash dishes and scrub the stove, collecting dishwater to flush the toilet. I knew Dad hated this behavior, but had given up saying anything about it. These daily annoyances nibbled, termite-like, at his affection for her. By the time I was born, it had all been eaten away.

In my memory, my childhood home was always quiet. Only inanimate objects spoke—the TV, washing machine, and coal stove. After we got a phone installed, I used to long for someone to call Dad so I could hear his voice. Sometimes he even laughed. I admired the people who phoned, for being able to make him laugh. Mom and I lacked that ability. My parents didn't talk much. Mom was chatty, but whenever she tried to start a conversation, he'd kill it.

"You don't understand." "Don't ask any more." "Can't you leave me in peace?"

These were the words Dad said to Mom most often. Sometimes she'd force a smile in response, then go over to the window and shut the curtains tightly, or else sigh emptily, pick up her clippers, and start cutting her nails. She never seemed to get angry. She'd put her self-respect away long ago, tucking it somewhere it couldn't be seen. Her indifference made pity impossible. I never once felt sorry for her.

Not only that, I hated how she'd dragged me down with her. Dad didn't love me because he didn't love her. I tried my best to draw a clear line between us: sneering at her countrified habits, correcting her whenever she used the wrong word, mocking her peasant taste. I thought this would please Dad, but I never got a hug from him, let alone a kiss. Some mornings, I'd look at his stubble and imagine how it would feel to be pressed against his cheek. He never made me laugh or cry. No emotions passed between us. We never played games, it never occurred to him that I might have liked to, just as Grandpa had never thought that about him. They both treated children like adults; the concept of childhood didn't exist in their world.

Dad sometimes traveled for business, but never brought me and Mom. The farthest we ever got was to my other grandma's house in the countryside. He didn't bring me to the playground or to the movies. Our one family outing was to see the lanterns on the last day of the New Year, but I was so short, all I got to see was other people's legs. Unlike the other dads, mine didn't lift me above his head so I could grab at the colored streamers trailing from each lantern with riddles written on them. Nor did he pluck me a stick of candied hawthorn. He didn't know a single one of my friends' names, had no idea how good my compositions were, and loathed math problems about chickens and rabbits sharing a hutch.

It was as if he'd decided early on that I existed in a different sphere, like a goldfish in a bowl whose owner never bothered pressing his face against the glass. I might have been no more than an ornament in his life. Our only contact was when I got my allowance. I liked asking him for money—he was much more generous than Mom. She liked me asking him too, because then it didn't have to come out of her housekeeping. I'd tell him exactly what I planned to buy: a hardcover diary with a heart-shaped lock made to look like ancient bronze, available in dark or light blue, but I'd pick dark because I preferred the night sky; a box of thirty-six color pencils, the sort that blurred when you ran a wet brush over them, great for twilit clouds and misty forests; a box of liqueur chocolates, which I planned to devour with my best friend in class, because she'd shared hers with me. As I described these objects, I felt I was describing a part of myself, as if that could help him get to know me a little better. Perhaps that would make him like me. They were sold out of dark-blue diaries so I ended up getting a light-blue one. I left it on our coffee table for quite a few days, and though Dad would have seen it every time he picked up his newspaper, he never once said: I thought you were getting a dark-blue one?

I know, I know, adults never listen to what children tell them, and wouldn't remember a detail like light or dark blue. If it had been Mom, this wouldn't have bothered me at all, but I was sensitive and fragile around Dad, and kept getting hurt.

At home, there was a clear class difference between him and Mom. He was high up, in a position of ultimate power, and his love was impossible to compel—it could only be a gift. I longed for it so much.

I knew his favorite time was late at night, after Mom and I had fallen asleep. Once, I got up to use the bathroom, and saw him watching TV, a beer can on the coffee table. He was slouched on the sofa with his legs over the armrest, his face flushed. The house was full of steam—he'd just taken a shower and was in white long underwear, looking like a giant mollusk that had finally crawled out of its confining shell. He saw me standing in the doorway and said softly, Go to bed. Outside the shell, his voice was moist and tender.

Dad rarely brought Mom to gatherings of colleagues or classmates, but her occasional appearances made them sit up and take notice. They fit the classical image of love, the scholar and the beauty. Everyone assumed they must be happy together, but Dad didn't want to pretend. The only exception was when we visited Grandpa.

Mom would take me clothes shopping before the New Year, in preparation for this visit. One year, I wanted a moss-colored sweater with a pocket in front like a kangaroo, but Mom said I'd worn something green the year before, and she didn't want them thinking I was in the same outfit.

On the last day of the year, I started getting dressed around noon. New clothes, new shoes, a new headband, even a new hair ornament. The one I remember best is a shiny satin ribbon tied in a thick bow studded with little pearls that quivered as I walked, making me feel like a fine lady from the imperial court. My favorite hair clip was red with dark-green checks, but my mom wouldn't let me wear it to Grandpa's place because it was too small. She made me wear enormous ones instead, like hands grabbing the back of my head. As if a bigger hair ornament would make me look happier.

When we were both dressed, we'd stand in front of the mirror, and Mom would say smugly, "This ought to annoy them."

"Why would they be annoyed?" I asked.

"Because they don't want to see us doing well. They thought your dad would suffer after marrying me."

Which meant we had to look like we were doing well. Although Dad never actually said so, I could sense this was what he wanted. But what did that mean? All the way there, my heart was in knots, wondering how I should behave. Then we arrived, and it came to me naturally. Helping Mom brush flour off her clothes after making dumplings, taking Dad's hand when we went onto the balcony to see the fireworks. At midnight, when the firecrackers went off, I'd cover my ears and bury my face in his chest. Mom would ask Dad to help roll up her sleeves, or take off her ring and give it to him for safekeeping before doing the washing up, casually mentioning to my grandma and aunt that this was Dad's latest gift to her. Dad silently went along with whatever we were doing. During the meal, he'd serve Mom with his own chopsticks—a breach of etiquette in that household, where every dish came with communal chopsticks.

I knew none of this was real, but it genuinely made me happy. I looked forward to New Year's Eve: the costumes, the performance, the three of us starring in our own variety show.

The year I turned seven, Grandma turned to Mom at the start of the meal and asked how work was going at the kindergarten.

"I told her to stop doing that," said Dad. "That place was short-staffed. She had to do the cleaning as well as taking care of the kids. It was exhausting her."

That was the first time I heard my dad lie. Mom hadn't resigned, she'd been fired to make way for a graduate from the Teachers' Training College. This was before my aunt and uncle left the country. My aunt, a professor at the Medical University, offered to ask around to see if there was something Mom could do, perhaps on the support staff. Dad shook his head and said that was men's work.

"There are jobs for women too," protested my aunt. "In the cafeteria or the dorms ..."

"No need," said Dad. "Let her relax at home for a while."

After we'd finished our dumplings, Grandma got out the envelopes of New Year money for me and Peixuan. As the grown-ups sat in front of the TV watching the year-end variety show, we went to the outer room to open our red packets. The new banknotes had a sweet fragrance. The people on them looked pure, their faces unwrinkled. When we counted our notes, I had five and she had three. That was too big a difference to be accidental. I went to tell my dad right away.

His face darkening, Dad turned to look at Grandma. She put down the apple she was peeling, and hastily explained that as Mom was out of work, she'd given me a little extra. The room grew very quiet, apart from the waves of applause and laughter from the TV. I looked sideways at the screen, where two men in Zhongshan suits were performing a crosstalk comedy routine. One of them started reciting an entire dinner menu in a single breath, and I felt hungry again.

A bang brought me back to the room. Dad had smacked his teacup down hard on the table.

"What are you doing?" Grandpa glared at him.

Dad glared back. I'd never seen them look directly at each other. Most of the time, each preferred fixing his gaze as far from the other as possible. Dad wrenched the red packet from my hand and flung it on the table. "Thank you for your good intentions, but I can still afford to keep my wife and child." He stood and said to me and Mom, "Get your coats, we're leaving."

We walked out of the front door and across the compound to the garage, where we'd left our bicycles for fear of having them stolen. The sky glowered down at us, no longer snowing, although it was still cold. I followed behind my parents, shivering as I buttoned my coat. It was very close to midnight, and trails of blazing light were already shooting from many of the balconies around us. People in the street lit the fuses on snakelike coils of firecrackers, then ran off with their fingers in their ears. As we passed through the smoky streets, fireworks went off above us, turning the sky green then red. The watchman had his hands stuffed into the sleeves of his padded jacket as he listened to the variety show on a portable radio. The crosstalk was over, and the host was now reading out New Year greetings sent in by border troops, in a quavering voice.

"Aren't you going to finish watching the show?" the watchman asked.

Mom grunted something in response. Dad jumped onto his bicycle, and Mom hoisted me up behind him, then got onto her own bike. We cycled through the compound, now strewn with red debris from the firecrackers.

The area around Southern Courtyard was still quite desolate then. Apart from the family quarters, there were no other residential buildings. Looking up, I could see a smidgen of the fireworks, but they already seemed very far away, in a different sky altogether. The two bicycles sailed through the deserted streets. Dad went very fast, and Mom had to pedal with all her might not to get left behind. Against the wind, she turned to say to Dad, "They're such bullies." She sounded like she wanted to cry, a sort of provocation. Dad said nothing. Sitting behind him, I suddenly burst into tears.

If only I'd waited a little longer to tell Dad about the red packets. Just a few more minutes, and we'd have made it to midnight, my crucial scene: as the clock struck twelve and the firecrackers were at their loudest, I'd have covered my ears and buried my face in Dad's chest. On all those New Year's Eves, it was only in those minutes that I could forget I was only pretending.

Cheng Gong

Remember when we were kids, and the area around Southern Courtyard always seemed so sad and empty? The university's at the eastern edge of the city—beyond this there's only the power plant, and then wheat fields and villages. The villagers sold freshly picked apples and peanuts at the university gates. One always had a little bag of newly laid free-range eggs—Dabin's dad worked at the cafeteria, and this guy would trade him the eggs for a few buckets of slops. Back then, there weren't any high-rise buildings around here, let alone the electronics and technology industrial park. Just the two chimneys sticking up from the power plant, which seemed closer then because there were no buildings in the way. On clear days, smoke rose from them at a diagonal. Through sandstorms, rain, or snow, they looked terrifying, like alien legs striding towards us, like the world was ending.

This used to be one big campus, not different zones like now. Family quarters were across from the university. The grown-ups called that Southern Courtyard, so I did too. My granny and your grandpa both lived here, but at opposite ends. In the middle were the cafeteria and the bike shelter, and a tiny wooded area. We met there every morning, and headed to school together. The elementary school was in the south-west corner of Southern Courtyard, so we had the shortest commute of any student.

Dad sent me to Southern Courtyard when I was six, and your mom brought you here when you were eight. You weren't crazy about that—when you first got here, you spent all your time sulking. You didn't want to know where the post office or the bookstore were, and you refused to chat with the clerk at the convenience store, not even to tell her your name. When our class went on a spring outing, you hid behind a rock rather than being in the group photo. You told us you were only here temporarily, and your dad would come to take you away again soon. Whenever I looked at you, I saw myself two years earlier. Once again, I started fantasizing that I would be leaving any day now. Then three years later, you really did go, and I stayed another twenty-four years. One time, when Dabin said I'd grown up in Southern Courtyard like him, I had to correct him: I moved here aged six. He pouted and said I was splitting hairs. But no, that was an important distinction. I might not remember much of my life before turning six, but I want to keep it separate in my mind. I don't think I ever told you this. For some reason, I never told you the most important things.

According to the fortune-teller, my destiny was activated at the age of six, after which began the cycle of my fate changing every ten years. Before activation, my existence had been weightless, meaning I could easily have died. Life truly begins when a person's fate is activated, like a tree's roots getting a firm grip on the soil. I'd rather not have put down roots. The idea of my destiny beginning felt like a horse being bridled, as if I were being led on a rope, walking down a path that had been laid out for me long ago. I became nostalgic for the time before fate had caught hold of me.

"Mommy only has Gong, and Gong only has Mommy." When I was little, my mom would say that all the time, then she'd pull me in for a hug and gently stroke my mop of hair. "That's how it is, isn't it?" When I nodded yes, she'd sigh in relief. There was no need to ask, but the question came up again and again.

Mom and I lived in a tiny, cramped space, but I thought it was the size of the world. I hadn't started kindergarten yet, and never went outside to play. Mom had no friends and didn't see her family. Even when she bumped into a neighbor, she only exchanged a few words. I could count all the people I knew on the fingers of one hand. We mostly stayed at home, two little rooms—less than thirty square meters, crammed full of stuff. Mom loved buying things, the one pleasure she allowed herself even when money was tight. She got a friend who worked at the export store to help her buy a carousel music box and a doll with a parasol. At the gates of the glass factory, she grabbed discounted chipped vases. From the antique market, she bought an old radio that could no longer produce a sound. Every few days she'd show up with a new object, a swallow building its nest. This useless crap was prominently displayed while regular things—shoes, umbrellas, basins—were found aesthetically lacking and hidden away. There were so many items stuffed under our bed, sometimes one would poke its head out to catch its breath. Our home was sealed tight as a tin can, keeping time out, and the days passed extraordinarily slowly.

Apart from pointless ornaments, Mom also loved clothes, though many of these were also purely decorative, and never worn. Coats with exquisite collars, flowing dresses, wool sweaters so soft I wanted to bury my face in them. Mom gave me a peach sweater she'd never put on, having decided the color was too bright, and I used it as a pillow. I liked its scent, the sweet rot of apples. I had nice clothes too, though not as many as Mom. A little waistcoat that tied at the back, a jacket with red and black checks, a white sweater with an anchor embroidered on the chest. They were all too big for me. Mom said I would grow into them. The few times we went out, Mom insisted I get dressed up. One time, we ran into Auntie Meizhen who lived downstairs. "Look at you," she said, enviously stroking the collar of Mom's camel coat. "Another outfit from your overseas relatives?" Mom smiled but didn't reply. I looked up at her. What overseas relatives?

Most days, I forgot I had a dad. He only came home late at night, reeking of alcohol, eyes so red I thought they would start spurting blood. Despite never holding down a real job, he was always busy with what he called his transport business. In reality, he drank and gambled, as if that was the only way to get rid of his surplus energy. Whenever he had any left, he would hit Mom.

As far back as I remember, I was always watching Mom getting hit, and I saw her get used to it. All she asked was that he delay his violence till I'd fallen asleep. If I hadn't, or if I was startled awake, she wanted me to lie there perfectly still anyway, not crying or screaming, just letting it be over soon. So I did that, obediently holding my breath in the dark, not stirring a muscle. As a reward or compensation, when the beating was over, Mom would come into my bed and let me put my hands on her bosom as I drifted off. In the moonlight, her small, pointy breasts looked pure white, like the domes of a temple. When I rested on them, the nightmares stayed away.

But there were also nights when she didn't come to me. I would jerk awake between dreams and find her in the other room, in the big bed with Dad, his brown hand on a temple dome.

In the morning, she'd be back in my bed, sitting up as usual, hugging herself and staring into space. I'd run my fingers gently over the blisters on her arms, where she'd been burned with cigarettes. The shiny little bumps felt mysterious to the touch. I counted her bruises, like dark clouds before the rain. New ones, old ones, I don't think I ever saw her completely healed. It was much later that I realized not all women had skin like Mom's: almost transparent, revealing fine blue veins, so fragile the slightest pressure could break it. I thought that she looked especially beautiful when she'd been injured, that she liked herself that way, that she'd come into this world to be hurt.

I later found out that Mom actually *did* have an overseas relative: her grandfather went to Taiwan in 1949, and from there to the USA. As far as I know, he never contacted her. Her father was an only child, and her grandmother raised him alone. Not long after Mom was born, her grandmother and father got ill and died, then her mother starved to death during the Three Years of Natural Disasters. She was raised by her grandfather's little brother's son. During the Cultural Revolution, this uncle was constantly tormented because her grandfather lived overseas. This was the atmosphere of terror Mom grew up in, perpetually afraid of abandonment.

This fear lingered in her eyes, like the footprints of some creature from the Cretaceous Period fleeing for its life. Her beauty existed alongside this terror. When my father first saw her outside the exhibition hall where she was working as a guide, did he see something in her that made him want to go in for the kill? Mom had been dependent on others for a long time, and must have yearned for a home of her own—perhaps that's why she was willing to entertain this guy who was pestering her. She soon realized he was a bastard, but she was pregnant by then, and rather than give her uncle any more trouble, she married him. Many years later, accompanying a girl I'd knocked up to the clinic, I had the sudden thought that if the morning after pill had been around back then, I'd never have been born.

Dad's thuggish ways could be traced back to his childhood. Before graduating from elementary school he was already hanging out with the Red Guards, doing all kinds of horrible things. Even after the Cultural Revolution had ended, he found he couldn't stop, but kept picking fights with people. Rather than getting a proper job, he found ways to cheat or extort money. He stabbed someone in the arm and broke someone else's nose, and of course he got injured himself: he walked with a limp from a broken leg. Everyone in Southern Courtyard knew who he was, and they hid when he came along. Behind his back, they called him Death-Defying Cheng. People must have warned you about him when you moved here?

I never saw this with my own eyes, but I feel like Dad wasn't actually any good at fighting. He was just full of hatred and didn't know who to aim it at, so he sprayed his uncontrollable rage in all directions. One summer, the three of us went out together for once, to celebrate Granny's birthday at Southern Courtyard. It was a scorching, windless afternoon. Standing near us at the bus stop was a very attractive woman, a little younger than Mom, in a white dress whose frilly collar scooped low in the back. "What a slut," Dad said quietly, glaring at her.

He drew closer to her and stood on tiptoe, screwing up his eyes as if he was trying to make out the bus stop sign. Casually raising his hand, he allowed his smoldering cigarette to rest on the woman's collar. She was looking out for the bus and didn't notice—nor did anyone else. Only Mom and I watched as flames devoured the frills. Mom clenched my hand tight, afraid I would make a sound. For a very long minute, we somehow forced ourselves to remain where we were. A chunk was now missing from the back of her dress, leaving a blackened ring like teeth marks. Mom only let go of my hand when the bus arrived and the woman got on.

I suspect this malignity, coming out of nowhere, might be genetic. When I moved to Southern Courtyard, I found out that Granny was even more notorious than Dad. Everyone remembered how she'd humiliated a young nurse from the University Hospital who'd offended her in some way, scaring her so badly she had a miscarriage. When the head nurse tried to defend her junior, Granny took to flinging the contents of a spittoon at her front door every day. Everyone said she only became so fearsome after my granddad was attacked during the Cultural Revolution and ended up in an unresponsive state. That said, before this incident, Granddad had been the autocratic deputy director of the University Hospital, and had a reputation for running the place with an iron fist. Everyone was scared of him. So was Dad's disposition genetic or not? It's hard to be sure.

Granny loathed Mom, though she'd honestly have hated anyone Dad married. She believed all people apart from blood relatives were evil, and therefore her enemies. When Mom married into the family, she naturally wasn't exempt. Granny made her kneel on a washboard all afternoon, then whacked her with a rolling pin. Mom soon got used to this treatment.

By contrast, Auntie was the only normal person in the family. Naturally timid, she had a lot to put up with, though Mom joining the household did take some pressure off her. They became friends for a short while, though it was Auntie making all the effort: taking advantage of her job to get Mom various medicines and passing her coupons to use the university bathhouse. She worshiped Mom for being elegant and well spoken. Mom was very good-looking, like an expensive necklace you wanted to take a closer look at or maybe try on, even if you could never own it. Alas, fantasy is followed by disappointment, and Auntie could never resist criticizing Mom in front of Granny, which soured their relationship.

The biggest wedge between Auntie and Mom, though, was me. As far back as I could remember, Mom was always keeping me away from Dad. She hoped to surround me with only good things. Auntie came to visit not long after I was born. Mom was sunning me on the balcony, and orchestral music was playing on the radio. Mom put her finger on her lips to shush Auntie till the tune was done. Look, she said, he's completely rapt with Beethoven. He's a baby, what does he know, said Auntie, who found the whole thing ridiculous. He knows a lot, Mom insisted, smiling, He's always surprising me. She played me classical music, read me fairy tales, and covered the walls with Van Gogh and Chagall prints. She had plans to turn me into some sort of genius, though these ambitions faded as I got older, and the cruelties of daily life rubbed away all her patience.

I don't remember the first time Mom went to Taikang Food Store. If Dad hadn't kept asking, I might have forgotten the whole thing. All I know is Mom was always bringing me there in the afternoon to buy snacks. The guy behind the counter dealt with candy all day long, so he always smelled sugary, and his words were sickly sweet too. I never learned his name, I just called him Uncle Candy. Every time we went, Uncle Candy would scoop a big handful of cellophane-wrapped sweets right into my pocket.

"That's too many, just a few will do," Mom simpered at him. "I won't dare to come again if you're like this."

Two days later, we were back, and I had more candy in my pocket. The shop was mostly empty in the afternoons, so Mom could lean across the counter and idly chat with Uncle Candy. The counter was taller than I was, and I sat under it eating my candy, flattening the cellophane wrappers and folding them into little figures. Suddenly, I heard Mom sobbing, and her shadow wavered on the ground. I reached up to take her hand, but he was already holding it.

Uncle Candy gave me more candies as I left. So many I couldn't finish them. I fell asleep with one in my mouth, and my dreams were scented with licorice.

One day I woke up from a licorice dream to find the house empty. Mom had left in a hurry, not taking anything with her, though it didn't feel as if she'd left anything either. All I had to remember her by was a couple of cavities from all that candy.

I don't know why she didn't take me with her. How had I

let her down so much for her to abandon me? For a long time, I didn't believe she'd actually done it. Surely she'd come back for me once she'd settled in? I wanted to wait at home for her rather than going to live with Granny, but Dad didn't ask my opinion—he just wanted somewhere to dump me.

One evening on the cusp of spring and summer, I stood in the doorway watching Dad hurl everything we owned into a couple of plastic sacks. As the sun set, shadows filled the cavernous space, and the bare white walls, empty of photographs, no longer looked so stark. I quietly rescued a clockwork frog and a few marbles from the junk pile. Dad strapped the sacks to his bicycle and we set off for Granny's, him riding and me running behind. He went slowly at first, then as we passed through a crowded market, he got impatient and sped up. I had to sprint, almost crashing into a fruit stand and knocking a little girl's pinwheel from her hand. The marbles jolted from my pocket and rolled across the ground, but I was too afraid of losing him to stop.

Granny's apartment also consisted of two small rooms, and I wondered if that's what everyone's home was like. She didn't have much furniture, only cardboard and wooden boxes of all sizes, making the place look like a warehouse. I looked around for a vase or picture frame, but the only ornament I could see was a square clock on the wall whose face read, in red, *Commemorating the 90th Anniversary of the Medical University*. Granny loved this red writing, which also adorned her tea mug, washbasin, and flask, some commemorating the school, others the Party.

It was dinner time, and several dark bowls sat on the table. There were only three chairs, so Auntie fetched me the stool from the sewing machine. Granny grumbled that Dad had promised to get her another chair after smashing the fourth one, but never had. Then she began enumerating all of Dad's promises that hadn't materialized, from buying her deep-fried rice cakes to paying for her gold teeth. She'd remembered every single one. Granny spoke without apparently using her tongue—rather than being bitten into shape, words seem to hurtle from her throat, a peculiar sound that reminded me of a partridge or some other bird. Dad calmly ate his dinner, as if he simply didn't understand this language.

Dad left right after dinner. As he walked out, Granny shouted after him not to forget my monthly living expenses. I stacked the dirty dishes and brought them to Auntie in the kitchen, then wiped them dry after she'd washed them. I thought it would be easier to get on her good side than on Granny's. Soon the dishes were done, the stove was wiped, and the kitchen was all tidy. I followed Auntie back into the outer room.

It was so dim here, I felt oxygen-deprived. The only light came from a fluorescent tube above the dining table, whose dusty bean-green shade cast a shadow like a bat spreading its wings. The black-and-white TV hummed. Granny lounged beneath the window on a dilapidated sofa, many of its bamboo strips snapped and jutting out at odd angles. In the middle of the sofa was a large dip that wrapped itself around Granny's squat little body, like a bird's nest in the crook of a branch. I thought she'd fallen asleep, but just as I was breathing a sigh of relief, she jerked upright and squinted at me. Then the partridge voice issued from her wrinkly face: "Remove all the clothes he's wearing!"

Before I understood what was going on, Auntie had caught hold of my arm and was undoing my shirt buttons.

"Don't bother with that," said Granny. "Just rip it off!"

Auntie tugged the shirt hard, and the buttons popped off onto the floor, allowing her to wrench it off me by the collar.

"The trousers! The trousers too!" yelled Granny.

Auntie knelt and held me with one hand, while the other ripped off my corduroy trousers.

"You think these clothes your mom gave you are so

precious? Ha!" Granny spat on the floor. "They were taken from dead children! You stink of rotting, maggoty dead kids! The eggs will have hatched by now, soon you'll have maggots crawling into your ears."

"That's not true!" I shouted.

"Your granny's telling the truth." Auntie picked up my shirt and turned it over to show me the label, which was covered in scribbled English writing. "Your mom bought these at Haiyou Market. Everything they sell there comes from containers of trash from overseas."

I stood there stunned, allowing Auntie to lift my legs and pull the trousers off. She lifted them between two fingers. "Look, the color's so bright, you can tell it hasn't been washed many times. If it hadn't come off a dead body, why would they throw out a perfectly good pair of trousers like these?"

"Stop waving that around, it's filthy!" said Granny, jabbing Auntie in the shoulder. "Go through his bags and get the other corpse clothes. Take them downstairs and burn them."

Auntie yanked open the plastic sacks and pulled out a sweater with an anchor embroidered on it, a hoodie, a cap, holding up each item as if to give me one last look. They smelled familiar, but now I wasn't sure if that was my mom's scent, or the dead children's. Auntie stuffed them into a cardboard box and took them downstairs.

"I've never heard of such an evil mother, giving her own son dead people's clothes."

Granny yawned, expelling rancid breath, stretched, and headed into the room she slept in.

I stood in the middle of the room in my long underwear. After a while, I burst into tears, though I couldn't have said why I was crying. Because I'd lost the clothes I loved, because maggots were crawling into my ears, because Mom deceived me. I thought of the peach sweater I'd fallen asleep cradling. Did its rotten apple fragrance come from a dead woman's perfume? All my sweet memories were now horrifying. Mom felt like a stranger too. I didn't think I could love her in the same way anymore.

Tired from crying, I slumped over the sewing machine stool and fell asleep. After a while, I heard movement. Auntie was placing the chairs alongside the single bed, extending it. From a wooden chest at the head of the bed, she produced a quilt.

"Come here, we'll share the bed." She lifted me off the floor and studied me. "Your granny will want to get rid of that underwear, too. Here ..." She handed me a maroon thermal shirt. "Wear this for now. We'll get you new ones tomorrow."

I just stood there haplessly, so she did it for me. When she accidentally pulled down my briefs along with the long underwear and my little genitals were exposed to the lamplight, she flushed bright red and quickly pulled the shirt over my face, as if afraid I would see.

It was a woman's top, which, on me, became a nightshirt that reached to my ankles. Auntie reached into the flappy sleeves to pull my arms through.

"Done." She sat on the side of the bed, looking at me. I turned my face aside.

"Here, this is for you." She reached into the pocket of her cardigan and put a piece of candy in my hand. The cool, waxy wrapper rubbed against my palm. I looked down—it was one of Uncle Candy's.

"I found it in your trouser pocket while I was burning your clothes," she said. "There was only one. If you like them, I'll buy you more."

"No thanks." I withdrew my hand and took the candy into my sleeve.

Before going to bed, Auntie pulled the rubber band off her braid and shook it out, then turned off the light and lay next to me. In the dark, her distinctive bulbous forehead and high cheekbones were hidden by her long hair, and she looked a bit like Mom. I had to fight to keep my hand from reaching for her breast. After a while, I heard snoring.

Rustling in the dark, I unwrapped the last piece of candy and popped it in my mouth.

Li Jiaqi

When I was very young, I had a sort of premonition that Dad would leave us one day. I even came up with the simplest way for him to do that—falling in love with one of his students. Apart from teaching, his duties in the Chinese Department included acting as a counselor, which naturally meant asking students about their lives, allowing girls with long hair like flowing water and books of poetry clutched to their bosoms to open their hearts to him. An old-fashioned phrase, "open their hearts"—it reeks of the eighties, when our hearts weren't buried so deep and could still be brought to the surface.

Dad never brought students home, and Mom and I weren't invited to join their gatherings, so I never met the girls he taught. My only knowledge of them came from the yearbooks he brought home, hence I didn't get to know them until they'd already graduated. It never felt like they'd truly departed, because of the words they left: *Our story hasn't ended yet,* or *You'll always be my hitching post.* Inscriptions that felt like love notes. In the afternoon sun, I squinted at those little pictures of girls hugging their knees and staring into the sunset or sitting on lawns in sunhats, as if I were choosing a stepmother from a catalog.

I believed they were superior to my mother, even though she was hard to beat in the looks department. This wasn't because of their youth, but because they weren't country-side folk. I never considered the possibility that they'd grown up somewhere rural, and perhaps hadn't even been in the city as long as Mom. They didn't seem like country folk, deploying fancy metaphors like "hitching post" that my mother could never have come up with.

Yet the student who was supposed to steal my dad away never showed up. In 1990, he resigned from the university, having decided to go into business in Beijing. Just before he left, I met his students for the first time.

That night, seven or eight of them came to our home. Dad wasn't back yet—his friends were throwing him a farewell dinner at a nearby restaurant. The students filled our tiny living room, their lips compressed and expressions grim, not taking a single bite of the watermelon my mom served them.

"We're sorry to disturb you, Mrs. Li, but we really wanted to say goodbye to the professor," said a girl, her eyes swollen as if she'd been crying for a long time.

"Yes," said another student. "You have no idea how kind he's been to us."

Mom smiled at him in confusion, uncertain what to say.

The boy continued, "Last summer, when we went to Beijing, he was the only one who supported us. And now those people are using that against him ..."

Mom didn't know anything about Dad being punished, though that didn't matter anymore. What worried her was their mention of Beijing.

"Will there be any problem with him going to Beijing now?" she asked.

The students assured her there wouldn't be, but still she worried. As far as she was concerned, *Beijing* was just another word on the *Xinwen Lianbo* daily news, like *nation* or *world*. In her mind, Beijing was a place to do important things—conferences with leaders of other countries, hosting the Asian Games, inspecting the troops on National Day—and she couldn't imagine actually living there. She urged them to say more about the city, asking if the roads were as wide as she'd seen on TV, and if the Square was always so crowded. Really, the students had only been to the capital that one time, but they sounded as if they'd spent half their lives there when they told Mom about their two-week visit.

I lurked nonchalantly behind my mother, twisting the arm of my plastic dolly. Round and round, like winding up a gramophone. I sped up as their mood intensified, until all of a sudden, the arm slipped out of its socket and flew through the air, landing at a student's feet. They stopped speaking and stared at me, as if they'd only just noticed I existed. Blushing, I walked over hesitantly. A boy took the doll from my hand and, carefully lining up the limb with its cavity, shoved it into place.

"Here, stop fiddling with that." He handed it back to me.

After that little interruption, the room sank into silence. The air around us seemed to stiffen. Our voltage was low, and the lights kept flickering. *Bzz, bzz.*

Dad was drunk by the time he got home, a scarlet miasma of alcohol in the air, like a burning coal sizzling as it consumed him. He stepped through the door, still despondent from having left the previous gathering, only to cheer up instantly when he saw the roomful of students. This was the sort of happiness only a drunk person could muster, a hollow enjoyment of bustle. Mom brought him a chair, but he kept staggering around. I worried this would make him look bad, but the students continued gazing at him with the utmost respect, along with a sort of sorrow, as if fully aware of his pain. I was jealous of how well they knew him—they seemed more like his family than Mom and I.

"How many times do I have to tell you, my resignation

had nothing to do with you!" He waggled his finger at them. "I just saw through everything." He shook his head. "It's completely meaningless."

The students bit their tongues, not saying a word. A girl started weeping quietly.

"Don't cry, Little Feng. You mustn't cry." Dad's voice turned tender. He finally sat and stared into space for a moment, then suddenly burst out laughing.

"Let's not hope for anything more," he said.

In my memory, that tragic evening concluded with those mysterious words. But actually, that's when Mom dragged me off to bed, while the others kept talking.

I hadn't understood much of the conversation, but for some reason I remembered the words they'd used. Many years later, Xu Yachen was astonished that I was able to recall everything they'd said about their trip to Beijing, including some details that had vanished or shifted in his own memory. He said, perhaps many things are destined to inscribe themselves in our minds even without us meaning them to.

I reconnected with Xu Yachen four years ago, while I was working as an editor at a fashion magazine and ran into him at a charity auction. As usual, it was full of wealthy businessmen, socialites, and nouveaux riches. A showcase of wealth. Everyone was vying to bid on jewelry worn by movie stars, premier cru wines, and pieces by trendy artists. The proceeds were going to build an elementary school for the children of rural migrant workers. Love is priceless, the emcee kept saying, although every measure of love there had a price tag on it. Xu Yachen went all in on a statue by a famous sculptor. When the emcee invited him up on the stage, he looked tenderly at the schoolchildren seated in the front row.

"This is just a tiny effort on our part, but it could change these children's entire lives," he said.

Thunderous applause rumbled across the room. I couldn't

say why this felt wrong, but I was sorry for those kids. How insignificant they must be, that their whole lives could be altered by someone else's tiny effort.

Xu Yachen was in a gray shirt, its top button fastened with difficulty, collar tight beneath his round head like someone strangling him to demand his money. I forced myself to remember that unremarkable face, so I'd be able to go up to him in the dispersing crowds later. He was the owner of a food and beverage consortium, and had been in the headlines after his business started doing well and he got into a dispute with his cofounder. My chief editor wanted me to interview him for our "New City Million-aires" column. After the auction, I wandered over slowly with a champagne flute in my hand, waiting till the hand-ful of people talking to him had wandered off before I approached. He readily agreed to the interview. I felt awk-ward running off right after accomplishing my mission, so I stayed for a bit of small talk. He asked where I was from, and I said Jinan. He said he'd studied there, and told me which university, which department, which year. Every piece of information correct. Finally, I had to ask whether he knew Li Muyuan. That's my professor, he said. And my father, I said.

"The professor's daughter!" he yelled with some emo-tion.

My hand shook, almost spilling my drink. It was moving to be named in that way, as if I was one amongst my father's students.

Yachen said the last time he'd seen me, I'd been a shy little girl. I couldn't place him until he suddenly recalled how he'd reattached my dolly's arm. I was shocked, and com-pletely unable to reconcile the man in front of me with the boy from back then.

"You were so young then, you probably don't remember what I looked like," he said.

"I do, actually."

"Then I must have got old and fat." He smiled sadly.

It wasn't that either. I'd never imagined he would own a food and beverage consortium. I couldn't have said what sort of person he'd become, but it shouldn't be someone so successful. That night had been so melancholy, I'd assumed the rest of their lives would follow suit.

One of the organizers came over and asked Yachen to pose with the statue he'd bought, a figure of a girl, maybe ten years old, in a red dress, leaning forward with slightly bent knees and closed eyes, as if to sniff an invisible flower. She looked intoxicated. The artwork was titled "Dream." Yachen did as the photographer asked and reached out to embrace this "Dream" with a dazzling smile.

A few days later, I met him for our interview. This ended with him taking me out to dinner at one of his restaurants. It was on the sixty-fifth floor, and through the large windows the city lights might as well have been at the other end of our lives, as if the ground were as distant from us as 1990. Neither of us dared bring up the past. He chatted about red wine, travel, collecting art, just as he probably did with every girl he met. It was a happy conversation, but I knew I wasn't going to retain any of it. After dinner, he gave me a lift home. As his car sped down Chang'an Road and the vast emptiness of the Square, the deep red walls looked the color of rust. It was very quiet, just the wheezing of the air-conditioning. He turned to ask if I wanted to come to his place for a drink, he had a lot of excellent red wine. All right, I said.

He'd gotten a divorce not long ago, and now lived alone in this huge villa. We sat in his garden drinking. It was a June evening, and after the rain earlier in the day, the air felt fresh and clean. A light breeze blew across my face, keeping me from getting too drunk. As he opened the second bottle, he started talking about my father. I stared at the rim of my glass, not wanting to miss a single word.

Several years after graduation, they heard about Dad's

death. The whole class got together and had a mini memorial service. Every one of them wept for him, a bout of tears to mark the end of youth.

"Not just our youth, it was the end of an era too," he added.

"The end of an era," I repeated softly, pressing down on the words, as if I'd finally found a sufficiently weighty sentiment to attach to my father's death.

Neither of us got drunk that night. We only drank enough that I could spend the night without feeling embarrassed.

Yachen and I made love like we were searching for something in each other's bodies. Traces of those ideals that burst like bubbles, the sincerity and generosity people used to treat each other with, vestiges of a bygone age. We wanted to use each other to return to the time and space of our last encounter. I wanted to go back so I could finally understand all those things I'd never been able to grasp; he wanted to remember everything he'd forgotten.

"Professor's daughter," he murmured, body pressed to mine, reminding me there would always be someone between us.

"Dad," I said indistinctly to the man solidly occupying the empty air.

We stayed awake all night, lying in bed, remembering that evening in 1990. My memory was much clearer than his. I could repeat everything they'd said.

"And then you asked who remembered how many magnolia-blossom lamps are on every streetlight on Chang'an Road? Twelve, you said. Because that long night in the Square, you'd counted them over and over," I heard myself say, though that husky voice didn't seem to belong to me, but to a tape recorded many years ago. The sharp memory abruptly became a strong beam of light, shining on Yachen and making him look feeble. He said he could see his former self. "See," not remember, because that self was still back there in the long ago.

"Part of me died along with that time," he said.

I shut my eyes, but I knew it was almost dawn because the darkness pressing down on my eyelids was beginning to lighten.

As the sun rose, he pulled on his clothes, becoming once again a complete person. He gave me a tour of the house, showing off the rosewood furniture and newly built wine cellar. He even opened a locked door on the second floor so I could appreciate all the art he'd acquired at various auctions. The large room's thick curtains were drawn to protect the valuable photographs from light damage. A sunless room reeking of imprisonment. The oil paintings covering the wall were cages containing young women, early summer landscapes, overripe fruit. Statues of all heights like stone figures in an ancient tomb. He hadn't bothered removing all of them from their protective plastic packaging. In the farthest corner of the room was his most recent purchase, the little girl named "Dream." She hadn't been unwrapped either, and duct tape covered her smile.

Yachen seemed extremely satisfied with his current life. Like many successful individuals, he believed all the setbacks he'd suffered had been in the service of his subsequent accomplishments.

"Luckily I was sanctioned, and couldn't join the Party," he said. "With my personality, I'd definitely have wound up becoming a minister. Imagine being on edge all day long, for that little bit of money. Completely meaningless."

Completely meaningless. My father had said this too. But it was possible these two men had different ideas of "meaning." Still, it had been eighteen years since my father had spoken these words. If he were still alive, if his business had been successful, he'd be a wealthy entrepreneur now as well. And looking over everything he owned, would he be similarly grateful for the punishment he'd suffered back then? Would he have long forgotten the emotional farewell with his students? Perhaps that evening was destined to slip from the memory of everyone involved.

I had one more question, but the moment had passed. I wanted to ask, if my father were still alive, would part of him have died anyway, along with that vanished era? Or would it have died even before that, making this a second death?

After so many years, Yachen still worshiped my father, but the focus of his reverence had changed. Now he respected Dad's "wise, far-sighted choice" to resign and join the first generation of businessmen in the People's Republic. I thought Dad had merely been exiling himself. According to Yachen, most of Dad's colleagues didn't get on with him. Not content with sanctioning him for defending his students, they thought of other ways to get at him, even preventing him from teaching. Dad must have been utterly disheartened. When he talked about "seeing through everything" and it being "meaningless," he must have been thinking not just of the political situation, but also his strife with the department. That's why he resigned without much thought for what came next.

It was 2008 when I met Yachen again, not long after Tang Hui came back to Beijing. Tang Hui was a schoolmate, three years older than me. We'd started dating at university and had been together quite some time. After graduating, he went to Shanghai for further studies, while I chose to stay in Beijing, though I couldn't have told you what was so good about this vast, impractical city. Maybe because of Dad, I'd always felt an unshakable bond to this place. For a number of years, Tang Hui and I spent more time apart than together, yet our feelings for each other remained remarkably strong. I only cheated because I felt so empty. He never noticed. He believed in our relationship with the same certainty he did in mathematical principles. After he finished his PhD, he finally came back to Beijing and started teaching at a university here. Before that, I'd spent years sharing with roommates, moving every now and then. Renting an apartment with him brought to an end that peripatetic phase of my existence. "Our first home." In the empty, light-filled room, he hugged me from behind. The love he gave me was as soft as the palms of his hands, and I felt soothed to be wrapped in it.

We'd only just moved into our new apartment. The green curtains were being altered to fit our windows, the gardenias and freesias on our balcony had just started to bloom, and the wine we were brewing from Jiangshao green plums wasn't ready to drink yet. I bought a toaster oven and a tamagoyaki omelet pan, and printed a thick stack of recipes I'd found online. Our tranquil life together had just begun. The walls still smelled faintly of fresh paint, a chemical scent that gave a sense of spaciousness. There were huge blanks that would be filled by what was to come.

The night I stayed over at Yachen's place, Tang Hui was in Shanghai for business. I don't know why I chose to interview Yachen while my boyfriend was out of town. Maybe I'd sensed from the start that something was going to happen between us. Even so, it needn't have left a trace. That night was too long, and we'd said everything we had to say to each other. It should all have ended at daybreak. That's what I decided as I left the next day, hugging Yachen with the melancholy of knowing we'd never meet again. In the taxi home, sunlight filled the back seat, and my heart filled with bottomless sorrow. Not seeing Yachen again meant I'd never be this close to my father again. As I sped away, I felt a curtain fall and cut me off from the past.

That night, I dreamed I was eight or nine, my hair in fuzzy braids—the way it was when I first met you—sitting on an empty train. In the dim light, a matryoshka doll rolled along the tattered carpet. I picked it up. Swaddled in scarlet paint, the wooden doll had an oily smile on her face. "Open it." A woman's shrill voice. I twisted it open to find a smaller doll, then an even smaller one. Sweat beaded on my forehead. "Open it! Open it!" Discarded doll halves rattled at my feet.

I awoke in an icy puddle of sweat, Tang Hui gently shaking my shoulder. "You were having a nightmare."

I pressed my face to his chest. It was impossible to say what the dream meant, but I had an inkling that this couldn't be the end. Sure enough, Yachen called a week later.

"I want to see you," he murmured into the phone.

That very afternoon, he picked me up and we drove to a restaurant in the countryside. It was a bright summer's day, and the air was fragrant with grass. We zoomed down a wide road, lush fields of wheat on either side. As the crimson sun sank below the horizon, Luo Dayou's "Childhood" played on the radio. I felt alive all of a sudden, as if we'd been released early from school.

The restaurant was surrounded by trees, and cicadas chirped loudly. Little white candles stood on the open-air tables and purple lilies floated on the lake.

"We've known each other for eighteen years," said Yachen. "Isn't that hard to believe? I've kept thinking about you these last few days. You make me remember many things about the past. When I'm with you, I feel real."

"To feeling real." We clinked glasses.

My will dissolved in the wine as it disappeared, inch by inch. I forgot the promise I'd made myself and followed him home again. We made love, and fell into a drunken sleep. Luckily, I woke up thirsty in the middle of the night and saw my phone flashing on the bedside table. Jumping out of bed, I flung on my shoes, yelled goodbye and rushed out the door.

I made up a stupid lie for Tang Hui, something about going drinking with my coworkers.

"They said we should get together more often," I said, laying the ground for future absences.

"I'd better learn to hold my liquor," said Tang Hui. "Wouldn't want to embarrass myself in front of your friends."

"You wouldn't like them," I said. "They're ridiculous."

Yachen called again at the weekend. Standing before the mirror, holding my hair up, I didn't recognize myself. The room, too, looked unfamiliar. Perhaps it was the curtains we'd just hung. The color was too bright, too insistently green. As my eyes swept across the mirror, I realized a pair of eyes was staring at me from the gloom.

"Dad!" I spun around. He was sitting there, in the coffee-colored waistcoat he'd worn all those years ago, his head gleaming with hair oil. A little patch of green-tinted sunlight wobbled on his leather shoe. He gazed at me in silence, expressionless.

"I don't know what to do, Dad," I said. "I just wanted to be a little closer to you."

The patch of greenish light fractured in my tears. As it flared, he disappeared.

This visitation, even if it was just a hallucination, was meant as a pardon. A little closer to him. What could be more important than that?

After that, I saw Yachen at least once a week. It always went the same way—he'd pick me up in the evening, we'd go for dinner, then back to his place to drink, make love, and reminisce. I was only really interested in the last item, and would have liked to shorten the preceding steps, but Yachen placed a lot of importance on dinner. He chose our restaurants with great care—a balcony full of bougainvillea blossoms, a classical Chinese courtyard with stippled bamboo stalks, a Michelin-starred chef visiting from abroad, the outlandish innovations of molecular gastronomy.

"I want to take good care of you, for the professor's sake," he once said, in all seriousness, glancing up from his menu. Yet sitting in these extravagant places, enjoying all this expensive food, filled me with guilt. Looking at him in his dapper clothes, swirling the wine in his glass, I'd be suddenly consumed with rage. How could we be so happy and comfortable? It wasn't right. There ought to be a bass note of tragedy. Just like that evening in 1990. We should be in a room with drawn curtains, harrowingly making love, excruciatingly revisiting the past. Only by being steeped in pain could our lust be reasonable, my betrayal noble.

I worked hard to control myself. Keeping my head down, I cleaned my plate. At last, the waiter took our plates away.

"I don't want dessert," I said. "Let's go back to yours now."

He smiled slyly. "No rush, finish your wine first."

As soon as we stepped in the door, I began dragging him towards the stairs, and we stumbled into the bedroom. I ripped off his shirt and loosened his belt. His plump body stood exposed in the gloom, like a ruined building.

"You want it so badly?" he said softly.

"Uh huh." Although what I wanted and what he was offering weren't the same thing.

Rough and hysterical, I squeezed my misery dry. I wanted him hollowed out like a sacrifice.

"You're a bandit," he said weakly.

Desire ebbed, and our bodies were scrubbed clean. At certain moments, from certain angles, he did look a little like the undergraduate I remembered. His ruddy, angular face intoxicated me with disappointment. I wanted to hug him. If only this affection would linger a few minutes more.

"Tell me more about back then," I said. *Back then*. A phrase we often used, although not quite in the same way. His "back then" meant his university days, while mine was the three years my dad had spent with him.

"What should I say?" he asked.

"Anything."

He shut his eyes and began to remember. He had a blurry memory of a time when he'd been drinking a lot after being dumped, and had even got into a fight with the guy who'd stolen his girlfriend. Dad summoned him for a talk, but just chatted about love instead of scolding him.

"What did he say?" I wanted to know.

I waited in the darkness until I heard him snore.

He wasn't able to wander too far into memory—that was more strenuous than running a marathon. He could only handle the past in small quantities, a little spice in his otherwise monotonous life. In fact, it might not have been recollection that he liked, but rather the instant of returning from former times to the present. Finding brightness in a baroque crystal chandelier, warmth in a fireplace bought at a Sotheby's auction, Lady Luck's kiss amidst 180-thread-count Egyptian cotton sheets and down comforters.

I knew I ought to have left long ago, but I stayed. Perhaps I was waiting for Tang Hui to find out. One stormy Friday, when the rain was at its heaviest, he phoned but I didn't pick up. The news said many roads were severely flooded, and he got worried enough to call my coworkers.

I got home just before midnight. The storm had quietened down. The living room window was open, leaving a puddle on the floor and the curtains drenched. Tang Hui was on the sofa, one arm propping up his head. He turned to look at me, watching as I took off my high-heeled shoes.

"Another gathering?" His voice was raspy.

"Yes."

He shook his head gently. "No."

"What?" I took off my earrings.

"There was no gathering."

I turned to look at him.

"Looks like you have an important appointment every week," he said. "I'd like an explanation."

He looked at me expectantly, as if urging me to paper over the cracks in my lies. I bit my lip, unable to speak.

He chuckled sadly. "Looks like we're in trouble."

The rain stopped. A cool dampness seeped into the room. We sat at either end of the sofa.

"He was one of my dad's students. I feel so warm towards him. I couldn't help wanting to get closer to ..." I began.

"Your dad had lots of students. Are you going to get close to every one of them?"

He stormed out, slamming the door behind him.

I remained in the sitting room, staring into space. I didn't fall asleep till three in the morning. It was a light sleep, too shallow for dreams, yet the matryoshka doll showed up again with its vermilion face. "Open it, open it!" screamed the shrill voice.

I woke up to find Tang Hui staring at me.

"There are so many things I never knew about Dad," I whispered. "I wanted to find out …"

"Jiaqi, he's been gone for twenty years!" he roared.

I didn't say anything, just hopped out of bed and walked barefoot to the living room to get my cigarettes. When I came back, Tang Hui had calmed down.

"Tell me what you plan to do," he said.

"I'm going to find the people my dad did business with. They might know …"

"I meant about us." He looked into my eyes. "Are you going to stop seeing him?"

"I don't know. I only like one tiny part of him, the part connected to Dad."

Tang Hui pulled me towards him and cupped my face. "Would you give up these deranged ideas?" He said there were still a lot of things waiting for us. We'd never gone on vacation together. Maybe we could spend New Year on a Thai island. Then Paris next summer. Buy a house in the suburbs a couple of years from now, with a little courtyard where I could plant fig trees and we'd have summer barbecues in their shade. We'd get a Labrador … He painstakingly outlined this picture of our future, but I just stared blankly at him. Defeated, he slumped against the headboard.

"Your father," he said. "I've always known he'd be our biggest enemy."

Two days later, I moved out of the apartment that still smelled faintly of paint. It was a gloomy morning. Bleary with sleep, Yachen opened the door, and took in the sight of me standing there with my luggage. There was a flash of surprise, then he reached out to give me a big hug. I only planned to stay with him for a little while, until I'd used up the rest of my yearning.

Yachen gave me a key and introduced me to his driver and cleaning lady. The cleaner, Xiaohui, had worked for him many years, and was now completely citified, smiling politely as she stealthily looked me up and down, trying to work out how long this new mistress would stick around. She quickly realized I was different from my predecessors: skincare products didn't take over every surface of the bathroom, but remained in my washbag. Clean clothes didn't go into the wardrobe, but remained in a pile in the corner. I hardly said a word about her cooking or ironing, and never asked her to do anything differently.

I began seeking out people who'd done business with Dad back in the day. Yachen helped by calling round his friends, and soon I'd got hold of a few names. I phoned and arranged to visit them, and our conversations yielded more leads. I was constantly distracted, and couldn't focus on my work. When I didn't show up for an interview I'd arranged with a movie star, she was so outraged her agent phoned to yell at the magazine, and my chief editor asked for my resignation in order to placate her. I didn't look for a new job right away, deciding instead to spend my time tracing Dad's acquaintances.

Yachen had business events almost every night. On his rare free evenings, he'd gather friends for food and drink. He liked bustle and needed lots of people around him. The rich can get companionship anytime they want. Even with all this company, he insisted I come along too.

"She's my professor's daughter," he'd tell his friends, as if this was the most distinctive thing about his new girl-friend.

"A classic romance," said a friend.

"Our Yachen is a nostalgic soul," said another. Everyone nodded.

Alcohol has a magic power—it makes everything sound sincere and even the most boring moments sparkle. As if nothing exists but this night. Every word is moving, and ought to be remembered forever. The gravity of existence fills everyone with life, taking away their weariness. When Yachen got drunk his face took on an expression of pure decadence, beaming and swaying his head, the way I remembered Dad. Or perhaps it was because I was drinking too that I perceived this in him. I began to love alcohol. The drinking gene, long dormant in my blood, was suddenly aroused. Whenever we went out for dinner, I'd return more than a little tipsy.

I was very fond of the journey home, the night's excitement still blazing in the air. Yachen and I in the back seat, arms entwined, those moments spent passionately yet noiselessly kissing. The cramped, sealed space made this feel illicit. Alcohol turned my tongue into a snake. As the car sped down the wideness of Chang'an Road, I counted twelve magnolia blossoms on every streetlight.

Through all this, I had enough restraint not to get completely drunk. I didn't know what would happen if I let myself go that far, but instinct told me not to try. Unfortunately, telling myself not to do something only made it more alluring, and I succumbed at Yachen's college reunion.

He'd arranged the reunion because my reappearance had made him wistful for that period of his life. I was looking forward to seeing so many of Dad's former students. Yachen's plan was not to tell them who I was at first, then when everyone was sufficiently merry, to lead me to the stage and announce that I was the professor's daughter. Before that point in the evening, though, I'd already had far too much. Without waiting for him to take my hand, I ran up on stage by myself and grabbed the microphone.

No one had encouraged me to drink. I'd done it all myself,

hoping to lose myself in alcohol. The atmosphere wasn't what I'd imagined. Everyone was grumbling about property prices, sharing stock market tips, and comparing notes on which country would be best to emigrate to. Some of the women huddled together discussing their children's education and which anti-aging skincare products worked best. People kept coming over for a toast with Yachen, clapping an arm across his shoulders, speaking in tones of pure flattery. This felt like a regular dinner party. No one was thinking of the past, and no one mentioned Dad. No one, no one at all. I drank glass after glass as everyone around me praised Yachen's success. Even so, I swear I hadn't planned on rushing the stage. Feeling too hot, I'd decided to step outside for a breath of fresh air. As I passed by the stage, someone was thanking Yachen for the opportunity to reconnect, saying she hoped his business would continue growing, and maybe they could do this again next year, say at a beach resort like Sanya ... Her face was warped, or maybe the floorboards were tilting, anyway something was off and I had to stop it. I marched up on stage and snatched the mic from her. That's where my memory cut out. I awoke in Yachen's guest room, darkness spread across the window like sealing wax. I went into his room and sat on the edge of the bed. His back was to me, but I knew he wasn't asleep.

"I was drunk," I said. After a moment's thought, I added, "I'm sorry."

He rolled over to stare at the ceiling.

"It must be hard for you, being with someone like me."

"I truly was drunk, maybe I said something I oughtn't have ..."

"*Maybe?*" he thundered. "Calling me uncultured in front of all those people? Vulgar? An empty soulless husk?"

"I said all that?"

"Didn't your parents teach you how to behave? Oh, I forgot, your father died before he had the chance." He turned to face me. "If he could see you now, he'd look away in shame. You're an embarrassment. I only took you in because I felt sorry for you."

"Like one of your charitable works."

"Yes, like those children I support. Not one of them is as ungrateful as you."

We stared at each other. Finally, he shut his eyes wearily, and said like a plea, "You should leave tomorrow."

I woke again just before noon. Maybe because I was about to go, I'd slept extraordinarily well, with no dreams at all. After I'd packed my things, I let myself into the second-floor storeroom and went up to the still-wrapped sculpture. I'd brought a box cutter with me, and started slicing open the plastic sheeting. The door crashed open and Xiaohui walked in.

"I thought I'd find you here," she snapped. "Now I've caught you."

"What do you mean by that?"

"You know very well what I mean. Go if you're going. But you wanted to help yourself to a little something on your way out."

I glared at her and kept cutting.

"What are you doing?" she demanded.

I ripped through the last layer, and the plastic fell to the ground. The statue stood exposed in the darkened room. The girl was still leaning forward, her face tilted up, eyes shut, smiling with intoxication, as if inhaling the scent of this strange environment. I flung down the knife and walked out.

Cheng Gong

Whenever I start drinking, I feel the need to get drunk. Soberness is a barrier that exists to be smashed. Being drunk is infinite joy and sorrow, a precious experience I hope to share with you sometime.

I think I've drunk enough to talk about Granddad. The farther he gets from me in time, the more it feels like there's a desert island in the middle of my memory where I can put anything to do with him—the most visible location, but also completely cut off. Now I need to plunge into the icy water and hold my breath as I swim across.

I didn't know he existed till I was six. Auntie was working at the hospital, and she brought me along one day. As we went through the gates, she asked if I remembered being here before, then said I'd been born here. I thought about it and regretfully informed her I couldn't remember being born. She laughed and said, You came here after that too, silly, to visit your granddad. He lives on the third floor of this hospital, she said, pointing out the window. Did I remember him? I didn't, but I was curious, and asked if we could see him.

We walked down a long corridor. The doors on either side were open, and when I peeped into the rooms as we went past, I saw a man's plaster-cast leg being hoisted up to the ceiling, then a scrawny man with his head wrapped in so many layers of bandages he looked like a cotton swab. There were between four and six patients in each room, along with a howling infant, a groaning old person, and various family members squabbling with the nurses.

Granddad was at the end of the corridor, a little apart from the other rooms. On his door was the number 317 in bright red, clearly painted by hand as an afterthought, the numerals smaller than for the other rooms. I would later find out that this had been a nurses' office, but they'd converted it when they needed somewhere to put Granddad.

It was very quiet inside. The room wasn't very large, but because it only contained a single bed it felt cavernous. The person in the bed must be Granddad. I went over and studied his large, pale face, his eyes like raisins. Though his eyeballs moved, his gaze only went from one part of the ceiling to another, never to us.

"Granddad." The word felt insubstantial in my mouth, hollow as an empty bean pod.

The last time I said that word I'd probably only just learned to speak. Auntie said when they brought me here before, Mom pointed at the man in the bed and told me that was my granddad, and, as if I'd been given a new toy, I'd shouted excitedly, "Grand—dad!"

"Stop that!" Dad had said. "He can't hear you."

Auntie explained that Granddad was in a vegetative state. "That means he can't speak or move. Just like those." She pointed at the withered orchids on the window sill.

I went back to the hospital alone the next day. Grabbing a water bottle, I clambered up onto the bed and poured its contents over Granddad from head to foot, then waited to see what color flowers he would sprout.

Eventually, a nurse came in and grumpily changed his soaked bedclothes. Next, she put a long pipe down his throat and poured in a brown slurry. So that was how Granddad got his nutrients.

For a long time after this, I snuck into Granddad's room almost every day. When I stood by his bed, he looked at me, and when I blinked, he did too. I winked, and after a while, he blinked again. I tried with the other eye, but he just stared at me. No reaction. At three, the nurse came in and shooed me out—she didn't want me to see him piss and shit, a process I could only imagine.

Grandpa seemed like a sort of plant that had been placed in someone else's home, and I felt I had a duty to visit him. I hoped I'd be able to train him to do something: squint, raise his eyebrows, even smile. After two weeks with no result, I gave up.

Sometime later, a hedgehog stole my affection. I was buying some steamed buns for Granny when I saw a hedgehog by the side of the road. I crept over, scooped it up in the steamed bun bag, and ran home. Granny wouldn't let it into the house, so I had to keep it in the back yard in a cracked pickle jar with a stone slab across the top. Each day I fed it tomato peel and cucumber stems, and carefully stroked it with my gloves on. Now I had a pet, I quickly forgot about Granddad. Then one Sunday, Auntie and I were on our way to visit one of her coworkers when it began to storm. I ran all the way home, but the jar was already overflowing and the hedgehog was floating belly up, spikes limp from their soaking.

I was sad for a few days, then I remembered Granddad. No one ever went to see him or even mentioned him, I realized. They'd forgotten he existed, which must be the saddest thing about being in a vegetative state. Would the nurses forget him too? I felt guilty. What if he'd quietly died and we hadn't noticed? The hedgehog's death had made me realize life was unpredictable. Finally, I confessed my worries to Granny and Auntie.

"Let him die," said Granny, rolling her eyes. "That's the only thing left for him to do."

"The nurses will remember to feed him every day," said Auntie.

I persuaded Auntie to let me go to the hospital after lunch, and promised Granny I'd get all my chores done by then. Auntie put a rug on the floor of Granddad's room, and I would have my afternoon naps there. It was dingy in the summer, when the lone window got choked with ivy. The damp made paint peel off the walls, like giant moths. The bed was shedding too, white paint flaking off the metal frame.

On these long afternoons, I sat on the rug and played with my only toy, a set of faded building blocks, or colored in the line drawings in my *Journey to the West* comic book.

Otherwise I picked bobbles of brown yarn off the rug, examined the ants scurrying by with their bounty of crumbs, and scribbled my red crayon over a scrap of gauze I'd scrounged from Auntie then tied round my head to scare the nurses. When I got really bored, I'd slump on the window sill and watch the black heads bobbing in and out of the gate, counting them till I fell asleep.

I started elementary school in September. At first I was excited to have more playmates, but it only took me two days to realize this place wasn't for me. The classes lasted too long, and the silence as the teacher wrote on the blackboard made me want to scream.

Finally, the weekend came and I could go back to the hospital. I charged gleefully into the room, only to find a man sitting cross-legged on my rug, shoveling the contents of a packed lunch into his mouth. It was my dad.

"You scared me, you little devil." He swatted the back of my head. "But what a good son. I guess you came as soon as you heard I was here?"

My dad owed money to loan sharks, and had to find a new hiding place every few days. Then he'd had a brainwave: they'd never think to look for him in Granddad's hospital room! And Auntie could deliver meals to him here.

"I was in need, and the old man's spirit protected me!" he said. "You're always better off having a dad around than not."

I blinked. This wasn't a sentiment I could agree with.

As far back as I could remember, Dad had always been in debt—as if "debtor" was his profession. When I was two or three, a couple of thugs barged into our house and scoured the whole place. When they didn't find Dad or any valuables they could swipe, they flung a chair through our TV set. I was watching a cartoon about a little mole when the screen suddenly went dark and caved in. The men stormed out. I sat staring at the chasm for a long time, but the mole didn't return.

Now Dad had taken over Room 317. He'd brought a radio from home, and kept it on all day long, lazing on the rug as he listened to book reviews and ball games. When the isolation was too much for him to bear, he'd wait till dark and sneak out for a few rounds of mahjong. The nurse kept reminding him that visitors weren't supposed to stay overnight, but he pretended not to hear her, and a couple of times even looked like he was going to hit her. Then she found out more about our family's past, and closed one eye to his presence.

I brought dinner each evening. He'd snatch the food, and crouch down by the wall to gobble it. When he was done, I emptied the scraps into the trash can and put the greasy container back into my bag. He ate fast, but even those ten minutes or so felt like an eternity to me. I couldn't look away from the rug he sat on, the magic carpet where I'd had so many strange dreams. Now it was spattered with food, and a cigarette had burned a hole in one corner. He'd destroyed it.

I began to loathe these visits. One time, I swung the bag so hard it tore and two steamed buns rolled out. The corridor had just been cleaned, and a sheen of disinfectant still glistened on the floor. When I picked up the buns, they had a faint chemical smell. I put them back in the container anyway. That night, I dreamed Dad was bleeding from every orifice after eating the buns, while I stood nearby watching calmly, plotting how to dispose of his corpse.

Dad finally paid off his debts that winter, but unfortunately he'd gotten the money by swindling a restaurant owner who reported him to the police. He got six years. He'd been in and out of lockup these last few years and we'd always known he'd be put away for real sooner or later. Now it had happened, we let out a sigh of relief, counting ourselves lucky he hadn't done anything worse.

On the coldest day of the year, Granny, Auntie, and I went to see him at the prison on the outskirts of the city. Tiny flakes of snow drifted across the sky. We brought two sweaters Auntie had knitted for him: navy blue, brioche stitch. Dad was clean-shaven, and I'd never seen his hair so short. When he looked down, I could see his scalp, which had an inch-long scar. He was more cheerful and less agitated than I'd expected, and Granny was surprisingly cordial. Don't worry about anything while you're inside, she said, I'll take care of Cheng Gong, and I'll keep track of what he costs me—you can pay me back when you get out. Six years will pass in no time. The mention of "six years" made Dad's face twitch, and Auntie hastily reminded him it would be less, he'd get time off for good behavior. Sounding sad, Dad said, Tell Yajuan to wait for me—she hasn't come to visit me, not once. Yajuan was the widow he'd been seeing. I'd heard she was bucktoothed and unattractive, but Dad seemed besotted, and went to be with her in Hangzhou when he got out. She and a friend had set up a garment business there, with a little factory of their own. Dad looked after their warehouse. She didn't seem to like his family, and told him not to get in touch with us too often. That's why we never heard from him except when he sent a little money and called us on festive occasions. He never offered to pay for my living expenses, which of course Granny objected to, but at least she no longer had to worry if he was okay, which must have been a relief.

Peace returned to Room 317. I could have resumed my visits, but I'd gotten interested in chess, and would go to the hutong by Southern Courtyard every afternoon to watch the players there. Granddad and Room 317 were relegated to the back of my mind. Little did I know Granddad would always find a way of coming back to life and reinserting himself into my existence every few years.

His next resuscitation began with school. Remember when you started coming to the elementary school and were shocked at how shabby it was? Just a two-story building and a row of rooms around a tiny courtyard with a basketball hoop fixed to one wall, our lone piece of athletic equipment. The pupils were mostly children of the Medical University staff and faculty, and our teachers were mostly their family members, many of them female—like our homeroom teacher Mrs. Yang. She'd gotten herself transferred to this compound so she could be in the same place as her husband, and teaching was the only job they could find for her. Other teachers had just arrived and still had thick country accents, which we gleefully imitated. As for those students who were the offspring of teachers, we all gave way to them as if they were armed with magic swords.

The school may not have been impressive, but it was the first community I belonged to. I was excited to have so many classmates instead of being all alone. Then I realized how stuck-up they were—they often didn't answer when I talked to them, and would shriek at small things like seeing a gecko on the classroom wall. Even so, I tried to make them like me, until I understood that they never would, no matter what I did. Because our parents either worked at the university or the teaching hospital, we knew all about one another's families—which meant they'd heard the stories about Dad. One boy had lived next door to Granny, and said that his dad had given mine a loan. When Dad vanished, the other man hadn't dared to demand that Granny repay the debt—but when this boy saw me in the corridor, he'd yell that I owed him money. Another girl's mom worked in the management department, and had had to issue Granny a warning when she put up a structure that blocked all the light to her neighbor's house. As a result, Granny began tormenting her—pouring leftover food into her bicycle basket, flinging soda bottles at their house till the yard was covered in broken glass. This girl said her mom had become a nervous wreck, often bursting into tears. The persecution only stopped when they moved. This girl and her friends were always huddling together after class, whispering then falling silent when I appeared. Soon, everyone was avoiding me. Even the teachers began looking at me warily, as if I might cause trouble.

Completely isolated, I played alone and walked home alone. When we went on our spring outing, everyone else joined in the games while I sat gnawing a bun. In our class photo, I stood right at the end of the back row, my neighbor twisting away from me. I hated school. Whenever we had group activities, I pretended to have a tummy ache and got Auntie to write me a sick note. She soon guessed what was going on, and told me a story about someone she'd known when she was a little girl, who'd also been a pariah because of her family background. That was the first time I heard Wang Luhan's name. No one wanted to be Luhan's friend, Auntie said, because her dad was a murderer. She told me to find a way to become part of the group, otherwise my self-esteem would get so damaged, I'd never recover. I told her I would, but did nothing.

What finally turned things around was an essay I wrote in class. The topic was "My Family," and the teacher said mine was so good, she read it out in class.

"My grandfather is a zombie." All my classmates looked up. My essay described Granddad as a martyr who'd tried to keep his comrades safe on the frontlines of the Korean War, and ended up in a vegetative state after an enemy strike— luckily the other soldiers managed to bring him safely home rather than abandoning him on the battlefield.

There was silence when she finished reading. After class, two girls came up to me and said I wrote really well. Then during study hall, the boy sitting next to me nudged me and asked what kind of rifle the enemy had shot Granddad with.

"One of those long ones." I mimed it. "They pulled so much shrapnel from his brain. Granny keeps it in a little wooden box. I'm not allowed to touch it, or I'd show you."

Over the next few days, my schoolmates kept asking me questions about Granddad. I hated repeating myself, so I made up a new story each time about how he'd ended up in his current state—he was shot, it was a bayonet attack, the enemy ran him over with a truck, he was flung from a high wall. I was moved by each of these fantastical tales, and came to believe they were all true.

One drizzly evening, I brought seven or eight classmates to see him. Only family members were allowed to visit, but we managed to sneak in while the nurses and security guards were on their dinner break. In order to create more atmosphere, I'd bought a Party flag and draped it across his torso beforehand. Everyone gathered round the bed, staring at him with such respect, he might have been a Party leader. Granddad accepted their attention with equanimity while his own gaze remained fixed to the ceiling, where a gecko slowly crawled across his field of vision.

Granddad's heroism was enough for my classmates to overlook Dad and Granny's misdeeds. Now they asked me to play with them after school, and happily passed me the ball during gym class.

The good times only lasted a short while. One morning, a girl pounced on me as soon as I walked into class. "My granddad says your granddad never fought in the Korean War. He's unconscious because he got beaten up during the Cultural Revolution."

"Nonsense!"

"My granddad said he must have done something really bad to get tortured like that ..."

"Stop it!" I clapped my hands over my ears and ran out.

After school, two boys blocked my way, rolling their eyes up so the whites showed and letting their tongues loll out of their mouths. "My grandfather is a zombie," they chanted, mimicking my voice. "He's a martyr of the Korean War, he bravely fought the enemy ..." They bent over laughing.

From then on, Granddad was a punchline. When I had to see Auntie at the hospital, I avoided the wards, and I swore never to set foot in Room 317 again. I blamed Granddad for not being a war hero. I didn't ask Auntie what happened during the Cultural Revolution. What was the point? All that mattered was he wasn't a hero. It must be because he was useless and weak, I thought, that they'd done this to him.

Li Jiaqi

Earlier on, you said everyone has a moment when their fate is activated, and after that they're being led around by a rope. For me, that probably happened when I turned eight. Dad left Jinan in the fall and traveled alone to Beijing. From then on, I had no home.

Dad didn't actually know anything about business—he was just throwing his lot in with a cousin he didn't even know that well. Grandma's little sister had moved to Beijing early on, got married and had kids there. This cousin of Dad's was her eldest son, and he didn't fit into our clan at all. He hadn't done well at school and refused to get a proper job. Instead, he hung out with his loser friends, and speculated in various goods. To Grandpa, *speculation* and *swindling* were basically the same word, so it must have been a shock when Dad said he was going into the same line. This was an unforgiveable breach.

I hated the things people called Dad: speculator, profiteer, and so on. I always mentally corrected them: he was a businessman. Back in 1990, this sounded like a fancy word you might see in a book. I'd certainly never met a businessman—the hawkers who sold puffed corn sticks and cartoon stickers outside the school gates probably didn't count. In fairy tales, though, the main character was often the daughter of a merchant, living a life as luxurious as any princess. She might get into trouble because of her beauty and innocence, until a handsome, brave man showed up to save the day. Unassailable good fortune, as if her father had paid a bribe to God. So, I would be a merchant's daughter—surely that meant I would have a good life.

After leaving for Beijing, Dad called once a week on Sunday evenings. Mom and I would wait by the public phone at a nearby convenience store. He was supposed to call at six, but was often late. Standing awkwardly there, we bought snacks out of embarrassment: fruit leather or haw flakes. By the end of winter, even these phone calls had stopped, because Dad was now traveling to Moscow for business, and the train took an entire week to get there. We only heard from him when he got back to China. Mom joined him in Beijing that spring because he needed help, and I was packed off to Grandpa's house. That was Grandma's idea—she thought it might repair Dad and Grandpa's relationship. Besides, Peixuan was living with them too, and could serve as a role model for me. Dad didn't want to owe them anything, but he had no choice—each trip to Moscow took half a month, and there was no way he could have brought me along. He only agreed on the condition that he would send Grandma money each month for my living expenses.

I didn't want to live with Grandpa. I'd much rather have gone to Beijing, even if that meant being stuck in a boarding school and only seeing my parents twice a month, but no one asked for my opinion, and I don't remember protesting either. I wasn't sure I had the right. If I'd complained, Mom would probably have said this was all for the sake of my future. A strange idea—I only wanted a better present. My childhood was the only part of my life they controlled completely; if they couldn't make me happy now, how could they make promises about the future?

We completed the transfer paperwork, and Mom took me and my suitcase to Grandpa's house. This was only for a short while, she promised. When they were settled in Beijing, she'd come and get me.

You're right that I made no effort to fit in. This was only supposed to be temporary, so I had no expectations or desires for my situation. Playing with you guys was just a way of annoying my grandparents and Peixuan. Sometimes I'd be having fun, then I'd look at your faces and wonder how we'd become friends. I was always screaming for no reason. Maybe I wanted to hide in the noise and cut myself off from you. I was completely out of control for those two years, running wild. Looking back, it might have been the happiest time of my life, though I can't remember how that actually felt. Memory is selective, and my memory would rather cling to suffering.

Everyone said Dad was making plenty of money. All I knew was he regularly went to Moscow and came back with new stock.

"He's lost his way," Grandpa said at dinner.

"He'll turn back when he runs into an obstacle," said Grandma.

"Hasn't he already met plenty of obstacles? It hasn't done any good."

As far as I can remember, I saw Dad once during this time. His business expanded and needed more capital, so he decided to sell our house. He came back alone, took care of the paperwork, and stored our stuff in a friend's warehouse: family photo albums, journals that had published Dad's poems, my old diaries, dolls. The warehouse caught fire a couple of winters later, and all our possessions were burned, leaving no material evidence of the years I'd lived with Dad.

On that visit, Dad showed up with a video player he'd gotten someone to bring back from abroad, a thank you to my grandparents for taking care of me. This was his first gift to them in years, but he plonked it on the table and said, frostily, This is for you. Grandpa left the room without even looking at it. Grandma asked Dad to stay for dinner, but he said he was meeting friends, which I knew was a lie. During the meal, I imagined Dad sitting in some little restaurant eating a bowl of noodles alone.

That night, Peixuan and I tested out the player with a video tape Dad had brought too, a film about a man who lost his teeth and sprouted fur all over his body as he slowly turned into a fly. Each day, he stood before the mirror silently examining his transformation, a strange exultation on his face at being cut off from the rest of the world. I was reminded of Dad.

Mom visited regularly, always with something special from the friendship store: chocolate, Swiss fruit candies, Ma Ling luncheon meat. She'd lost weight, gotten a perm, and wore knee-high low-heeled boots. Even her accent had changed—she now added *er* to ends of words, like Beijingers do. I pestered her for travel stories, and she told me the train was very dangerous, full of bad people. She didn't enjoy those journeys. Moscow, she said, was nothing but cold, cold, cold. I overheard her complaining to my aunt that Dad stayed out all day drinking, until he was so wasted he couldn't find his way home, so would sit on some steps and wait for her to find him. He was always going to gambling dens, sometimes losing every ruble he'd just earned. Aunt sighed and said money can alter a person's character.

I didn't believe what they were saying—Dad couldn't have changed like that. At the time, nothing would have made me happier than riding a train with Dad. Of all the people who'd never been on the K3 service, I must have known the most about it. It set off every Wednesday morning from Beijing, and arrived in Moscow the following Tuesday. I could have recited the name of every stop along the way, and knew the train skirted Mohe City around sunset on Thursday. On Saturday you could see Lake Baikal from the window, and on Sunday you passed the Yenisei River. The route was as clear to me as the lines on my palm. I spread out my map, knelt before it, and traced it with my marker, filling the skinny crescent of Lake Baikal with blue, imagining its surface thick with ice, glistening with snow on freezing nights.

All my fantasies about faraway places ran along these tracks. I imagined Dad in a woolen coat and leather boots, standing on the windswept platform with his briefcase. A grizzled pickpocket slouched in a corner of the dining car smoking, hat pulled low over his eyes. A green-eyed prostitute in vertiginous heels tap-tapping her way along the scarlet carpet. Dad shrugging off his coat and pouring himself a glass of vodka in a Moscow hotel room. Dad pushing a towering stack of chips across the table at the famous Crown casino, while a lady with blonde wavy hair expertly dealt the cards.

Thieves, hookers, drunkards, and gamblers—the ingredients for my imaginings all came from Mom. She must have regretted mentioning the prostitutes as soon as the words were out of her mouth. In any case, everything she said made me imagine a life full of peril. A wayward life, according to Grandpa. Yet danger and waywardness seemed foreign and exciting to me. They stirred my childish heart, like the scent of poppies.

I never got the chance to take the к3 or to see Moscow, but these images stubbornly persisted into adulthood. You might find it hard to understand, but my eyes grow moist when I hear the word *Siberia*. It makes me think of an ending. Dad didn't die there, but when I think of his actual death, everything goes white and there's a humming in my ears, like a train speeding along the tracks.

The к3 train between Beijing and Moscow ferried the last few years of Dad's life. In Russia, that frozen country, the train is a metaphor for destiny. Anna Karenina's soul wanders the platforms. The first time I read that novel, I thought I might run into her if I ever got to follow Dad to Russia. Sadly that never happened, and I don't know that I'd have recognized her anyway. If I'd had the chance, though, I'd have asked her what it meant to be a soul.

Dad's final trip to Russia was in November 1993. The country's vast body had come crashing down, and the fallen flag had been tucked away where no one could see it. The hammer and sickle had grown rusty. A month later, the double-headed eagle, dating back to the Byzantine Empire, was back on the national crest. In that last month, everyone lay in the rubble of the old order, losing themselves in cheap vodka, bidding farewell to the Bolsheviks. As life ebbed away, Dad arrived, wanting to share in their pain and confusion, because just like them, he believed in nothing.

That's just how I imagined it, of course. Ridiculous, right? When I told this to Tang Hui, he said, That's very moving, but also laughable.

"I have a question," he said. "You're always linking your father's life to great historical events, as if that's the only way to give meaning to his existence. When you can't find a connection in China, you reach for world history. Why not untie him from the past? Give him a bit of freedom?"

After all, he reminded me, Dad wasn't in Moscow to share their pain and confusion, but their money. He was fervently speculating away, swindling rubles by the handful from the pockets of the Russian people. I objecting to the word *swindling*, but he insisted, "That's exactly what he was doing—selling them shoddy merchandise."

Tang Hui's a Beijinger. One of his relatives ran a wholesale business on Yabao Road in the nineties, selling goods to people like Dad who'd transport them to Moscow. "The down jackets we sold the Russians were stuffed with rotting chicken feathers, often from infected birds. Not one scrap of duck down. As for the leather jackets, they were cardboard with a layer of shiny paint. Just imagine, the suffering, confused Russians you described shivering in the snow, thinking they're cold because the collapse of their country has weakened them, not because they're wearing knockoff coats. Then they finally get into a warm room, the snow melts into their jackets, the 'leather' cracks apart and disintegrates before their eyes. You said they don't believe in anything. Why would they? After watching a leather jacket turn to scrap paper under their nose?"

"Not all businessmen were like that," I said without much conviction.

"Why do you think so many Chinese people got attacked in Moscow afterwards? The Russians hated those deceitful Chinese traders, that's why. Okay, maybe your father had a different way of thinking, but he was doing the same as everyone else—taking advantage of the disaster to line his pockets."

I hadn't been dating Tang Hui long when we had this conversation in a coffee shop near the school. I looked up, biting my straw. This was my first inkling we might not be compatible—he had a sense of righteousness I would never possess. Already he understood I'd built Dad up into an impossibly great idol whose looming presence threatened our relationship, which is why he wanted to topple it. In fact, he thought he'd already done this and that it was just a matter of time. Tang Hui was an optimist, and that was probably the most fundamental difference between us.

Mom never talks about doing business in Russia—she doesn't even seem to remember she once lived in Beijing for a year. In the last few years, I've met a lot of people who were also in Moscow around that time, such as Auntie Ling, who knew Dad well. Like many others, Auntie Ling and her husband made a ton of cash, though he later left her for a younger woman. I took the metro to the last stop to meet her—she grumbled that the city was expanding too fast, and had gotten too full of outsiders. She missed the Beijing of the nineties with its dance halls, bars, friendship stores, and foreign currency coupons. Sitting in her chilly living room in a quiet suburb, she reminded me of a white-haired courtesan sitting by the palace walls reminiscing about her heyday.

"The train was a moving bazaar. As soon as we crossed the border into Russia, we'd haul out our bundles of coats at each station. The platforms were packed, and the crowd swarmed towards us before the train had even stopped moving. Each stop was less than ten minutes—not enough time to disembark, so we traded through the windows. A few words of Russian, hand gestures, move fast, grab the money and toss it into the sack, no time to count, fling the garment out. If you were unlucky, someone snatched a coat and ran off with it—there was no way you could go after them. Once, your father had a whole bag stolen. He ran after the thief, didn't catch him, then had to run back to the train as it started—he barely made it back on board."

Memory brightened Auntie Ling's murky eyes. In an instant, she was back on the к3, stopping at a small station, every moment a battle. I looked away from her face, out the window. In order to stop myself interrupting, I'd been chain smoking, staring at my cigarette ash as it crumbled off. Her narration was too realistic, and it hurt my dignity. I couldn't imagine Dad leaning out a window, brandishing a down jacket and calling his wares, chasing down a thief and having to grab the railing to clamber back on a moving train. Even if I accepted what he was doing, I didn't need to think about what it was actually like to sell each garment.

He was a solitary man, said Auntie Ling. The other traders hung out during the weeklong journey to Moscow, but Dad didn't join their nightly boozy games of cards. He had no patience for their vulgar jokes. He enjoyed drinking, but preferred doing it alone in his compartment. The others complained he thought he was too good for them because he'd been to university. It annoyed them that he was doing well, so they ganged up and got the suppliers to give him the worst merchandise. Between that and his growing alcoholism, his business went downhill.

Dad might have been a good professor, but he was a terrible businessman. When the university squeezed him out, he exiled himself and entered a different profession, only to find himself ostracized there too. He was a born outsider. He dealt with disappointment by walking out, and so his life was one departure after another. Sometimes I thought if he'd just stayed put, and decided not to make any decisions, his life might have gone much smoother.

The K3 train still runs today, leaving Beijing each Wednesday, arriving in Moscow the following Tuesday. Passing Mohe on day two, Lake Baikal on the Saturday, and the Yenisei River the day after. Not many people are willing to spend six days on the journey nowadays, and so there aren't as many passengers as before.

Every time I pass Beijing Station, I think to myself I'll ride the K3 someday. Really, though, I'm waiting for the service to vanish from the timetables. While it exists, it's a threat to my fantasy.

Cheng Gong

I remember very clearly the day you transferred into our elementary school. It was spring, and the vendors had started selling silkworm snacks at the school gates.

The teacher brought you in during second period. You stood by the door, tall and thin, a beam of sunlight whittling the left side of your face. Like a figure in an overexposed photograph, your features were hard to discern, making you solemn and mysterious.

You hardly said anything to introduce yourself. Everyone stared for a moment before applauding.

The only empty seat was in the back row, next to mine. The teacher ushered you there—just for now, she assured you, as if these were dangerous conditions. You seemed unbothered.

I turned to look at you during class. Your hair, parted on one side, hid most of your face, and I could only see your protruding nose. Your nostrils trembled faintly, agitating the air. You kept pressing down on your sky-blue mechanical pencil, stabbing the lead into the paper till it snapped. Then you reached into your pencil case, inserted a couple more lengths, and kept going. Your desk was covered with bits of shattered lead, like an ant colony. You didn't open your textbook once all morning.

After school, Li Peixuan appeared in the doorway. You scooped up the bits of lead, put away your pencil case, and followed her out. Peixuan was the year above us, but we all knew who she was—the only city-level triple-good student in the whole school (remember "triple-good"? Good morals, good grades, good health).

We soon learned that she was your cousin, which meant your grandfather was the famous professor Li Jisheng. Everyone at the Medical University knew him. Before long, all the girls in class were asking you to jump rope with them and inviting you on weekend excursions to the countryside—but you didn't seem interested in these offers.

By then, I was no longer lonely, but had formed a little gang with Dabin and Zifeng. Our teacher used to say the classroom was a small society, and indeed, we had divisions of social class too. The three of us were on the lowest rung. This pecking order was decided by our parents' professions. My dad used to be a driver for the university, working alongside Zifeng's dad. Then he decided it was too tiring and stopped doing it, but no one dared to fire him, so he was technically still a university employee. Zifeng's dad now drove ambulances instead of goods trucks, and no longer had to do overtime. Dabin's dad was a cook at our cafeteria, and stood each day stirring a pot the size of a bathtub. All manual laborers, in other words. Only parents who worked with their brains were respected. The elite of our class were the offspring of university administrators and professors. In the middle were the children of regular teachers, and at the bottom, us. The upper tier quickly formed a little circle, which the middle group tried hard to ingratiate themselves into while strenuously avoiding us. When I realized this was happening, I decided to unite those of us at the bottom of the heap.

Dabin was frightened of everything: rodents, insects, even blood—if anyone in the class had a nosebleed, he'd look like he was about to faint. Worse, he was way too emotional. When the class went to see *Mama Love Me One More Time*, he sobbed the most fiercely and it took him several days to recover. He cried at *Liu Hulan* too, and kept asking why they couldn't have spared Liu Hulan's life. At least he was generous—the sort of person who, if he only had one eraser, would break it in half to share it with you.

Zifeng was the opposite—he felt nothing at all, and couldn't understand why people wept while watching a movie. I heard he didn't even shed a tear when his beloved grandma died. His own parents thought he was cold-blooded. But I'm not, he told us more than once, I just don't know how to react—could you tell me when I ought to cry? I said, If your mom suddenly abandoned you, you'd know it was time to cry. She wouldn't do that, he said, not even when my dad hits her. Well then, I said frostily, I guess you'll never find out. Zifeng sighed dejectedly.

To be honest, I'd never have chosen these people as my friends, but you're always better off having friends around than not. I needed allies.

Our little group frequently got together. They sought me out between classes and talked earnestly about boring things. I noticed you glaring at us—probably our classmates had warned you to keep your distance.

That's why I wasn't surprised you didn't say a word to me that first week—I thought that's how things would be between us. Then one afternoon the following week, Dabin came by between classes to invite me to his house after school—his dog had just had puppies. After he left, you abruptly said, "What kind of dog?"

"Wolfhound," I said, startled, then hastily added, "I'm sure the puppies are cute, though."

You nodded, then just before our final class of the day, you asked if you could come see the puppies. You still looked unfriendly, and turned away immediately after you'd spoken. I actually wondered if I'd hallucinated it.

That evening, you patted Dabin's growling dog, and kissed the puppies. Then, like the rest of us, you scooped puffed rice snacks into your mouth with grubby hands.

Dabin and Zifeng took to you right away, but your friendliness felt forced to me, like you were performing. From then on, you often hung out with us after school. It wasn't till later that I realized you were trying to avoid going home, and so you chose to join us, kids who could also stay out late.

You enjoyed games that involved running—tag or throwing sandbags—as well as climbing walls and trees. Only when you were sweating and covered in dirt did you seem to feel you'd had fun. Sometimes, without warning, you'd let out a shriek, not drawing breath, until your voice gave out. Then you'd look smugly at us, as if you'd torn a hole in the sky. I learned to spot the signs, and would hold your mouth shut. Your teeth felt slimy against my palm.

Soon, you were dictating how we played our games, constantly changing the rules—sandbags could only be thrown with one hand, you had to turn around before throwing.

One time, during hide and seek, I ran to the bamboo grove behind the library and sidled in. It was early summer and the leaves were growing thickly. Just as I was feeling pleased with myself for finding the perfect spot, you squirmed in from the other direction. We stood side by side, pressed against the wall. It had rained the day before, and the air was still damp. Shadows from the bamboo leaves swayed across your face. All of a sudden, your hand shot out and a crooked finger slipped into my armpit. I twisted away, rustling the bamboo, and when you giggled, I clamped your mouth shut. We tussled in silence until we heard Dabin's footsteps. We held our breath, but a long stick reached in toward us. Standing in the gloom, waiting for the bamboo to part, you took my hand. Your palms were damp, like mushrooms after the rain.

"Do you know," Dabin said to me many years later. "It felt like I'd caught you in flagrante." He should know. He was married to a TV presenter who'd had several extracurricular encounters, and had trained himself to sniff out her incipient infidelities like a hunting dog.

"I think you already liked Jiaqi back then," he said.

I shook my head and said I didn't know. My feelings were complicated. Sometimes your face took on the weariness of a much older person as you studied your surroundings impatiently. I felt uneasy with your early maturity, as if you were running far in front of me. A faint sense of competition pushed us apart. In a few years, as our desires matured, that competitiveness might have turned to a desire for conquest, and I might have fallen hard for you. But at the time, there was no outlet for these emotions, and I didn't know how to handle them.

After a month, the teacher moved you to a different desk, but it was too late—we were friends, and our classmates looked at you with pity. Some of the well-meaning girls tried to talk you out of your fallen state, but you refused to repent.

Naively, we assumed you played with us because we were more fun than other people. Actually, what amused you was the dramatic gulf between us, the granddaughter of a famous professor and some lowborn brats.

Everyone could see you were rebelling against your family and disliked your grandparents, though you never said so. You never mentioned them at all. And you hated Peixuan, their emissary. You wanted to be the opposite of her, a disappointment—the only way you could hurt them.

Peixuan quickly learned about our friendship, and took it upon herself to urge you back to the path of righteousness. Each day we'd see her waiting for you outside the school, like a parent. After she'd dragged you home a couple of times, we began leaving school before the last period, looking for secluded areas where we could play. Unfortunately, we lived on a college campus, and all the secluded areas contained undergraduates making out. We kept having to retreat as pimply boys yelled at us. Where could we go? Then we thought of Dead Man's Tower.

Everyone knew it. The Germans had built it as a water tower when they occupied Jinan, then it stood abandoned for several years before becoming storage for the cadavers and spare organs used in dissection classes and experiments—at our university and two nearby ones too.

As a driver, Zifeng's dad sometimes had the task of hauling fresh corpses here from the execution grounds. Zifeng told us each time he went out—who'd have thought so many people got sentenced to death? We finally believed that criminals actually did face the firing squad, then their bodies would get taken here and cut into pieces for medical students in their coke-bottle glasses to prod at. Dead Man's Tower purified your spirit—anyone who came here would be afraid to commit any crimes, especially capital ones. I came up with the hazy notion that it wasn't easy to squander your life and not leave behind anything of value—they could always come and gouge it out of your remains.

A rumor had gone round the school about older students sneaking in there one night and subsequently coming down with a mysterious illness.

Dead Man's Tower was in the south-western corner of campus, surrounded by tall brick walls. The only entrance was a metal gate on the west side, so low a grown man would have to bend over—probably because most people would be carried in horizontally. There were no trees anywhere around it, and even the grass was sparse. A bald patch in an otherwise lush campus, as if someone had wrenched a chunk of hair off a scalp. Auntie told me the undergrads had paid special attention to this area during one of the annual Tree Planting Days, but all the saplings had died, apparently because the soil was permeated with formaldehyde.

It was deathly silent when we came here in the evenings. A row of houses stood near the gate against the western wall, dilapidated from long abandonment. Broken glass dangled from a high window, quivering as if it might fall at the first breath of wind. Us boys piled rocks and bricks against the house till we could climb up to the window sill, and from there reached for the roof tiles to haul ourselves up. You followed.

From the rooftop, we could finally see what lay within the walls. On one side of the yard was a mound of bodies— more accurately, body parts. There were faces cut in half, decapitated heads with their eyes shut tight. I noticed a corpse with moldy nipples. The other side was a lake of formaldehyde in which scattered limbs were soaking. Mottled green skin with strange bronze patterns. You shrieked—not from fear, but exhilaration. I eyed Dabin, worried he would faint, but though his face went pale for a few minutes, he soon recovered. Progress, I thought. Later, I would find out he was still terrified of bugs. Corpses weren't living things, he explained, so there was no reason to fear them.

Our adventure couldn't end on the rooftop, but there was no way down except to jump. Zifeng had the longest legs so we shoved him off the edge. Staggering, he found some wooden crates to stack. They rattled as he moved them. He pulled a lid off to reveal they were full of skulls, some so dainty they must have been children's, perhaps younger than us. Did anyone that young get sentenced to death? We looked at each other, shuddering.

The tower's wooden door was locked, so we couldn't get any further. On another expedition, though, we found it standing ajar, with the padlock on the ground nearby. We stood listening for a long time until we were sure there was no one inside. Someone had forgotten to lock up. Inside, we climbed the narrow wooden stairs, avoiding the skeletons that littered each landing. On the second floor were wooden shelves on which brownish jars of various sizes were laid out, various human organs preserved in liquid. It was hard to believe they'd come from warm bodies like our own.

A jar the color of tea held a child so minuscule it must have died before being born. Bent over, trying to hug itself, a picture of loneliness. Its head was large, its tiny fingers and toes finely molded.

"A baby," you murmured.

"Fetus," I corrected you.

"What's the difference?"

"A fetus lives in the water, a baby has crawled up onto land. Same as tadpoles and frogs."

You were fascinated by a half-brain, pale and rigid as a tinned monkey-head mushroom. You brought the jar over to the window, turning it to study it from different angles.

"It's badly damaged." Crinkling your brow as though you were a pathologist, you pointed out some cracks and a hole the size of a bug's eye. Why preserve a broken brain?

"Because it contains this person's memories."

"Do you mean," you looked at me, "the day will come

when we'll be able to look at this chunk of brain and know what happened to this person as a kid?"

"Maybe."

You thought about it and said earnestly, "Then I'll let them dissect me when I'm dead, so my memories can live on too." You nodded firmly, sealing the deal.

I had no idea why you'd want your memories to live on, but it felt like a high-minded notion. Before you'd said it, I'd never thought of such a thing. Once again, you were ahead of me. Dejected, I said icily, "What makes you think people in the future will even care about your memories? Bet they aren't interested."

"Doesn't matter, they can just live here," you said. "Someone will care, eventually."

A cloud drifted aside, allowing sunlight to shine through the thick brown glass and onto the pale brain. Just like that, it was almost transparent. I squinted and thought I could see something throbbing beneath the murky surface.

Light hit those sealed memories. They snuffled, rolled over, and went back to sleep.

The next time we went back, the door was locked again so we played in the yard. Blind man's buff. Only you could have thought of that. Someone had a red scarf tied over their eyes and had to hunt down the rest, which meant the blindfolded person might end up grabbing a severed arm or half-torso.

The yard was too small and cluttered for our games, and we eventually just sat on the rooftop enjoying the scenery. Four of us in a row, legs dangling. The lack of trees made the tower stark, tall and slender like a monk in grey robes. The world suddenly felt much older.

The setting sun scorched the western sky red. Dusk settled over us.

"They'll never eat again," I said, gazing at the cadavers.

"Look on the bright side," said Dabin. "They won't get hungry either."

Did sitting so high up make us look to the future? Our conversation drifted that way. Dabin wanted to be a cop with a gun. Zifeng wanted to be an author, to probe people's rich inner lives. As for me, I wanted to be accomplished, to gain people's respect. You spread your arms wide and proclaimed, "I want lots and lots of love."

We were making wishes. But why here? Maybe the presence of the dead connected us to a supernatural realm, though the dead hadn't even been able to keep their own limbs connected to their bodies, so who knows?

As the semester drew to a close and exams loomed, Peixuan showed up. She seemed startled to see us up on the roof. After searching everywhere for you, she'd finally gone down that deserted path, but hadn't thought we'd be atop the wall around Dead Man's Tower. She stopped a few meters away.

"Go home and start revising," she said, head tilted up to you. "I don't want to see you get held back a grade."

You invited her to join us. There were so many cool things to see in the yard: corpses with staring eyes, severed hands and feet, children's tongues. Peixuan grimaced.

"Enough nonsense," she muttered.

"Come see for yourself!" You swung your legs with gusto.

"We're going home. Now."

"See? She doesn't dare!" you crowed.

"The flag-raising girl is a scaredy cat," I said.

Our laughter was like a basin of filthy water we'd flung down onto her. She stood perfectly still, seeming to shrink, her gleaming dignity tarnished. I felt a glimmer of glee, as if I'd smashed a beautiful porcelain vase, or spat into a sparkling clear brook.

As she turned to go, you called after her, "Don't be a tattletale, now!"

She stopped and swung around. "Li Jiaqi, your life is going to end up a tragedy."

"You mean *your* life, right?" You glared at her.

When you got home that night, everything was normal. Peixuan hadn't said a word to your grandparents.

The good times didn't last much longer. There was a Parent-Teacher meeting after the exams, and as it ended, our class teacher asked our guardians to stay behind.

The kids waiting in the yard departed with their parents as they emerged. Finally there was just Dabin, Zifeng, you, and me left.

When our folks finally came out, an elderly lady was striding ahead of the others, looking like she wanted to get away from them. Her ferocious gaze pierced me like a harpoon. She said your name and led you away.

That night, your grandmother told you she didn't mind you spending time with the backward students—you might even be able to help them—but you weren't to go near Cheng Gong. She wouldn't answer when you asked why and, when you pestered her, she finally said, Look at the household he grew up in—I'm afraid there's something dirty in his heart. He might hurt you.

You repeated those words to me the next day.

"She's right." I shoved you away hard. "You should stay far from me."

You came closer and sighed. "It's almost summer. They're going to lock me up again."

I walked you home on the last day of school. We promised to write each other, and to hide the letters in a disused concrete ditch hidden by shrubs for the other to find. It was a rainy summer, and the paper I pulled from the ditch was often sodden, the writing blurred beyond recognition. Your thoughts and feelings became an unguessable puzzle.

One day towards the end of July, I ran into your grandmother at Kangkang Convenience Store. I'd just bought a packet of salt and two buns when I saw her walk in with three empty yoghurt jars. She lowered her eyelids and swerved to avoid me, but I deliberately brushed against her and gleefully felt my sweaty singlet touch her arm.

I had a terrible dream that night: three people in white coats locked me in a lab and debated what kind of fluid they should preserve my heart in.

"Why are you doing this?" I yelled at them.

One of them answered, through a mask, "There's something dirty in your heart."

Li Jiaqi

I remember that summer vacation, although in my memory it wasn't a ditch we put the letters in, but rather a huge fig tree on the east side of Grandpa's building. There was a cavity near its roots, facing the wall, that you'd miss if you didn't know where to look. Our correspondence was stained green and smelled vegetal. I climbed the tree and read your words nestled in its branches. Even after several days of heavy rain, the letters didn't get damp—they were wedged so far in, they might have survived for years. After I moved away, I dreamed several times that I had come back to Southern Courtyard and found a new letter in the hollow. I wandered aimlessly this afternoon, maybe looking for the tree—but the whole building had been torn down, so of course the tree was gone too. I was disappointed, as if I'd missed your final letter. But now you've said it was a ditch, I'm not sure there ever was such a tree.

Anyway, while writing you letters that summer, I suddenly realized how strong my feelings for you were. For just a moment, I wished I wasn't moving away soon—but that quickly passed. You couldn't compete with my longing for Beijing.

It was only the beginning of autumn, but I couldn't wait for winter break. That's when Dad had promised to fetch me for a family New Year in Beijing. I promised to bring you all chocolates and filled candies from the city's friendship store, which I imagined as a vista of shelves even bigger than the school field, a place selling the latest of everything. I also wanted to visit Beijing Maxim's and eat a bloody steak in its dim interior. The day drew closer and closer, then, a week before I was due to leave, Mom suddenly returned.

Anyone could see she'd been crying—her eyes were so swollen she could barely open them. She stood at the school gate, clutching a limp travel bag with both hands. No gifts from the friendship store this time.

Dad hadn't come home two days in a row. Mom had wandered the long wintry streets searching for his drunken figure slumped on the sidewalk, but he was nowhere to be seen. He wasn't in the warehouse either, nor his shared shopfront. She asked the other tenants, but no one knew where he was. Early the third morning, just as she was about to call the police, he showed up. Mom asked where he'd been, and he said with another woman.

"The whole time?"

"Yes."

She didn't know how to respond to this frank disclosure. Flustered, she went into the bedroom and shut the door. Though they hadn't been intimate in years, she'd never expected this. She lay in bed sobbing, afraid he'd come in but also hoping he would, until she heard the front door slam. It turned out the business had gone bust. Stocks were piling up in the warehouse, and creditors began coming by to demand that Mom pay his debts. She almost stopped answering the door, but what if Dad had lost his keys? She knew no one in Beijing and had nowhere to go. All day she lay in bed, fully dressed, crying herself to sleep. This went on for a long week, until Dad showed his face again. He sat gingerly on the couch, like a guest. She only asked if he was hungry, if he'd like her to make dinner. Scurrying into the kitchen, she allowed herself to hope the whole thing had blown over, until she opened the fridge and saw it was empty. From behind her he said, "Let's get divorced."

She stood for a moment, helplessly shaking her head, then sprinted into the bedroom and locked the door. "Can't we just talk?" Dad wheedled. The next morning, she tossed some clothes into a bag and fled back to Jinan.

Recounting all this at Grandpa's house, she had to pause several times because she was crying so hard. Grandpa frowned, like he was on her side but didn't pity her. Grandma wanted to know who this other woman was, but Mom had no idea.

"I don't want to know," she kept muttering.

"Maybe his friends led him astray," said Grandma, sounding like she didn't really believe that herself.

"Yes!" Mom clutched at that theory like a piece of driftwood in the middle of the ocean. Dad was always drinking and gambling with his rotten friends, and she'd heard those men were customers of the whores on the Moscow train. Surely everything was their fault. Couldn't Grandpa have a word with him? "He won't listen to anything I say," Grandpa coldly replied.

They left a message for Dad to call them back, but he never did. Mom slept on the living room couch. I woke to find her already sitting by the phone. When I brought her breakfast, she grabbed my arm. "Why is he doing this to us?"

I yanked my hand away. I didn't want to be yoked to her, to be part of "us." Sad as she was, I couldn't muster any sympathy. Nor could anyone else. Everyone thought it was her fault—she'd lost Dad because she was so useless.

Her arrival disrupted Grandpa's placid existence. He was in the middle of writing a medical book, and it shattered his calm to hear Mom endlessly complaining and sobbing. Finally, he snapped at Mom: Stop avoiding the problem, go back to Beijing and deal with it.

"But you ought to stand up for me."

"Everyone has to sort out their own problems," said Grandpa. "No one can help you. Go back to Beijing tomorrow."

Furious, Mom accused Grandpa of being cruel and heartless, then began digging up old grudges: how they'd always looked down on her, how much humiliation she'd had to swallow, and now they were abandoning her.

Ignoring her, Grandpa shoved his manuscript into his briefcase, intending to work at his office.

"Pack your things, Jiaqi," said Mom. "We're leaving now!"

I began putting away my stationery as Peixuan watched sympathetically. No one asked what I thought. No one ever had. I was like a potted plant, getting carried back and forth.

"Could you tell Cheng Gong and the others?" I asked Peixuan, picking up my schoolbag.

Mom brought me to my aunt's house, where we had a miserable New Year. On the eve itself, my uncle insisted I had to go watch him set off fireworks. The roof of their shed leaked, and melted snow had soaked the fireworks. No matter how many matches he lit, they just fizzled out. I kept waiting for flames to rip the night apart, but it remained dark, as if I was wearing an iron mask. I gave up and stopped covering my ears with my hands.

Thinking back to New Year's at Grandpa's house, I understood how hard-won that fake happiness was, the result of everyone's effort. Now they'd stopped trying.

Winter vacation was short that year, and school started soon after New Year's. I was sent back to Grandma's house, while Mom went to Beijing with my aunt for what she said would be a final conversation with Dad. An ominous word, *final*. I knew it was probably hopeless, but could only hope pity would change Dad's mind.

I rejoined the gang and found I'd missed all kinds of things over the winter break. You and Zifeng had learned how to ride bikes, and Dabin's dog was pregnant again.

"Same father?" I realized as I was asking what a weird question that was.

"No, a more handsome dog this time, pure white with long hair."

Even dogs could choose better partners for themselves.

You noticed I seemed sluggish—I was waiting for news. A few days later, it finally arrived. In the living room after dinner, Grandma told me Mom had agreed to the divorce.

"I wasn't going to tell you yet, but your grandpa made me," she said.

"What about me?" I asked right away. "Who will I stay with?"

She looked at me strangely. "Your mother. Your dad ... might not be back in Jinan for a while."

I shook my head.

"I've told your mom you should stay with us for now."

"No! I don't agree!" I ran to my room.

I ought to have known, from the day my mom showed up in tears, that this is how things would end. Yet I'd believed some enormous force bound me to Dad, and that they wouldn't be able to keep us apart. How could he disappear from my life?

They finished divorce proceedings in March. Dad came back to Jinan for that, but only for a day, and hurried back to Beijing that same night. He stopped by Grandpa's house before leaving, but no one had told me, and so I stayed out playing. Luckily, Peixuan came looking for me—the first favor she ever did me. Without stopping to explain to the rest of you, I ran home.

The living room was empty—they were all in the study. The door was ajar. I crept closer and heard Grandpa thunder, "Absolutely not. You can't marry Wang Luhan!"

My heart sank.

"Did I ask your opinion?" said Dad. "I'm just letting you know."

"You can marry anyone you like—except her!" Grandpa roared.

I burst in and grabbed Dad's hand, trying to drag him out. His last moments here ought to be spent with me—why was he wasting time arguing? He didn't even look at me. Pulling his hand free, he stepped forward, eyes wide and fixed on Grandpa's. "How dare you try to keep us apart? Why don't you think about what you've done? Or have you forgotten?"

Grandpa was shaking. Through trembling lips, he said weakly, "I've left you alone. But listen to me, just this one time."

Looking pale, Grandma dragged me out, but even through the closed door, I could hear Dad laughing, a terrifying cackle that stopped abruptly a few moments later. Spitting out each word, he said hoarsely, "How can you live so comfortably?"

"Peixuan," said Grandma. "Take Jiaqi out."

Before I could say anything, Peixuan's hand was clamped in mine, and Grandma was shoving us out the front door.

I banged on the door while Peixuan tugged at my shoulders. "Let's go play?" she said.

"No!" I screamed. "You don't know anything."

She looked at me calmly. "If the adults don't want us to know something, it's better that we don't know."

"I don't care who he's going to marry! But he'll be gone soon, don't you understand? I might never see him again." I held my breath to prevent myself from crying. I had to keep my tears in reserve for when I said goodbye to him.

"Let's go play," she repeated robotically. In the dark stairwell, she looked like a marionette.

We sat on the steps as nightfall slowly dyed the air. A bicycle approached and stopped in front of us. Mom jumped off and said I had to go to my aunt's house now. She didn't want Dad to see me again. That was the only way she could get back at him.

"She has school tomorrow ..." said Peixuan. I wasn't sure if she was trying to help me see Dad one last time, or if she was just worried about my homework.

Mom promised to bring me back after Dad was gone. When I refused, she said my aunt was making my favorite, sweet and sour carp, and my uncle had bought me a beautiful kite.

"I'm staying here," I said.

Stalemate. I heard footsteps behind me and turned to see Dad. Mom pulled me closer.

Dad looked terrible, as if the quarrel were clinging to him. His eyes drifted away from Mom's hateful face and lighted on me. When he came closer, Mom's grip tightened on my shoulder.

"Goodbye, Jiaqi." He smiled grimly. "Take care of yourself."

"Goodbye, Dad," I said softly.

He reached out and quickly ruffled my hair. I wished I could have kept hold of his hand, but it had already left me. Just two seconds. He was walking away. I wanted to run after him, but Mom was clutching onto me for dear life.

"He doesn't want us." Mom bent to hug me. "Don't you see? You have to remember that."

This wasn't true. I didn't want to waste my carefully hoarded tears on these lies, yet I was crying. Huge droplets fell from my eyes, washing away Dad's figure as it vanished into the dusk.

Cheng Gong

That winter felt particularly long. Halfway through April, the first flowers hadn't yet bloomed. You were feeling low because of your parents' divorce. We'd stopped playing games. In the evenings, we sat on the wall around Dead Man's Tower. There were now more dismembered arms among the body parts in the courtyard. We reached for them with a grappling hook, pulling them into the shape of a thousand-handed Goddess of Mercy.

We'd run out of steam. Dead Man's Tower had lost its mystery. We needed a new hangout.

One day, a storm started in the afternoon, and was still raging after school. We wouldn't be able to go to Dead Man's Tower. Dejected, we headed home. You and I trudged along, sharing an umbrella. I tried desperately to think of somewhere else to go. A burst of wind snatched our umbrella and flung it to the side of the road. As we ran after it, a light went off in my brain as it must have done for my dad, backed into a corner with creditors on all sides.

"I'll take you somewhere!"

We made our way to the hospital. I flung open the door of Room 317 and waved you in.

You walked slowly to the bed and stared unblinkingly at comatose Granddad, as if he was a riddle you needed to work out. "Is he ticklish?" you asked.

"No idea. See for yourself." I was delighted that you found him fascinating.

You thrust your fingers into his armpit. No response.

"Does he feel pain?"

"Try it."

You got a sharp pencil from your case and prodded his palm, then his face.

"Does he dream?"

"Um ..." I wasn't sure how we would prove this.

You pursed your lips and considered him. "It would be better if he was dead."

"That's what everyone says, but he's stuck."

"Stuck how?"

"Like a cassette tape. He can't go forward or back."

"Why's he stuck?"

"Maybe his bed in Hell isn't ready yet."

"It might be better, being stuck. After you die, you get reborn, and you have to learn to talk and read, then go through elementary school all over again. I get tired just thinking of it."

"He didn't go to elementary school," I said. "He grew up in a farming village, and then he joined the army."

"He'll have to go to school if he's reborn."

"Right." I nodded. "Maybe he got himself stuck to skip school."

We burst out laughing.

Room 317 became our after-school refuge. Neither of us mentioned this to Dabin or Zifeng to start with—we didn't want to share our treasure with them. Instead, we both pretended we had to go home early, and as soon as they were out of sight, we ran to the hospital.

You remember swaddling Granddad in bandages? That took us a whole Saturday afternoon. You hadn't brought enough bandages from home, so we had to wrap his legs with scraps of cloth leftover from Granny's sewing. He looked a bit like a parrot. Then we dressed up as Egyptian grave robbers, and played at finding this mysterious mummy in a tomb.

Another afternoon, we propped him up on a stool and scribbled made-up words all over his back. A secret Kung Fu manual, carved into human skin, lost for many years. We were the wandering warriors who'd found it in a hidden tunnel.

We also turned him into Sleeping Beauty with some lipstick I'd stolen from Auntie—she'd never used it, anyway. We stuck his eyelids down with tape, but neither of us was willing to kiss him, so in our version of the story, Prince

Charming got waylaid and never woke the princess.

Room 317 was our theater. We were both directors and actors, while Granddad was our prop and sole audience. His small, staring eyes watched us running around.

"Don't you think he has a baby's eyes?" you said one day, out of the blue. "So pure, like they've never seen anything dirty."

I couldn't imagine my enormous granddad as a baby, but he also didn't seem like a grandfather. Pale and plump, not a single wrinkle on his round cream-frosting face. Though he wasn't smiling, there was something cheerful about him. Such pinchable cheeks. I felt calm when I saw him.

He roused something maternal in you, and you kept insisting on playing house. You were Mommy, I was Daddy, and Granddad was our precious baby.

You tied an apron round Baby's neck to serve as a bib, and aimed a milk-filled syringe into his mouth. Mischievously, he spat it out. You cradled his head and sang lullabies. I stood to one side, unable to help, getting told off by you for talking too loudly.

"Shh!" you'd say, frowning. "I just got him to sleep."

In fact, Baby's eyes remained wide open. His gaze was blank, free from desire—pure indeed. I felt I'd experienced the gamut of human emotions, as if I really was a father. A heavy sensation, but also a new one, and I didn't resist it. Many years later, accompanying a girlfriend to get an abortion during yet another short-lived relationship, I sat in a long hospital corridor, my heart like wood. For some reason, I suddenly recalled playing Daddy in that room, the only time in my life I'd willingly experienced fatherhood.

From spring to fall, we acted out every scenario we could imagine. Then we stopped, having finally run out of stories.

Even so, Room 317 remained our favorite spot. We sat side by side on the floor, doing our homework with the bed as our desk. Sometimes Dabin and Zifeng sought me out for a game of chess. While we did that, you listened to the radio or played cat's cradle by yourself. Now that we no longer needed him for our games, Granddad was more like a superfluous piece of furniture. Occasionally, we did find a use for him—in late spring, when they'd turned off the heating but the air was still chilly, you leaned against him for warmth. His large, soft body gave out abundant heat with each breath.

"I'm falling asleep." You stretched lazily.

The room was less than ten square meters, its only furniture the iron bed and the patient in it. The bed had been painted white, the patient was in white pajamas, and the curtains and water jug were white too—all now yellowed from age, humanized. The room was also old, and had a dampness that wouldn't go away. When we leaned against the wall, paint flaked off like ringworm, reeking of illness and medicine. Outside, the leaves of the parasol tree moved as one when the wind blew, scattering sunlight throughout the room.

Across the street were a florist and a fruit store next to each other, with their displays of bouquets and fruit baskets, then a shop for funeral goods, a little wreath dangling from its sign. From our third-story perch, they looked bright and full of color, as if every day were a festival celebration. Ambulances drew up, sirens blaring, and white stretcher beds were wheeled out to welcome the newcomers. Patients arrived and departed every day, though of course some never left. Like an enormous sieve, the hospital chose who would live, retaining the elderly and superfluous. God would take them and replace them with new ones, like the milkman collecting empties.

In the next room to these births and deaths, we played our games. The man in the bed was neither living nor dying. His childlike eyes were like some eternal creature's, reaching us from outside the mortal realm. Shrouded by his gaze, we were cut off from the world, and not even the smallest shred of time could reach us.

That was an illusion, of course. Time always finds a way in, and nothing is eternal. Our game continued until the day came when our blindfolds were abruptly wrenched off. Blinking in the daylight, we knew playtime was over.

It was a Monday in September. Rain spattered in the windows that wouldn't close tight, bringing with it the scent of leaves and soil. Dabin and I were playing chess by the window, and you were on the floor listening to the radio. You'd tuned in punctually every day for a serialized novel you were hooked on, a tragic tale about a white-haired courtesan deep in the palace reminiscing about a love affair of her youth that had come to nothing.

After two rounds, Dabin hurried home to watch *Knights of the Zodiac*. This anime seemed to have cast a spell over every kid's heart. Come evening, no matter where they were, they'd hear its summons and rush back home. You and I might have been the only ones not watching Saint Seiya. We didn't like cartoons, didn't enjoy TV, and most importantly, didn't want to go home.

"Sure, go hang out with Goddess Athena!" I jeered after Dabin's departing back.

I put away the chess set, the pieces clacking as they tumbled back into the box. Silence. The radio was off, the rain had stopped, and you were so quiet you might have stopped existing.

You were still there, of course—it was your presence causing the silence. I looked at you, sitting by the bed, staring unblinkingly at its occupant. I noticed you'd undone some of his buttons, revealing his chest, which your eyes were fixed on. Had you come up with a new game? But no, you were looking more solemn than I'd ever seen you.

You slowly bent down. I opened my mouth to call your name, but nothing came out. You rapped lightly on his chest, *dok dok dok*, like quietly knocking on a door, head tilted, listening.

"What's going on?" I had to ask.

You didn't answer, More knocking. A long wait. Your face was full of emotion.

"What are you doing?" I was getting scared.

You finally raised your head, though your eyes remained fixed to his chest. "I heard ... his soul move," you murmured to yourself.

I stared. I knew the word *soul*, but it seemed as distant from our lives as a planet in another solar system.

"I knew it, his soul is trapped in there," you said.

A crow cawed sharply outside the window, sounding like it had been hit.

The earth stopped turning for a few seconds, stunned that someone had guessed its riddle.

You froze too. You'd stumbled on the answer, but had no idea what the question was.

The damp night seeped in, gathering around us like walls. The room grew smaller, the air sticky. I shivered, feeling as trapped as Granddad's soul.

We looked at each other in unspeakable sorrow.

It started to rain again. We listened to the plop of raindrops on the leaves, which drooped like hands that couldn't grasp anything.

We stayed a long time at the hospital that evening. It was still raining as I walked you home. You asked, "What do you think a soul actually is?"

"Who knows?" I watched the light ripple in a puddle of rain.

You nodded thoughtfully. "I've been trying to understand, but I just get more confused."

"You have?" I was angry you'd never mentioned this. "How did you think of it?"

"Remember the half-brain in Dead Man's Tower? I couldn't stop wondering what happened to its soul. Then today, I started imagining what your granddad's soul is doing in there."

I said nothing.

You looked down, opening and closing your umbrella. It was a while till you spoke again. "Never mind, you wouldn't understand. One day you'll realize this world isn't how you think it is."

You sounded like an adult speaking to a child: jaded, worldly, evasive.

I watched a rainwater puddle eddy, imagining the raindrops had bored into the concrete. I raised my foot and stepped into it.

Walking home alone, I took the longest way I could, to delay my arrival. The rain had stopped, but the air still felt heavy. After a long time, I found myself at Dead Man's Tower. Just as well, I thought, I'll get some fresh air on the roof.

The moon was out, resting huge and round by the tower, like a head stuck on a scalpel blade. I shuddered. When I looked again, fog had rolled in, covering most of the moon like a secret that shouldn't have been revealed.

For the first time, I found the tower frightening. But how could that be? I hadn't been scared when we were playing there every day. Perhaps it wasn't the tower but a thought that had flashed through my head, or not the thought exactly, but how it made me feel. What was terrifying about that feeling? I couldn't say.

Some familiar things had suddenly transformed, becoming unrecognizable.

Instead of approaching the tower, I ran home. Even though I didn't look up, the moon filled my peripheral vision. The sky was so low I thought it might touch my head. The world felt impossibly heavy, crashing down on me from some far-off place.

Li Jiaqi

I'd never imagined Mom would want to marry again. Perhaps subconsciously, I wanted her to keep suffering from Dad's departure, just like I was. Besides, I felt she lacked the ability to find happiness—but it turned out happiness was still able to find her. She was attractive enough that she didn't need to make any special effort, just standing there sufficed.

After the divorce, Mom found another job as a kindergarten auntie. It was a boarding kindergarten—the parents only came to get their kids at the weekend—which meant the aunties had to live in too. That was the main attraction as far as she was concerned. Dad had agreed to buy her the apartment we'd lived in before, but we'd have to wait till he could sell off his merchandise—his money was all tied up for now. Within two years, he promised. Mom kept reminding me about this arrangement, and said she'd definitely come get me. In the meantime, I had no choice but to live with Grandpa, and I could tell she felt guilty about that. Everything will be okay when we have our home, she said, hugging me. I actually didn't care. Nothing she said gave me anything to look forward to. I kept my mouth shut, though. Her sadness was so exhausting, I didn't even have the energy to hurt her. I stood in silence, enduring her arms around my neck and her tears running down my cheeks. This reminded me of being a child, holding my doll and telling her stories. Mom's affection for me was more or less the same as I'd felt for that doll, entirely one-way. I suspected Dad's love was the same. I was beginning to realize that most of the love in this world is a failure, all of us throwing basketballs and missing the hoop.

Of course, sometimes there were successes. Take Uncle Lin and my mom. She was singing the first time he saw her. It was afternoon nap time at the kindergarten, and she was sitting by the beds crooning to the children. She'd made an effort with her appearance and was in a dress, with her hair in a flawless braid. The bright spring sun blurred away the torment on her face, and erased the burden she was carrying on her shoulders, making her look like an innocent young girl.

She kept repeating the few songs she knew, even though the children were sound asleep, until the inspection team from the education committee was out of sight. Finally, she breathed a sigh of relief, leaned back against the wall, and rubbed her sore neck. All of a sudden, one of the inspectors doubled back and appeared in the doorway. She jumped to her feet, wondering for a confused moment if she ought to start singing again. Looking embarrassed to have startled her, he gestured at the briefcase he'd left on the window sill. Before leaving, he turned to look at her again, and her heart clenched. Maybe she should have sung.

The briefcase man showed up again a couple of days later. Mom saw him through the window standing in the courtyard, and wondered what else he could have left behind. Only when the director called for her did she understand he was here for her. Would she like to see a movie with him? Before she could refuse, he was already walking away, adding with a grin that he'd already asked her boss if she could take the rest of the day off.

This sudden love felt like an assault, and Mom instinctively wanted to flee. After the movie, she began avoiding Uncle Lin. Whenever he came, she'd hide in the storeroom and get her coworkers to say she wasn't there, but he appeared again and again. She thought about quitting her job, but everyone told her such good men were rare, and she ought to hold on to him. Yet she was fearful that all men were prone to abandonment and she would end up getting hurt. Then one weekend, Uncle Lin mingled with the parents coming to pick up their children, and went up to Mom before she had a chance to get away. She finally agreed to give him a little time, and when the last child was gone, they sat in the empty kindergarten to talk. Actually, Uncle Lin did all the talking. He was divorced, he said, with no kids. His ex was a restless woman who'd kept wanting to leave the country. Three years ago, she'd had the chance to visit the US on a work trip, and ended up staying. The plan had been that he would leave his job to join her, but next thing he knew, she was living with an American man two decades older than her—maybe she'd fallen in love, or maybe she just wanted a green card. In any case, she asked for a divorce.

Wasn't this exactly what had happened to Mom? She turned her large, long-lashed eyes on this despondent man. Happy people each have their own joys, but sad people are all sad in the same way. Their identical sadnesses made her feel a little more secure. Although her feelings were beginning to shift, she was still afraid to be near him. Whenever he showed up, she panicked and ran away. Still, Uncle Lin didn't give up. I bet it was Mom's fearfulness that attracted him. She was as flustered as a virgin. It was the permissive nineties, and he'd been scarred by a liberated woman. Mom's prim, old-fashioned ways were enchanting.

This game of hide and seek stretched on into the summer. One day, a storm blew up at noon and continued till evening, trapping everyone in the kindergarten—including Uncle Lin, who was visiting. It was Mom's turn to cook. Uncle Lin stayed for the meal, then helped her do the dishes and clean the kitchen. Beneath the dripping eaves, as thunder rumbled, he confessed his intense feelings. Mom kept her head down, barely listening, reminding him of the problems they would face. I have an eleven-year-old daughter, she kept murmuring. Uncle Lin placed his hand on hers. I know, he said, but let's deal with this together.

It was fall when they finally began seeing each other for real. One Sunday, Mom brought me to meet Uncle Lin. He must have done some homework to find out my likes and dislikes, because at the restaurant, he ordered all my favorite dishes and patiently peeled my prawns. Even so, I could tell he didn't like me, and wouldn't have no matter how lively or warm I had been. My existence destroyed his image of Mom as a blushing ingenue. Besides, Mom cared too much about me. She gave me all her attention, neglecting him. Naturally, I hated him too. He was the opposite of Dad: he talked too much, waving his hands around, and smiled a lot. A very simple man, no mystery to him at all. He was happy and warmhearted, full of enthusiasm for life, but I thought that was just skin-deep.

After lunch, Uncle Lin took us to a reservoir on the outskirts of town, a half-hour's drive away. When we got there, a film crew was shooting a TV series, blocking access to the waterfront. There was a hill nearby, so Uncle Lin suggested we go climbing instead. He talked nonstop, like a radio that couldn't be turned off. When Mom went over on her ankle, he knelt down to rub it, then ran to find her a branch she could use as a crutch. We stopped for a rest, and they offered an apple back and forth to each other. I sat on a stone nearby, watching the peeled apple slowly turn brown. I was tired and wanted to go home, but Uncle Lin said no, we had to reach the top. He reckoned it would be good for my character to persevere. He kept encouraging me the rest of the way, telling me how beautiful the scenery was, and what a sense of accomplishment I would get from conquering nature. Seriously, "conquering nature"? That sounded childish even to me. When we did get to the top, there was nothing there at all, just a maddening wind. And still Uncle Lin smugly asked whether I felt a sense of accomplishment like he'd promised. I stared at his greasy face, shiny as jellied pig skin, and was hit by an inescapable truth: Mom's boyfriend was a moron. Worse, she was besotted. All of a sudden she'd gone girlish, even her voice had turned fluty. She got excited over the smallest things, and was always asking Uncle Lin to teach her how to do stuff, as if she'd newly arrived in this world.

Maybe that *was* the case—she seemed reborn, learning existence anew from this idiot. The marks Dad left had been wiped away. She'd recovered, and was no longer in pain. How could it be that easy?

Actually, I'd already known it would be this way. Even right after Dad left, when we were sobbing together, it was clear her suffering was not the same as mine. She would never understand a noble love like ours. I didn't envy her shallow pleasures, not at all. I didn't want to feel better. I only prayed she and this foolish man wouldn't barge into my world and attempt to paint over everything. Unluckily, my prayers were in vain.

On the way home, Mom finally noticed I was in a bad mood, but she put that down to me not wanting to get packed off to Grandpa's house. Trying to cheer me up, she told me some "good news" she'd been planning to share later: Uncle Lin was pulling strings to get me transferred to Fifth Street Elementary. That was the best school around, she said, and he'd put in a lot of effort. The two of them beamed at me expectantly, waiting for me to gush with gratitude.

When I remained silent, Uncle Lin said awkwardly, "You might find it hard to settle in, at first. Things might be different here from your old school—the teaching methods, the curriculum, the quality of the students. It's normal if you feel out of place." He struck a pose, the consummate educator. "If you can't keep up, fear not—I've found you the very best tutors for languages and math. Whatever subject you're having trouble with, we'll get you help."

"I don't want to change schools again."

"I know." Uncle Lin nodded. "You'll miss your friends. I've got a couple of old classmates whose kids are your age. They're doing well at school. I'll introduce you."

Huh. Turns out he'd even chosen my friends for me.

"Fifth Street is only two blocks from Uncle Lin's home. When we've moved in"—Mom glanced quickly at me—

"you'll only be five minutes' walk from school." She blushed, embarrassed to mention shacking up with Uncle Lin.

"You can move in with him; I'm not going to." I turned to look out the window.

After a long pause, I heard my mom crying. Even this sounded more delicate than usual.

"Didn't I tell you?" she choked. "This girl's stayed too long at her grandpa's house, now she's so strange …"

Uncle Lin put his hand on her shoulder, which just made her howl more loudly.

"What mother wants to send her daughter away? I had no choice, truly, or I'd never have left her there where no one cares about her, no one loves her …"

"That's all in the past," said Uncle Lin, taking her hand. "It will be better from now on."

We were back in the city now, surrounded by gray buildings. Pigeons flapped their wings, wheeling past windows sealed off by iron bars. The twilight was damp as moss. The water vapor in the air seemed to thicken before my eyes. I realized I was weeping too. How could that be? Now they'd think I was sad because no one loved me. But that's not why I was in pain. God knows why I was crying at such an inopportune moment. How immature I must have seemed.

It was exceptionally cold that day, as if to warn us the rest of the winter would be bitter. In that cruel season, Mom would have her second wedding. Or her first, strictly speaking—Dad's parents had opposed the match, so she married him without a ceremony, just a meal with close friends. She didn't even wear a gown. She must have resented that all these years, and now finally she'd get to make up for it. At the age of thirty-six, with a child in tow, she was going to get married in splendor. This was redress for Uncle Lin too. He hadn't been able to hold his head up ever since his wife had left him for an old American guy with false teeth, but this wedding would restore his reputation. He wanted to put my mom's beauty on display.

For a couple eager to tell the world how very happy they were, this wedding was essential. Uncle Lin didn't begrudge the expense of booking out the finest restaurant, nor spending several evenings on the guest list, making sure they'd invited absolutely everyone.

The people my mom most wanted to be there weren't her poor relatives from the countryside, but Grandpa and Grandma. She wanted them to see how well Uncle Lin's whole family treated her. They wouldn't come, of course, so she hoped to use me as a mouthpiece to let them know all about it. Although she could easily have done this after work, she insisted on waiting till the weekend to try on her gown, so I could accompany her—she assumed I was dying to see her in it. I didn't care. The red qipao with gold trim would have looked the same on anyone. She showed me the ring Uncle Lin's mother had given her, a chunky gilded thing that looked ridiculous on her finger. She never wore it, just kept it at home and took it out to feel its heft from time to time. Instead, Uncle Lin bought her one in the latest style, with finely etched flowers clustering around a gemstone. I didn't see what was so great about it. All gold jewelry looked equally tacky to me, and I swore I would never wear anything like that, not in my whole life.

Another weekend, she took me to see "our new home," where Uncle Lin had lived until his divorce, when he'd moved back in with his parents. It had stood empty for years, and was now being redecorated in honor of the wedding. When we got there, the paint was still drying on the walls, and the new fridge hadn't been plugged in. I would have the south-facing room. Through newly hung gauze curtains, sunlight seeped through a small window onto a lavender bedspread. Sweet and vulgar. I imagined myself sleeping in that bed night after night, having mediocre dreams, growing up to be an insipid young lady. Meanwhile, Mom was dragging me out to the yard for what she called a big surprise. She'd lived so many years in the countryside that she had an unbreakable attachment to the soil, and had always yearned for a ground-floor apartment with a small garden, just a few square meters to plant melons and soybeans, to gaze out at in the summer and enjoy the lush vines. That, to her, was happiness. I envied her concrete joys, so straightforward you could have written them out as a list. Now she'd ticked off every item.

"Look, the roses you like, those pale pink ones." She tugged my sleeve and pointed at the foot of the wall. I hated roses, along with all scented flowers.

It was evening by the time we left Uncle Lin's place. The streetlamps were on and the roads were bustling. Three girls around my age came out of a convenience store with tubs of yoghurt, sandwich cookies, and other snacks.

"Those must be Fifth Street students," whispered Uncle Lin. "The middle one is in their uniform, I think."

"Really?" said Mom.

"I'll go ask," said Uncle Lin.

"Don't—" I said, grabbing at his sleeve, but he was already striding over. Smiling, he chatted with the girls, turning once to point at me. Their eyes swung towards me and looked me over quizzically. I squirmed and felt my ears grow hot, and wished I could burrow into the ground. Uncle Lin hollered, "Come over here and meet these young ladies!" He beckoned, looking pleased with himself, as if he'd just done me a great service.

"Go on," said Mom, nudging me. Instead, I turned and ran for the other end of the street.

As I sprinted, wind whistled past my ears. I wished I could keep running, but I had nowhere to go. After two blocks, I stopped and sat on the curb. They caught up with me soon enough. Looking stricken, Mom hauled me to my feet and demanded that I apologize to Uncle Lin. I kept my mouth shut and tried to struggle free. Out of nowhere, she slapped me across the face. Even she seemed surprised. Her hand hovered for a while before she put it down again. She'd never hit me before, and appeared a little uncertain if she was allowed to do that.

"Come on, let's talk this through. No need for violence," said Uncle Lin.

Mom was staring at the road to avoid meeting my eyes. "This girl's so disobedient. I have to teach her a lesson, don't I?"

I didn't cry, and all I said to her was, Okay, are you done? Now let's go to Grandpa's house. We'd been supposed to have dinner with Uncle Lin's parents that night—my first meeting with them. Now, though, there had to be a change of plan. Uncle Lin agreed to drop me off at Grandpa's place. He probably knew that dragging me along with such fury in me would only make things worse. It must have cost him a lot of effort even getting his parents to agree to see me.

"No rush," he said, stroking Mom's shoulder. "There'll be plenty of time to discipline her when she's moved in with us."

*

I didn't tell you I was changing schools because I knew you'd get angry and start ignoring me. I didn't want this to come between us. And yet a barrier had formed without me realizing it—you were silent and moody, as if something was bothering you. I didn't ask what, because I thought we'd reached the age when we each had our own secrets.

Instead, I sought out Peixuan. I had to do something before they put in the transfer paperwork. This was the first conversation I initiated with her. Usually she was the one running after me, stern-faced and insisting, "Jiaqi, we need to talk." She loved talking. As the study leader of her class, she excelled at encouraging and correcting the weaker students. It made my scalp prickle the way she looked loftily down at everyone else, but there was no one else I could turn to. I hoped she could plead with Grandpa to let me stay where I was. He didn't exactly like me, but he didn't hate me either. Apart from an extra place setting at the dinner table, my presence wouldn't affect his life. If Peixuan was willing to speak for me—say if she pointed out that my grades had recently gone up, and this progress would surely be lost if I had to start over at a new school—he'd probably agree. Did he care about my grades, though? I wasn't sure. Even after two years under his roof, I knew almost nothing about him, except how much he loved his work.

Would Peixuan be willing to help? Her overdeveloped sense of responsibility meant she worried endlessly about my studies and moral development. My departure would probably come as a relief. Still, she was always saying nothing was more precious than family, and how wonderful that we could grow up side by side, supporting each other. Sounded fake, but maybe she meant it. I waited all evening for a chance to speak with her, but she was completely immersed in studying for a math competition, not even pausing for a sip of water. I poured her a fresh glass and stood behind her, watching. She kept scribbling away. I thought she was just pretending not to see me, but when I cleared my throat, she jumped in fright. I asked if we could talk, and she said okay, but only after the competition that Saturday. She was taking this very seriously. At dinner, she told Grandma she was staying back at school for the next few days—the mathletes were getting extra coaching.

"Our school's never won before," she said, looking ready to go into battle to wrest glory for us all. I found her community spirit laughable—words like *school* or *family* felt hollow, meaningless. Just ways of referring to other people, that's all. Of course, if Peixuan could understand this way of thinking, she would no longer be Peixuan. Although Grandpa's household was full of very different personalities, the one thing we all had in common was our stubbornness.

I had no choice except to wait for Saturday—but something happened before that.

On Thursday afternoon, hurrying to mail a letter to Uncle before the post office closed, Grandma slipped and fell on the stairs. Peixuan came to see me during study hall with red-rimmed eyes. Grandpa was in Beijing for a consultation, and when the hospital hadn't been able to get hold of him, they'd called Peixuan at the school. Grandma was still unconscious, with a concussion and broken leg.

Peixuan sobbed quietly all the way to the hospital, but when we were almost there, she suddenly stopped, steadied her breathing, and wiped away her tears. Taking my hand, she said, don't be scared, I'm here, it'll be okay. As if she'd just remembered to be a big sister to me. Where had this ludicrous sense of duty come from?

Still, looking at her pretty, innocent face, I felt a little moved.

Grandma had woken by the time we got to her room. Her right leg, encased in plaster, hung in midair. Even as she lay there immobilized, she fretted about who would get us dinner. We bought packed meals from the hospital cafeteria, and went back to her room. She tried to get us to go home, but Peixuan refused. Instead, she plopped herself down and got on with doing her homework, using the edge of the bed as a desk. Pointing at the other side, she said, You can go over there. We stayed till the nurses chased us away.

The wind had risen, and the trees had shed a lot of leaves. They crunched beneath our feet as we walked down the quiet street.

"I'm dropping out of the math competition," said Peixuan abruptly.

I was startled. "Because of Grandma?"

"I won't be able to see her if I have to stay back for extra coaching."

"I can do that."

"You can keep her company at the hospital, but I'll need

to make her bone broth at home. The doctor said bone broth is good for broken bones."

"Grandpa will be home in a few days."

"He's always busy. Grandma said he had quite a few surgeries next week."

"Surgeries are usually in the morning. Maybe in the afternoons he can ..."

"I don't want him to be distracted, don't you understand?" she said anxiously. "He won't be able to concentrate if he's thinking about Grandma, and his work is far more important than any math competition."

I stared at her. My cousin, just six months older than me, so noble I couldn't breathe.

Everyone tried to talk her out of it, but she really did drop out of the competition. Grandma was discharged a few days later, while Peixuan went on doing all the grocery shopping and cooking. She moved a stool into the kitchen to use as a desk, poring over her textbooks as she rinsed vegetables and peeled garlic, completing her homework while keeping an eye on the simmering soup. I helped out too, and came straight home after school each day. It was harder for me to give up playtime than for Peixuan to sacrifice her competition. Still, this was the perfect opportunity to show I could contribute to the household, which might persuade them to let me stay. I didn't tell you my twisty reasoning, only that my grandmother was injured and I had to help take care of her. In response, you said nothing. You had something going on anyway, I thought—you disappeared every day after school, and even Dabin and Zifeng didn't know where you went. I'd noticed, of course, but didn't have the bandwidth to worry about you.

During this time, I got to know Grandpa better. To be accurate, I should just say I got to know him a little—previously I hadn't known him at all. I still remember his expression the night he got back from his work trip, walked into the room, and saw Grandma lying in bed. In that moment, something hidden within his personality seemed to come to the surface—a sort of disgust. There was no sympathy or affection, only a desire to get away as quickly as possible. A moment later, his face softened, and he sat by the bed and asked Grandma how she was doing. He ought to have known how to treat a patient, but now he seemed helpless. He almost let Grandma fall while helping her to the bathroom. Another time, he'd painstakingly laid out a towel and fresh clothes before he realized the water the nurse had put on the stove to heat had boiled dry. Grandma seemed stunned by this attention, and kept telling him not to bother with this or that, Peixuan could do it. It struck me that he might never have done anything for her before—not just her, but for the family. He didn't even know where we kept the toilet paper.

The night he got back from his trip, Peixuan asked him to hold the cover as she stuffed the quilt in, and the frustration on his face was plain to us all. He had no patience for these mundane chores. Peixuan had to assure him we could take care of everything ourselves, so he could focus on his work. The next morning, he got up at his usual time, ate the breakfast Peixuan made him, and went off to the hospital. His routine didn't change at all, apart from having to pick up the newspaper and mail himself. He got home late, and sometimes brought work with him. Soon it was time for another business trip.

In my memory, there were no adults around for a while—just me and Peixuan, immersed in the minutiae of running a household:

"Do eggplants need to be peeled?"

"Are you sure the fish is cooked?"

"Should I turn off the fuse before changing the light bulb?"

"Do you know where the water meter is?"

We got into arguments over things like the best way to boil turnips. Her spoonfuls of salt were leveled off perfectly flat. She couldn't stand the way I tossed a pinch or two into the pot without measuring, while I found her need for precision equally maddening. She was less annoying than before though. When I saw her turn a pot of potatoes to mush and burn a hole in her apron, I even thought she was a little adorable. There was nothing hypocritical about her rectitude and high-mindedness—that's just how she was. It was still ludicrous, but I resolved not to make fun of her anymore.

Two weeks later, I finally felt able to ask Peixuan if she'd speak to Grandpa on my behalf. I was sure by then she wouldn't refuse, because I'd done enough to prove I could be useful. She needed me to stick around and help out.

"You're so selfish," she said when I was done, shaking her head. "All you care about is yourself." I tried to defend myself, but she cut me off. "Haven't you realized how much trouble we're making for Grandpa and Grandma, just by being here? When Grandma's able to walk again, she'll go back to how she was before: making all our meals, doing all our laundry. Why do you want to tire her out like that? She needs rest, and Grandpa needs a quiet house so he can concentrate on his work."

"Do we affect his work?"

"Of course. He doesn't like having so many people around."

"Wow, you really understand him—even better than he does himself." I sat on my bed, sulking. "I knew it, you hate me. You want to get rid of me. Why not just say so, instead of these crappy excuses? If they need peace and quiet, why don't *you* leave?"

"I plan to. I've been talking to my father, and he's bringing forward our move to the US. I've got my visa. After the winter break, when Grandma's leg has healed, I'll be gone."

"Are you serious?"

She came over and sat next to me. "It's time for us to leave, Jiaqi. The good times in Southern Courtyard are over."

*

Peixuan ended up staying till the New Year, having delayed her departure so the wound on her face could heal—apparently she'd had some kind of fall.

Actually, she healed before that, but needed time to adjust to her appearance. She didn't know how to explain the scar to her new classmates, nor how to regain the pride she depended on. It must have been a difficult time for poor Peixuan. Though I felt pity, there was also a sort of pleasure in attaching the word *poor* to her name, like seeing a magnificent building crumbling to the ground right in front of you.

She mailed me a letter two weeks after getting to the States, telling me about her new school. Her classmates were great, she said, even if her English wasn't good enough to fully understand what they were saying. Near the end of the letter, she mentioned a field behind their house where she liked to go in the evening, and sometimes there were deer there, beautiful creatures staring at her motionlessly then suddenly vanishing into the dense woods. I thought I sensed something sad in there I hadn't seen in her before, but chose to believe I must be mistaken.

Many years later, when I saw her scar, I thought about that letter: Peixuan in a strange country at twilight, standing alone in a field. She must have hoped I would comfort her. It showed a lot of trust to make herself vulnerable like that—perhaps she thought we were close.

I never replied. I was stuck in a torment of my own, one I couldn't tell anyone about. I lost the ability to put words together, and cut myself off from the world. I'm not saying our destinies were bound by blood or anything like that, but it's true that right after leaving Southern Courtyard, we each went through the most difficult times of our childhoods.

Whenever I think back to this period, my mind always goes to the afternoon Peixuan told me she was moving to the States.

There we were, side by side on my bed, the sun streaming through a window and creating a neat little square. I'd been fiddling with a button on my sweater, and when she said "the good times in Southern Courtyard are over," the thread suddenly snapped.

The button fell to the floor, bounced a couple of times through the sunlight, and melted into the shadows. I'll look for it later, I thought. There was a roaring in my heart, and I felt a great sense of loss. The curtain had come down on something, though I had no idea what. Later, I would understand: this was an ending. My childhood was over.

Cheng Gong

Mind if I smoke? We could open the window a little. You're not still cold, are you? Alcohol really does warm a person up. Where was I? —From the day I realized my grandfather's soul was still inside his body, my life suddenly took on a new seriousness.

I skipped class the next day and headed for the medical library, where I scoured the shelves for any books on the soul.

"These might be a bit advanced for you, kiddo," said the librarian as he recorded my loans.

I went straight to Room 317. The nurse had just left, and the room still reeked of antiseptic. Putting down the books, I walked over to the bed. Before this, Granddad had seemed like an object—a prop for our games, or a cushion to lean against. Everything was different now. He had a soul. He was a human being. Gazing at him from the foot of the bed, it sunk in for maybe the first time that this person was my grandfather. If he hadn't been in this condition, he'd surely have been a good Granddad—kind, generous, fond of me. He'd have taken me fishing at the reservoir, or to the zoo to see the elephants. Bought me new sneakers or a Transformer. Never have allowed Granny to bully me.

I put my hand on his chest, and felt his sturdy heart beating in his frozen body. Then, just the way I'd seen you do it, I rapped with one knuckle like knocking at a door. *Dok dok dok.*

"You can hear me, can't you?"

Although there was no indication, I chose to believe he could. He surely could.

His soul is trapped. His soul is trapped. I said this to myself over and over, and a mission grew in me, something I'd never felt before: I had to rescue him.

All that afternoon, I flipped through my library books. Although there weren't many sections I actually understood, a solemn sense of satisfaction lay coiled between these incomprehensible words. Of course, rescuing a soul wasn't going to be an easy task.

After school, you showed up at the hospital, where you'd guessed I'd be, and asked why I hadn't been in class. I said no reason, I hadn't felt like going. You looked at my stack of books, but said nothing. As usual, you walked over to the window and turned on the radio, then sat down and resumed work on your little drawing. I went back to the volume in my hands.

We were both striving hard to make this afternoon as normal as possible, yet the atmosphere of the room was somehow different. Even the antiseptic stench seemed more piercing. I couldn't take in a single word—all my attention was on the bed, just visible out the corner of my eye. Through its iron bars, I could see Granddad's legs, moving gently from side to side. When I finally couldn't resist and looked up, you were staring in the same direction. Our eyes met, and immediately darted away from each other. We quickly bent over our work again. There were three people in the room now—we could no longer ignore Granddad's presence.

Everything became misshapen, deformed. Even the radio felt the need to remind us of its altered existence. It was playing a song by Tsai Chin, whose voice I liked—she sounded a little like my mother. I was fully absorbed in the music when it started wavering, finally drifting into white noise. After some time, the sound came back, no longer Tsai Chin but a gloomy middle-aged man reading the news in a soporific drone. Then his voice, too, faded into static. You went over to twiddle the knob back to the original station, but Tsai Chin disappeared again after a couple of bars. You kept trying, with no luck. The radio was possessed, wandering the airwaves of its own volition, chopping voices into tiny fragments.

Some form of interference was filling this room. I abruptly remembered a line from one of the library books: the soul is a type of electromagnetic wave.

Leaving the radio to its spasms, you pushed open the window, as if trying to disperse something. A strong gust of wind blew in, rustling the pages of my book, asserting its presence. All non-living things were suddenly animate. The ward felt cramped, forcing us to face each other. You turned, and our eyes met. You finally seemed willing to acknowledge the strangeness between us. Walking over to the table, you began leafing through the books. "All right then, what are you up to?"

"I want to rescue Granddad's soul."

You shrugged, scornful as a grown-up. "Who do you think you are? Ultraman?"

"No, that's why I need these books."

"You might as well give up."

"You mean, you don't think this will ever happen, right?"

"I don't know." You shook your head, your disdainful expression making me hate you. "Even if you could rescue his soul, do you think that would bring him back to life?"

"It might," I insisted.

"All right, say you pull it off. Are you sure your granny and auntie would want that?" Your eyes darted towards me. "If he woke up right now, that would create problems for a lot of people."

I snatched back the book you were holding. I'd used to think you were a little mean, but now I realized you were an exceptionally cruel person. I'd never speak to you about rescuing Granddad's soul again, I decided. All heroes who accomplish great deeds go through a period of being misunderstood. At that moment, I felt their anguish.

"Why not just forget it?" Your voice was low, as if you were afraid of being overheard. "There might be things we're not meant to know about."

Neither of us said anything after that. The room was completely silent, apart from the radio cycling tirelessly through the stations, though the human voices were gone, leaving only the dull crackling of static, a pitch black tunnel through which one walked alone.

That was the first time we went home before the sky had completely darkened.

When I came in the front door, Granny was by the window, tramping away at the treadle of her sewing machine, which rumbled like a helicopter. Seeing me, she took her tiny foot off the pedal. "You're early today."

I noticed she was wearing a cozy sleeveless winter jacket, dark reddish-brown, the woolen fabric washed threadbare, leaving two sturdy pieces of something more like tightly woven felt, stiff as a suit of armor. The thick scent of camphor told me this garment had just come out of the storage trunk, which meant Granny had cracked them open a little earlier than usual.

Every autumn, Granny dragged her feet till the central

heating was about to come on, before finally bringing out our winter clothes, a major undertaking.

"Getting through winter takes away half my life," she'd say.

We had no wardrobes or cupboards at home, so everything went into boxes. This was supposed to be a space-saving measure, but even if we'd moved into a mansion, Granny would simply have bought more boxes. Her logic was: nothing in a wardrobe truly belonged to you, only things in boxes counted. She was constantly afraid of our home being raided. Our valuables were in boxes so we could easily bring them along if we had to flee. Other than a dining table and beds, these two rooms contained only boxes, filling every inch of space, stacked on top of each other all the way to the ceiling, leaving only the narrowest possible space to pass between. The items we used most were in the topmost ones; our winter clothes, untouched for half the year, would have sunk to the bottom layer. Retrieving them meant heaving off all the ones above.

Granny sat through chilly autumn evenings in her thin outfits, shivering with cold.

"We'll move the boxes tomorrow," she'd say through chattering teeth.

Then next morning the sun would make an appearance, and she'd decide we could wait a few more days.

"Did you ever hear the story of the lazy squirrel who delayed building its nest, and froze to death in the end?" I asked her one time.

She glared at me. "I was the one who told you that."

"No, it was Auntie."

"It was me," she grumbled. "You don't understand. We should cover up in spring but endure the cold in autumn— it's good for us."

Switching feet, she began working the treadle again. It was hard to believe someone as lazy as her was prepared to spend several weeks sewing a patchwork quilt that wouldn't even keep out the cold. This was because someone had told her working a foot-operated machine would keep dementia away. She pedaled frantically, scared we would bully her if her mind started to go.

Running out of thread, she came to a halt. I solicitously rushed to get her sewing kit.

"Granny?" I asked casually, standing to one side with the box held out. "I'm sure you must be hoping for Granddad to wake up?"

"I'm hoping he dies soon," she answered, not even looking up. "He's a hardy old bugger, still clinging on after lying there all these years. If he'd died sooner, the hospital would have given us proper compensation. Now they've changed directors a few times—who knows if the management will still take responsibility?"

"You really don't wish he'd wake up, not even a little bit? If he came round, we'd be"—I searched my brain for the right word—"reunited."

"Reunited? Ha!" That voice like a partridge. "Where would he live? The hospital would stop sending funds. What would we eat? You're not planning to support us, are you?" She spat with sudden violence, glowering at me with her beady eyes. I ran into the inner room and looked around wildly. Boxes everywhere. No room for another bed.

After a while, Auntie came home. I took the bags of groceries from her and followed her into the kitchen.

"Auntie, if Granddad woke up, would you be happy?" I asked tentatively, rinsing a cucumber.

"That's not possible," she said. "His brain's been removed."

"It has?" I'd always thought he'd been hit on the head or something.

"Not all of it, maybe half."

"But I mean maybe. If he did wake up, just imagine ..."

"Mm." Auntie lit the stove, then swiftly beat some eggs in a bowl. "Then I'd be out of a job. I got my post in the hospital to replace your granddad. And now there are all these new people, younger and better qualified than me. They'd love to squeeze me out. If Dad regained consciousness, they'd have an excuse to send me packing." In the hot oil, the egg mixture was emitting yellow bubbles, like little scorched suns. Auntie stood frozen, still holding the spatula. As the stench of burning filled the air, she shuddered violently. "It's impossible, impossible," she muttered over and over. "No one wakes up after having half their brain cut out. You know I'm not brave, don't frighten me like that."

I gobbled up some charred omelet before hurrying into the other room. My library books were laid out on the desk, but I didn't have the energy to look at them again. No one wakes up after having half their brain cut out—I tried to force myself to accept this fact. And I had to admit you'd been right: no one was hoping for Granddad to regain consciousness. Once again, you'd thought of something that had eluded me. You were still ahead of me. I hated you.

There was no longer a place for Granddad in this family, on this earth. The thought sent a trickle of sorrow through me. In comic books, children were always being kidnapped by an assortment of demons or aliens, heading off to fairy kingdoms or distant planets for adventures before coming home. I'd always envied those children, and walking down the street I'd look out for strange or suspicious individuals, hoping they'd take me away. Now I understood you couldn't just leave like that, you might return to find the world could no longer accommodate you. Suddenly, I had another realization: Granddad, immobile on his hospital bed, was still supporting us. If he wasn't in a vegetative state, Granny wouldn't be receiving payouts from the relief fund, and Auntie wouldn't have a job, which would mean they couldn't pay my school fees. We'd traded half his brain for these things. Without that sacrifice, we wouldn't have our present lives. Hang on … I suddenly thought of the pale cerebellum we'd seen in Dead Man's Tower. It couldn't be Granddad's, could it? I shivered. How had Granddad fallen into his coma in the first place? I had to get to the bottom of this.

At bedtime, I pestered Auntie to tell me. "A nail," she muttered, before dropping off.

From then on, I barraged her with questions every night. If she wasn't too tired, she'd tell me a little, but it cost her a lot of effort. Her memory seemed to have been run over by a tank, shattered into tiny fragments. I gradually grew used to her jumbled version of events, which often mixed up cause and effect, and the many long silences that filled her narration, sometimes ending in snores.

Besides, she was obliged to spend a lot of time defining certain terms, such as *Cultural Revolution* or *cowshed*. The latter I quickly made sense of, but as for the former, her explanation made me more and more confused, because an endless stream of strange words ran through it: *big character poster, rebel factions, Red Guards.* I had to keep interrupting to ask what they meant. In the end, I only half understood—but as it turned out, it was perfectly possible to be confused about the Cultural Revolution and still grasp what happened to Granddad.

Granddad came to grief in 1967, when the Cultural Revolution was underway. The hospital staff had split into two factions. As part of management, Granddad was considered a *conservative*, while the others were *rebels*. These two words were actually not unfamiliar—when Dad used to play cards, these were the sides he and his friends would take, and they sounded incompatible as fire and water. The rebels denounced the conservatives in *struggle sessions*, another incomprehensible term. Auntie explained it to me as torturing a person, body and soul. Granddad was abused in this way, then locked in the cowshed. To start with, I'd imagined this must be a place containing livestock, or at least that it was a sort of cattle barn, but it seems any location could be a cowshed. This particular cowshed was in Dead Man's Tower, where we would later play every day. At the time, it was still an ordinary water tower with no corpses or formaldehyde pool. During the struggle session, he was beaten up, leaving him covered in injuries, and locked up again. The next day, when Granny came to fetch him, he seemed disoriented and sensitive to light. He couldn't speak and was vomiting nonstop. Granny thought he was still in shock and would be fine after a few days, but things only got worse. He lost sensation in one arm, then his legs grew numb, leaving him unable to walk. A few days later, he lost control of his bowels and bladder, and could only make little stammering sounds.

They brought him to the University Hospital, but the doctors there couldn't tell what was wrong either. His condition worsened, day after day, and soon his entire body was immobile. He could still blink, and his heart was beating, but otherwise he was no different to a corpse.

The hospital summoned specialists from every department to carry out a thorough examination. Finally, an x-ray revealed a two-inch iron nail in his cranial cavity that must have entered through his temple, leaving a scar so small no one had paid it any attention. The nail had rusted, spreading infection through his brain tissue. The operation to remove it would carry a certain amount of risk, but after studying his condition carefully, the hospital decided it would be best to go ahead. No matter what they said, Granny refused to give consent.

"At least he's alive now. What if the surgery fails and he dies?" she repeated over and over.

Back then, Granny evidently lacked an understanding of what it meant to be "a living corpse." All she wanted was to avoid widowhood. If she could have foreseen how the second half of her life would be ruined by her husband's prolonged existence, she would surely have gotten out of their way, praying for the surgery to fail so Granddad's heart could stop its involuntary beating.

The hospital sent one of Granddad's colleagues to persuade her, and assured her that if anything went wrong, she and her two children would be taken care of. Too tired to cause any more trouble, she finally signed the consent form.

The surgery successfully removed the nail, which had stirred his gray matter like a swizzle stick, swirling rust and germs through it. The rotting brain had begun to stink. The doctors tried to remove as little as possible, preserving at least a third of the cerebrum. Yet Granddad's condition was exactly the same afterwards—he neither woke up nor died.

Auntie said there were quite a few medical case studies in which patients who'd had part of their brain removed found the empty space being filled with interstitial fluid, while the remaining tissue took over the missing functions, meaning mobility and thought processes were unimpaired, allowing them to live normally. Most of these, though, were children whose brains hadn't fully developed, and the excised portions were of secondary importance. It was clear that Granddad couldn't expect such a miracle. The doctors were fairly certain he would never wake up.

It took a few days after the operation till the police began their own investigation. The crime likely took place after the struggle session crowd had dispersed. Someone must have gone to Dead Man's Tower and hammered the nail into his skull. Because he'd been badly beaten and was sprawled unmoving on the floor with his mind still clouded, he probably didn't resist. The perpetrator seemed familiar with the principles of anatomy and must have been an experienced surgeon in order to pick exactly the right spot, avoiding all major blood vessels so Granddad didn't die immediately. The wound had also been treated to speed up its healing. Afterwards, people joked that this might have been the most sophisticated procedure ever to take place at the University Hospital, but it was a shame no one would ever know who'd wielded the lancet. Everyone at the struggle session was a suspect, but the police looked elsewhere too. They asked Granny who might have had a grudge against her husband. She gave them a long list of names, but that wasn't the half of it. The vast majority of doctors at this hospital loathed Granddad. According to Auntie, he'd done well in the war, but had never properly studied medicine. Despite his lack of skills, he was put in charge of far superior doctors. Naturally, they found this unfair. Granddad didn't like them either—so what if they knew a bit about medicine? That didn't give them the right to be so arrogant, looking down on their own Deputy Director. And so he took it out on them. The better their surgical skills, the less likely it was they'd ever see a scalpel. Let them be talented—they'd never get to show it off. These people were filled with hatred for him, and were constantly looking for ways to rebel.

Going by Granny's list of names, the police expanded their inquiries. One night a short while later, one of the people she'd mentioned hanged himself at home with a drip tube, a physician named Wang Liangcheng. No one could believe he was the culprit. He was normally smiley and pleasant, a cultured guy who enjoyed drawing and playing the violin—a bit of a nerd. Then a witness reported seeing him walk towards Dead Man's Tower the afternoon after the struggle session. He'd held an umbrella against the rain, next to someone in a raincoat whose face was hidden. Presumably his co-conspirator, or possibly the mastermind. Wang Liangcheng's wife said over and over that he'd told her he hadn't done anything. Her words weren't worth much, but after all Dr. Wang specialized in internal medicine and didn't have any surgical experience. In the end, the police questioned everyone they ought to question, but found nothing suspicious and no new clues, so the matter died down. Suicide was an admission of guilt, wasn't it? They closed the case. My father insisted the police continue investigating until they'd found this accomplice. He went down to the station and plonked himself down at the entrance, refusing to leave. After a few days of this, they tried to chase him away, so he raised his fist to an officer's face, then kicked the man in the belly a few times. Another policeman tried to pull him away, but my father snatched his arm free and charged at him. Like a mad dog, he couldn't have stopped if he'd tried.

My father was thirteen at the time. Vicious energy rattled around inside him, unable to find a way out. It was around then that he turned violent, quick to anger, punching anyone who got in his way. Auntie said the whole family had been afraid of Granddad, who'd had a similar temper, rising out of nowhere. When he fell into his vegetative state, this rage transferred to my father. Later on, I wondered whether this was because Granddad was no longer around to protect him against the injuries and assaults of the outside world, so he turned himself into his father to fend off the terror of this enormous loss. Not long after that, my father joined the Red Guards, and finally his anger had an outlet. The red armband gave him license to be violent. He was addicted to ransacking houses. As soon as the order came, he'd rush over to the address. Whenever there was a period of inactivity, he'd grow restless, sometimes even smashing things in his own home. After the Cultural Revolution, when the other Red Guards had gone back to being regular people, he couldn't apply the brakes, but went on in his destructive, combative way. Learning all this, I began to see him differently. I couldn't forgive him completely, but felt a little more sympathy toward him. It helped to know he hadn't always been like this.

While my father was hanging round the police station demanding answers, Granny spent her days loitering outside the Director's office. She wanted an explanation too, but a more pragmatic one—she wanted to know how the family would be compensated. Granddad had been an employee of the hospital, and the incident happened here, so of course the hospital ought to take responsibility. She brought a little stool with her, and sat in the corridor outside the office from morning till night. Lacking my father's powerful fists, she brought her own weapon: tears. Hysterical sobs that seemed to swamp the world, raggedly howling out Granddad's name, screaming for him to wake up, to see how his fatherless children and widow were being mistreated. She cried so long and so loudly that her voice turned terrifying, partridgelike. In the end, she got what she was after.

The hospital agreed to provide Granddad dedicated care for the rest of his life, and a sum from the relief fund to be paid out each month. This kept Granny quiet for a while. From then on, whenever anything happened to make her unhappy, she'd get her stool out and head back to the hospital to cry some more. The two rooms we lived in were earned with her tears, and so was Auntie's job. Even the two gold teeth in her mouth she'd obtained by weeping.

One way or another, the matter was settled. Time moved forward in great strides. Every day, a page got torn off the calendar like a shred of dead skin. To start with, the entire family went to see Granddad daily, standing around the room as a nurse gave him a sponge bath, making sure she didn't cut any corners. Then it became once a week, and finally not at all. Not visiting brought its own peace of mind. The whole thing ought to be the hospital's responsibility, anyway. If the family allowed themselves to worry about it, it felt like they were being taken advantage of.

It would have been better if Granddad had died then and been burnt to nothing. Nothing to see, nothing to touch. The sense of him being completely gone—that would have made the grief last longer. But instead he just lay there, staring out of those expressionless eyes, taking unimaginably smelly shits. No matter what happened to the family, it had nothing to do with him. That was an enraging thought, and bit by bit, the family stopped caring about him. Being in an unresponsive state was like falling into a ditch between life and death. The living have birthdays, the dead have anniversaries, but the comatose celebrate neither birth nor death. There's no date to remember them by.

And yet, he existed. A sturdy, unavoidable existence. This only truly hit my grandmother when she wanted to remarry. It seemed my Granny's whole life had been a battle against her destiny of becoming a grass widow. She was born to a penniless family in Shandong's Cao County. The year she turned sixteen, her father arranged her marriage to a landowner's son from the neighboring village. This boy had suffered a serious bout of childhood polio, and both his legs were shriveled, leaving him bedridden. Such a marriage would be practically widowhood from the start, but the dowry was generous, and her father wanted the money to build a house. Little did he realize what a spitfire his daughter could be. When the wedding party arrived at their house, drums banging and gongs clanging, she clambered up onto the roof holding a grenade she'd dug up from a cache in the hills behind the town, where the anti-Japanese Eighth Route Army had buried it. She yelled at the incomers to get the hell out. Before they knew what was happening, she'd pulled the pin with her teeth. The grenade arced through the air, landing neatly on the roof of the empty sedan chair, which an instant later exploded into a thousand pieces. Debris flew everywhere, ripped shreds of red satin fluttering towards the sky. My grandmother stood above it all, suddenly realizing the power that had lain concealed inside her. As twilight descended, Granny walked through a cloud of sulfurous dust, dragging her weary body out of the village, finally free. She went through a phase of being a vagrant, wandering with no destination in mind, begging for food to survive, sometimes reduced to eating tree bark and grass. Just when she was at her lowest ebb, she encountered a division of the Eighth Route Army, and fell in with them.

"I hear you've got a good grenade-pitching arm?" These were the first words Granddad spoke to her. He was also a new recruit; like her, he'd joined the revolution in order to feed himself. Granny was mesmerized by his bulging calf muscles. Out of nowhere, the strapping man in front of her filled her with conflicting emotions.

When they were given their rifles, Granddad's talent showed itself. He never missed, and became famous within their division for his marksmanship. This talented couple walked together through a chaotic world, leaving a bloody trail. I heard they killed dozens of Japanese devils between them. If Granddad's left leg hadn't been injured in battle, relegating him to the rear and then the medical corps, he'd surely have reached at least the rank of major by the time of Liberation. And because Granny stayed behind to keep him company, she wasn't able to continue with her exploits on the frontline.

After Granddad was left comatose, Granny would often think back to the glory of those revolutionary days, banging the table and cursing the cowardice of Granddad's attackers, who hadn't dared attack him head-on with a gun or knife. They'd seen it all, and slaughtered their share of Japanese devils, so what was there to be afraid of? Instead, his assailants chose this underhand method. The era of flinging a grenade and blowing the enemy to smithereens was gone forever, but Granny couldn't get used to these peacetime ways of killing, so elliptical and secretive. She'd fought the Japanese and the Kuomintang, and now had to do battle against her fate. After half a lifetime, she'd circled back to where she'd been at sixteen, and ended up a grass widow anyway.

When Auntie was a little older, she began to hear people gossiping that Granny was always flirting with men. Getting a prescription filled at the pharmacy or buying flour from the provision shop, she'd linger at the counter, chatting and simpering, teasing the men who worked there, coyly pawing at them. When she heard the knife-sharpener plying his trade downstairs, she'd summon him into the house and ensnare him in a long conversation. Everyone knew she was lonely, but by not even attempting to conceal it, she was making herself a laughingstock. One time, she was glued to the counter as usual, jabbering away at the provision shop man, when his wife happened to walk in. The other woman yelled at Granny to keep her distance and sneered, I know you're man-crazy. Granny lunged at her and scratched her face, drawing blood. From then on, all the guys in town stayed away from her.

Granny sat in her solitude for a very long time, before finally meeting a man who wasn't someone else's husband. He worked at the iron foundry and his wife had died of lung disease, leaving behind a plump little boy a year older than my aunt. Auntie recalled that for a while, this man often came round for dinner, bringing boxes of food from the factory cafeteria. Each time he visited, Granny would turn tender and warm. Sometimes he spent the night and his son would stay too, squeezing into my aunt's bed, his flabby arms rubbing against her. In the dark, his mouth hung open as he breathed laboriously, like a fish getting ready to swallow her whole. His bulk made my aunt afraid, but also gave her a sense of security. Granny told father and son to leave their dirty clothes for her to wash, and even helped shave their heads. In return, the man hefted sacks of flour and honeycomb coal back home for her. The two households seemed ready to merge. Unfortunately, that wasn't possible in the end. Granddad was still alive, and there was no way to divorce him, which meant my grandmother wouldn't be free until the day he died. Yet he showed no signs of wanting to leave this world. Quite the contrary, under the dedicated care of the nurses, he'd put on a fair bit of weight, and now had a double chin and ruddy cheeks, like a Buddha.

The man began to waver. He wanted to give his son a proper mother, after all ... he said hesitantly. Granny sobbed and clutched his arm, begging him not to leave. His heart was soft and he stayed a little longer, but Granny knew she was just dragging it out. There was no way to keep him, unless ... The grenade she'd thrown aged sixteen had left her with the firm conviction that violence solved all problems. If that missile could win a teenage girl her freedom, why shouldn't a fruit knife cut her bonds now? She stuffed the knife into her bag every time she left the house, even just downstairs to buy a bottle of soy sauce. The hospital was across the road, and a short walk would bring her to his room. She could stick the knife into his heart when no one was around, and make it back home in time to cook dinner. Perhaps she really did go there, but always encountered the nurses—it was summer, and they were rubbing him down assiduously to avoid bedsores.

Then one day, Auntie recalled, they went shopping for fabric. On their way home, it started to rain. As they got off the bus outside Southern Courtyard, Granny looked up at the gray sky and abruptly said she wanted to visit Grand-dad. At his building, she handed the umbrella to my aunt and said, wait here a while, I'll just pop upstairs. Auntie stood beneath the eaves, listening to rain tumble on her broken umbrella, *pak-tak*, *pak-tak*. The sound scratched at her scalp. As it echoed faintly in her ears, she thought she heard a faint, sharp scream rushing at her through the ragged raindrops, piercing her like a needle. She froze for a few seconds, then dashed up the stairs. When she opened the door, Granny was standing by the bed, the knife in her hand. Her face went white when she saw my aunt. Shuddering violently, she dropped the blade.

"I wanted to help him," she wept. "The sooner he dies, the sooner he'll reach the next life."

And so, like an envoy from the gods, my aunt saved my grandfather's life. But what truly got Granddad out of danger was Granny's lover. He finally found a real mother for his fat son, a woman several years older than Granny, plain-featured but still more desirable—she was an actual widow, not the grass variety, her husband having died once and for all. The widow was a bus conductor. The foundry was on the west side, and father and son often wound up on this bus in the mornings. Standing beneath the bus-stop sign, they'd watch the vehicle approach, the conductor waving from the window, her smile enchanting in the dawn sunlight. The bus stopped by the entrance to the Medical University, near Granny's apartment. Gradually, they no longer alighted at this stop, nor at any other—the bus was now their destination. The widow gave the son a plastic ticket clipboard, loaded with colorful stubs. He clutched it proudly to his belly, like a rich man, now and then ripping off a couple of tickets to bestow on others. When he and his father came to see Granny for the last time, the conductor had already become his mother. Granny clutched at the man, weeping and clinging to his leg, but it was no use. When she grew exhausted, her hands slowly released him. Father and son hastily said their good-byes, and my aunt silently saw them to the door. The boy turned around, bit his lip, and ripped off a thick wad of ticket stubs for her.

From then on, Granny accepted her fate and no longer wished for Granddad's death. Even if he were to die, she had nowhere to go. As far as she was concerned, freedom was useless. Love would never come again, leaving her with hatred, her only sustenance. She didn't know who she ought to hate, so she hated everyone. She loathed the conductor, so she stopped taking bus number 1. She hated the ironworker, and his fat son too, whom she cursed and hoped would choke to death. She detested the neighbors, certain they were laughing at her, so she flung rocks at their windows. She spurned her trouble-making son and timorous daughter. Of course, she reserved the bulk of her hatred for my grandfather. Every few days, she'd swear at him, wishing he'd die quickly, blaming him for everything bad that ever happened to her. When rage got the better of her, she'd stamp her feet and grab the knife, yelling that she was going to kill him, but of course Auntie always stopped her. This became a game they played at regular intervals, a rehearsal for murder. This allowed her to siphon off a little of the hatred from her brimming heart. All this anger, yet she forgot to hate the attacker. She wasn't the only one. As time went on, most people forgot one of the culprits was still at large.

"What happened to the other attacker?" I rolled over in bed to ask my aunt softly. "He's still in Southern Courtyard, isn't he?"

No reply. She'd fallen asleep. I was alone in the dark with a huge pile of questions.

He must still live in Southern Courtyard. I'd probably laid eyes on everyone who lived here, so I'd seen him before, maybe bumped into him often. Lining up for steamed buns in the cafeteria, returning yogurt jars to the corner shop, selling cardboard boxes to the scrap merchant. Perhaps all those times, he'd been standing not far from me, staring coldly in my direction. Noticing my tattered school bag, the grubby school uniform sleeve I wiped my nose on. Staring as I swiftly picked up a coin someone else had dropped, and stuffed it into my pocket. He must surely know I had no father nor mother, that my teachers gave me a hard time and my classmates jeered at me, that I was eleven but still sleeping in the same bed as my aunt. When he looked at me, would he feel a sense of accomplishment, that everything I had was because of him? He was responsible for us being lowly as ants, so vulnerable anyone could step on us.

I tossed the covers aside and jumped out of bed, and walked barefoot to the window, which was open to the night sky. Moonlight wandered carelessly amongst those battered wooden trunks, like a scavenger walking through a ruin, searching for something valuable but finally leaving disappointed. Ever since a violent summer storm shredded our curtains, these windows had gone uncovered. We didn't need curtains because we had no secrets. Besides, no one was curious enough about us to look in. Only those doing well had hidden parts of their lives, aimed at provoking curiosity in others. Granddad's attacker was surely leading his life like a riddle, behind thick curtains.

I slumped against the wall between two tall rows of boxes. The moon couldn't reach in here—it was like the bottom of a well. In the past, I'd come here whenever I felt sad. But this was the first time I truly understood my circumstances. My whole life was taking place in a narrow shaft. I had nothing at all. Even my few friends, you and the others, my moments of happiness, were all temporary. There'd come a day when you'd all leave me for a better life. I'd be stuck in this room full of broken boxes and curtainless windows. Perhaps I'd end up like my father, drinking and hitting people, frittering away my abundant, useless energy. I pulled myself together before I got completely swamped by self-pity, and grew incredibly angry instead.

I'd never hated anyone. Not the mother who abandoned me, my tyrannical father, my cruel grandmother, my sadistic teachers, or the classmates who made fun of me. I just accepted that's how things were. If the gods deal you a terrible hand, all you can do is play it as best you can.

Now I understood this hand hadn't been dealt by the gods. "If your Granddad hadn't been attacked, for all we know he might be the chancellor by now." Auntie's words echoed in my ears. I clung onto this unverifiable supposition, and imagined the alternate life it presented: high status, a happy family, a life full of freedom and plenty. I believed these were the cards we ought to have had, but someone had swapped them around. All our misfortunes came from the same place: that nail, and the person behind it. The culprit who sent my entire family careening down a different track.

Sitting in my desolate corner, I felt my desire for vengeance blaze like a bonfire. I huddled closer, until my whole body was burning with it. My veins were thrumming, like ropes pulled taut. Something ancient and slumbering in my blood roused itself. Now it surged in waves towards my head. Listening to the tides in my body, I felt an enormous force crashing against my chest. Faint blue flames danced up and down. In my wavering vision, I saw a large group of people surrounding the bonfire. Flimsy, transparent shades. I'd never seen them before, but I recognized them: my ancestors, Granddad's kin, staring at me with searing eyes. When they left, their gaze stayed behind. Those eyes would always remain, gleaming like eternal temple flames. Before going, they walked over to me as if to say goodbye, not actually speaking, just putting their hands on my shoulder, conferring strength. It hurt where they touched me. The pain spread slowly through my body, and with sudden anguish I understood I wasn't a child anymore. I woke at dawn, curled up in that space between boxes, feeling like I'd slept for a long time. Yet I could detect the faint aroma of ashes on my body, and a lingering pressure on my shoulder. I believed there truly had been a visitation.

Kin. During the long day that followed, this word kept churning around my mind. To me, it was a remote, almost over-emotional term, only seen in books. My household comprised two small rooms, Granny and Auntie. A broken, tattered household. It had never crossed my mind that I had anything like kinfolk.

Auntie said Granddad had had two older brothers. One died suddenly when he was three, the other caught bubonic plague when he was twelve and passed away too. Only Granddad lived to adulthood. His village was suffering famine, so in order to feed himself, he left home and joined the revolution. After liberation, he was deployed to the Medical University, and settled down in the city. The next time he visited his hometown, his parents had died—he now had no living relatives. He stayed a few days, hiring workers to restore the family graves. Granddad had a strong sense of kinship. He'd always hoped to have a few more children, repopulating the Cheng clan. During the war, Granny got pregnant twice, but miscarried both times. This put future pregnancies at risk, and after she gave birth to my father with great difficulty, she lost two more children. Just as she was preparing to have her tubes tied, my aunt came along, and she decided to take the risk of carrying her to term. She spent several months flat on her back, taking god knows how many pills to keep this baby safe. Granddad had been hoping for a boy, and when it turned out to be a daughter, he pinned all his hopes on his only son. Apparently, he'd hoped to borrow a rifle from his old army friends, so as to pass on his sharpshooting skills to my father, firmly believing these would come in useful someday. He wanted my father to become a soldier when he was old enough, or a policeman, anything that would have got him his own gun. If he'd known my father would never get a gun of his own, but would instead end up being arrested by armed men, what would he have thought? I guessed that he did know, and that his spirit, imprisoned in that immobile body, must be hopping with rage. He'd probably given up hope in his useless son, and had turned his sights on me.

He'd been looking at me all along. Hadn't he?

"Little Gong is different from the other kids." I remembered my mother saying. She always declared this with absolute certainty.

I'd finally found out just how I was different: the entire family's mission rested on my shoulders. This broken, defeated family was waiting for me to rescue it. I had no choice but to find the other assailant. I told myself I had to take revenge. As to how I would do this, I wasn't sure, but simply thinking of the word *revenge* already filled me with pleasure.

No one knew who the second culprit was. Apart from

Granddad, anyway. Even if he was immobilized at the time, unable to resist, he must have known who'd pushed the nail in. The scene must have been etched in his brain. But he had no way of telling us. His soul was trapped, imprisoned in that paralyzed body. If we could only communicate with his soul, we'd have the murderer's name. A mighty plan floated into view—I would invent a machine to speak with Granddad's spirit.

I thought of the perfect name for it: a spirit intercom.

Even if I'd lost my journal from when I was devising this machine, I'd still remember very clearly when I started. November 1993, though I recorded it as: '93, Brumaire. Much more dashing, as if my destiny was intersecting with Napoleon Bonaparte's. To be honest, back then I hardly knew anything about this famous, diminutive man, just what I'd read in a newspaper article I'd stumbled across, which was enough to make me worship him. As a little child, poor and puny, with his heavy rural accent, Napoleon was mocked by his classmates. But the heavens had a grand mission for him, and granted him the ambition to conquer the whole of Europe. This article described it mundanely, but it made my blood churn. Poverty, classmates jeering, a mighty calling, fierce ambition. How stirring, to have these things in common with him.

It sounds hilarious now, but at the time, inventing the spirit intercom felt as noble as imposing imperial rule over Europe.

From then on, I plunged into a fever of invention. At noon each day, I rushed home to gobble my lunch, then dashed to the library to grab more books. Anatomy, mechanics, Buddhism, alchemy ... The librarian gaped at the range of fields I was researching. He was a man in his thirties with a prominent red nose, which ought to have made him look jolly, except it was the only cheerful part of his decidedly glum face. He always had a book with him, *New Concept English: Volume One*, which he'd read whenever no one was at the counter, tongue protruding between his teeth as he tried out new words. He was curious as to why I wanted all these books, but I refused to give him an explanation.

"It's good to read more," he said encouragingly. "If you manage to leave the country, all this knowledge will surely come in useful overseas."

"Why would I leave the country?" I asked.

"That's the only way to live a good life." He tweaked his swollen scarlet nose viciously, and let out a long sigh. He suffered from chronic rhinitis and dust allergies. Spending each day amongst these piles of old books was torture to him.

I shook my head. "I want to live a bit better, but here."

"You won't have a good time here. You're still young, you'll understand when you grow up." He gently stroked the tattered cover of *New Concept English*.

I'd been pitying him, but now he'd gone and said the words I detested most: "You'll understand when you grow up." Whenever I asked Auntie anything she didn't want to answer, that's how she'd shut me up. A child's world is full of No Entry signs and forbidden zones, our age the only explanation needed to keep us out.

I flipped through these mystical books, but gleaned virtually nothing. The few volumes that mentioned souls invariably made them sound like an abstract fantasy, with no practical advice about how to rescue an actual trapped soul. One book referred to the "primordial spirit," but I couldn't make out whether this was the same as a regular soul. According to that author, certain curses and chants could cause the primordial spirit to appear. I was suspicious of this approach, which seemed insufficiently scientific. In my imagination, the spirit intercom would be a tangible object, exquisitely designed. After wandering in a big circle, I ended up at my starting point: the soul is a type of electromagnetic wave. I didn't actually know what an electromagnetic wave was, but according to the few books I was able to understand, it wasn't too different from a sound wave. The station-hopping radio in Room 317 inspired me. I saw the soul as a physical presence, a blazing little planet shaped like a seed, and when it spoke, it sent out a stream of sound waves, causing the air to stir. We couldn't understand because we had no way of receiving these waves. Our ears weren't attuned to their frequency. From a book about electromagnetism, I understood the air was full of waves we couldn't detect. That is to say, if I built the right machine, we'd be able to intercept these other waves.

I began sketching in my notebook. Spirit Intercom Model One. Model Two. Model Three. When I made a mistake, I crumpled up the page, and when all the pages had been torn out I got a new book. Finally, I had a pretty good idea what my machine would look like: a black box to receive electromagnetic waves, its walls perforated with little holes, with wires connected to speakers and electrodes.

My blueprint was perfect, but reality didn't match up. The black box ended up being a metal cookie tin I got from a junk seller. Imported cookies, apparently—the outside of the tin was covered with English words, which the librarian smugly read to me. "Made in Denmark." How far away that was, Denmark. I only knew it as the home of the Little Mermaid. This metal tin must have been entrusted with an important mission, to sail across the ocean from such a distant land. Its destiny was here, to be part of my spirit intercom. I went to a cobbler, who squinted at my sketch as he painstakingly pierced the tin full of tiny holes.

The speakers were supplied by the same man, who had a real treasure trove of gadgets. They looked like police walkie-talkies, complete with serial numbers. I asked why he hadn't turned them in to the station, and he said public property got replaced by the state. Walkie-talkies rarely went missing, though—in all his years, he'd only come across these. How had they ended up here? Surely they'd also been sent to fulfill the great plan of my spirit intercom. I truly believed this, and so when the junk man said he couldn't just give them to me, I didn't mind smashing open the piggy bank full of coins I'd been hoarding for years.

Then there were the electrodes, the sort you stick to your body when doing an ECG. These were easy to get—I just asked Auntie for them, making up a story about listening to a rabbit's heartbeat for biology class. She seemed suspicious, but didn't ask any questions. Probably a harmless game, she must have thought. She brought home a set, but warned me she'd need it back when I was done.

As for the electromagnetic wave receiver, that would naturally be the radio in Room 317.

My preparations took place in secrecy. I didn't say a word to anyone, not even you. You'd had all this time to ponder the question of the soul, but still hadn't talked to me about it. You had your secrets, now I had mine—a bigger, more weighty one. If I'd told you, you'd have laughed and poured cold water over my scheme. I decided you'd only find out when I was successful. Ah, what a wonderful project. I imagined your stunned face, mouth gaping open, and that cheered me up. What a perfect chance to strip away your arrogance. I'd have your respect forever.

Two weeks later, I left the house at dusk with a huge plastic bag and hurried to the hospital.

The corridors were very quiet. I went into Room 317 and gingerly shut the door behind me. Very carefully, I pulled my mighty machine from the bag. Watching closely, I thought I saw Granddad's expression change. He seemed to be watching, his little round eyes giving me a quick blink. This tiny gesture seemed significant.

"You know I've come to rescue you, don't you?" My eyes twitched, and I felt about to cry.

The machine stood on the bedside table. All sorts of wires protruded from the round, gray-blue metal box, like tentacles from some deep sea squid. Mysterious and eerie.

From my pocket, I produced a chart of human anatomy I'd ripped from a book, with the acupoints marked, and propped it up next to me. Following the diagram, I placed the electrodes on Granddad's body, then set up the walkie-talkies. Everything was as it should be. Sticking my hand into the cookie tin, I solemnly turned on the radio.

Static. Humming from the speakers. The room filled with noises, yet still felt terrifyingly quiet. I turned and stood ramrod straight at the foot of the bed. "Granddad, let's begin."

Clutching the receiver tightly, I held my breath and listened with great attention. I believed I could hear every speck of dust in the room.

Li Jiaqi

The most significant event of winter 1993, as far as I was concerned, was Dad's return—the week before Mom's marriage. One afternoon in December, he showed up at my school and asked for me. I ran all the way to the gate. He was smoking some distance away on the other side of the metal fence, in a long black coat whose upturned collar hid half his face. Even before I could get a proper look at him, I had a feeling he wasn't doing well. I felt a twinge in my heart, and tears came to my eyes.

Seeing me crying, he lowered his head and stamped out his cigarette. Perhaps my tears made him feel awkward—expressing strong emotions was forbidden in our relationship.

He'd lost a lot of weight and gotten tan; his hair was longer, and there was stubble on his cheeks. He seemed exhausted, sucking hard on his cigarette, which he'd lit as soon as the last one was extinguished, patting himself all over to find his lighter. I noticed his hands tremble.

"I only have study hall this afternoon," I lied, meaning I was free to leave with him.

"Okay." With that, he led me away.

We didn't actually have anywhere to go. After wandering aimlessly down a few streets, we saw a park with a lake in it, bought a ticket, and went in. The wintry park looked desolate, the willow trees by the water like pencil scribbles in a sketchbook. The roof of the pavilion on the opposite shore dipped down at the corners, as if trying to see its reflection in the lake, only to be rebuffed by the ice.

Dad went to the kiosk for cigarettes, and on the way back he bought me a roast yam. I warmed my icy hands on it as I slowly nibbled. We ducked out of the ferocious wind into a covered walkway. On either side of us, withered vines gripped square pillars. I imagined them in the summer, thick with leaves; we could come back then and row on the lake.

"We've been here before. Do you remember?" he asked.

"No, we haven't."

"We have, when you were little."

I wanted to ask if we'd come in the summer, but he was so sunk in memories I couldn't bear to rouse him. His expression had turned tender, as if he missed our past. Was that possible? I felt unsure of everything. I still couldn't believe he'd come to my school. You have to understand—I'd had a dream where this happened, and he'd been standing at the gate exactly like in my dream, although dream him wore a coffee-colored sweater and had very short hair. He'd pressed his face to the fence, waved at me, and said, let's go. But he wouldn't actually take me away—any fantasy I'd had about that was long extinguished. Yet here he was, which at least meant he must miss me, a stronger emotion than I'd expected. I'd wanted to say something to him as we walked to the park, but then stopped myself, afraid he'd be able to tell how overjoyed I was, and despise me for it. He thought anything remotely childish was stupid, and I had to do my best to keep it hidden. I was always reminding myself to be more mature around him.

I thought Dad had come home because of Grandma's injury, but when I mentioned that, it was clear he had no idea what I was talking about. No one had told him—he hadn't even planned to go to Grandpa's house.

"I ought to see her, I suppose?" he muttered, as if fishing for encouragement. I suggested that he come with me that evening, and he agreed. Then I asked when he was going back to Beijing.

"In a few days," he said vaguely. It seemed he didn't have a return ticket. An awful thought flashed through my mind: if Grandma were more seriously injured, maybe he'd stay longer.

"Mom's getting married next week," I said as casually as I could, trying to gauge from his face if he already knew this. Had he come back for the ceremony? He wouldn't be welcome there.

"Oh, really?" he nodded. "What's he like?"

"Very ordinary."

"You don't like him?"

I shook my head and peeled a patch of skin off the roast yam. "They want me to live with them and not with Grandpa. I'm starting at a new school next semester." I was in a hurry to impart this information, so he'd know not to look for me at my old school.

"Do you already have a school place?"

"Yes, near Uncle Lin's house." I didn't think I needed to explain who Uncle Lin was.

"That's good," he said, after a pause. He seemed distracted, indifferent to Mom's marriage. If he wasn't here for the wedding, then why?

"How about you?" I asked. "Are you married?"

"Uh-huh." He tapped his cigarette. Sparks landed on the ground and flickered.

"Are you happy in Beijing?"

"I'm all right." His mouth tightened a little, as if he'd just had a spoonful of bitter medicine.

His greenish eyebags made him look weird in profile. I stared at him, trying to fix this new feature in my mind. He wasn't happy—of that I was certain—which comforted me a little. We hadn't been able to make Dad happy, but this other woman, Wang Luhan, couldn't do it either. It was in his nature to be unhappy, and perhaps I'd inherited that. A tragic thought.

Icy wind tousled his hair like a pair of wizened hands. I looked at the stubborn undergrowth of his stubble. He looked like an escaped convict. I had a bizarre thought: this wasn't my dad but a stranger who was kidnapping me, and it didn't matter where to, anywhere but here.

"Do you want to ride the Ferris wheel?" asked Dad. "It's over there. I'll wait here for you."

I said nothing, just bent over my wrinkled roast yam skin. The yam flesh burned like a fireball in my stomach. After a while, Dad seemed to realize it was on him to break the silence. "Are you cold? How about we go for a walk around the lake?"

I lied and said I wasn't cold, and as we set off along the bank, I quietly slipped my hands into my sleeves. The sky was dark as a bruised knee. There was no one else in the park—I couldn't recall seeing anyone else all afternoon, which seemed to indicate this day had been specially designed for the two of us. The sky gradually darkened. Dad walked faster and faster, until I was forced to jog to keep up with him. He had a destination in mind, and it seemed urgent. He was keen to prove something. This was a duel against himself.

We moved from the west side of the lake to the north

side. The final glimmer of daylight was taken away. Abruptly, he stopped.

"Forget it, we won't make it," he said. "I hadn't realized how far away the pavilion is. We rowed there before." Panting, he got out his cigarettes, looking sorrowfully into the distance. I was heartbroken to see him admitting defeat.

"Let's keep going, we'll get there soon," I said.

"No." He shook his head.

"We can definitely get there. Let's go," I wheedled, then suddenly burst into tears.

It wasn't as simple as unhappiness. His whole body reeked of decay. Something had died—his passion, faith, fighting spirit. Irreversibly gone. He understood this very clearly, but had still wanted to give it a try. I didn't know why it mattered that we reach the pavilion, but it was important to him. This tiny achievement would have comforted him a little.

But now I was the one who wanted to get there, and I pleaded with him to take me, sobbing as I tugged at his sleeve. He stood there unmoving.

"Stop it, will you?" he finally said. "You're old enough to know better."

I froze. These were the words I dreaded hearing. I wanted him to think I was grown up, the way he wanted me to be. Now I'd ruined everything.

I kept crying as we walked out of the park. He saw a restaurant across the road with its lights still on, and made for it. Weren't we going to Grandpa's house? I asked. We ought to give them a call if not. He didn't seem to hear me as he hurtled inside.

The restaurant was minuscule: just four tables and an open kitchen. A middle-aged woman stood by the doorway cleaning vegetables, while a young man scooped a live fish from a tank, dropped it on a board, and whacked its head with the flat of a cleaver. Its tail thrashed frantically, flicking water droplets everywhere. As soon as we sat down,

Dad asked for a small bottle of baijiu. The waiter was too busy dealing with the fish to take our order. Dad couldn't stop fiddling with his lighter, so antsy he could have been sitting on a bed of nails. When the waiter finally brought the liquor, he took a few quick gulps. Only then did he calm down, and his eyes lit up. The fog that had clung to him all day dispersed. He slowly cheered up, swaying a little.

"Would you like some?" He waved his glass. "You'll feel warmer."

Without waiting for a reply, he got the waiter to bring another glass. Although he poured carefully, he still spilled some. Again, I noticed his shaky hands.

"Is this enough? Mm, should be." He handed it over.

I took a small mouthful and sparks danced on my tongue. Dad's order began to arrive, and soon the table was covered in dishes, but we ate very little. He seemed unenthusiastic about the food, and the yam was still swelling in my stomach. Besides, it would have saddened me to see empty plates and cups, meaning the meal was over and we would part.

Even as I sank into worry, he relaxed, face flushed and eyes tender.

"Cheer up, would you?' he said. "Trust me, whatever kind of man your mom's found, he'll be better than me." He looked melancholy for a moment, then he grinned.

"I don't care who she's with." I raised my glass and took a sip. "I don't care if he likes me or not. It doesn't matter."

His eyes were fixed on the glass in front of him, as if he hadn't heard a word I'd said.

"But I'm not changing schools," I muttered. "I don't want to leave my friends."

"Friends!" His attention snapped back. "They aren't important, not one bit." He shook his head firmly.

As we reached the end of the bottle, he began shifting in his seat.

"Should I get another one? Yes, let's." He seemed to enjoy answering his own questions. As if to forestall my protests, he said, "That's not too much, is it? Oh, right, I didn't touch a drop this afternoon."

I watched the waiter fetch another bottle. This was bad for him, but at least he seemed happy. This mood was like a thin sheet of ice. It would shatter with a single touch.

His beeper went off. He stopped it and took a big mouthful of baijiu. Before he could put down his glass, the beeper sounded again. He slammed it against the table, but it wouldn't stop shrilling. He ignored it, turning back to his glass. I could tell he was irritated. The good mood had been destroyed.

"Where were we?" He looked up at me. "Oh, right, changing schools. You'll be fine, don't worry. You're going to find out that it doesn't matter where you are. It's all exactly the same."

The pager buzzed and twitched like a dying animal using the last of its strength to crawl a short distance across the table.

"Shut up already!" he spat. Swaying, he rose to his feet, and said he had to make a phone call. He walked a few steps, then turned back to grab the baijiu bottle.

I sat and watched the waiter kill a chicken. I'd never seen one getting slaughtered at such close quarters. Its long, stiff neck suddenly went limp, and blood began gushing from it. Chickens were more intelligent than fish, I thought, they knew to close their eyes at the moment of death. The chicken had its feathers plucked, its head and rump chopped off, and its body hacked into little pieces, which were thrown into a pot. As it boiled, the waiter scooped the bloody scum that floated to the surface.

It was clear to me that my dad was a drunk, and although I didn't fully understand what that meant, I knew it could destroy a person. He may already be destroyed. The clear-headed, wise, ambitious man no longer existed, leaving only this numb, confused husk. For the first time, I understood how everything a person had was fragile and unstable. Our natures were not fixed, our talents could be taken away, our virtue could be polluted. Anyone could become a completely different person. Someone you knew inside out could turn into a stranger—a horrifying thought, though it seemed magical and heartwarming that I hadn't stopped loving him. Even with him completely transformed, my love hadn't been damaged at all. I was proud of my rock-solid love. Surely such enduring love would have its uses. I believed I would be able to do something for my father.

I thought through so many things while my dad was away from the table, I could feel myself growing up. If only this burst of maturity had taken place earlier that day, I might have handled myself differently and made our afternoon less of a disaster.

It was getting colder. The restaurant was eager to close, but still there was no sign of Dad. The waiter came over a few times to ask where he was. Had I been abandoned? I gathered my courage and asked the waiter if I could go look for him. He stared at me dubiously, and decided to come with me.

Dad was right outside, sitting on the ground with his back to the icy wall. Head on knees, empty bottle next to him. I shook him for a long while before he looked up.

"I fell asleep."

The waiter took his money and walked away muttering darkly about unfit fathers.

Dad staggered to his feet, but pushed me away when I tried to help him. We walked slowly back the same way we'd come. When we got to Grandpa's building, he said he wasn't coming up—he'd visit another day. Just as well, I thought, I didn't want my grandparents to see him in this state.

I walked alone into the dark doorway. When I turned back to look, he was standing in the same spot, swaying slightly, black coat flapping in the wind.

"I'll come and see you again in a couple of days, okay?" His voice was gentle, almost a plea.

I wished I could write those words on a piece of paper and stuff them into his pocket, because I was scared he'd forget his promise once he'd sobered up.

Cheng Gong

"Granddad? Hello? It's me, Little Gong."

I stayed in Room 317 past midnight that day, till the walkie-talkie batteries went dead. No response. Or rather, there must have been a response, I just wasn't able to hear it.

I couldn't deny that the experiment had failed. But that's normal, isn't it, to fail on the first attempt? Some of the world's greatest inventions only succeeded after thousands of tries. That's how I comforted myself, though I still felt despair.

The problem was the radio—it was so old that it only received a few local stations. Even broadcasts from the next city were beyond it. How could it possibly detect the voice of a soul? I needed a more up-to-date, sensitive model that could pick up the faintest electromagnetic waves.

I spent a few days feeling dejected, then pulled myself together and went in search of a better radio. The trash collector told me everyone had stereos these days, all these old-style radios had been sold off or tossed out. He suggested I try the flea market.

That Sunday morning, I got the number 11 bus to the end of the line, on the westernmost side of the city, where there was a huge independent marketplace. The flea market was tiny, in the north-east corner. I walked around the stalls looking carefully, and though there were a few radio sets, they were all about the same as the one in Room 317. Battered, worn out, oozing damp and bygone time. I hated them. They reminded me of Mom and those beautiful, soiled clothes.

Then I spotted a second-hand German radio set that didn't have this stench. Even from a distance, I already thought it looked special. I headed straight for the corner stall, not looking away for even a second in case it suddenly vanished. It was very old, but in a dignified way. Like an ageing dandy in a spiffy suit, still full of spirit. There wasn't a speck of dust on the speaker mesh or the slender screws of its longish exterior, the aerial wasn't rusty at all, and the tea-colored plastic shell gleamed warmly. The top and sides were covered with switches and knobs whose uses were unclear, and a row of white letters on the bottom right corner were so scuffed, even someone who knew German might have struggled to make them out. This only added to its mystique, like a secret code. This was it! There was a small electrical blockage, but the stallholder swore than when this was fixed, it would even be able to pick up signals from Korea. It had been confiscated more than twenty years ago from some capitalist's home. He hadn't been able to bring himself to sell it—it was his most valuable item.

After a round of the market, I ended up back at this stall, picking up the radio for a closer look. The stallholder squinted at me, a shriveled cigarette butt drooping from his lips. "Yours for four hundred yuan."

I gave him a quick smile and walked out. Brand-new radios cost a little over two hundred—decent-looking ones, made by a state-run company. They clearly couldn't compete with this German product, though, not because of workmanship or materials, but simply because they were everywhere you looked. It was far too easy to lay your hands on one. How could the insides of a mighty invention like the spirit intercom come from something so commonplace?

After that, the German radio set nagged at my heart. As soon as my eyes opened each morning, it would appear before me. Never in my entire life had I felt such fierce desire. But could I get four hundred yuan? Even if I could persuade Granny and Auntie to give me an allowance, it would take several years to save up that sum. Borrow it? My friends were all as poor as me. You were probably the richest—you might have looked no better off than us, but everyone knew your Dad was earning tons of foreign currency in Beijing, enough to fill a truck. You said he loved you very much, so he must have given you some of that cash. I didn't know how to broach the subject, though, and if you did give me a loan, I knew you'd lord it over me. If my invention succeeded, you'd take all the credit.

Who else was there? Ah, the red-nosed librarian.

"What, you're inventing things now?" he said loudly in the afternoon stillness of the library. I looked around in a panic, but luckily no one else was around. He was getting worked up—his eyes were turning bloodshot, and his nose was even more crimson than usual.

"That's the right thing to do!" he said. "You have to learn things your own way. Don't trust your teachers, whatever you do. Nothing you can read in a book is worth anything."

"Mm-hmm." I nodded.

"I wish I could help, but I'm already in all kinds of debt because I've been preparing to leave the country." He deflated a bit at this sad thought, then perked up again. "The National Patent Office! Write them a letter explaining your device. Maybe they'll be interested."

"I can't wait that long."

"Then there's nothing else you can do, my young friend. If you can bear to take my advice, put this aside for now, and think of a way to leave the country. There's no point inventing anything here, there's no hope for this place."

"I don't want to leave the country," I said. "There's nowhere I want to go."

It was evening by the time I left the library. The wind was rising, and withered yellow leaves swirled through the air. The sun lurked on the horizon like a dictator clinging to power, its rays a defeated army.

The school field was full of people—there was some kind of competition going on. Somewhere in the distance, I heard a basketball hit the ground. *Thud. Thud. Thud.* Then a few seconds later, a riot of cheers. Such joy at winning a match, or maybe even a well-executed three-pointer. I envied their ability to live in such simple happiness. Like Dabin and Zifeng, who might right then have been sitting in front of a TV set, clutching their joysticks, directing a tiny man with a big nose to jump on toadstools and eat gold coins. They kept inviting me to join them, but I felt it was shameful to waste time like that. It was a bitter thought, that our paths were already diverging, yet it filled me with pride.

Of course, said a voice in my heart, you're completely different from them.

If I couldn't borrow the money, should I steal it? I gave it some serious thought. I'd once seen a boy get caught pickpocketing someone's wallet at the market. They twisted his arms behind his back and ripped the wool cap off his head. A crowd formed around him, and an old lady yelled, Disgraceful, how will your parents ever hold their heads up again? Her look of hatred was branded on my brain. I was doing this to rescue my family—I couldn't bring shame to them.

So that road was blocked too, and hope was evaporating. In the absence of a miracle, my invention could only ever be a fantasy. But wait ... a miracle. Why hadn't I thought of this before? There was a church next to Southern Courtyard!

That Sunday, I hung around outside the church after the service. Other people were there too, waiting to speak to the pastor, but they weren't as determined as me, and wandered off when the cold wind rose. Soon, I was alone—even the magpies had flown away. A plump woman came out and told me to go, she had to lock up. I wasn't going, I said, I wanted to see the pastor. She tried to catch hold of me, but I ducked aside. She chased me round the yard until she had to stop, panting. "Fine, stay there and starve to death for all I care." She walked out the gate and locked it behind her.

After a while, I got bored of waiting and lay down for a nap, but visions of crispy golden fried fish kept appearing to me, and my stomach gurgled. Was I really going to starve to death? What if they forgot about me, and no one came all week? Next Sunday, they'd find my corpse propped up in a corner, already stinking a little. Maggots burrowing into my sunken eyes, wriggling between my parted lips. How would they deal with me? Dump me in Dead Man's Tower? Then you'd see me on your next visit there.

Goodbye, Jiaqi. I rehearsed the moment of our parting, and these words felt familiar to me, as if they'd always been hanging up somewhere in my mind, ready to fall at the slightest touch like paint peeling off a wall. A strange, inauspicious feeling. As if it was inevitable that we would be parted. God had written this scene and locked it in a drawer, but I'd accidentally opened it ahead of time. I shuddered and sat on the ground, shaking my head to dislodge these awful thoughts. The sun was no longer overhead, I realized. Soon it would be evening, the light would fade, the rising wind would shake the branches vigorously, and I'd be shivering in my thin school uniform.

Goodbye, Jiaqi. I couldn't dispel the words whirling round my brain. In what circumstances would I speak them? I couldn't imagine. What could separate us, apart from death? But did you feel the same way? I wasn't sure. We'd begun to drift apart ever since I started experimenting with the spirit intercom. It wasn't just you, I'd drifted apart from the world. This enormous secret had cut me off. I'd turned my back on my duty to revive my clan, and was walking alone down a dark path. How far would I have to go? Did this path have an end? Perhaps I would be left in eternal darkness. This was frightening. What if you were right, and there were things in this world we weren't meant to know about, such as souls? A chill went down my back. As dusk fell on the yard, I suddenly missed you a lot. I wanted to see you right away, to make sure you hadn't changed. Just like that, my stubbornness melted away. I had to get the hell out of this place.

The walls separating me from the street were too high. Even if I piled up enough stones to get to the top, I'd injure myself jumping down on the other side. Before daylight faded entirely, I crept along the narrow, overgrown path by the side of the church to reach the back, where the wall was lower. I had no idea what lay on the other side, but I could smell cooking, and the aroma of fried onions made my empty stomach clench. I made a stack of stones, shakily stepped onto them, and pulled myself atop the wall. Ahead of me was a siheyuan courtyard. All the curtains were drawn shut and I couldn't see inside, but the lights were on so at least I knew someone was home. Stepping carefully across the cracked tiles, I leaped down into the courtyard, twisting my ankle but not too seriously. I'd landed heavily—surely someone would have heard me? I froze, but no one came out. Creeping over to one of the lit windows, I peered through a gap in the curtains and saw the plump woman from earlier, talking to a man in black—the pastor.

"It was the boy," I heard her say. "The one Xu Huiyun's been helping."

"What does he want?"

"How should I know? Probably more money."

"That can't be, he doesn't know where the money comes from. I've always given it directly to his aunt, anyway."

The woman sighed. "I've never understood why this has to be a big secret."

"I've explained this to you. She ... owes a debt to the boy's family. She feels responsible for the boy's suffering. She made a confession to me." The pastor lowered his voice. "Apparently, a man was left in a vegetative state—you know, back during the free-for-all of the Cultural Revolution. And it was her husband who did it—"

"What, Li Jisheng?"

Your grandfather's name. I shivered.

"So Li Jisheng's been supporting the boy?"

"No, Xu Huiyun has. Her husband doesn't know."

"Why not? Wasn't this all his fault?"

I turned and ran for the wooden gate in the far corner of the courtyard, and once I was out, went straight home. Without pausing to put down my bag, I dashed into the kitchen and shoveled cold leftover fried rice into my mouth. Next, I wolfed down two sausages, a few slices of stale cake, and some wedding candy Auntie had brought home god knows how long ago. I gobbled everything edible in the fridge, eating as quickly as I could to stop the thoughts from coming. Then I went into the bathroom and had a shower, letting the rushing water drown the voices in my mind. Finally, I went to bed and put a pillow over my head, pressing it down hard until I fell asleep.

The fog was heavy all that winter. I opened the window each morning to nothing but grayness, like TV static. Everything turned gray: rooftops, streets, electric wires, even the pigeons as they flapped about, as if they were in mourning for someone. Fog felt different from other weather—unlike rain or snow, which were pure and fell from the sky with the scent of far-off places. Fog felt like something the city excreted, the filth of humanity. It was 1993, and this industrial city was beyond help. Our springs ran dry, the river round the city stank to high heaven, the large-bellied chimneys of the power plant belched thick clouds of smoke, high-rise buildings were being constructed everywhere, and cranes were hauling rubble up into the sky, scattering dust back down to earth. I couldn't help thinking the end of the world might soon be upon us.

Your grandfather kept appearing in my mind. Walking along, torso ramrod straight. Narrow face deeply creased with wrinkles, eyes as cool as a deep pool, not the slightest hint of a smile in them. For years now, these eyes had been quietly watching my family's lowly, degraded existence, which he'd bestowed upon us. Behind his stern expression, he must have been laughing his head off. I didn't understand why he'd stuck a nail into Granddad's head, rather than simply killing him. Maybe such a quick ending would have been unsatisfying, and he'd devised a way to prolong his entertainment. This farce had now been playing out for almost thirty years—surely that was enough? Didn't he feel any guilt? No matter which way I looked at it, I couldn't understand. Your grandmother knew everything and was covering up her husband's sins. True, she'd confessed to the priest—but that was just putting on a show for God. When she saw me, I felt no sympathy from her, she avoided me like the plague. I'll never forget the disgust in her eyes when she looked at me. She'd been quietly sending money to my family all these years, so I wouldn't be driven to crime. Not that she cared if I became a criminal—what she feared was that I'd take revenge.

I remembered the strange dream. The blue bonfire. The transparent people. The hand on my shoulder. Revenge had felt abstract before that, but now it had been turned into something passionate, the desire to invent a spirit intercom. I actually liked the idea of revenge—it rendered my life no longer boring and pointless. If only this could continue—but everything changed the second I learned who the other attacker had been. Vengeance reeked of blood, it bared its sharp teeth, clawing at my nerves. "You know who the culprit is. Now you can take revenge."

For several sleepless nights, I rolled across the bed, unbearably hot, to press myself against the wall and stare at the bloody splotches from the mosquitoes I'd killed in the summer. In the lower bunk, Auntie turned over, ground her teeth, snored. Each sound shattered the peace and tortured me. I wished I could wake her and ask what she would do if she knew who the other attacker was. But I couldn't. She'd instantly suspect I knew something, and I couldn't tell her the secret. For all that it was wearing me out, I couldn't let it go. What did having this information mean? I didn't know either, but I dimly sensed this revenge was my personal affair, and there were things I needed to do. Where should I start? No matter what, I had to do something. The thought nagged at me. All my energy went into appearing normal. I had to be careful talking to you—I was terrified of letting slip any hint of strangeness. After saying goodbye each evening, I'd walk home alone, breathing a sigh of relief that the curtain had once again fallen on an ordinary day. Nothing had happened, I told myself, greedily relishing this moment of quiet.

To be honest, even if I had behaved oddly, you probably wouldn't have noticed—you were immersed in your own worries, never saying a word, frowning all day long. Even Dabin, not the sharpest tool in the box, noticed. With great confidence he said you must be distressed by your mom's marriage. Ever since you went on that outing with her and her fiancé, you'd been all gloomy, which made Dabin think you didn't like your would-be stepdad. I mean, *obviously* you didn't like him, how could anyone replace your dad? But you had to accept facts—the wedding was in a month. You would be trussed up in a fancy dress and thrust in front of the happy couple for photographs. Maybe they'd humiliate you further by forcing you to call the man "Dad." Was that what was troubling you? If it was, why couldn't you tell us? So maybe you had a different secret. When did that start? Back when we were talking about the spirit intercom? Before that? I didn't have the energy to probe—I was too absorbed in my own secret.

On the surface, nothing had changed. I waited for you at the junction each gray morning. You appeared, and we walked to school together. Now I began to notice the fog, which turned the world into an old man with clouded lungs. We couldn't see our own legs—we were ghosts, suspended in midair. Into this blankness, houses and trees popped out like specters, startling us. The air smelled of burning foliage. A woman swept dried leaves from the sidewalk into a heap, rustling away. We walked in silence, side by side. Even if one of us had spoken, it felt like the other wouldn't hear. The fog trapped everyone in their own jar, and we sank into our own thoughts behind glass, our minds guttering like flames smoldering from lack of oxygen.

It was secrets that drove a wedge between us. We were a species of beast that hunted secrets to survive. The day was always going to come when we would fall out over a prey and go our separate ways; this moment had now arrived. Many years later, when I thought back to this winter, I'd see us walking side by side through the fog—heavy, desolate, endless. Maybe this was the truest representation of childhood. Walking through a fog made of secrets, stumbling along a path we couldn't see, not knowing where we were going. Growing up felt like making it through the fog and seeing the world clearly—but actually, that wasn't the case. We'd just wrapped that fog around ourselves, each of us spinning it into a cocoon.

On Sunday morning, I went back to the flea market, but the space where the corner stall should have been was empty. I asked the neighboring stallholder, who told me the man I'd spoken to before had quit—he owed too much rent, and had gone into hiding. I asked if she knew where he'd gone, at which she rolled her eyes—if anyone knew where he was, how could he be in hiding?

So it seemed the spirit intercom was destined not to be invented. Maybe the point of this whole crazy plan had been for me to learn who the other attacker was. If I had made contact with Granddad, that would surely have been the first thing he'd have told me.

Before classes started on Monday morning, the uncle from the gatehouse came looking for you. You hurried off with him, and still hadn't come back by the end of the day. This had never happened before. We were usually inseparable, and you'd never disappeared for so long. I kept looking away from your seat during class, so I could forget it was empty. All afternoon I was distracted, and sliced two erasers into rubble with my metal ruler. After school, I waited around till it got dark. Finally, I put your pencil case and textbooks into my bag and took them with me. When I passed the gatehouse, I thought of seeing if the uncle knew any more, but they'd changed shift and someone else was on duty.

The next day, you told me your dad had shown up—that mysterious, glamorous man I'd heard so much about. He took you to the park, then to a restaurant by the lake for dinner.

"We had so much fun, you can't imagine!" Your smug face made me furious. What right did you have to be so happy when I was suffering? It wasn't fair that I carried such a heavy burden while you got to be light and free. You should have been the one to discover the secret. You ought to be filled with doubt through sleepless nights. You ought to be ashamed and unable to face me. Now it seemed as if this had nothing to do with you. As if some strange force was keeping you separate from this filth. "We ordered so much food the table was completely full, then we had some baijiu ..." You chattered on, looking rapt, not bothering to pretend you weren't bragging, as if you wanted me to understand how it felt to be pampered, something I'd never experienced. You were reminding me you weren't an unloved feral child like me. You'd never done this before, yet here you were, casually hurting me. Who gave you the right? Was my family destined to be insulted by yours forever? When you got to the bit about your dad taking you out again before he left, I interrupted. "Why aren't you leaving with him?"

"He's doing business in Moscow. He'll send for me when things are less busy."

"No way." I shook my head.

"What do you mean?"

"You're bluffing. He'll never send for you."

Your face twitched, and the joy in your eyes faded.

"He doesn't want you," I forced myself to say. "Stop lying to yourself."

A dull, painful sound came from you, and your face contorted.

"They were right about you," you said slowly. "There's something dirty in your heart, Cheng Gong."

I burst out laughing, getting so carried away I bent in two. I didn't allow myself to stop until you were out of sight.

Li Jiaqi

December 16, 1993. I left home at five-thirty, wearing a dark-green coat and a white beanie, with my usual schoolbag on my back. Forty-eight hours later, Peixuan was sitting at the police station, animatedly telling an officer about the last time she'd seen me. I hadn't quarreled with my family that evening, she kept emphasizing, nor had I been behaving unusually. No one knew where I'd gone. The only witness was an old man who'd been selling newspapers by the entrance to the family compound, who said I'd walked past his stand around seven-thirty. He was mistaken, though, because at that time, I was already on a train heading for Beijing, staring through the foggy window of Compartment 9 at the nighttime city flying past.

To this day, I can't say what compelled me to get on that train. Mom blamed herself for slapping me—she thought I was acting out to protest her marrying Uncle Lin. Although I never tried to correct this impression and rescue her from the depths of regret, my leaving had nothing to do with her. She didn't cross my mind a single time that night, and I even forgot the wedding was in three days. The only flicker of anticipation I'd felt for this event had been for what I was going to wear: a tartan jacket and a dress with pearls beaded on its ruffled skirt. Now that I was leaving, though, I didn't give this outfit a second thought. Of course, you couldn't say this had nothing to do with me changing schools. After Peixuan refused to help me, I'd been filled with despair— my future seemed dark. That alone wouldn't have made me skip town, because I had nowhere to go. I kept saying Dad would soon come and get me, but you're right, that was never going to happen. I wasn't lying, though, just ... avoiding this truth. You ought to know how cruel those words of yours were. A dagger in my flesh, from you of all people. As I turned and walked home, longing to never see you again, the idea of going to Beijing to see Dad flashed into my brain for the first time. If this had occurred to me before, I'd have immediately thought, what about Cheng Gong? But at this moment, you'd hurt me enough that I was ready to abandon you.

It didn't cross my mind to try leaving with Dad—no one would have agreed to that. My plan was to persuade him to let me come to Beijing during winter vacation. This brief reunion would be enough, and you'd realize how ridiculously wrong you'd been about him. Dad seemed unlikely to agree, so I had a backup plan: I would get hold of his Beijing address so I could visit anytime. But how? Should I pretend I wanted to write him or send him a card? I couldn't bring myself to say anything so cringey around him.

An even more pressing concern was Dad might break his promise to come see me before he left. I spent the next few days distracted, waiting for him to show up. He didn't come to my school, and he didn't come to see Granny. I paged him and waited an hour by the public phone, but he didn't call back. Just as I was beginning to fear he'd already gone back to Beijing, he showed up one afternoon.

He was unshaven, in the same black coat as before, holding a small bag. As usual, he was smoking, but a different brand this time, only two left in the pack.

"When I called, the guy at the convenience store said you'd already left," he said. I could faintly smell alcohol on him.

"How have you been these last few days?" I asked in the voice of a grown-up.

"Not too bad. Saw some old friends."

"Former coworkers?"

"No, the people I was sent down with. They're doing well in business now." He tossed aside his cigarette butt and put his hand in his pocket. "I can't stay long, I want to see a couple of them again before I leave. Here, I got your grandma some health supplements, pass these to her."

"Don't you want to see her?"

"Next time. I'm leaving tonight."

I looked down. "What time's your train?"

"Eight twenty-five," he said. "Listen, I want you to study hard in your new school, alright? Make sure you do all your homework. You've got my pager number, call me if anything comes up."

I took the bag from him without a word, not even asking him to stay a little longer. I didn't say goodbye, just stood there without moving. The glowing numerals of his departure time were taking up all the space in my brain. I repeated them silently to myself, feeling them grow strange. After a while, I began to wonder if he'd actually said another time altogether.

From that moment, I forgot I was annoyed with you, and no longer worried about things like changing schools. My body was being controlled by a burst of intense emotion— exultation, passion, similar to how cult members must feel as they hurtle towards martyrdom. That's what made me run all the way home, drop off the nutritional supplements, then dash straight off for the train station without a pause.

I'd told myself that one day I would understand my feelings for him, and that day had finally arrived. There were no portents, nothing to prepare me, but I knew this was it. He'd looked frail, unlike his usual self, which made me believe he needed me now, more than ever. Or looking at it selfishly, this was the best opportunity I would have to get close to him, when he was most likely to understand how I felt. How could I miss this chance?

As for the consequences—a scolding, punishment, getting sent home—I didn't have time to think about them. My head was full of more important things: How would Dad react? What would we do on this nightlong journey? What was his home in Beijing like? What should I say to his new wife when I met her?

I crossed the road from Southern Courtyard and got the number 8 bus all the way to the end. The train station was round the corner from the terminus. Everything was going incredibly smoothly, as if I'd rehearsed it. Cold wind gusted across the broad platform, and passengers hunched over as they shuffled by with their suitcases. I leaped onto the train and ducked into an empty compartment. The window was fogged up. I wiped a corner with my hand and looked out. A lot of people were walking this way, but I didn't see Dad. It was very warm here. My cheeks were scalding, and my palms grew damp. Two men came in with their luggage and looked at me strangely.

"Where are your parents?" said one of them, a balding guy.

"Are you sure you're in the right place?" said his companion. I kept my lips clamped shut, staring at my shoes.

"Answer, or I'll call the conductor," said the first man.

I barged past them, pulled open the door, and fled. Seeing the ticket inspector approaching from the other end of the corridor, I slipped into the toilet and locked the door. The light switch was outside, so I stood in the dark staring at the faint glimmer of water in the toilet bowl. Someone tried the handle a few times, then walked away. Finally, the whistle sounded and the train began to move. A couple of people were talking outside. I waited a very long time, until they left. Only when there was complete silence did I open the door.

One by one, I pulled open the door of each compartment and swiftly scanned the four beds inside, as their occupants gaped at me. I worked my way down the corridor, and as the number of remaining doors went down, my heart thrummed like a galloping horse and the scene before me began swaying violently. I must have been too dizzy to see clearly. If not, why would I have closed the second-last door? I then stood frozen for more than ten seconds, until someone yanked it open again from inside.

I looked up. "Dad."

The pungent smell of tobacco enveloped me, so delicious I could have wept. And then I did begin to sob.

*

"Didn't you stop to think I might have changed my ticket? What if I was on a different train?" said my father, when his rage had simmered down.

"I had to try my luck."

"Try your luck?" He smiled, as if he approved of this way of thinking.

"I didn't even bring my piggy bank," I said. "I felt you would definitely be here."

"You mustn't be too optimistic—always expect the

worst. You'll understand some day."

"How could you say that to her?" said the woman from the opposite bunk, smiling. "Can't you see she's terrified?" She reached into the plastic bag by her side and handed me an apple.

This woman, the only other passenger in the compartment, wore a wine-red woolen coat and kept butting into our conversation. She'd been chatting with Dad and realized she'd been a couple of years below him at university. She claimed she'd heard of him, like everyone else, and had even read his poems. This display of blind adoration moved my father, and he offered her one of his beers. Naturally, she then moved from the upper bunk to the unoccupied lower one. Her friendliness was the sort that felt oppressive, but she wasn't bad-looking, and smelled faintly of shampoo—I couldn't tell what Dad thought of her. To start with, I was grateful she was there—having an admirer around meant Dad had to keep his temper in check. Besides, she kept speaking up for me, insisting I must have my reasons for doing what I did. Soon, I realized her presence was ruining this night, which ought to have belonged to me and Dad alone. I had so much to say to him, but this clearly wasn't the moment for the scalding words tumbling in my chest.

When the woman understood that Dad's greatest wish was for me to return to Jinan as quickly as possible, she took it upon herself to say she was in Beijing for a three-day business trip, and she was happy to bring me back with her. Dad seemed to think this was a great idea, though he asked a few times if she was sure that wouldn't be too much trouble. Not at all, she said, her hotel was only one subway stop away from Dad's apartment.

"Alright, then it's settled," said the woman. She asked Dad for the address, and arranged to pick me up at 7 p.m. in three days' time.

Through this whole process, neither of them asked what I wanted. I was nothing more than a package to be handed from one person to another. It broke my heart to see how relieved my dad looked, as if he'd managed to offload a huge burden. Although the problem was now solved, he wasn't prepared to forgive me. Still frowning, he went out to buy me a ticket, and came back with a bowl of instant noodles. My stomach hurt, but I managed to eat a little. He didn't urge me to eat more, but smoked his cigarette in silence. "When you're done, you can sleep in the upper bunk." No punishment in the world could be more cruel than his indifference. I think he knew that, and that's why he spoke in such an icy tone.

I climbed up the ladder with my bag and the apple. From this moment, it was as if I no longer existed. The two of them sat at the small table, chatting and drinking beer. They kept their voices low to start with, but as the alcohol took hold, they got louder and louder. They began reminiscing about the cafeteria and communal showers at their university, and spoke nostalgically about the wise but sharp-tongued older professors in the Chinese department. When Dad mentioned his glorious time in the poetry society, the woman's face once again took on a look of adoration. I peered through the gap between mattress and guardrail, and saw Dad swaying gently, smiling with his eyes shut, drunk and lost in these pleasant memories. Going over worn-out stories with this random woman instead of comforting the daughter who'd gone to such pains to seek him out. I understood now that there were many things that could make him happy: alcohol, recollections, her ludicrous admiration, but not me. My confidence had completely evaporated—he didn't need me. I wrapped myself in the musty blanket and cried softly to myself, before blearily dozing off. Not long after, I jerked awake. I felt hot and achy all over, and as I pressed my face to the compartment wall, I realized I was getting a fever. Good, I hoped I was properly sick, that might soften Dad's heart and make him regret how he'd treated me. If only the fever would lay me out for the next three days, so I couldn't go back to Jinan. As I sank into my tragic imaginings, their voices grew farther and farther from me.

Just before dawn, I heard a rustling as they swept the melon seed and peanut shells into the trash. Dad opened the window a crack to let out the cigarette smoke. A brisk morning breeze stirred the curtains and gently stroked my forehead. I touched my face, but it didn't seem warmer than usual. Perhaps I'd only dreamed the fever. The aches were real, though. We were almost at Beijing, and for some reason I was filled with anxiety. I wished I could delay our arrival. I was going to be disappointed, I now knew with certainty. The train sped on, and the sky lightened oppressively with every passing second. I rolled over and tried to retreat into my shallow sleep. Hazily, I heard Dad say, "It's strange, I keep running into old friends recently. It's like experiencing the past all over again."

We left the station and got into a taxi. I pressed my face against the window and looked out at this city I'd dreamed of so many times. It looked silent and vast through the gray-blue fog. The buildings were twice the size of the ones in Jinan, the streets so wide you couldn't see the other side. Dad opened a window to smoke. The chatty driver asked him this and that, but Dad only answered briefly. His brow was furrowed, and he kept tapping ash off his cigarette.

The taxi stopped in front of a dark-red building, and Dad led me all the way inside. He walked very slowly, and paused to light another cigarette when we reached the staircase.

"When we get upstairs, I want you to call your mom and grandma." He shook his head. "You shouldn't have been so thoughtless. You just do whatever makes you happy. Can't you think about other people?"

"Sorry ..." I said. "You did tell me you wanted to bring me to Beijing."

"But not now. My life is a mess." He smiled grimly and dropped the cigarette butt.

At the third floor, he spent a long time searching for his keys. He ran his hands up and down his body, and finally found them in the side pocket of his bag.

It was very dark inside—the curtains were drawn. The floor was covered in bags of stuff, like rolling hills. I didn't dare to move, so I stayed still waiting for him to turn on the lights, but he didn't. Stepping over the bags, he headed for the window. Only then did I notice there was someone on the couch: a woman, slumped over with her head on her knees.

"Go to bed." He lifted her to her feet, but after swaying for a few moments, she shoved him away hard and fell back on the couch. Dad wrapped his arms around her shoulders and tugged, like trying to uproot a tree. She got her arms free and they tussled in the dark, vigorous but silent. She lashed out and kicked him, but still Dad clung to her. Guttural moans came from her throat, then she slowly calmed down. Dad kept his arms around her. They stood there, perfectly still.

I ought to have turned my face aside or shut my eyes, but I stared unblinkingly at them, as if this were a fleeting eclipse. I'd never seen Dad hugging anyone, let alone with such emotion. The only sound in the room was my heart thumping. Perhaps they heard it too, but that wasn't enough to remind them of my existence.

"Why did you come back?" said the woman, freeing herself from my father's embrace. "Didn't you say you weren't coming back?" Her voice was raspy, as if she hadn't spoken in some time.

Instead of answering, Dad said only, "Is she still asleep?"

That's when I realized there was a fourth person in the apartment.

"Why did you come back?" she said again. "It's over. That's what you said."

"I was angry. You said some awful things too, didn't you? Anyway, I'm back now."

"It's too late." She began to sob. "It's really too late. I took a pill to get rid of the baby."

"Okay, enough nonsense."

"You think I'm just trying to scare you?" She grabbed his shoulders and shook him. "Listen to me—our child is gone! Washed from my body into the sewers."

Dad stared at her. "You're insane. Just like your mother."

"You didn't want it. You said it was all over." She was shouting now. "I stayed home for a week, waiting by the phone. If you'd ever done that, you'd know what despair feels like."

"Blame, blame, blame. Everything's always my fault," said Dad. "It wasn't easy for me to gather the courage to come back. And what do I get? This endless tantrum. I've had enough." He turned to look at me, as if to say: You see? This is my life.

The woman's eyes landed on me. "Who's she?"

"My daughter. She'll be staying a couple of days. Let me get her settled in, alright?" He sounded very tired, almost pleading.

"Oh right, you don't care, you already have a child of your own ..." the woman mumbled.

Dad led me to a storeroom piled high with bulging bags, some so full they couldn't even zip shut. The sleeve of a padded jacket spilled out of one, a toy panda's head from another. Dad pulled one aside and it toppled over, spilling pandas onto the ground. They were identical, reaching out as if they wanted a hug. One by one, Dad moved the bags out. Finally, he produced a folding bed from behind the door, which just about fit into the space he'd cleared. Onto this went some bedding from the cupboard.

"I'll go back to the station and see if I can get you a ticket for tonight," he said. "I'll tell the attendant to keep an eye on you. When you get to Jinan, you can take a bus home."

I said nothing.

"Wait till I've sold off my merchandise and paid my creditors. I'll move to a bigger place, and you can come stay with me for a while. I promise."

"You owe money?"

"It's normal for businesses to go into the red, now and then," he said a little impatiently. "This is grown-up stuff, don't worry about it. Understand?"

"When can I come and stay? Next summer?"

"Sure thing. I'll head back to Moscow in the spring. I couldn't survive another winter there."

"Do you really promise?"

"Yes. I'll get rid of this stock soon. Yes, very soon." He nodded, as if trying to convince himself. "Go to sleep. I'll be home late."

He shut the door behind him. I sat on the bed. The mattress was so thin I could feel the chilly metal frame through it. I wasn't sleepy. Listening carefully to the sounds from outside, I heard the woman faintly sobbing, Dad saying something to her in a quiet voice. Then the front door slammed. Dad was gone. My heart sank. I locked the storeroom door. It was completely silent outside. A few times, I felt the urge to open the door and look out, but resisted. The woman was too scary. She must be Wang Luhan. I'd been expecting someone completely different. She was neither young nor as beautiful as my mom, and she wasn't gentle at all. Hysterical, in fact. What did Dad love about her? I couldn't understand. Maybe he was already regretting it, and wouldn't be back again.

But then I remembered the way he'd hugged her, and grew uncertain. There was passion there, and some kind of force keeping them bound together. That's why Dad was suffering so badly. What should I do to help him? I felt sad every time I remembered I'd be leaving that night, after which Dad's life and everything about Beijing would have nothing to do with me. I looked around the cramped little room, which was cozier than I'd first thought. I went over to one of the bags and knelt to study the panda head poking out. This panda had been very popular for a while. Back when the Asian Games were going on, a classmate brought one of these to school, and everyone passed it around during class. Out of a weird sort of dignity, I pretended to be indifferent, even though I'd wanted one too. If my classmates back then had known I would one day be facing hundreds of these, they'd surely have died of envy. I took the pandas out of the bag and arranged them on the ground. Looking closely, I could spot minute differences between them. One had eyes a little closer together, another had a slightly smaller mouth, and one seemed melancholy in a way I couldn't have put into words. I held it in my hand and a name jumped into my mind: Tata. I'd never been one for stuffed toys, but Tata and I could suffer through this together. I decided to bring it back to Jinan and keep it forever.

Hugging Tata, I went over to the window and looked down. This is Beijing, I said to myself, trying to memorize everything—but all I saw was just another unremarkable northern city. Murky gray sky cut into squares by electric wires. Blockish old brick buildings with pigeons standing solemnly on their roof terraces. The only difference was the roads looked a little wider than in Jinan and, because no one was walking by, it felt desolate. I didn't know where the nearest market was, and couldn't see any post offices or eating places. The people here didn't seem to have human needs. Thinking of eating places made my stomach clench. I was so hungry my head was spinning. There wasn't even a bottle of water in here.

In a corner, behind an extra-large bag, was a pile of books—I happened to notice a glint of light reflected off their white covers. I picked up the top one. It was covered in dust, so I tapped it against the wall till the title appeared: *The Compendium of Contemporary Chinese Fiction, Volume 2.* Beneath that was Volume 5, and then Volume 7. There were thirteen altogether. I opened one and saw on the cover page, among the names of the editors, *Li Muyuan.* Dad had edited these books! He must have brought these with him from Jinan. I'd never seen them before. I checked the date at the front: last year. He must have done a lot of work on this series, then quit before it got published. I arranged them in order, then checked the contents page of the first volume, and turned to the story with the nicest-sounding title, "Love in a Fallen City." This sounded like it should have been a touching romance, but instead the female protagonist was divorced at the start of the story. I felt disappointed. A story about a divorcee finding love reminded me of Mom. She would be calculating and scheming, not romantic in the slightest. I pressed on but didn't enjoy it at all. Making sure to remember the author's name, I promised myself I'd never read anything else by her.

The sky remained gloomy, and there were no clocks in the room, so I couldn't tell if it was noon yet. When I couldn't hold it in any longer, I dashed out to the bathroom and bolted the door. It was pitch-dark inside, and though I groped around the wall for a long time, I couldn't find the light switch. I stood astride the toilet, but before I could squat, I suddenly saw it—the bloody clump of flesh. It had been expelled from her body and left there. The white porcelain of the toilet gleamed coldly, like an operating table.

I could have pretended not to know what it was—there was nothing to identify it. No body, no name. It had yet to gain these things. On the way into this world, it had been told not to bother coming.

It didn't understand why. It clung grimly to the edge of the water. Clenching itself into a bloody fist, refusing to let go of this corner of a heartless world.

It looked up, this featureless face, forcing me to acknowledge it. Through the veins that hadn't yet formed flowed the same blood as mine. These blood ties could never be denied. It wanted me to remember this.

Now it was staring right at me. Tiny eyes like raisins, peering at me through a slick of blood, brimming with hatred.

I backed up against the wall. Something in the dark banged into my head. I almost screamed. Then I steadied my nerves and looked. It was the chain for the flush. The green plastic handle swayed in the air. I gathered my courage, took hold of it, and pulled hard.

Water flooded in from all directions, submerging it, prizing loose its little fingers.

Intuition told me this was my little sister.

The flow licked away the last trace of blood, and swirled down the drain. The water stilled, leaving a cavernous darkness with a few glimmers of light across it, as if the clump of flesh might resurface at any moment. Not daring to pee, I rushed out of the bathroom.

Back in the living room, I hesitated by the balcony door, then pulled it open and stepped out. I squatted by the railing, where there was a little drain. Over the howling of the wintry wind, I could hear the tinkling of my pee. Steam rose from around my feet, a tragic breath of life. I stood and scraped the soles of my slippers dry. When I turned to go back into the living room, a pallid figure stood in the half-open doorway, staring straight at me. I let out a cry.

"Don't be scared," said the figure, though she seemed quite frightened herself—she was shaking violently. Using the door as a shield, I cautiously stuck my head out. A very, very old woman, squeezed dry by time, like a sheet of seaweed.

"Don't be scared, it's okay," she repeated like a chant, backing away. "Don't be scared." She shook her head as she retreated, sending hair clips clattering onto the floor. Startled by the noise, she looked down at them, then began stomping her feet as if to crush invisible bugs. When she lifted her head again, she seemed alarmed to see me there, and ran from the room. I heard a door slam.

Many years later, when I told Tang Hui about this day, he refused to believe me. Wang Luhan couldn't have left it in the toilet, he said, I must have imagined the whole thing.

But if I hadn't seen it, why would I have been so scared that I went out onto the balcony to pee? And if I hadn't done that, how would I have bumped into Granny Qin by the balcony door? Each event in the chain of memory joined to the one before. Also, what else could explain my lingering fear of the watery depths of the toilet bowl? Even with the bathroom light on, I didn't dare look. I found the sink scary too, and couldn't look down while I washed my face, which meant I was always getting my sleeves wet.

Tang Hui said once a false memory had been implanted, it would function exactly like a real one, giving rise to the same habits and phobias.

"Your subconscious has an innate sense of guilt." After we got together, Tang Hui became fond of psychoanalyzing me. "You believed you'd participated in the bad deed carried out by the adults, so your recollection gradually shifted until you convinced yourself you'd seen the drowned fetus and got rid of it."

It was true, I did feel guilty, but was this innate? Or was it the result of layer after layer of memory? I had no idea. I definitely had a strong desire to walk among these adults and take on their burden of culpability. Maybe because my life was so empty, I needed to enter a world that didn't belong to me in order to find meaning.

Dad took a long time to come home that day. After my shock, I went back to the little room, and lay down hugging Tata. Despite my hunger and the uncomfortably cold bed, I fell asleep with one of the bulging sacks as a pillow. I was hazily aware of someone singing. I thought that might be a dream, but when I opened my eyes the sound persisted. A woman's faint, sweet warble, slipping warmly into my ears. I wished I could ride it back into sleep, but instead it pulled me towards wakefulness.

"*Stars fill the night, the crescent moon gleams bright ...*" Just those two lines, over and over. They made me feel uneasy.

I climbed out of bed, and after a brief struggle with

myself, found the courage to open the door and walk out. In the living room, Wang Luhan was brushing the hair of the old woman who'd frightened me earlier. The old woman was sitting on a bench by the window, staring at the black hair clips in the palm of her hand, as if worried they'd be snatched away. Her mouth was opening and closing—I realized she was the singer. If I hadn't seen for myself that this gentle voice was coming from that pair of withered lips, I wouldn't have believed it.

The song surged up from somewhere deep within her, where there might be a version of her that hadn't gotten old or lost her mind. Wang Luhan stood behind her, holding a curved cow horn comb, translucent and amber. Sunlight passed through it like honey and dripped onto her grizzled hair.

"*Stars fill the night, the crescent moon gleams bright ...*" I'd lost count of how many times she'd repeated these two lines when the old lady abruptly remembered the rest of the song. "*The production brigade has a meeting, let's speak of our ills. The evil old society, the blood and tears of the poor. A thousand worries besiege my heart, bitter tears fill my chest ...*"

I shuddered—what a horrifying song. Luckily, she lost the lyrics again, and went back to the stars and moon. Distracted, Wang Luhan kept running the comb through the old woman's hair.

The old woman was Luhan's mother, Granny Qin. Years later, Xie Tiancheng would tell me the first sign her mind was going came when Luhan noticed she was staying up all night long. Every evening, before dusk, she would sit at the window and sing this tune to the sky.

After what felt like a very long time, the song finally ceased. Wang Luhan put down the comb, took the clips from her mother's hand, and fastened them at her temples. With the tangled hair out of the way, the old woman's wrinkled face was revealed, barren as a dry well.

Wang Luhan grabbed a hand mirror from the sill and

handed it to Granny Qin, who studied herself intently. With her little finger, she lifted a wisp of hair from beside her left ear. "You missed this."

Luhan pulled a couple of silver clips from her mother's hair, and tidied away the stray strands.

"Done," she said.

"Done," Granny Qin repeated, as if she were passing on a message from her daughter. She continued turning the mirror this way and that, examining herself.

Wang Luhan went over to the couch and sat down. She was wearing a flannel nightgown, the bright pink of lotus roots, with a scoop neck that revealed her collar bones. The deep hollows beneath them looked like an empty set of scales. She was far too thin, and looked like some sort of ice-cold implement. Rusty too—there were splotches of brown at her temples. The afternoon sun shone fiercely into the room, and though she wriggled to the farthest end of the couch, she couldn't escape it. Finally, she gave up and slumped back, looking exhausted. Tilting her head back, she shut her eyes, allowing the sunlight to peck at her face like a flock of pigeons.

Granny Qin had belatedly realized that the discolorations were on the mirror, not her face. Taking a corner of her sleeve, she began diligently wiping at the glass.

After a while, Wang Luhan opened her eyes and reached for the cigarette packet on the coffee table. Putting one between her lips, she lit a match and bent to the flame, then took a long breath in. Raising her chin a little, she allowed a thin puff of smoke to escape her lips.

I'd never seen a woman smoking before, except on TV, which didn't count. All of a sudden, I remembered my class monitor, a girl named Jiang Lailai. She'd transferred into the elementary school around the same time as me. She was repeating the year due to family problems, though I suspected this wasn't the first time she'd been kept back, because she was clearly a fully developed young woman.

Her boyfriend, a middle school guy, was the leader of a gang of young hoodlums who hung out in billiard halls and video parlors. After school, as everyone watched, Jiang Lailai would climb onto the back of his motorbike and wrap her arms around him. One time, you told me you'd seen them standing by the billiard hall on a rainy day. Lailai took a lit cigarette from the boy. You didn't dare to keep watching, in case he beat you up, so you held up your umbrella and quickly walked by. She looked so cheap, standing there smoking, you later said to me through gritted teeth. But that sounded like the highest praise to me. Now, watching Wang Luhan puff on her cigarette, I thought hazily that Jiang Lailai could be a younger version of her.

Luhan turned to look at me. Her eyes lingered for a while. Ash accumulated on her cigarette and broke off onto the floor.

"You don't look like your dad at all," she said.

She sounded pleased about that. Probably she wanted my father all for herself.

Offended, I said, "Have you seen pictures of him at my age? He looked just like me."

"Oh, really?" She smiled.

"Yes. If you saw the photos, you'd agree."

"I don't think so." She looked directly at me, her smile abruptly gone. "I knew him when he was your age."

My heart chilled, and my mouth dropped open. They'd been childhood friends. Into my mind came the image of Jiang Lailai and the boy standing outside a billiard hall, sharing a cigarette. Rain dripping off the awning, lust swirling through the damp air. Was my dad like that boy when he was young? I couldn't imagine him and Luhan together at that age. Maybe they were already in love back then. I got jealous, imagining someone already having had a place in my dad's heart.

Granny Qin dropped the mirror back onto the sill and pointed at me. "Who's she?"

"It's fine, Mom. Just one of the family kids."

"Her hair's so messy." Granny Qin stared at me, wild-eyed. "You ought to comb it."

"Enough nonsense, Mom," said Wang Luhan coldly, stubbing out the cigarette.

"It's too messy! That won't do!" Grabbing my arm, Granny Qin pulled me over to the window. "Quick, comb her hair." She was shaking, and her eyes were bulging so badly I thought they might pop out. I tried to struggle free, but her grip was firm.

"Stop it!" Wang Luhan roared. "Are you trying to drive us all mad?"

The old woman didn't seem to hear her, but kept mumbling that this wouldn't do. She pulled the elastic bands off my fuzzy plaits and unraveled them, then grabbed the comb and plunged its teeth into my hair. I shook my head so she couldn't pull it through.

"Come on, let me," she said. "Your hair's so messy, they'll think you're a madwoman. They'll lock you away." I turned to stare at her. Her eyes were full of sincere terror. She wasn't trying to scare me—which was actually more frightening. I stuck my fingernails into the hand on my shoulder but she didn't react, as if she felt no pain. "Such nice hair! If you just let me …"

She was tugging painfully at my hair, and Wang Luhan wasn't lifting a finger to stop her. I knew she was watching. Gripped by a sudden urge to make her angry, I ran my fingernails viciously over the back of Granny Qin's hand and bright jewels of blood appeared on her white flesh. Still her hand remained clamped to my shoulder, like a dead bird.

Wang Luhan watched us quietly from the couch. A great weariness passed over her face. She seemed happy for me to punish her mother however I chose. For years now, her mother's behavior had grated at their relationship, scraping away the tenderest, most sensitive parts. Her love for her mother spoiled in the rancid air, turning cold and brittle.

Of course, I only understood this much later. At the time, I had a confused sense of what was happening, but couldn't have put it into words. All I knew was it made me sad, so I began to cry.

"Don't worry, we'll make your hair look nice, and everything will be fine." Granny Qin parted my hair in a neat line, and pulled it into two pigtails, practiced and assured. Perhaps she'd done the same for Luhan when she was young. She produced a card of black hair clips from her trouser pocket, and brought them one by one to her mouth, to be prized open with her teeth. These went across my hairline, keeping my bangs off my forehead. When she'd used them all up, she got another set from a different pocket. How many clips did she have on her? Were they meant to keep her insanity in check? In the end, my hair was as smooth and glossy as her own, not a strand out of place.

By the time she was done, the afternoon was almost gone. The sun was setting, and its light had retreated to a small pool by the window. I sat in the chair, feeling the clips tugging at my scalp, making my head feel huge and heavy. Granny Qin seemed tired too. She sat next to Wang Luhan, and the room grew very quiet.

"I'm hungry, Han," said Granny Qin, looking at her daughter a little resentfully. Wang Luhan stood and went into the bedroom. She emerged in a coat with ink-green and persimmon-orange checks, over a black woolen dress. Surprisingly, she'd put on lipstick, even though she was just going downstairs. The smear of red seemed to give her a burst of energy, leaving her less frosty than before.

That was my first understanding of makeup. A sort of ritual, a way of taking pleasure in life. Just as hair-combing was, for Granny Qin, a ritual to assert she hadn't lost her mind.

Slipping on a pair of low-heeled leather boots, Wang Luhan went out with a thermal flask.

I've always believed that Wang Luhan must have felt

hopeful as she stood at the mirror to apply lipstick and put on her coat that winter afternoon. She was back in fifteen minutes, nose red, outside cold clinging to her. I had to admit she was beautiful in that outfit. Not my mom's innocent, guileless beauty, something more world-weary.

She put the food container on the table, and got three bowls from the kitchen.

"Come eat," she said, looking at me through hooded eyes. "If you wait for your father, you'll starve."

I hesitated, but I was so hungry my legs brought me over to the table of their own volition.

The square table stood against a wall, and we sat at its other three sides. In front of me was a large bowl of wontons, scattered with jade-green cilantro leaves. After not having eaten all day, the steam and aroma rising from them made my heart twinge. I gobbled them down, and drank all the soup too. Granny Qin nibbled at the skins, and made each dumpling last several mouthfuls. She ate elegantly, not at all like a madwoman. Wang Luhan didn't have any wontons —she said she just wanted a bit of hot soup, but even after the soup had turned cold, she hadn't touched a drop. Her hands were wrapped around the bowl, as if she were warming them. After she'd eaten, Granny Qin's expression softened, and she even looked a little kind.

"You're a pretty girl. You remind me of someone." Her brow crinkled, then she smiled in embarrassment. "I can't remember who."

She reached out and stroked my cheek, as if I were made out of some kind of special fabric. I didn't pull back, but obediently allowed her to touch me.

"Go have a nap, Mom," said Wang Luhan, frowning. "Remember what you promised me?"

The older woman shuddered and shrank back. "I'm going, I'm going. Please don't make me take the pills."

"Quickly, go."

Granny Qin slowly got to her feet and went into her room.

The living room was completely dark now. Wang Luhan lit a cigarette. Her face was in shadow, and I couldn't read her expression. All I could make out were those thin, brightly colored lips, like a silk flower bent out of shape. She looked at me. The glow of her cigarette winked bright then dim, like a third eye in the gloom.

"You're very fortunate." Her voice sounded like she'd left it in the rain and it had gotten rusty. "What's your name?"

"Li Jiaqi."

"You're very fortunate, Jiaqi." She kept looking at me. "You got to be born. My child didn't." She smiled mysteriously. "You know why? Because it was cursed."

I thought of the bloody clump of flesh, and a chill went down my spine.

"A cursed child. That's what your father called it." She stubbed out her cigarette viciously. Her lipstick had left a heart-shaped imprint on the butt, a sort of decadent beauty. I couldn't stop staring at it.

"He never wanted the baby. He wanted to get rid of it, then when I did, he blamed me and said I was mad." She shook her head. "I am mad. He drove me mad. You're lucky, you really are. You don't have to live with him. He has darkness in his heart, like your grandfather did."

"Why don't you leave him, then?"

She turned to look at me. A long silence as I waited for the explosion. Instead, she nodded. "You're right, I ought to have left him long ago." She pressed her lips together, and seemed to come to a decision. Her eyes were fixed on something ahead of her.

I stood there a moment longer, then fled back to the storeroom.

It was pitch-dark inside. I groped my way to the folding bed. I didn't want to mess up my braids—Granny Qin might insist on combing my hair again—so I lay face down. The feverish sensation came again, and my cheeks seemed to glow with heat. My heart was beating violently. It comforted me to know Wang Luhan had made up her mind. Now Dad would be free. He probably wouldn't come back to me, though. Where would he go? How would he live alone? My head grew heavier and heavier. Unsettled and in discomfort, I drifted into sleep.

In my shallow, gray drowsiness, I saw the vague outline of a figure in black approaching my bedside trailing long sleeves, bending to look at me. I couldn't make out its face, and somehow I knew that this wasn't a face I would be allowed to remember. It reached out, apparently asking me to leave with it. Its hand was very pale, as if it had shed a few hundred layers of skin. It hovered over me and slowly descended, like a circling bird, onto my forehead. Then it slid over my neck and shoulder, trying to make sure of something. When the hand rose up again, its fingertips were red. The figure looked at its hand for a moment, then turned and left the room.

I woke up to quarreling. Dad was back. My back and shoulders ached when I sat up, and my body felt it might fall apart. Moving as quietly as I could on heavy legs, I crept to the living room.

"I never said that!" Dad thundered. "All I said was this isn't the best time to raise a child. Isn't that the truth?" He'd had quite a bit to drink—his face was flushed, and the glass in his hand was shaking so hard, its contents almost spilled.

"The truth is you never wanted this child. You thought it would get in your way." Wang Luhan spoke icily from the couch, a cigarette between her lips.

"If you'd had the child, it would be living with a lunatic who might explode at any moment. Do you think that's okay?"

"A lunatic? Ha! So now you're throwing her under the bus. Remember what you said when she came to live with me? You wanted to make it up to her and give her a good life. And now? You stay as far from her as you can. You won't even look at her! And when her illness flares up, you tell me to get rid of her. You called her a lunatic. Tell me, what made her mad?"

"There you go again. Will you give it a rest? Do you want me to kneel before you and confess my guilt every single day? Is that what it would take?" He walked briskly over to the cabinet. More booze gurgled into his glass. He shook his head as he poured. "This is pointless."

I'd heard him say this before.

He began gulping his drink. Wang Luhan watched him expressionlessly. I tensed up, wondering if I ought to sprint over to grab the glass from his hand.

Wang Luhan pulled herself together and sat a little straighter. In a low voice, she said, "We should split up."

"Are you sure?"

"Yes."

"Fine."

"We knew we shouldn't be together, but we had to try. Now we've both gotten hurt. Every time we quarrel, you walk out and slam the door. I feel like I'm going to die." She choked on her sobs. "You'll never understand this despair. If this goes on, one of us really will die. It's best if we're apart. Then we'll both be free."

I'd been holding my breath. To think I'd been afraid she wouldn't go through with it.

"Your mind seems very clear today." Dad shook his glass, swirling the dregs.

"My mind's always clear. You're the one who gets smashed every day."

"Making up your mind all of a sudden. Very good. Mm, is there some other reason?"

She looked up. "What other reason could there be?"

"Seriously? Haven't you got another guy lined up?" Dad smiled.

"What are you talking about?"

Dad swayed a little and steadied himself against the cabinet. "Why else would you decide to get rid of the child behind my back? I suppose you can't wait to run off with whoever it is."

Wang Luhan hurled the ashtray at him. It smashed to pieces against the cabinet, gouging a chunk out of it.

"You're a bastard, Li Muyuan," she said with emphasis.

"You stayed with me so you could destroy me. Happy now?"

"You think *I* destroyed *you*? Who destroyed our family?"

A door slammed and Granny Qin hurtled past me into the living room. She flung her arms around her daughter. "What's wrong, Han? Don't be scared, everything's going to be alright."

"Who do you think you are, Luhan? You're a criminal's daughter too, aren't you?"

Wang Luhan pushed Granny Qin aside and grabbed the front of my dad's shirt. "Don't talk like that—heaven is watching! Aren't you afraid of retribution?"

Granny Qin wept and covered her ears. "It's alright, nothing to be scared of."

"What retribution could top being with you? Nothing could be worse!" Dad shoved her away and stumbled towards the front door. He froze when he saw me—he'd only just remembered my existence. "Jiaqi, let's go!"

I sprinted into the storeroom and grabbed my coat. Granny Qin followed me in and caught hold of me. "You're a good girl. Don't be scared, it's alright. The bad people won't find us here!"

"You're the bad person! You're a crazy old woman!" I threw her off, but she moved to block the door. I grabbed her arms and tried to pull her aside.

"It's dangerous out there. Good girl, do as I say ..." She clung tightly to the door frame, even as I kicked and punched her.

"Please let me out, Dad's waiting," I said, sobbing.

"It's dangerous, you're not safe," she kept repeating robotically. She was shaking hard, her shoulder bones thumping against the door, as if she were under a spell. Her eyes were fixed on the air in front of her, bulging wildly from fear. I stared at her, terror-stricken, until the front door slammed, snapping me out of it.

"Dad's gone! Let me out, let me out!" I tugged at her legs, pummeled her stomach, clawed at her face. She remained perfectly still, as if she'd lost all sensation and turned into a statue. Beads of blood oozed from her face where I'd scratched her, a horrific sight.

I ran out of steam and sat on the floor, howling. I don't know how much time passed before she finally opened the door and bent down to pat my head. I ducked past her and rushed out. Flinging the front door open, I screamed, "Dad! Dad!"

No answer—he was long gone. The corridor was silent. The landing window was broken, shards of glass clinging to the frame, stabbing at the sky. Wind gushed through, pushing open the door behind me.

My legs were blocks of wood. I dragged them back into the living room, where the standing lamp seemed dimmer. The sizzling filament of the bulb let out a faint moan. Wang Luhan was lying on the couch, eyes shut, hands clasped to her chest, breathing vehemently. The last traces of lipstick were vanishing from her mouth as it gently opened and shut. In an instant, something seemed to engulf it, and it vanished completely.

*

Fifteen minutes later and four blocks away, my father's Volkswagen Santana collided head-on with a truck. The car was flung quite a distance, and landed with its wheels in the air. Dad's skull was smashed, and glass from the windshield sliced open his forehead. Alcohol-rich blood poured over his face, as if to get him drunk one last time.

As the ambulance with its stark purplish lights came

speeding through the hospital gates, tiny flakes of snow began falling, and my father's breathing stopped. Next to him, the passenger seat was empty—a place the god of death had reserved for me.

The truck driver only had a few cuts on his face. As far as he could remember, he hadn't realized that Dad was driving under the influence. While waiting at the intersection, he'd seen the Santana stop behind the line across the junction. Then the lights changed, and they both moved forward, neither going particularly fast, a lane apart. As they approached, the Santana abruptly swerved towards the truck and sped up.

Years later, when I thought about the accident, I felt I'd been there myself. There I was, beneath the overturned Santana, face down, trapped and immobile in the passenger seat. All I could see was a little patch of road, swaying through the shattered windshield.

The temperature was plummeting. I could smell the damp scent of fallen snow mixed with the sharpness of blood. I didn't know where my fingers were, but they were touching blood. As blood cools, it becomes less sticky. I saw a pair of legs stride across the little patch of road, walking my way. My field of vision narrowed. I didn't wonder what was going on, but accepted it like a dream.

This was all a hallucination, of course, but it didn't come out of my imagination. Anything I imagined repeatedly shifted—details would change, there'd be additions or amendments. No matter how many times I revisited the accident, though, the scene before me remained resolutely the same. Hence I believe I may have died in that car.

I'd tailed my father all the way to Beijing so I could die with him. For years now, I've tried to parse the meaning of this trip. It wasn't because of what you'd said, and it wasn't my willfulness. A voice from beyond commanded me to go to the station alone, and board a train departing Jinan. And the final destination of this spontaneous journey was that Volkswagen Santana.

Granny Qin saved my life. As she grimly held the door shut, what had those staring eyes seen?

Each time I think of the accident, I feel a pang of guilt at surviving. Tang Hui said that's why I kept placing myself in the scene. Perhaps that's true. Even all these years later, I can't and don't want to walk away from the moment of my father's death. I ought to have been a part of it.

*

The following afternoon, I was in the storeroom when someone knocked on the front door. I didn't go out, but sat on the edge of my bed, listening to the visitor talking to Wang Luhan. I heard Dad's name, something about the road, the hospital, the mortuary, as if he were an item in a production line, passing down a conveyor belt. A short while later, the door shut. Wang Luhan must have left with him. The apartment grew very quiet.

I lay back in the bed, perfectly still. The bad news settled around me like snow. Still loose and fluffy, not cold yet. I was afraid to move. If I touched it, that would make it real.

I closed my eyes tight. An image gradually formed in the dark: a summer evening just before I started elementary school. Dad was showing me the route I would soon be taking to school. We walked past a memorial archway, up a long set of steps, turned the corner to a street with parasol trees on either side, through a crossroads, another turn, and the school was on our right. We stood at the gate and watched. The students were cleaning up. A girl was chasing a boy with a broom, and everyone was squealing and giggling as they raced around the schoolyard. On our way back, Dad said, there's a shortcut where you won't need to cross any roads, come with me. He led me along a winding lane, and when we got to the end, made me read the street name and memorize it. A woman cycled past, a head of jade-green celery in her bike basket. Two old guys sat by the wall playing chess. The fragrance of frying garlic wafted towards us.

We turned into an alley with no name. On one side was a high wall, on the other an unbroken row of red brick houses. No windows, just a wooden door towards the end of the street. There was no one around except for Dad and me. We walked side by side, a little closer together because the alley was so narrow. Or perhaps that's just how it felt to me. The sun had set, and there were a few clouds in the gray-orange sky. It felt oddly cool and silent here. A gust of wind passed overhead like a flock of swallows, hollowing out my heart. I felt a melancholy sense that summer would soon be over. As we approached the wooden door, I saw it was embedded deep in the wall, tightly shut. Large flakes of dark-green paint were sloughing off it. I guessed this must be a warehouse. After we'd walked past, Dad said, That's the mortuary, where they put dead people—are you scared? I shook my head. People turn into goods when they die, I thought, to be stacked up in a warehouse. We left the alleyway and turned a corner. Past a fork in the road was the familiar street that led to our home. Dad stopped walking and looked back the way we'd come, and so did I. He said to me, "Now I've shown you the way, you can walk it alone."

Cheng Gong

While you were busy running away from home, I carried out a little revenge of my own. Although looking at the consequences, especially after all these years, it wasn't actually that little. At the time, though, it didn't feel like enough—quite the opposite, it was just the beginning. A door opening quietly in an unseen corner.

The day after you went missing, Peixuan waited for me after school. She said you hadn't been home all night, and asked if I knew where you'd gone. This was the first time Peixuan had ever spoken to me. She didn't meet my eye, and her tone was frosty, as if she might get dirty just by being near me—exactly like your grandmother. Right away, I was furious.

"I know where she is," I said. "But I won't tell you."

I walked on, but she ran after me and stopped me again. Her whole family was frantic, she said, and they were looking everywhere. I didn't answer, just stepped around her and kept going.

I got to the grove and sat at the stone table. The sun hadn't come out for a few days now, and it was cold as a crypt in the shade. I was certain your disappearance had something to do with your dad. You'd said he was coming to see you in a couple of days, though I hadn't expected he would take you away with him. I didn't know how you'd persuaded him, but I vaguely felt this was aimed at me. You wanted to rub in my face this big difference between us, and show that you could leave me without a moment's thought. I felt completely abandoned, like when my mom walked out. The memory is still crystal clear: early morning in that empty room, screaming for her. Like a nightmare I'll never wake up from. I'm still in it now. Of course, my feelings for you are different than those for my mom. With you there's hatred, and a competitive spirit that will never go away. Still, you're the only person who could have made me feel the way I did when Mom left: a sharp sensation I was all alone.

Lunchtime came and went, but I kept sitting there, the stone bench ice-cold beneath my bum. I picked up a twig and scraped viciously at the hard soil, imagining it was a bleeding face covered in scratches. That's right, I needed more blood. A few days before this, I'd been troubled by thoughts of revenge—wondering how I ought to deal with you. Now that meant nothing. You'd struck first, and I couldn't do anything about it. Ever since deciding to find Granddad's killer, I'd tried time and again to gather the courage to do something, but each time I would find out there was nothing I could do except passively accept things as they were. Now I was raising a little fist filled with strength, but had no idea where to aim it.

After school the next day, Peixuan was there again. She said I should go to the station—the police wanted to have a word with me. If she hadn't needed to get home to take care of your grandmother, I'm sure she would have dragged me there herself.

As soon as I stepped into the police station, I saw your grandfather. This was my first sight of him at close quarters. I shut the door behind me, and while my back was turned, tried to get my breathing under control. Someone had been boiling vinegar, and the air was filled with its sharp reek, which combined nauseatingly with the cigarette smoke. I stuck my hands into my pockets, and didn't know where to look: at the peanut shells on the floor, the banners on the wall, or the teacup in the officer's hand? My eyes made a round of the room, and finally settled on your grandfather. He was sitting by the wall and had taken off his glasses to rub his eyes.

The hand holding the glasses was very pale and a little too small for his body. It looked delicate, and gave the impression that he'd never done any physical labor. I was trying to store up more impressions about his appearance when he abruptly raised his head. My heart shrank, and I hastily moved my gaze away. In that instant, I'd been looking at his face. He looked weird with his glasses off, his features somehow too stark. It felt uncomfortable seeing his eyes without anything in front of them, like learning a secret. I couldn't have said what was distinctive about them, only that they seemed even more elderly than the rest of him, as if they'd already spent many years in the world before he came along.

He put on his glasses, and once again he looked the way he did in my head. "I really can't think of anyone who would do that," he said wearily.

The plump officer at the desk nodded. "It's not very likely she was kidnapped, but we can't rule out the possibility. If you think of anyone suspicious, come and see me anytime."

The officer beckoned me over, opened a folder, and was about to start questioning me when someone outside called for him. He told me to hang on, stubbed out his cigarette, and left.

Now it was just me and your grandfather in the room. My limbs felt cold and stiff, and all the blood in my body seemed to surge to my head, where it bubbled like molten lava. It was alarmingly quiet. I hoped the north wind howling outside and the ticking of the Compas wall clock would cover the sound of our breathing. But no, I could still hear every rise and fall of your grandfather's body, which made my hair stand on end, especially because he was behind me and I couldn't see his face.

Without warning, your grandfather stood up, and my blood solidified. What was he doing? In my pockets, my hands clenched into fists, ready to lash out. He walked past me to the officer's desk. The cigarette hadn't been completely extinguished. He pressed it firmly against the ashtray, stared at it a moment to make sure it really was out, then looked up. He was right in front of me now, and I knew he was looking at me. I ought to have looked back with razor-sharp eyes, with a stare that would have left him sleepless and trembling whenever he remembered it—but for some reason, I couldn't. My eyelids were weighed down, and I couldn't raise them. So my eyes remained fixed on the red cigarette packet on the desk. On it was the word *Peony*, though I'd been staring so long it had stopped making sense. Your grandfather went back to his seat, and the officer came back into the room. Only then did I start breathing again. I realized my hands were still in fists and my palms were sweaty. Surely he should have been the one who was afraid to look at me? But I'd flinched. My evasiveness must surely have delighted him.

My heart filled with despair. I decided I wouldn't tell them a single thing about where you'd gone. I wasn't trying to protect you or anything high-minded like that. Still stinging from your betrayal, I wasn't ready to see you again—and if I told them what I knew, they'd surely find you very quickly. Besides, I couldn't do what your grandfather wanted me to. He wished to know where you'd gone, but I wouldn't tell him. Let him fret, let him be unable to eat or sleep. I couldn't miss this opportunity to make him suffer, especially after the pathetic performance I'd just put on. Unfortunately, it seemed your absence wasn't causing him too much distress—at least on the surface. The police officer poured him some tea, and he slowly sipped at it, blowing aside the tea leaves floating on the surface.

"Is this the boy who knows where Jiaqi went?" he asked the officer.

Didn't he even know my name? We'd lived in the same compound all these years, and bumped into each other many times. He'd seen me go to school with you more than once. How could he not know who I was? Was he not aware that your grandmother and Peixuan had tried to stop you from hanging out with me? Impossible. He must be pretending because he was too afraid to face me.

The officer said yes, and told him my name.

I turned around and, out of the corner of my eye, watched his face. Even if he hadn't recognized me, there's no way he didn't know who Cheng Gong was. There were several names that ought to have made him uneasy, and mine was one. Again I was disappointed—his expression remained calm.

"Cheng Gong." Your grandfather repeated my name. "Does your family work at the university?" He looked at me equably.

Either he was a superb actor, or he truly didn't know. I was baffled. Still, that didn't explain why I was doing so badly—all I did was nod and say yes. Why hadn't I glared at him and said my grandfather's name was Cheng Shouyi? What was I afraid of?

"Cheng Gong!" The officer banged on the desk. "I asked you a question!"

I rubbed my sticky palms together and stared hazily at him. They must have thought I was an exceptionally shy child. I was utterly disappointed in myself.

I told the officer you would definitely have gone to the bookshop across the road from Southern Courtyard after school, because you'd been saying a few days ago that you wanted the new issue of *Doraemon*. It was true that we used to pool our money and get the latest comic book at the end of each month. The officer asked if I'd seen you go there, or if that was just a guess. I said it was a guess. He asked why I hadn't told Peixuan, and I said I hadn't been certain—after all, I hadn't seen you myself.

"One more question," said the officer. "I've heard that you and Jiaqi are good friends. Has anything about her seemed strange recently?"

I said I hadn't noticed anything. The officer asked your grandfather if he had any questions, and when he said no, he closed his folder and said I could go. I stood, but he called me back. "If I find out you lied to me, kid, I'll come get you. Don't try to keep anything from us. Got it?"

How absurd, to say such a thing in front of a man who'd spent more than twenty years beyond the reach of the law.

"Got it," I said.

A woman brushed past me as I left, moving so fast I didn't see her face.

"Have they found Jiaqi?" Through the half-open door, I

saw her rush up to your grandfather and agitatedly clutch at his sweater. "Where's my daughter?"

Stony-faced, your grandfather shoved her hand away and straightened his sweater. The officer pulled your mother aside and told her to calm down, the police were searching everywhere. When your mother found out you'd been gone for two days, she got worked up all over again. "You're trying to hide this from me! Why didn't you say anything when I called last night? You told me she was at a classmate's house! What are you playing at?"

Your grandfather's face flushed red. "What good would it have done? It was late. Look at you now! Stop embarrassing yourself, or at least have the decency to wait till we get home."

This stunned your mother into a few seconds of silence, then she sneered. "I haven't been part of your family for a long time now. I'm not embarrassing you. What do you care?"

Your grandfather shook his head. "Hopeless." He grabbed his coat from the back of his chair and left. Your mother tried to follow, but the officer stopped her. "Hang on, we still need you to give a statement."

The officer walked your grandfather out. When he saw I was still there, he glared at me. "Isn't it your dinner time?"

He shut the door, but still I stood there, watching your grandfather mount a battered 28-inch bicycle and head back to Southern Courtyard. During the argument, which I thought your mother had won, I'd glimpsed your grandfather's dignity. She was scared of him, or at least had once been scared of him, and her ferocity seemed like a reaction to having been held back a long time. Your grandfather had a loftiness that made everyone else feel inferior. Anyway, I was completely disappointed in myself. My timid behavior earlier was now a stain on my life that I could never wash off. Whenever I thought about it after that, I felt ashamed all over again.

Through the door, I heard your mother sobbing. She

sounded so sad, I found myself wondering if I ought to tell her what I knew. A moment later, I had dispelled this notion. She loved you so much, and yet you'd never mentioned this, as if it meant nothing to you. But to me, this was an unspeakable luxury. Do you remember when we would fight over whose mom was more beautiful, and I wouldn't rest until everyone had agreed mine was the prettiest? Laughable. Where was this most beautiful of mothers? I'd never had a love like this. I wish I'd never seen it. I headed home, not looking back.

On the fourth afternoon of your disappearance, I saw Peixuan outside the school once again. As I walked past, she glared at me. After a few hundred meters, I realized she was following me. I sped up, then pretended I needed to tie my shoelace and glanced back. She was still there. I made a detour around the grove, and headed for Dead Man's Tower.

The morning fog had lingered, refusing to dissipate, and now it was getting dark. We were all waiting for snow. Once again, the weather forecast had lied.

The road narrowed, the trees grew sparse, and there was the lead-gray tower up ahead. The brick wall around it had lost its bloodstains, and the squat houses by the wall had gaping holes where their windows had been. Everything was just as we had left it in the summer. In this deepest corner of the compound, no vegetation grew. The seasons did not touch this place, and time had been sealed out. Not in order to preserve our happy times here—even though our joyous cries still echoed through the air. As far as I was concerned, this place could never be anything other than the scene of a crime.

I tossed my schoolbag aside and leaned against the wall, watching Peixuan approach. White coat, immaculate ponytail. Her beauty really was the dullest thing in the world.

She stopped five meters from me. "You lied to me."

"So?"

"The old man at the gatehouse said a man came to see her

at the school. Did you see him? What did he look like? Was it her dad?"

"Why not ask her dad?"

"I can't get hold of him. I keep calling, but he's not answering his phone, and no one knows where he lives in Beijing." She shot me a look. "Did Jiaqi leave with him?"

Ignoring her, I went over to the end of the wall, and began piling bricks under the windows of one of the houses.

"What if they're in danger? Have you thought of that?" She took a couple of careful steps closer. "You're her good friend. Aren't you even a little worried? Come on, tell me what you know."

Using the bricks as a staircase, I climbed up to the window ledge, then pulled myself from there onto the top of the wall.

"I'll tell you if you come up here."

"Do you know how scared everyone is right now? Her mom's losing her mind! You think this is the moment to play childish games? Don't you have any compassion?" She turned to go.

"You're right, there's something dirty in my heart." I began laughing.

The daylight was almost gone, and a washed-out new moon floated in the sky, sharp as a canine. The pool of formaldehyde gleamed darkly, and cold air rose from the liquid. Peixuan, stark white as a lie, was disappearing into the distance. I shouted, "I know a secret about your grandpa. An enormous secret." I paused, then raised my voice. "Your grandpa did something terrible."

Peixuan stopped walking and turned to look at me. "I'm warning you, Cheng Gong, stop talking nonsense."

"Why do you think your grandma is always going to church? She has to repent because of what he did. It's been so many years, and her conscience is still uneasy."

Peixuan was facing me now.

"Ha! Such a huge secret, and you're the only one who doesn't know," I said.

She paused and started walking back towards me. "Did Jiaqi tell you this? Is that why she ran away from home?"

"Doesn't your neck ache, having to look up at me like that? Come on up, so we can talk properly," I said. "I'm not going to hurt you. I just want you to stop being so high and mighty."

She slowly walked over to the wall, looking resentful.

"You can put your bag on mine. Come on, I'll give you a hand." I straddled the wall and reached down to her.

She looked sharply at me, trying to tell if I was lying. Finally, she shrugged, stepped onto the pile of bricks, and grabbed hold of the window frame, carefully avoiding the glass shards. It took her a moment to decide whether or not to take my proffered hand—grubby, ballpoint-pen scribbling on the back, dirt under the fingernails. At no other time would she have imagined such a hand could have anything to do with her, but now she had no choice. She took a deep breath and gave me her hand—a hand from a medical family, on which virtually no germs could survive. As she settled on the wall, I could hear that her breathing was raspy from fear.

"All right, tell me." She flashed those large, innocent eyes, so at odds with her intelligence. "Is this what my uncle told you? Did he take Jiaqi away?"

"Don't you want to know what your grandpa did?"

"No. I wouldn't believe you anyway. My uncle doesn't get on with Grandpa." And yet her eyes remained on me, as if waiting for my answer.

"They say your grandpa ..." I kept my voice low.

Her lips were pressed together. She looked very anxious.

"He's a murderer," I said slowly.

Her face twitched, and went very pale. What I'd said was unwelcome, but not totally unexpected.

"That's ludicrous," she eventually said. "Grandpa carries out at least three major surgeries a week. He's been doing this for fifty years. Do you know how many lives he's saved in that time? No one values human life more than he does, understand? I don't know what my uncle told you, but it can't be true. Jiaqi's been living with Grandpa, she ought to know what sort of person he is. Why would she believe my uncle's lies? Just ask anyone at the hospital. They'll tell you Grandpa pours his whole heart into his work and gives all his time to his patients. He's the most remarkable person I've ever met. Don't repeat this nonsense to anyone else." She'd said all this in a rush, facing straight ahead. Now she turned to look at me.

The wind had disheveled her hair, and her sleeves were stained from the climb. This made her seem a little more human, but hadn't dented her dignity—in fact, though I was higher up than her, I still felt as if she were looking down at me. This reminded me of meeting your grandpa the day before, and a strong sense of shame washed over me.

Her chest was all puffed up with passion for your grandpa, which made her look warm and safe. I didn't understand. What a foolish way to feel. How could she have these emotions and still appear so lofty? I truly wished I could pity her—that would have made me feel better, but her inexplicable pride prevented me. I couldn't see any reason to give way.

"Excellent performance—I can see why your school sends you to elocution competitions," I said. "I have to go home now. Maybe you should say these things to the dead people on the other side of this wall." With that, I slid down to the window ledge, jumped onto the bricks, and then the ground. One by one, I flung the bricks away.

"What are you doing?" By the time she realized, it was too late. "Put them back!" Her voice was sharp from terror. I chuckled, imagining her reciting Monday's National Flag speech in this tone.

"I heard that in this very place," I said quietly, "your grandpa killed a man. The body is still floating in that pool of liquid in there. Look for yourself if you don't believe me."

She shrieked, clapped her hands over her ears, and curled up into a ball. I dusted myself off, retrieved my schoolbag from under hers, and sauntered away.

"Don't you dare go!" she shouted. "Come back here immediately! You have to help me down."

Whistling, I followed my shadow to the streetlights. The screams behind me grew fainter. Disappointingly, before they faded away altogether, I didn't hear a single plea. I'd been wondering whether I'd turn back to help her if she begged, or even just said something nice to me. I needn't have bothered. As if high-and-mighty Li Peixuan would ever lower herself like that.

Not long after I got home, it began to snow. Finally. I leaned against the window sill, watching clouds of snowflakes soaring through the air, an overwhelming sight. Behind me, Auntie was rifling through our possessions, looking for her artificial leather boots. Their uppers had worn through, and their fur rims had rubbed away, but still she searched frantically for them whenever it snowed. She believed they were the only things that could prevent her from falling. She'd fallen once, before buying these boots, and knocked out her two front teeth. Now she regarded snowy weather as the enemy.

"Luckily I'm not on night shift today," she muttered, pulling out the innermost box, coughing from the dust. She thumped her chest and turned to look at me. "Has your granny gone to sleep?"

"Not yet."

"If she starts acting up and wants you to go out for candied chestnuts, tell her you saw them putting away the stall earlier. Understood?"

"Mhm."

Occasionally, despite her age and personality, Granny would turn girlish—for instance, on snowy days, she loved to sit by the window peeling piping hot candied chestnuts.

"The ground's wet, you're sure to fall over," said Auntie. "Good luck to anyone who has to go out in this."

I opened the window and stuck my head out. Right away, tiny needles of ice jabbed into my neck and the backs of my ears, shooting down the collar of my sweater. The ground was completely white. The snowflakes were dazzling in the streetlights, as if they'd been set alight. Dizzyingly they spun and fell, like crazed white moths.

Was Peixuan still on the wall? I resisted the question, because compassion was a type of cowardice. Still, my exhilaration had faded away, and a faint worry began to manifest itself. Naturally, I'd thought about how she might be able to get down. The best thing would be if someone happened to come along and rescue her—but who would go there on such a cold evening? And the snow made it even less likely. She could lower herself from the roof onto the window ledge, and jump to the ground from there—it actually wasn't too far. Surely fear and hunger would eventually make her grit her teeth, shut her eyes, and do it. She wasn't going to sit there and freeze to death, was she?

"What are you doing? You'll catch your death!" Auntie yelled. "Help me get the boxes from under your granny's bed."

I happily accepted this task, with a faint hope that Granny would demand roasted chestnuts. That would give me an excuse to go out. I told myself I would just go and see if she was still there—I wasn't going to help her, no matter what. Unfortunately, Granny had already fallen asleep.

"Granny, Granny, it's snowing!" I tugged at her blanket.

She snorted, gently kicked me aside, and rolled over.

Auntie not only found the boots, she also brought out a whole pile of winter clothes. She folded them one by one, and stacked them on a chair. As I climbed to my upper bunk, she was still pulling them out of boxes. The bed was half-covered in them.

I'd planned to get up in the middle of the night to see if it was still snowing, but when I woke up, it was dawn. I drew the curtains and saw it had stopped, but there was more than a foot of snow on the ground. I got dressed, grabbed a steamed bun, and dashed out, crunching over thick snow to Dead Man's Tower. Peixuan was gone, of course, and the snow there was pristine, with not a footprint in sight. I dug through the snow with a branch, and found the bricks where I'd flung them, with none under the window ledge. This meant no one had rescued her. I refused to give it any more thought—she'd gotten down safely, that was the main thing.

Even so, I couldn't rest easy. At school, I walked back and forth past her classroom, trying to look casual, but I didn't see her inside. When the bell went, her teacher chased me away. Feeling uneasy, I went to class, but my eyes kept turning to the door, as if it might swing open at any moment— someone would call my name, I'd go out, and there would be the plump police officer, jabbing a finger at me and saying, Hey, kid, you're in big trouble now. But no. One class after another went by, and the door remained shut.

It was Saturday, so there were no afternoon classes. After lunch, Dabin and Zifeng dragged me into a snowball fight. We played for a while, then I said we should make a snowman. They were enthusiastic—but where to do it? Zifeng suggested the woods, but I said there wasn't enough space. Dabin said the field had plenty of room, but I thought too many people walked past there, and our snowman would get destroyed. Finally I said, How about behind the bicycle shelter? It was near all our homes, and for as long as the snow didn't melt, we'd be able to see it every day. Dabin laughed and said he'd been about to suggest that. As we walked over, Zifeng said, Cheng Gong, I know what you're thinking, you want Jiaqi to see it when she comes back. I said that was nonsense. Dabin looked sad, and said, Isn't it strange that she and her cousin are both missing? I said, Wait, Li Peixuan is missing? Yes, he said, She didn't come to school this morning—her teacher asked me to help carry some books to her classroom, and I noticed she wasn't at her desk.

We made a snowman almost as tall as us. Dabin sacrificed two of his bouncy balls for its eyes. "They glow in the dark," he said. "Jiaqi and Peixuan will see them even at night."

"Let's pack the snow tightly," said Zifeng. "Otherwise the wind might blow it over. Jiaqi might take a few days to come back, we want it to last till then."

On Monday, everyone was startled to see someone else raising the flag—a short, scrawny girl whose nerves got the better of her. She managed to get the flag twisted up in the rope, and had to start over again. As they played the national anthem for a second time, I moved my lips mechanically. Well, there's trouble now, I told myself. The strange thing was, I felt very calm, and the frenzied mouse that had been running around in my heart was finally still.

*

I didn't see Peixuan again till the following March. She only missed a week of school, and was soon back at her flag-raising post, not to mention topping the whole school in the end-of-semester exams as usual. What I mean is, although I saw her in the distance at assembly, I never ran into her close up. Probably that was a mutual effort—I didn't want to speak to her, and I suspect she felt the same way, so we avoided each other. When we did meet, it was while I was deliberately taking a detour away from the school. It was unseasonably chilly that day, and I decided to go home for a sweater. Not long after setting out, I saw her coming towards me.

The road was narrow, and there was nowhere to hide.

I recalled the day she came back to school. Dabin had peered into her classroom, and from there the news of her facial injury spread far and wide. Dabin rushed over to tell us she was wearing a mask that covered everything but her eyes. During phys ed that afternoon, Dabin claimed he had an upset stomach and ran over for another look. She still had the mask on, and when he asked her classmates, they said she hadn't taken it off all day. Zifeng said, I bet she's not going to—won't it be weird if she raises the flag on Monday with the mask on? Dabin shook his head and said surely she wouldn't be doing that anymore.

But there she was on Monday, maskless. As usual, she walked steadily to the flagpost with the flag held high, and stood very straight as she watched it rise up. Everyone stood on tiptoe to catch a glimpse of her face, but we were too far away. I felt relief—she was probably fine. Later, Dabin went to her classroom again, and reported that he'd seen many schoolmates from different classes clustered there, asking after her, some bearing fruit candies and stuffed toys. Peixuan came out to magnanimously thank everyone for their concern and accept the gifts. Dabin said everyone was shocked by the sight of her face. He gestured to show us how long the scar was, how red and swollen, like a blood-sucking lizard. She must have seen their horrified looks, but smiled as if nothing had happened. Dabin said, Why was she in such a hurry to remove her mask? Just to raise the flag? Why not wait for the scab to come off, so she doesn't look so scary?

Dabin burst into tears, and Zifeng said, So you care about her. Dabin said, Yes, I like her, so what? She's so brave, everyone admires her. Zifeng said, But she's a top student. Again Dabin said, So what? I'll just study harder from now on. Zifeng said, That's fine, not many people will want to marry her with that scar on her face, you can jump ahead on the list. Dabin said, I don't want to marry her either, if I had to look at that scar every day, it would make me sad.

"How did she get hurt?" I asked.

"She fell from a wall and cut her face on some glass," said

Dabin. "I don't believe it. Whoever heard of Li Peixuan climbing a wall?" He was silent for a moment. "Someone must have cut her. If I find out who did it, I'll slash his face to pieces!"

I'd spent the last week bracing myself for trouble. Would it be a teacher or the police who came to find me? Probably the police—this seemed serious. For the first few days, when there was no news of Peixuan at all, I'd even thought she might be dead, so it was a relief to find out she was only injured—but I might still get brought in for questioning. "Come on, why did you do this?" Her grandpa would be at the station again, this time for his other granddaughter. Would he show the same restraint when he asked me if I was the boy who hurt Peixuan? Would he pretend once again not to know who I was? I wanted to see him get angry. If he lost his composure, that would reveal his true face, the evil one, and lay bare the enmity between us. It's ridiculous, I know. I felt I needed a little rip in his dignity before I could attack him.

Naturally, I was also prepared to become Dabin's enemy. This would be a great test of our friendship. I was almost certain he would choose to remain by the side of his goddess. It wasn't like I treasured our relationship, but over the years, I'd gotten used to having this idiot around. Anyway, I was ready for the whole world to set itself against me. A tragedy to fulfill my dreams of heroism.

No police officers or teachers came looking for me, which made me more and more anxious. Was your family planning their own revenge? Remembering what your grandpa had done to mine sent shivers over my scalp. I kept a pencil knife in my pocket at all times, just in case. One day went by after another, and still nothing. Then Peixuan came back to school, and everything went back to normal. I couldn't believe it. I thought I'd punched a hole through the entire world, but in reality, all I'd done was thrown a pebble into the sea. It hadn't even made a sound.

I've never found out why Peixuan covered for me. Was her silence absolution or mercy? How much did she know about the wrong that lay between our families, if anything? That was a mystery. Peixuan herself was a riddle—no one knew what she was thinking. Her body was a black box, containing an enormous force, enough to obliterate all the pain that came her way. Nothing could destroy her. That March afternoon, when I saw her walking towards me, I understood this.

It was very cold, and the sky was overcast. The grass hadn't grown in yet, and the air didn't smell of blossoming flowers—winter was persisting. Only Peixuan's pale yellow cardigan had a springlike floral scent. I didn't realize it was her at first—I'd never seen her wearing such a bright color. Besides, she was taller and more developed, a young woman now. Then I recognized her steady flag-raiser's gait, her upright posture like a sapling. She saw me too, and didn't hide or hesitate, just strode ahead, looking levelly at me.

When I was too far away to see her face, I could pretend nothing had happened. Then she drew closer, her features came into focus, and I stared at the scar—my handiwork. It looked huge from any angle, dwarfing her narrow chin. Being slightly raised, it made the lower half of her face look sunken, as if a meteor had crashed into it. I'll admit that when I saw that scar, I thought it would settle any scores between us, no matter how large. The guilt swiftly faded because even at that moment, I couldn't pity her. She looked unflappable, scarred chin lifted, proud gaze eviscerating as ever.

I'd expected her to say something like, You see? Nothing can defeat me. And that would put an end to it. Instead, she murmured with implacable firmness, "My grandfather never hurt anyone. Don't you ever say that again."

Li Jiaqi

The afternoon after Dad's accident, I got a fever. Steeped in memories, the fuses of my consciousness burned out one by one. I lay drowsing, unable to stop sweating. Dreams came one after another, thin ones, like padding spilling from a torn winter coat. My body was so hot it woke me. Still dazed, I sat up and saw the glistening window. Thinking it was ice, I ran over barefoot and pressed my face to its surface. I don't know how long I stayed there, until my face felt less scalding hot, and my mind was a little clearer. It was dark outside, and clouds were blowing across the sky.

In the inky black room, bags were piled up on the floor like graves. Sleeves protruded from them like arms reaching from the soil. Terrified, I opened the door and fled. The passageway was dark too. I groped my way to the living room and turned on the lights. There were faint creases in the red couch, and the glass ashtray on the coffee table was stuffed full of upright cigarette butts, like tiny people in white robes carrying out a secret ritual. In my father and Wang Luhan's unlit bedroom, a stark white blanket lay huddled on one side of the double bed. I retreated to the passageway and saw a glimmer of light beneath Granny Qin's door. Without thinking, I pulled it open.

Granny Qin was sitting alone on the bed, muttering to herself. She didn't seem to notice me, but after a bit more mumbling she suddenly turned and spat viciously on the floor, before shrinking back fearfully and staring wide-eyed as if someone else had done the spitting.

"Old Wang seems like a good sort, but he can get pretty violent," she said.

"Stop talking nonsense or I'll rip your mouth to shreds!" Her again, in a different voice.

"So you'll do it, but you don't want people talking about it? Did you know this before?"

"Get out! Get out of here!" She stood and planted her feet

firmly, as if ready to chase someone out with a broom.

She was arguing with herself, playing both parts. Before, I'd have run from the room, but now I stood there staring steadily at her. Her expression moved swiftly from anger to hatred to glee to disappointment. This strange, exuberant behavior seemed to be her way of proving she was still alive. I slowly walked over to sit at her feet.

She slumped back onto the bed, still talking quietly. I felt her breath on my face, warming me. I rested my head against her legs. Her body was toasty too.

"I'm so scared." I began to weep.

"Don't be scared. It's alright." Granny Qin placed her hand on my head, and distractedly stroked my hair.

"I feel bad, and I don't dare to sleep," I said. "Scary things come whenever I shut my eyes. Dead people's hands reach up from the ground ..."

"If the police ask questions, tell them you don't know anything."

"I dreamed about my mom's wedding. Someone gave me a chocolate, but when I unwrapped it, there was a dead sparrow's head inside."

"Even if you had gone there, what would that prove?" She caught hold of my hands. "You didn't do anything. You have nothing to be afraid of."

"And I dreamed about a ghost, a ghost with no legs ..."

"Let them investigate," she said. "So what if the nail was yours? That doesn't prove anything!"

"Is there such a thing as a soul?" I asked. "My dad's dead. Do you understand? He's dead."

She shuddered. "Your dad's dead, your dad's dead." She chewed over the words, trying to find a hidden meaning. "No, that can't be—your dad can't be dead." She shoved me aside and pointed at the ceiling. "Quick, fetch the scissors, we have to cut the tube around his neck!" Her head tilted back. "A stool! Get a stool! It's fine, your dad will be fine." She took a couple of steps back and grabbed hold of me.

"Don't be scared, Han. Good girl. We'll bring your dad back down. He won't die, he'll be fine."

At the word *die*, I sobbed even harder.

"Don't cry, your dad will be fine." She knelt and swabbed roughly at my tears. Her wrinkled face looked like a paper lantern that had been trampled on. Her body sagged and she sat on the ground, still holding me, and started crying too.

The two of us sat there, hugging each other and crying. I smelled camphor on her sweater, and decay on her body. Like a burned-out building whose crumbling walls still smoldered.

As she wept, I felt I'd reached the bottom of her heart, clear as a mirror. She remembered and understood everything. I started to think she wasn't mad—that was just a label other people had put on her. Her hair remained immaculate, the black clips like shackles.

I gradually forgot we were crying for different people, different dads whose deaths were separated by time. Our sobs merged into a single sound.

*

That evening in December 1993, the deaths of my father and Wang Luhan's father became mysteriously intertwined. I was mourning my father, who'd just departed, but also a more distant death.

It rained heavily the night before the interrogation in 1976, and lightning streaked the windows. Unable to sleep, Wang Liangcheng paced around the room as his wife tried to comfort him. Just before dawn, the rain faded, and he finally lay down, only to jolt upright a second later. His wife drowsily asked what was wrong. He said he'd just remembered there were a couple of nails in a drawer. He had to hide them from the police. He looked in every drawer, but there were no nails. He upended them all, and crawled around the floor searching. Sweat poured off his face as he rummaged, his breathing frenzied. Suddenly, his palm landed on a length of rubber tubing, a fleshy brown color, warm as a body. The rain had stopped, and he felt very calm.

There was a small window in the bathroom, right up against the ceiling. He tied the rubber tubing to the frame, looped the noose around his neck, and kicked the stool out from under him.

His daughter found him when she got up to use the bathroom. He was dangling from the window, gray-green face slick with rain. She screamed and ran out.

It was Xie Tiancheng who told me this, many years later. He only knew the bare bones—after all, he'd heard it at several removes, and too much time had passed. Even so, I saw each scene as he spoke, as vividly as if I'd been there.

Xie Tiancheng arrived at Wang Luhan's apartment late that night in 1993. Years later, he still remembered turning on the lights and being surprised at what he saw. He'd expected chaos; Granny Qin cursing and hurling things around, me howling from hunger and fear. Instead, we were asleep in Granny Qin's bed, still embracing tightly. She'd curled up her legs so mine could rest on hers. He stood in the doorway looking at us, and forgot what he'd been going to do next.

I wasn't asleep, but didn't dare to move. Every so often, Granny Qin would cry out for Han, and I would answer, terrified she would realize I wasn't her daughter and chase me out. I thought everyone had forgotten me, that we were trapped in this icy place, and would quietly die, bit by bit. Our eyes would die, our teeth would die, our toes would die. I stopped feeling her arm under me, and only sensed the softest part of her, her drooping breasts, pressed against my face through a thin layer of clothes, loose as grave soil.

The lights snapped on with a click, and a tall man was in the doorway.

"Don't be scared," he said. "I'm your dad's friend."

"You're here." Granny Qin sat up. She seemed to know him. "Is it cold outside?"

"I'll make you something to eat," he said. "Luhan will be back soon."

I went to the kitchen and watched him slice cabbage. He turned to me and said, "Fried noodles okay?"

He tossed chopped onions into the wok, and steam rose from the hot oil. He hadn't taken off his coat and sweat was beading on his forehead.

He set a bowl of noodles on the table, gestured for me to sit, then brought a bowl to Granny Qin's room. I faintly heard him promise to bring her to see the lantern show on the fifteenth day of the New Year. When she was done eating, he got her to take her meds, which she docilely did. I heard the pills rattling from their bottle. He knew where they were kept, and the correct dose.

He came back out and saw me staring at the empty bowl. "Still hungry? There's more in the wok."

I shook my head and he took the bowl away. After a while, he emerged from the kitchen with two bowls of noodles and gave me the smaller portion. "I'm having some too."

He began slurping up his noodles, a loud, joyful sound. I found it touching. Even humble noodles seemed delicious now, and soon I'd finished my portion.

"Where's Wang Luhan?" I asked.

He put down his chopsticks and sat up straight. "I have something to tell you."

"My father's dead," I said.

He froze for a second, and nodded painfully. After a short silence, he said, "Luhan fainted. She hadn't eaten in a few days. A friend took her to the hospital, and I came straight here." He pulled me over and brushed the hair off my forehead. "What's your name?"

"Li Jiaqi."

"Listen to me, Jiaqi. All this will pass. Nothing in the world lasts forever." His hand rested on my forehead. "Do you have a fever?" He went over to the cabinet and found a thermometer, watched as I placed it in my armpit, and went to the kitchen for some warm water. I'd never hoped more to be ill, to express my anguish, to get even with Wang Luhan for fainting. I had to suffer more than her, to prove I loved Dad more. 36.8 degrees, he said, No fever. He poured me a glass of water and told me to go to bed.

"Are you leaving?" I asked.

"No. Don't worry. Go to sleep."

"Can I sleep here?" I sat on the sofa.

He went into the storeroom and came back out with bedding and a pillow. He indicated I should stand, and started laying out the bedding, but stopped.

"Did you get your period?" His voice was very soft.

I followed his eyes to a brownish stain on the couch.

He studied my face. "First time?"

I kept my mouth clamped shut.

He hesitated. "The convenience store downstairs might still be open. I'll go and see."

I grabbed his arm. "Don't leave me alone."

"Okay ... Do you want to change?"

The thought of going into the storeroom or bathroom terrified me, and I shook my head. He shrugged, and went to the bedroom for a towel, which he folded and set on top of the bedding. I lay down, and he pulled the blanket over me.

He turned off the lights, leaving only the one in the passageway on, and brought a chair over to sit by the sofa. "Go to sleep. I'll be here."

Seeing my eyes still open, he said, "You don't need a bedtime story, do you? At your age?"

"Do people really have souls?" I asked. "Can I see my dad's soul?"

He lit a cigarette and drew deeply from it. "When I was a kid, whenever the anniversary of my grandpa's death came round, my grandma would climb up onto a stool and pull all the nails from the walls, or she'd cover them in red paper. She said demons brought Grandpa back to the house at night, leading him by a chain around his neck, which they would attach to a nail. If there weren't any nails available, Grandpa could walk around freely rather than being strung up. She also left snacks for the demons; a plate of little fish, the ones with a lot of bones so you have to eat them slowly. That way, Grandpa could stay longer." Smoke drifted from his cigarette between us. "One year, I crept out of bed in the middle of the night and hid behind the door."

"Did you see your grandpa?"

"I fell asleep sitting there on the floor."

"I'm not going to fall asleep."

"It's okay, you'll see him even if you do. They come to us in dreams. Not just on special days, anytime. If you go to sleep quickly, you might see him soon."

I closed my eyes but didn't dream. In the dark, I heard the man next to me thunderously breathing in and out, enveloping me in warm air and making me feel safe. I'd always wanted Dad to stay with me as I slept, but instead this was a man whose name I didn't even know. The thought filled me with shame, as if I'd betrayed Dad. I felt a churning in my belly, and my shorts moistened. Of course, I had no idea what menstruation was, but it felt very far away. Shouldn't it have waited till I was older and ready to fall in love? But here it was, tied up with fear and sadness right from the beginning. It seemed to come from somewhere very deep within me, carrying with it a pain that came and went, reminding me of Dad, and of the clump of flesh. I imagined it flowing endlessly, until it was all gone. Perhaps I'd see him. On a night like this, bleeding could be a way of getting closer to him.

The sound of a key in the front door. The man jumped up from his chair, and I sat up too. Wang Luhan walked in, her orange-and-green-checked coat unbuttoned to reveal a sweater glistening with snowflakes. She stood there taking in the whole room: drinks cabinet, windows, couch, me. The way she looked at me, I felt like just another piece of furniture.

"Didn't Huiling come back with you?" said the man, going over to her.

Wang Luhan shook her head and hung her coat from the back of a chair. The man supported her as she sat, and poured her a glass of warm water.

"I need you to do me a favor," she said. She reached for her coat, not seeming to have noticed it had slid to the floor as she groped the empty air. The man picked it up and handed it to her. She took two slips of paper from the pocket. "Huiling got us these tickets. You'll have to bring the child back to Jinan tomorrow morning."

"But you ..."

"I'll be fine," she said.

The man knelt and put his hand on her knee. "I'll be back tomorrow night, and I'll stay with you after that."

I couldn't make out his face in the dim light, but I sensed the tenderness in his eyes. My heart chilled as I remembered what my father had said while quarreling with her: she had someone waiting for her. This man had come to take care of me and Granny Qin, but he wasn't Dad. He was replacing Dad as the head of this household. I glared furiously at his hand on Luhan's leg.

Luhan shoved his hand away. "It's late. You should go home."

The man put on his coat, but lingered. I ran over to him and pushed him out of the living room towards the front door. He walked out silently, and I slammed the door behind him.

Back in the living room, all the lights were on, illuminating every corner of the room. Luhan was by the liquor cabinet, pouring herself some vodka. Dad's warmth still lingered on that bottle. She held the glass in both hands. The spotlight above her spat out blinding light, licking the drink like a snake's tongue. The vodka trembled, and so did her shadow on the wall, a large, startled bird flapping its wings. She took a big mouthful of vodka, called me over, and told me about the car accident in the simplest possible way, as if this were an item on the daily news. Your dad is gone, she said somberly. It was as if we'd made an agreement that neither of us would cry. You'll go back to Jinan tomorrow, she said, and you won't be at the funeral—it's better that way, you'll understand someday.

I didn't argue. There was something very sincere in her voice that made me want to believe her. I didn't cry either. I just looked at her; I was closer to her face than I'd ever been. Her protruding cheekbones and nose bridge made her seem unfamiliar. Or maybe it wasn't the angle, maybe she was a stranger now. Before, she'd been Dad's wife. Now, she had no connection to us, like two planets in the same solar system breaking away from their orbits because their sun was gone. I studied her, this unlucky woman. Her father had killed himself when she was a little girl, her mother lost her mind, and now her husband was dead. These sorrows must have burrowed through her heart, turning it into a bottomless well.

"Are you going to kill yourself?" I asked.

She looked at me. "Why would you say that?"

"That's what happens on TV," I said. "When two people are in love and one of them dies, the other commits suicide."

She laughed, the glass in her hand shaking. "Do you want me to die?"

"I want you to live."

"I'm going to live," she said.

I hesitated. "Does that mean you didn't really love my dad?"

"I love him."

"But you were always fighting."

"We shouldn't have been together."

"Why?"

No answer.

"Because he was married to my mom?" I asked.

"No."

"Because Grandpa and Grandma didn't approve?"

She shook her head.

"Then why?"

"Stop asking!" She tipped her head back and drained her glass, then tried to pour herself some more, but it was down to the dregs. She shook the empty bottle. "Bastard. Should have left more for me," she mumbled. Her voice had softened, as if she was recalling something, and her eyes brightened. Then the brightness oozed from her eyes and trickled down her cheeks.

"Maybe I loved him so much because I knew it would never work." She coughed, choking on the vodka. Her face flushed red, and she thumped at her chest, finally getting her breathing under control. Her voice was hoarse, and she sounded like she was divulging an enormous secret. "Your dad and I are the same: twisted people who could only experience twisted love." The corners of her mouth lifted with what seemed like pride at these feelings that normal people couldn't possibly understand.

"Are you going to be with the man who came here earlier?" I asked.

"Who? Xie Tiancheng?"

"He likes you, I can tell."

"Relax, I'm not getting together with him." She put her hand on my shoulder. "You worry too much, little girl. You're afraid I'll die, you're afraid I'll be with another man. So tell me, what do you think I ought to do? It's not easy, living all alone, you know?" She smiled sadly, and another line of tears dribbled down. "It's so hard."

Her body slid down to sit on the floor, head leaning against the cabinet, next to the dent she'd left the day before with the ashtray. She ran her fingertips over its outline.

Near dawn, I ran out of steam and lay down on the couch, facing her. My eyelids grew heavy, but I resisted sleep, forcing myself to keep watching her. I wanted to know she was still there, and for her to know I was too. Maybe that didn't matter to her, but I believed if we were together, we had the power to make Dad come into our presence.

He never came, and in the end I fell asleep, only to be startled awake by Granny Qin's singing.

"*Stars fill the night.*" Mellifluous as ever. In Granny Qin's world, nothing at all had happened.

She came into the room, stared at me in surprise, then seemed to remember who I was and smiled. Once again, she pulled me over to the chair by the window to have my hair combed, and this time I didn't resist. These braids would be the only thing I brought back from Beijing. She worked even more intently than she had the day before, carefully sticking in the clips so they didn't scratch my scalp. This time I felt no pain at all.

Luhan turned off the lights that had been on all night, and went into the bedroom. When she came out, she was in a black coat over a black turtleneck.

"You look good in black." Granny Qin went over to her and straightened her collar.

Luhan went out and returned a short while later with soup dumplings for me and Granny Qin. I opened the plastic bag and inhaled the savory steam, but when I put one in my mouth, I tasted nothing but fatty meat. I managed not to spit it out, but didn't have any more. Luhan ate nothing, just held a glass of warm water. The sorrow of the night before had hardened onto her face, becoming permanent. Like Granny Qin, she would look like this even when she was happy. They hadn't looked alike before, but now there was a family resemblance. The dark day's gloomy light was a veil shrouding this pair of widows. I imagined their lives after I'd gone. Granny Qin would wake up in the middle of the night and sing while combing her own hair. In the morning, Luhan would pull herself together and go out to get breakfast. All afternoon, she'd be on the couch smoking one cigarette after another, until the ashtray was full of little red hearts and the sky began to darken. Then another long night would begin. To those in pain, nights are like walking through a very long tunnel. Only at daybreak can you climb back to the surface. Another dawn, more singing, over and over, day after day with no hope. This dimly lit apartment, rank with chicken feathers and the reek of paint, was a living grave. I knew I would be living in sadness back home, but the thought of leaving this place still brought me some relief. Of course, I would miss it too. I looked around, trying to remember every detail. The position of every nail in the walls, the peeling paint on the doorframe. Everything was connected to Dad. Whenever I thought of him in the future, I would recall this place, a container for memories.

"You remind me of someone." Granny Qin put down the dumpling she was eating and stared at me. "But I can't remember who."

Xie Tiancheng arrived, and Granny Qin told him to have a dumpling. He said he'd already eaten, and waved the plastic bag in his hand—he'd gotten me bean-paste buns for the road.

"Children like sweet things," he said.

"That's right," said Granny Qin. "Han is the same way."

I put on my coat. Granny Qin came over to straighten my hair clips, then suddenly froze.

"What's your name?"

"Li Jiaqi."

"Come back soon, Jiaqi," she said. "We'll have steamed dumplings tonight." She turned to Luhan. "Can we have steamed dumplings tonight?"

Wang Luhan didn't answer. She walked us to the door and thrust a black plastic bag at me. Inside was a packet of menstrual pads.

I stepped outside, but then doubled back to the storeroom, where I grabbed the topmost book from the pile and stuffed it in my coat pocket. As I left, I glanced at the folding bed, where Tata the panda was lying face down.

On the train back, Xie Tiancheng noticed I was pulling away from him. He kept offering me bean-paste buns and made me an instant black sesame dessert. I didn't know why he was being so friendly when taking me home was just a task he'd been assigned. He pointed out the window telling me where the train was passing by, what the local specialties were. He'd get off and buy some, he said, if there was anything I wanted to eat. I shook my head, but even so, when the train stopped for a few minutes, he jumped off and got me a box of Tianjin dough fritters, and then a couple of piping hot roast yams.

Unable to withstand his friendliness, I accepted one of the yams. At first, I'd only intended to warm my hands, but I couldn't resist taking a couple of bites. The whole journey, though, I didn't say a word to him. He walked me to Grandpa's building, all the way to the stairwell.

See you again, Jiaqi, he said behind me, but I didn't turn around. I didn't think we'd ever meet again.

Cheng Gong

Many things happened in the winter of 1993. You weren't the only person planning to leave this place.

One evening, Auntie cooked four dishes, which was unusual—what's more, they were all my favorites. She also got a crate of beer, which she shared with Granny. When I asked for a glass, she rapped my knuckles with her chopsticks. She kept topping up Granny's glass, encouraging her to drink more. Granny can hold her liquor—no one could drink her under the table. Even so, the room was very warm, and she got drowsy after a few bottles.

After Granny had gone off to bed, Auntie cleared the table and said to me, Let's get an early night too. I climbed onto the upper bunk, but I'd just lain down when her voice rose to me: Cheng Gong, I have something I need to tell you.

Tang is leaving, she said, and he asked me to go with him. I asked who Tang was, and she said, Didn't I tell you? He's one of the residents. It took me a while to remember. It had rained heavily one day that summer, and Auntie was doing the night shift alone in the pharmacy when she saw a young man sheltering under the eaves. She did have an umbrella, but didn't want to lend it to him. Every time she'd done this before, she'd ended up having to buy a new one. Then the man came inside and started talking to Auntie. She blushed, feeling he'd somehow sensed she'd had an umbrella in her bag. He tried to make conversation, asking if her shift lasted till dawn—he had a report to finish, and would probably be up all night too. Auntie said nothing, but abruptly reached into her bag and pulled out the umbrella. As she watched him walk away, she felt annoyed—he'd probably only started chatting to trick her into handing it over. Then the next morning, he arrived as she was finishing her shift and returned the umbrella. He'd even fixed it with tape where it had been ripped. They went to the cafeteria for breakfast, his treat. Life hadn't been easy for Tang—he was from a rural family, and as a child, he'd experienced hearing loss after a bad reaction to antibiotics. Though he could only understand a third of what his teachers were saying, he was determined to become a doctor, and repeated three grades before getting into university. In order to not fall behind on his work, he was now staying in the library till midnight daily. He would soon be graduating, but it would be a struggle to find work—the training hospital wasn't going to offer him a job. Another time, she'd mentioned how nice Tang was—his family back in Hunan had sent him some white pepper, and he'd given it to her. After that, Auntie put white pepper in everything she cooked, but never mentioned Tang again. I didn't pay much attention, I just thought she liked him—she liked everyone who was nice to her, from the male doctors to the doorman. If they so much as smiled at her or said thank you, she would talk about it forever.

Which is why I didn't fully believe her. Could this be one-sided? Maybe the guy was just being polite. I said, What are you going to do down south? She said, Tang wants to open a clinic, and I'll be the office manager. Good idea, I said. When are you going? Next week, she said, I've already got my ticket. Now I was silent. She said, I didn't tell you before because I didn't want your granny to find out, she's sure to break my legs. I said, You've told me now, aren't you afraid I'll tell her? She said, I was going to leave you a letter, but I couldn't find the words. I said, Oh, so you wouldn't have said anything if you'd managed to write it? She was quiet for a while, then I heard her crying. I don't know what to do, she said. What do you mean, I said, haven't you made up your mind? She cried a bit more, then said, I'd bring you with me but your granny's old, she can't be alone. Right, I said, so I have to stay behind. She said, When I get there, I'll send money home every month. There's a lot to do around here, it'll be hard on you. After a while, we'll bring you over to live with us. I hated that *we*. Even Auntie was part of a *we* now. I swabbed at a ballpoint pen mark on the wall and wondered when she was talking about. Would this have to wait till Granny died? She cried some more and kept saying she didn't know what to do. Go to sleep, I said, I'm tired. She wept for a very long time. I was drifting off when I heard her say, Don't blame me, Little Gong. Blearily, I thought my mom must have come back, because no one else called me Little Gong.

I woke up before dawn the next day, and lay in bed thinking about my situation. I couldn't believe Auntie was leaving. I'd expected everyone else to leave, but not her—like me, she had nowhere to go. She was like a shadow, like air—I hadn't spent much time thinking about her existence, but now that I faced a life without her, where I'd have to deal with Granny alone, I realized how terrifying that would be. Should I tell Granny? No, I couldn't. Maybe persuade her to take me along? After all, Granny was perfectly capable of taking care of herself. But then I remembered Grandpa, and scratched that idea. I couldn't go anywhere till I'd taken revenge.

Our dinners for the next few days were resplendent: deep-fried stuffed lotus root, chives and squid, sweet and sour pork ribs, steamed buns with a zucchini filling. All my favorites. As I ate a rib, Auntie couldn't hold in her tears any longer, and ran to the bathroom. Granny was gnawing at a rib too, and as she sucked the gravy off her fingers, she said, The meat's tough. Before falling asleep, I saw Auntie quietly pull a suitcase out from under her bed and fill it with clothes. We said nothing, and she didn't dare to look at me. The following afternoon, I was passing by the cafeteria noticeboard, and saw there'd be a screening of *The Little Flower* at the community hall that evening. I wondered if I should tell her—it was her favorite movie, and she'd been wanting to see it again—but then I decided not to. There wouldn't be time before she left.

That Friday, she told me before bed that she would be leaving in the morning. I'll send you a letter at your school, she said. Tear it up after you've read it, and not a word to Granny, understood? I said nothing. She said, Come down here, let me see you. No, I said. Come, she said, standing on tiptoe and reaching up for me. I curled myself into a ball as far in as I could go. She jumped and caught hold of a corner of the blanket, and thinking it was my shirt, pulled hard. It landed on her head and we both burst out laughing. Whenever we fought, I would sulk on the upper bunk, and she would catch me like this, then tickle my feet till we were friends again. Still giggling, she clambered up and sat next to me. The room was suddenly very quiet. She sighed, her mouth drooped, and she said, I've never made a decision for myself, not in my whole life, and I want to do it just once. She sighed again, hugging her knees, and I felt very scared. She brushed the hair off my forehead and said, Time for a haircut—when I'm not around, you'll have to go to the barber by the gate. She teared up. This is just temporary, Cheng Gong, I can't do anything about your granny, we just have to face the facts—I'll bring you both over when it's possible. What about Granddad? I said. Granddad? She froze. It was clear she'd forgotten all about his existence. I'm not leaving, I said, I still have things to do here. She asked what things, but I refused to answer. She patted my hand. Granddad has nurses to take care of him, she said. We can't take him with us, it wouldn't do any good ... I pouted and shook my head. It was getting dark, and the window frame left swaying shadows on the wall. White walls turn bluish if you stare at them too long. Translucent people dancing around a bonfire silently surrounded me.

Since you're going, I said, I have to tell you something: I know the other person who attacked Granddad. Her mouth dropped open in shock. Do you want to know who? I said. Who? she repeated, staring at me. Li Jisheng. As I said the name, I felt her hand tremble where it rested on mine. Don't talk nonsense. She looked at me, then immediately dropped her gaze. How do you know it's him? Never mind how, I said, I know. It can't be him, she said. There's no way, you can't make up stuff like this—you haven't told anyone else, have you? This can't just be swept away, I said, I want to take revenge for Granddad. What do you mean, revenge? she said. Don't scare me, tell me, what are you going to do? I looked her in the eye. You knew it was him all along, didn't you? How could I know, she protested, I don't know anything, stop guessing, it's all in the past, anyway, don't do anything stupid, I'm leaving tomorrow morning, don't you want me to go with an easy mind? She burst into tears. Go ahead and leave, I said, don't worry about my business. Promise me you won't do anything stupid. She tried to hug me, but I pushed her away. Go to sleep, I said coldly.

I couldn't get to sleep that night, and nor could she, I heard her tossing and turning in the lower bunk. I kept turning her reaction over in my mind: trembling fingers, darting eyes. She must have known. I suddenly felt you were all in on it: you, Peixuan, my aunt, everyone except me.

I was awake when Auntie left in the morning, but I didn't get out of bed. I heard her put on her boots and walk out with her suitcase. There was quite a gap between these two actions, during which the room was completely silent. What was she doing in that time? Looking around, quietly weeping? Whatever it was, I would take it as a goodbye, and I said farewell to her too, even though I still hated her a little. But then I thought I might never see her again, because I wasn't going to leave, and I knew she wouldn't return. She closed the door as gently as she could, but I still felt a crash in my heart. When I got out of bed, I saw she'd left me breakfast, and it felt like a normal day.

I didn't go to school. There was nothing stopping me from playing truant now. The most they'd do was call my guardian, and I had no guardians left. Granny definitely wouldn't be up for going to the school to get lectured by my teacher, and if a teacher dared to come round, she'd probably chase them away with a broom. She wouldn't care even if I got expelled. So why bother? Now you'd left, school meant nothing to me.

I walked out of Southern Courtyard and ambled listlessly eastward. Without meaning to, I ended up near Wenhui High. Everything beyond the market was Wenhui territory. I'd heard about Wenhui's reputation just a few days after coming to stay with Granny. They had everything you could imagine, from extortion to scams, from abortions to suicide. You took your life in your hands if you walked by the school gates, and the nearby movie theater and billiards hall were no-go zones. I noticed some kids in the field. A few girls were sitting on the bleachers, pointing at one of the boys and laughing. One of them was eating a banana. They seemed so free. A very pretty girl saw me and whistled, beckoning me over. The other girls shouted, Hey, kid, c'mere! I fled.

The loudspeaker outside the cinema blared the soundtrack of the film being screened. I'd heard they often screened pornos here, but I couldn't tell which ones those were. Anything with *lady* in the title seemed likely, though, so I bought a ticket and went upstairs. They were showing something called *Beautiful Lady Scary Ghost*. Disappointingly, everyone in it was fully dressed, though some of them had turned into ghosts. I did like the female ghost, who had a bit of fuzz on her upper lip. After the movie, before my eyes had adjusted to the light outside, I was accosted by a guy in a black baseball cap, who had a faceful of pimples and a squint. He was about my height, but definitely in high school. He shoved me into a corner and demanded all my money. I didn't bother saying anything, just emptied my pockets. He walked away, then turned back to ask if I could play billiards. I shook my head, but he made me go with him anyway.

We spent all afternoon in the billiards hall. He taught me how to play, but most of the time I was just watching him. I felt a bit sorry for him. He obviously didn't have any friends, not even to enjoy the spoils of his mugging. I don't think he meant me any harm, he just wanted company. Before I left, he asked for my school and class, and said I should come see him again.

I walked home through the dusk, thinking what an enriching day it had been—I'd seen another possible life. The world on the other side of the market had opened up and seemed to welcome me. I wondered if I should go back the next day to catch another movie. As I neared home, I began feeling uneasy. Granny would soon realize Auntie was gone, which would trigger an explosive rage, and I could expect to be interrogated. But I had no money on me to buy food, so all I could do was gather my courage and head in. The aroma of noodles in black bean sauce hit me, and Auntie ran in from the kitchen. Was I dreaming? She hugged me, beaming. You're just in time for dinner, she said.

It was just as well they'd got there early, said Auntie, that gave her time to change her mind before the train departed, and she could say goodbye to Tang through the window. She was crying so hard, it took a lot of effort to say, I ... I really can't. Tang smiled bleakly and said, I knew you wouldn't be able to leave, but I had to give it a try. Then he started sobbing too, and reached through the window to hug her. She'd expected him to scream at her, and didn't know how to react. There'll never be a better person than Tang in the world, she would say afterwards, and I didn't even say sorry to him properly. Was that her only regret? I never asked.

That night, we were back in our narrow bunks. It was as if we hadn't seen each other in a long time. I asked why she'd stayed, and she said, I was worried about you—what if you did some terrible thing? She stroked my ears the way she did when I had a fever, and tears came to my eyes. She was the first person who'd chosen to stay for me, when she could have left. I said, Do you remember when you had your fortune told, and it said you wouldn't go anywhere in this life? She nodded. I thought of that on my way back from the train station, and it must be true, otherwise why did my heart beat so fast when I saw the train, and my legs went soft, like I was on my way to be executed? I was sad after deciding not to leave, but my heart felt lighter. When I saw Southern Courtyard's gate from the bus window, I burst into tears, scaring all the other passengers. I kept bawling, I just couldn't stop, not even when I went to the market. Uncle Chen at the vegetable stall asked what was wrong. How could they know what I'd been through? I felt as if I'd already been all the way to the south and back. She smiled mournfully. I'm so useless, she said, I ought to have at least waited till the train got to Xuzhou before turning back, that way I could say I'd left Jinan once at least.

When she'd calmed down, I said, If you don't want me to do some terrible thing, tell me what you know. She said nothing, just looked down at her writhing hands. Even if you don't tell me, I said, I'll find out sooner or later. She sighed. I'd tell you if I could, but I really don't know anything. Did you know about Li Jisheng? I asked. She shook her head. I didn't, she said, though I'd guessed it might be him. I asked how she'd guessed. She hesitated a moment before answering.

After Wang Liangcheng's suicide, Li Muyuan would show up outside Wang Luhan's home, usually after dark. He'd stand for a while by the window, then leave. One time, Auntie walked by, pretending she was on her way somewhere else. He seemed panicked to see her, and left right away. Later, Auntie noticed him following Wang Luhan around. Not in a sneaky way—Luhan seemed to know he was there. He'd be right behind her as she went to the market, the grocery store, the pharmacy, but they never talked. One time, Luhan was coming back with some coal when her cart overturned. Muyuan went over to help her pick up the coal, but she shoved him away. He fell over, climbed back up, and tried again to help her, only to get pushed away again. He persisted a few times, until she gave up and stood aside. He picked up the coal, and pushed the cart the rest of the way.

Some time after that, said Auntie, your father began giving Wang Luhan a hard time, and Li Muyuan always stepped in to help her. He even got beaten up by your father, for his pains. People started saying Muyuan must have feelings for Luhan. Auntie shook her head. I knew it wasn't that simple. I asked what she meant. It was a shameful love, she said sternly, like a teacher catching a student in the act of cheating. This was more than I could comprehend—I didn't understand what strange feelings these could be, nor could I guess what this had to do with Li Jisheng. After a moment's thought, I said, Were you following them because you suspected something? Auntie's face changed and she said, sounding flustered, Who says I was following them? I just happened to see ... I said nothing—it was obvious she was lying. But why? I couldn't work it out, so I moved on to the most important question: If you'd guessed it was him, why didn't you tell Granny and Dad? I was scared, said Auntie. This man put a nail into someone's brain, who knows what he'd have done to us if I'd exposed him? What if they put him in jail, and he gave up even more names? What do you mean? I said. They'd get arrested, that's all. Auntie shook her head. If this blew up, there'd be no going back. I asked what that meant. She said, You don't know what it was like back then, you might get paraded through the streets or dragged into a struggle session at the drop of a hat, they'd denounce you for this today and that tomorrow, you never knew when the arrow was going to point at you. Your granddad ended up like that because he was denounced, remember? No one knew how anything would work out, no one was running things, do you understand? Even if you'd done nothing wrong, you might still end up the unlucky one. Best not to say anything, just keep to yourself. I said, Didn't you hate them, after what they did to Granddad? Granny said he could have been hospital director someday. Auntie sighed and said, No, he couldn't. I asked why. She said, It wasn't his fate, he was a regular person—he was very lucky he didn't get killed fighting the Japanese devils. Isn't everyone a regular person? I asked. Li Jisheng isn't, she said. Just look at him and you know he's special. I said, Did the fortune-teller say that? No, she said, that's my intuition. It's quite accurate too—when the Cultural Revolution started, I sensed our family was in trouble, and sure enough. And when your mom got married, I felt that was the end ... Auntie stopped, and glanced at me. She'd always been very careful not to mention my mother, as if the topic were a caged lion that would bite us if it ever got free. Abruptly, she hugged me. I'm here now, anyhow, she said, and I'm not leaving again. Remember what you promised me, forget about revenge. Trust me, we can't beat him. If you really want revenge, study hard, and achieve something great. I looked at her, confused. Auntie, I said, am I a regular person? No, she said with certainty, all my hopes are in you. Go to bed. She patted my shoulder. Thank god, she said, I can sleep soundly now.

I got under the cold covers. Back to school tomorrow. I couldn't help being sad that my life on the other side of the market was over almost as soon as it had begun. Auntie had said I wasn't a regular person, which made me want to do something extraordinary.

After a while, something struck me and I asked, What happened to Wang Luhan? Auntie took a while to reply, as if she needed to dredge this from her memory. Her elder brother took her away, she said, and she never came back to Southern Courtyard.

Before drifting off to sleep, I wondered why Auntie had lied about following Li Muyuan and Wang Luhan. A few days later, this question surfaced again. That afternoon, I got home to find Granny eating instant noodles. Auntie had said she had a stomachache, and had gone to bed without cooking dinner. I went into the small room, and she sat up in bed. Li Muyuan's dead, she said. He got hit by a truck. I asked how she knew. She said the church had held a prayer meeting for his mother, and someone who was there told her about it. She was wringing her hands, looking anxious, as if she ought to be doing something. After I'd gone to bed, she crept out of the room, and I heard the door shut. I ran to the window barefoot. It was very cold outside, and there wasn't anyone to be seen except Auntie, crouching at the base of a streetlight, lighting a match.

The strong wind blew out the match, and she lit another, shielding it with her hand. From her blouse, she pulled out a red diary, ripped out one page after another, and started a fire. She paused a few times, apparently reading what was written there. Finally, the red covers went in too, and the flames leaped higher. She squatted there until it had gone out. Then she stood, dabbed at her face, wrapped her arms around herself, and came back in.

Just like that, I realized she must have had her own *shameful love* for your dad. That's why she was following him. While everyone else was absorbed in tracking down the killer, she'd been enmeshed in affairs of the heart. Perhaps she'd thought she could stay clear of worldly troubles if she could only make this relationship happen, only to discover your dad and Wang Luhan were secretly seeing each other. With chaos like a net over everything, there was nowhere to hide. Did she keep the secret because she loved your dad? Maybe. She didn't want to tear apart his family and ruin his future. She must also have been scared of what would happen if this blew up. Fear and love made her stay silent. Your dad didn't know about either—he knew nothing. And now he was dead, he'd never know. Or perhaps she thought now he was dead, she could finally let him know. That's why she was in such a hurry to burn the diary. I thought I'd seen that red book in one of the boxes. Why had I never opened it? Maybe because I'd never imagined Auntie would have any secrets.

I still had a lot of questions for Auntie: How did she treat Li Muyuan after finding out the truth? Was she able to keep liking him while she watched him living his normal life even as her own had been destroyed? Did she truly never hate him? Had she felt the urge to tell him the truth? I realized my own situation now and hers back then were similar: we were trapped in the same story, like hamsters on a wheel. If a hamster knew it wasn't getting anywhere, would it still bother?

A few days later, you showed up again. It was a Monday, and it had started snowing early that morning. Before our afternoon Chinese class, Dabin ran up to me and said, Jiaqi's back, but she's changing schools, her mom's here to do the paperwork. That sent a jolt through my heart, but I wasn't surprised. I'd always known you would leave, and then it would be as if this place had nothing to do with you. You had that freedom. Dabin rubbed his reddening eyes and said, She's gone home to pack her stuff. She asked you to go see her at her grandpa's house after school.

The snow got heavier in the afternoon. The wind flung the classroom's back windows open, shattering the glass. The teacher cancelled assembly and sent us home early. Everyone else got their bags and left, but I stayed where I was. The seating plan had been rearranged the week before, and I was in the last row, right by the heater. Icy wind was sweeping through the broken window, meeting the hot air from the heater and eddying around me. I tore out the last page of my homework book and wrote a letter. It was just one line, but I called it a letter:

Li Jiaqi, your grandpa is the other murderer who hurt my granddad. But I don't hate you, we can still be friends.

I folded it into a little square, put on my coat, and walked out. Covered in snow, the school field looked endlessly vast. Snowflakes tumbled through the air, swathes of them smacking me in the face, making it hard to breathe. I pulled up my hood, held my coat collar closed, and strode ahead. This might be the last time I saw you, and I had a lot to say but I might not get the chance. Your mother would be hurrying you, and your grandmother would be glaring at us. How much time would we have? Ten minutes? Half an hour? How much of that should I spend comforting you, how much saying goodbye? I wanted to hug you. Was that too wild a wish when you were leaving? Then I'd press this letter into your hand and run away. There's not much time, said a voice in my ear, quickly, quickly. Yet I walked slower and slower, and when I got to Kangkang Convenience Store, I stopped altogether.

I heard a sad howl. It sounded like a dog, but I couldn't tell where it was coming from. The shop was dark, and the door was locked. They must have closed early because of the weather. I stood beneath the awning. A scrawny stray dog with a withered leg used to lurk under the wooden table there—you fed it quite a few times. I pulled aside the plastic milk and soft-drink crates under the table, but it wasn't there. The howling started again. I looked around and noticed the nearby ditch. Inside was a black, huddled thing, gently shivering.

"There you are," I said quietly.

The stray dog looked up at me and yelped a few more times.

I'll never forget its face. Its eyes and the top half of its muzzle were covered in a hardening shell, as if it were wearing an iron mask. The pus from its eyes had mixed with mud to form a thick layer that had frozen solid. Unable to see, it had blundered into the ditch, and because of its withered leg, it hadn't been able to climb out.

I squatted to take a closer look. Sensing my presence, it grew agitated, and barked as it tried to get to its feet—but after several attempts, it wasn't able to stand. All it could do was thrust its head towards me. Though it couldn't see, it wanted me to know it was looking at me, that behind the mask was a pair of hopeful eyes.

"Don't be scared." I brushed the snow off its fur, which was warmer than I expected. Obediently, it lay back down, making a whining sound in its throat.

It sensed me pulling my hand back and looked up in terror, searching for me. I stuck both hands into the bank of
snow by the ditch, and pushed it onto the dog. As it shook
itself frantically, I leaped across the ditch and pushed over
the snow there too. The dog was now buried up to its neck,
and could only stretch its head towards me. Now and then,
a bark came from deep in its throat, but the cold shrank the
sound to almost nothing. I stared at the black mask, imagining the fearful eyes behind it. What an insignificant life.
I fetched a basin from under the awning to use as a shovel.
The snow was heavy, mixed with soil. Each time the dog
tossed its head to get its face clear, I buried it again, and a
little less of the mask would reemerge. Finally it was gone.
Silence. I flung the letter into the ditch too, tossed more
snow after it, and pressed it down with the basin.

How much time had passed? When I stood up, my legs
were numb, and my hands were red and swollen from the
cold. It was completely dark. Snow was still falling rapidly,
like sand into the bottom of an hourglass. Bits of time that
no longer belonged to me. The streetlights blinked on, and
light poured onto the ground, revealing how filthy the
snow was. I replaced the basin, and with my hands in my
pockets, started walking back home.

I walked in the front door and saw Granny and Auntie
eating dinner.

"Is it cold out?" asked Auntie.

"Yes." I sat down without washing my hands. Auntie
split a steamed bun and gave me half. I sank my fingernails
into its white surface, like holding a clump of steaming hot
snow. I could feel my fingertips thaw, the deep creases on
my palm melting away. I let out a breath.

It's been years since I've thought about that dog. In my
recollection, I got to Kangkang and simply turned back for
whatever reason—the weather, or because I didn't want to
go to your grandpa's house. That stretch of memory got

erased, as if I'd never seen the dog, as if it never existed in the first place. Now I've remembered for the first time in almost two decades. That masked face, clear as anything. Such a pathetic life. Meaningless. Don't you think so? I felt I had a duty to end it. Did I feel satisfied afterwards, or more empty than ever? All of a sudden, I didn't want to see you. I couldn't explain why—a centrifugal force was flinging me off my orbit, away from the story that had already been written. The moment I threw the letter into the ditch, I was like a hamster that had finally decided to stop running, and so I came to a standstill.

Li Jiaqi

I didn't see Xie Tiancheng again until we met up last year, at the café next to Beijing Station. While I waited for him, I looked out at the crowded train station and saw myself, aged twelve, hurrying into the terminal. Tiancheng tried to take my hand, but I shook him off. He smiled awkwardly as if to say that was fine, he didn't mind. I've always remembered that smile, perhaps because of its gentleness. Like poor Blanche DuBois, I have always depended on the kindness of strangers.

When he showed up, I was gratified that he looked as tall as I'd remembered, though I didn't actually recognize him—it was just instinct that told me this was him. He'd aged a lot. His eyes were sunken, and there were dark splotches on his cheeks and the backs of his hands. I noticed them when he pulled out his cigarettes.

"It must have been twenty years since I saw you last?" he said.

"Eighteen."

"My daughter's sixteen this year," he said. "She's already started dating."

He'd also ended up doing business in Moscow. Like Auntie Ling, he'd dreamed of striking a big deal, but never managed to pull it off. Luckily, he'd bought some houses and cars with his first earnings, which brought in enough rent to support his family. This meant he had a lot of free time, which he spent dabbling in the stock market, playing mahjong, and meeting up with friends from the Moscow days for a few beers—anything to avoid going home to his nagging, menopausal wife, he said.

It got dark, but the *Beijing Station* sign was clearly visible through the gloom. We moved on to a bustling hotpot restaurant. He asked what I'd been up to, and seemed very interested in my work as a fashion editor—he thought it was a pity that I'd quit. When I said I'd still be doing interviews for the magazine, he wanted to know who with.

"Oh, Shu Qi, what a babe!" he exclaimed. "Those pouty lips. Is she as hot in person?"

In the hotpot grid, each ingredient bubbled away in its own compartment, like different people leading their own lives but all stewing in the same broth. Tiancheng took the cigarette from his mouth so he could put in a scalding chunk of mutton, followed by a mouthful of cold beer. It was strange—this man looked nothing like the way I remembered him, yet he exuded a nineties aura. Trains, Moscow, intoxicating dreams of striking gold. That was his golden age. Like Auntie Ling, he thought the best times were over, and the present was a confusing mess.

The hotpot restaurant was in a mall and closed early, so we went on to a bar. He picked the place: an Irish pub by the river, complete with billiard table and soccer on the TV.

"I ran into one of the old Moscow guys a couple of days

ago," said Tiancheng. "He mentioned your dad."

"What about him?"

"Your dad still owes him money."

"How much?"

"A lot, especially with interest, since '93. He's been looking everywhere for Luhan, and if he finds you, he'll probably pester you to pay up too."

"He didn't find Luhan?"

"Nope. I haven't seen her for more than ten years either."

"Oh, I always wondered if you were still together."

"No, just like you wanted." He laughed.

They'd kept seeing each other for two years after Dad's death, he said. She moved house, cut her hair short, and got a job at the cosmetics counter at a Wangfujing mall. When there weren't any customers around, she sprayed perfume onto a tester card and wafted it vigorously around. He went to see her a couple of times, and she asked what he smelled. Something sweet, with a hint of sandalwood, he said. Huh, she said, I can't smell it myself. She locked Granny Qin in the apartment while she worked. One winter's day in 1995, the old woman flung open all the windows while it was snowing and caught pneumonia. Half a year later, she was dead.

Tiancheng thought Luhan might start afresh, which she did—unfortunately, by falling in with a bunch of Christians. Not the quiet Bible study, church on Sunday sort, but the ones who spent every minute of every day thinking of redemption. She disappeared for a while after that, and her neighbors said they'd seen her leaving with a middle-aged woman, carrying a suitcase. Tiancheng started drinking heavily and seeing other people. A short while after meeting his current wife, they got married.

"I might not be as good as your dad, but if Luhan had stuck with me, she'd be doing okay," he said. "She's always been stubborn. Bashes her head against a wall and tells herself that's fate."

He met Luhan one last time, when she showed up at his apartment late one night. His wife, two months pregnant by now, was spending the night at her parents' home. Luhan hadn't eaten, so he took her to a nearby restaurant. Despite the heat, she was wearing a bobbled long-sleeved turtleneck. She looked fragile, eyes swollen and skin flaking off her pale lips. She'd quarreled with the Christians, she said, having finally realized they were just using her. Sweat was dripping off the tip of her nose. He handed her a napkin and said, I'm glad you've come to your senses. She said, They're ridiculous, they want God all to themselves, so you need to go through them to be saved. She ate fast, not seeming to notice what she was putting in her mouth. Lend me some money, she said, I was staying with a believer and now she won't let me have my stuff back unless I pay her rent. You can't afford to offend these people, they'll say bad things about you in front of God. He asked where she was going next, and she said she didn't know, but God would show her the way, he would cleanse her of sin. She took a long drag from her cigarette and blew smoke in his face. This would once have been entrancing, but he could see it meant nothing to her, and now it meant nothing to him either. Listen to me, Luhan, he said, you aren't sinful. Of course I am, she said agitatedly. That's why God kept me here, so he could cleanse me.

After the meal, he took her home. She took off her sweater and lay sprawled on the rug. Although his desire had faded, he still made love to her. It felt inevitable, a necessary ending, the most basic ending a man and woman could come to. Her body was stiff, and her eyes remained fixed to the turning fan. Just like when they were eating, she didn't seem to realize what was going on. Afterwards, she got her cigarettes and sat on the bed smoking, leaving ash all over the pillows. I know you like me, she said, but it's not possible between us, what happened just now means nothing. She seemed afraid he would love her, unaware she was no longer loveable. Of course it means nothing, he said. Just before dawn, he took her to the bank and withdrew some money. Not enough to pay her rent—he had a child on the way—but enough to placate the former roommate. And that was the last time he saw Luhan.

The night before I left Beijing, Luhan had promised me she would go on living alone. Maybe she was already prepared then to cut herself off from everyone but her god. In my mind, her life had come to an end after Dad's death. That might have been better—but no, life is long, and we must go on existing even in utter despair. Tears rolled down my face. "If it were now, I'd want the two of you to be together," I told Tiancheng.

That's the last thing I remember. Next thing I knew, it was dark and the chairs were upside down on the tables. A server was dozing off at the bar. When he heard me stirring on the couch, he looked up and said, Good, you're awake, your friend didn't know where you lived—he said to give him a call. I looked at my phone, but it was dead. Outside, it was almost light. I stopped by the flower stall at a roadside market and chose a bunch of pinks, then I sat by the river for a long time before getting the metro home. I'd been delaying my return, afraid not of Tang Hui's anger but his disappointment, that hurt look in his eyes.

I didn't explain, and he didn't ask. All he said was could I please stop seeing my father's old friends? I didn't reply. What was I supposed to tell him, that I'd started having dreams of matryoshka dolls again? That I thought I was getting to the heart of the mystery? I'd never be able to explain why this secret meant so much to me.

I did see Tiancheng again, and he told me the story of Wang Luhan and my father, as well as the bigger story around them. After that, instead of dreaming of Russian dolls, I lay awake at night, waiting for daylight to appear in the window. In those moments, I felt like hurrying back to Southern Courtyard and telling you what I knew—

but did you need this secret? Perhaps you didn't care. It had been so long, surely no one cared.

This is the story Luhan told Tiancheng after my father's death, probably not long after I left for Beijing. You might not want to hear this, she said, but I have to let this out—he's dead, after all—and you can forget it afterwards. But Tiancheng was a good listener. He knew he would remember every word, and carry the tale where it needed to go.

Half the stories in the world take place because of weather—in this case, a storm. It was raining so heavily that Grandpa and Wang Liangcheng could barely make any headway, even with their umbrellas. They ran to the nearest shelter: Dead Man's Tower. There, they found your granddad unconscious—his tormentors had gone, leaving him there. No one knows what happened next, but he ended up with a nail in his brain, and was soon in a vegetative state. Wang Liangheng killed himself. Out of fear or guilt? No one could say. But Wang Luhan believed what she'd heard him tell her mother: he hadn't done anything.

Later on, she often thought how if it hadn't rained that day, she and my dad might never have been anything to each other but neighbors—nodding to each other in the street, perhaps saying hi. Then they'd have been sent down to different parts of the countryside, been allocated different jobs when they returned to the city, married and had children, meeting up only when they came back to Southern Courtyard at the New Year, asking after each other's spouses and kids, then quickly departing. One of many, many acquaintances acquired over a lifetime, not even worth mentioning.

But it did happen. And that nail pinned them together.

In just a few months, Wang Luhan's world changed. Her father hanged himself, her mother hid in the wardrobe, and her big brother was stuck in Beijing. She was left to hold together the tatters of this family: taking care of her deranged mom, cooking and cleaning, doing everything around the house. One time, she lost their food coupons, and searched for them in the street till dusk. The next day, she had to steel herself to borrow some from their relatives. Another time, she was making her way home with a cart-load of coal when a couple of teenagers stood in her way as she was coming down the hill. One of them was your dad. He'd been hassling her in the name of revenge. They over-turned her cart so the coal rolled down the path and got buried in the snowdrifts, then they stamped on it for good measure before swaggering away. As Luhan was picking up the broken pieces of coal, Dad came along and helped her. He'd been following her from a distance, like a shadow, loyal and useless. While she was being bullied, he'd done nothing but watch. Head lowered, Luhan said, Go away, this is none of your business—aren't you all supposed to be avoiding me?

It's true, she was a pariah—but where should he draw the line? On the surface, they were very different—her father was a suspected killer who'd committed suicide, her mother had lost her mind, and her whole family was destroyed, while his was completely normal, just living peaceful lives. In reality, though, she was the daughter of a criminal, and so was he. His father refused to tell him any-thing, but he knew he couldn't evade responsibility. The difference was, he had to pretend to be a normal person. He told her about how unbearable this was, the weight he felt when he was with his classmates, how their fanaticism made him uncomfortable—he worried the day would come when they denounced him. He kept having the same night-mare: them hanging a placard around his neck and march-ing him around Southern Courtyard, then hauling him up onto a platform in the middle of the field. He didn't like being at home, where he couldn't breathe. His dad was always frowning and silent, his mom did nothing but weep quietly, then she'd place her hand on the Bible and pray, Lord Jesus, I plead for Your mercy. She can't have had much confidence in God, otherwise why ask him so many times and so loudly? His little brother tuned everything out, and sat beneath the lamp studying. He was just a couple of years younger than my dad, but he seemed completely unaware of what was happening—though perhaps this was a sign of maturity. At dinner, they bent over their food and didn't say a word to each other. The house was terrifyingly quiet, nothing but the sound of chewing, as if they were all gnawing on someone else's bones.

He said to Luhan, I know I can't help, but if I can at least be with you, I won't worry as much.

Every time Luhan stepped out of her building from then on, she'd look up at the second story window where it was very likely my dad was sitting, watching out for her. She'd start walking slowly, and before long he'd show up behind her, following her to the market, the grain store, the second-hand shop. They were always far apart enough that anyone seeing them would have thought they just happened to be walking in the same direction. Sometimes she'd speed up and dart around a corner, trying to shake him off. When this first happened, he got agitated, but then he learned to take a short cut and wait for her up ahead. She'd be unsurprised to see him there, and would walk past as if nothing had happened, then it would be back to the usual shadowing, right up till she went back into her building and disappeared from his sight.

This secret friendship continued until the day she went to the market by the river on the edge of town. Your dad and two other boys grabbed hold of her, tied her hands behind her back, and pulled an old woolen hat over her head, covering her face so she couldn't see. They spun her around by her braid so many times she lost count. Then the grip loosened, everything went quiet, and they seemed to vanish. Unbearably dizzy, she stumbled forward, trying to find a tree to lean against. Instead, she stepped into nothingness and plummeted weightlessly. As water covered her head, she heard my dad calling her name.

The river wasn't deep, but Luhan didn't know how to swim, and her hands were still tied. It was December, and the icy water was draining the warmth from her body. As her feet touched the bottom, she saw her father's pale brown eyes quietly watching her. She stopped struggling, no longer cold. She waited for him to come and lead her away, but instead he turned and vanished. Then a pair of hands took hold of her, and when she opened her eyes, she was being towed to shore. Although it was evening, and daylight was slipping away, it somehow felt like dawn, like the sun was struggling free of the clouds.

Many years later, Luhan ran into my dad at an embassy party. Someone was talking about going swimming in Beidaihe. Dad turned to Luhan and said, "Have you learned to swim yet?"

She shook her head. "My legs are strong, though, I can tread water a long time." They both laughed. After a while, she said, "I actually knew the river was in front of me. But I wanted you to show yourself, to let them all see you."

He smiled grimly. "I knew it."

"What did you know?"

"That once I got involved with you, I'd never be able to free myself."

That dawnlike evening, he'd followed her dripping wet to her home. She gave him some of her brother's clothes, and hung her own padded shirt over a chair by the stove. Her mother stuck her head out of the wardrobe to ask who was there. No one, she answered, undoing her dripping braid. Her hair was tangled, but she dragged a comb hard through it, relishing the pain, leaving snapped-off bits of hair all over the floor. He sat by the stove, gulping down his tea. She poured him some more, then warmed her hands on her own mug, not drinking. Her mother stuck her head out from the wardrobe and eyed them warily. A moment later, they heard a tinkling sound, and liquid trickled from the wardrobe. Luhan grabbed a towel and ran over.

"You did that on purpose," she said.

"I couldn't hold it in."

"You did it on purpose!" she screamed, then stormed into the bathroom to rinse out the towel. She didn't want to lose her temper at her mother, but couldn't stop herself. Her mother could get better if she wanted to. Luhan leaned against the sink, sobbing. Dad stood by the door a long time before going over and taking her wet hands. Cloth had been tacked over the bathroom window, and now the wind made it swell, like a frozen sun shining down on them.

From that day, your dad started bothering my dad too—asking why he was always with Luhan, trying to get him to admit he'd conspired with Wang Liangcheng. Dad allowed himself to be screamed at, and never responded. Your dad showed up at Grandpa's house with a gang. Grandma was home alone, and they started asking her about her relationship with the criminal Wang Liangcheng, until Grandpa came home and chased them away. Grandma was so terrified, she stayed in bed for days after that. She summoned Dad and told him to stop seeing Wang Luhan. Stay away from her, she said, or you'll ruin this family.

It's already ruined, said Dad.

To avoid any more interference from your dad and my grandma, he stopped following her around. Instead, he told her to stay safely at home and visited her every day, bringing charcoal, groceries, and other supplies. He also brought a little something pilfered from home, perhaps a steamed bun like a mantou or a couple of baozi, or if he was lucky, a strip of pork belly or some rendered lard, at which she'd clap her hands with delight. Later, he stole money and ration coupons, which he rolled up and smuggled in the lining of his padded jacket. One time, he was taking cash from a drawer when Grandma walked in. He quickly retreated from the room, but it turned out she'd known what he was doing all along, she'd just been pretending. After that, he regularly helped himself from that drawer. They had an unspoken agreement: she would leave him money and keep his father in the dark, while he would make sure no one saw him in public with Wang Luhan.

He started bringing books to Luhan's place, which they would read in the dim lamplight of the outer room. A classmate's brother was a leader in the Red Guards, and Dad borrowed some of the foreign novels he'd confiscated. Although she couldn't understand many of them, Luhan loved these —they gave her another world into which she could escape from her poverty-stricken home. *Anna Karenina* was her favorite. She was drawn to the train and Moscow, and senselessly adored the resonance and wintry cadence of the name *Vronsky*. Dad borrowed and returned the book quite a few times, until finally he traded it for a harmonica. He placed it in Luhan's hands one evening, and she kept it by her side always, eventually bringing it to France and Africa. When they reunited many years later, and she accompanied him to Moscow behind her husband's back, he noticed the book quietly lying in her leather suitcase, in the swaying train carriage. She smiled desolately and said, Maybe Anna Karenina is our destiny. The book met its demise during one of their regular quarrels: she ripped it to shreds and flung it out the window.

Dad often stayed for dinner. Luhan's dad had been an excellent cook, turning his wife into a picky eater. Dad quickly learned how to cook the Jiangnan way: always add an extra scoop of sugar and a splash of wine. He later began inventing his own recipes, mostly successfully—Luhan's mom would happily eat them and ask him to make the same thing the next day. Strangely, she didn't seem to remember who he was, but trusted him all the same. Soon he took over the cooking altogether, while Luhan did the prepping and washing up. They wore Luhan's parents' aprons, as if playing at being the man and woman of the house, while Luhan's mom was like their child, fussing over her food and throwing tantrums.

Whenever Luhan's mom had one of her attacks, this short-lived peace would be broken; Dad wasn't just staying late for dinner, but also because this was usually when they hit. When evening arrived and the building grew busy with people returning home—bicycle bells ringing, children running and screaming, sizzling and smoke from the many kitchens—Luhan's mom would pull down the tacked-up fabric to stare out. As the sky darkened and the windows lit up, she'd sit in the gloom and tremble, screaming her husband's name at the walls and empty air, imploring him not to abandon her.

"Don't be scared, it wasn't your fault. So what if it was your nail, you didn't do anything ..." she said over and over, as if repetition would change her husband's mind. Again and again she returned to that night, fruitlessly trying to wrest him back from the god of death.

To my father, these words felt like an accusation. Although Luhan's mother's eyes were unfocussed, he still felt her gaze on him. They had to hold her down and make her take her meds before she would calm down, otherwise she would start pulling out her hair and banging her head against the door, or charge into the bathroom and try to climb up to the window. They were always exhausted by the time she stilled. As Dad left, Luhan wouldn't meet his eyes.

"It's okay, Mom, everything's all right," she would say, gently patting her mom's back.

Dad knew Luhan blamed him for the family's situation, each of her mom's episodes a reminder whose fault this was. This was a wedge between them. If she hadn't had an attack for several days, Dad and Luhan would grow close again, only to be driven apart by the next flare-up, which caused the thawing sections of Luhan's heart to freeze solid again.

Eventually, Luhan delayed her mom's afternoon naps, then gave her a sedative so she'd sleep into the evening. This meant she wouldn't go to bed until the small hours of the morning, but Luhan willingly put up with this in exchange for peaceful afternoons belonging to her and Dad alone. She'd do the laundry as he read to her from a novel, urging him to repeat the loveliest sections, slower this time. He acted out the funny bits, sending her into gales of laughter. Or they'd share an apple, and compete to see which of them could get the longest piece of peel—until she got good enough to take off the peel in a single length. On sunny days, she couldn't resist removing the tacks and letting the light in as she wiped the sill, humming. Speckles of sun danced on her face. For a brief time she was able to forget her mom's existence, and recovered her lively disposition. Many years later, Dad told her that at these moments, her smiles were like comets soaring through the night sky, and he wished he had a jar to store them in.

One day, Dad gave her a shuttlecock. She'd intended to try it out for a minute, but was having so much fun she couldn't stop kicking it—until she realized her mom had woken and was watching her from the doorway. She hastily caught it and held it behind her back.

"Look at you, having so much fun," said her mom.

"I'm not, Mom."

"A little thing like that, cheering you up."

Luhan bit her lip and swept the droplets of sweat from her brow, removing the traces of her momentary happiness.

Is it dark yet? her mom muttered, going to the window and pulling aside the cloth. Almost, said Luhan. She felt something brewing inside her, like illness.

Her mother refused to leave her torment—that felt like betrayal—and she wouldn't allow Luhan to leave either. Any pleasure was disrespectful, and therefore forbidden. Her mother was an arm reaching from the past and dragging her back into the dark hole of memory. She understood a cruel truth: she would have to leave her mother for there to be any possibility of happiness in her own life. As an adult, she moved far from home partly out of circumstance, but also partly from self-preservation. Many years later, when she found out her brother had been diagnosed with late-stage cancer, her immediate thought was that this was a summons, and she would have to return to her mother's side.

Her brother, Wang Guangyi, had been in Beijing all this time. They'd sent him to the Ministry of Foreign Affairs after college. He didn't go home for a couple of years after what happened to his father. One time, he and a colleague were on a trip to Tai'an, and he didn't even get off the train when it passed through Jinan. He didn't want anyone to know about his family—it might drag him down. He'd always felt guilty about that. When the ministry allocated him an apartment in 1972, although it was small and run-down, he still wanted to bring his mother and sister to live with him. By coincidence, he came back to Jinan just after your dad had led a group of people to ransack Luhan's home. The stove had been kicked over and had set light to the curtains, leaving an entire wall scorched black. Shell-shocked, her mother had retreated into the wardrobe. Luhan was unfazed—she was used to these scenes. The strangest thing for Guangyi was that my dad was there, balanced on a stool, putting up new curtains. It was Guangyi who seemed like an outsider, standing awkwardly in the middle of the room and getting in everyone's way. He remembered who my dad was, of course, and this made him even more determined to bring his little sister away from this place.

Luhan didn't want to go, but her brother insisted their mother needed a change of scene for her health. She could come back in a few years, he said, when the Chengs had stopped making trouble. Luhan tried one excuse after another to stay behind, but Guangyi wouldn't listen, and bought them all tickets right away. They would leave in a few days. He asked, What are you so reluctant to leave behind? She avoided his gaze, shaking her head.

She spent the next few days packing, with her brother by her side the whole time, so she wasn't able to let my father know about the move. Finally, she slipped away, claiming she had to return her library books, and ran straight to Grandpa's apartment, where Grandma answered the door and was startled to see her. Before she could react, Dad had darted out the front door and was sprinting down the building stairs with Luhan. Just like before, they walked one behind the other to the rear of the library, where there was a vacant lot overgrown with thigh-high grass. Luhan told him everything that had happened. Dad was silent for a while, then he said, Actually, you ought to go, you'll only suffer if you stay here. Furious, she tried to argue, but Dad didn't seem to be listening. He wore a bitter smile, as if he'd always known things would turn out this way. I knew this would happen, he said. Picking up a pebble, he started scrawling on the wall behind him. Luhan tried to tell him about her feelings for him, but she hadn't done this in all these years, and now she found herself unable to. He'd said he knew this would happen. That meant he'd never expected to stay with her. Of course he hadn't—she was a criminal's daughter. She'd forgotten they weren't the same.

Holding back her tears, she said, Will you come and see me? I don't know, he said, still scribbling. She nodded. Fine, then I'm off. She walked very slowly, waiting for him to catch up with her. All the way home, she thought he'd surely take a shortcut and appear in front of her. Walking back up to her apartment, she strained to hear if he was calling her name. At home, she waited for him to visit. She didn't sleep that night, and kept going to the window to pull aside the curtain and stare out. The next morning, she waited downstairs for a long time. At the station, she put her luggage on the train, then ran out to stand beneath the *Jinan Station* sign. The attendant called her when the whistle went. Only as the train pulled out did she give up hope. Slumping against the seat in front of her, she burst into tears.

"Heartless. You didn't say a word to me when I left," she said when they met again many years later.

"I did. On the library wall."

"What did you say?"

"Not telling you."

Xie Tiancheng said when Luhan got to this part of the story, she paused and asked him, Do you think the words he wrote are still there? Should I go and see? Then she added, Muyuan wasn't heartless, just pessimistic, he didn't believe anything good could last, so when he was about to lose something, he'd already be defeated by despair and pride, and not realize he should try to hang on to it.

She tried to hang on. Three months after leaving Jinan, she wrote him a letter, which was probably intercepted by his mother. She wrote another, but that didn't reach him either. By the time of the third letter, he'd been sent down to the countryside. She made a trip back to Jinan in 1979, and learned that he'd been accepted into university and also gotten married. This wasn't surprising—she felt as if she'd heard the news she'd been waiting for all along. The day before she was due to leave, she went to his school. It was raining that day, and she was soaked by the time she got to his dorm. His roommate said he'd gone home for the weekend, and when he heard she was an old friend of Muyuan's, he presented her with a copy of the Poetry Society's journal. She took Muyuan's umbrella and walked through the lawns and shaded avenues of the campus, past the cafeteria and sports field. She paused in the shelter of the teaching block and flipped through the magazine till she found some of Dad's poems. When the rain stopped, she folded the umbrella and walked back to the gate.

The following year, she got married to one of her brother's classmates, who was eight years older than her. He'd majored in French and was also in Foreign Affairs. A year after that, she followed him to Algeria, and then Senegal. To the foreigners, she was just a diplomatic wife, a reserved Chinese woman. No one knew she was a criminal's daughter. They weren't able to have children, which was a shame, but the two of them had a good life. Sometimes her husband felt more like a travel companion—they were always settling down in new countries, saying goodbye to each new house just as it started to feel familiar. Time lost its moorings, and somehow twelve years passed. If not for the date printed on the bottom right corner of her photos from this era, she wouldn't have been able to put them in chronological order. Always in a dress and pearls, in one tropical country or another, smiling by her husband's side.

If she hadn't run into my father, Luhan said, she'd probably never have left her husband. But that night, she looked across the crowded party, and immediately recognized the man she hadn't seen for twenty years. She felt dizzy, and a jolt shot through her body, waking her from a very long dream. Then he was walking towards her, and her tranquil life of more than a decade collapsed explosively behind her. The happiness she'd relied on suddenly felt fake. She'd never go back to it.

The following week, she didn't accompany her husband on his next trip, but set off for Moscow with Dad instead. They snuggled together on the train, gazing out the window at the bleak mountains and snowy lakes. He looked at her and said, You make my life meaningful again. Her heart tightened. The man next to her was much more downtrodden than he'd been in his youth, his bright eyes now full of ashes. She pressed his hand and said, I'll always be with you, you'll be happy every day from now on. He nodded. Of course, he said, we'll surely be very happy.

After coming back from Moscow, Luhan asked for a divorce. Her husband received this unexpected news with sangfroid. Peering at her through round gold-rimmed glasses, he said, Do you need more time to think about it? No, she answered. Very well, he said, then let's do it before the end of the month, I'm leaving for France then. The next time she saw him, he was on TV, having been appointed the ambassador of some African country. By his side was a woman in a pearl necklace, smiling serenely.

Dad asked for a divorce around the same time, and though Mom said no, they knew it had to happen sooner or later. He moved in with Luhan, and they were happy for a while. Life together felt familiar, intimate, just as it had in her gloomy apartment. He read novels to her, they cooked together, standing by the window to share an apple—though any of these activities could be interrupted by a surge of desire. Sex replaced language, and became their most important means of communication. Even amid this ferocious joy, a strand of fear told her something would break them apart. She never told my father—some words, once spoken, become stone, and remain there forever. She chose to believe this feeling was a hangover from the dark past that would gradually fade.

When her brother got cancer and her mother had to move in with them, she must have realized this might endanger their relationship. Time had erased most torments, but she vividly recalled her helplessness in the face of her mom's episodes. To be honest, she hadn't missed her mom much during her time abroad. She knew her mom was being taken care of and was doing well, and that was enough for her. Sometimes a whole month went by without her phoning. She felt anxious when she heard her mom's voice, as if it might fracture and explode at any moment. And so she'd fled for more than a decade, but now there was no getting away.

Dad seemed fine with this development—back in the day, he reminded her, her mother had been part of their makeshift household of three. He'd missed her. They'd only felt helpless because they were still kids. Now he was a powerful grown man, he'd give her mother a good life. He said all this while he was tipsy, though. Drunks tend to be more optimistic. He promised to quit, but instead drank more after her mom moved in. They began to quarrel.

Tiancheng asked Luhan whether she and Muyuan would still be together, if her mom hadn't moved in.

There's no if, said Luhan, Muyuan was right, it was always the three of us—my mother always came between us.

Luhan extinguished her last cigarette in the ashtray full of heart-stained butts. As dusk fell, a song came from behind the closed bedroom door: *"Stars fill the night ..."*

*

Another time, I asked Tiancheng about the nail. Did Luhan tell him why Grandpa and her father wanted to harm Cheng Shouyi? No, he said, she didn't, but Cheng Shouyi was in charge, and often behaved tyrannically, so everyone hated him. Luhan claimed her father had been too tolerant to take revenge this way—which meant it was probably Li Jisheng's idea. This was a time when bad people did bad things, but good people did bad things too, and it's impossible to say what really happened. Wang Liangcheng ended up dead, so all the guilt got heaped onto him. I said, Maybe he killed himself in order to take the blame. Tiancheng laughed and said, Jiaqi, you think too highly of people. No, I said, I've heard and seen a lot that makes me think Wang Liangcheng really was like that. What about your grandfather? said Tiancheng, What do you think he was like? I was silent for a while. I don't know, I said. My idea of him is getting less and less clear.

Tiancheng said, I saw him at your father's funeral. He looked very stern—he frowned the whole time, and didn't shed a single tear. After the ceremony, while people were going up to Luhan, he went outside alone. I followed and offered him a cigarette. No thanks, he said. I lit my own cigarette and asked if he was staying in Beijing. He was leaving that night, he said. I said a few words of condolence and he thanked me very politely, looking straight ahead. Somehow or other, I felt his body exuded righteousness, which made me respect him—he didn't seem like the sly, treacherous man Luhan had spoken of. When everyone had left, he went up to Luhan and said, Muyuan's mother has a broken leg and couldn't be here, but she wanted me to tell you to come to us if you need anything at all. Luhan kept her head lowered, not saying a word. He handed her a fat envelope, put on his cap, and walked out.

Do you think Luhan forgave Grandpa? I asked. Tiancheng said, That's not important, the main thing is, she felt guilty too. As if someone had to take on those sins. Your dad was dead, so the burden fell to her.

Tiancheng and I sat beneath a parasol outside the coffee shop. It was springtime by then, and a light drizzle was falling. The air smelled of grass. Thank you for telling me all this, I said. He replied, I enjoy seeing you, so I've dragged the story out—but that really is everything I know. I said, I remember all your stories. On the anniversary of Dad's death, I cover every nail on the wall in red paper, then I sit and wait for him. He said, Don't forget to have some coffee so you don't doze off. Don't worry, I said, I won't.

Cheng Gong

Would you believe it, I met Wang Luhan too. You'll never guess where—Room 317. That place was like a little theater, and we all had our dramas there—you and me, Auntie and

Tang. Granddad's body had some magnetic force that drew us all there, so our stories could unfold in front of him.

Not long after you transferred out, I went to Room 317 and sat with Granddad for a while. Then I put the spirit intercom into a cardboard box, sealed it with tape, and stuffed it under the bed. I walked out, closing the door behind me.

Any memory connected with you remained shut behind that door. I didn't return for a year after that. Once, waiting by the hospital entrance for Auntie to finish work, I looked up at the easternmost window and saw two gray pigeons taking flight from the sill.

A figure in the window peered through the murky glass. A hallucination, I thought—no one entered the room now, except the nurse who came to feed him and stayed maybe ten minutes a day.

When Auntie appeared, I asked if she could see the person in the window. She glanced up and said no, then dragged me away. As we walked, I realized her eyes were full of tears, and when I asked why, she said Room 317 was where she and Tang used to meet. The autumn they were dating, their liaisons had been in the grove of trees, but the air was turning chilly. Then Auntie had a brainwave—her word—and she led Tang to Room 317. After that, they went there every day. I couldn't imagine them being intimate in front of Granddad, his beady eyes flicking past their passion.

A year after you left, the hospital built a new block of wards on the vacant land to the north, remember that? When they were laying the foundations, apparently they dug up a nest of white snakes. We went to have a look and didn't see anything, but kept spreading the rumor anyway. The new building was eight stories tall, full of beds. Now the block that 317 was in could be for long-term patients—those who were paralyzed, those with dementia, those who'd paid and cajoled their way in and now refused to leave—most of whom could not be treated, and simply needed to be kept alive. The hospital cared for them as a way of caring for its superfluous, useless workers, those who couldn't be asked to leave, dispatching them to the old building to perform these simple tasks. Auntie wept from terror, afraid she'd be relegated in this way, but they allowed her to remain in the pharmacy.

It was the women of fifty or so who got sent to the old building, bad-tempered and fraught from menopause. Food and medicine were delivered irregularly, and the sheets changed more seldom than they should have been. Patients who lost control of their bodily functions got shouted at. Relatives complained, but the resultant reforms were purely symbolic and ineffective. The director preferred to put his energy into opening more branches and applying for medical awards; no matter how well the old block was managed, it wouldn't help his advancement. Better to keep one eye shut, as long as they didn't actually lose any patients through negligence.

Everyone called it the ghost block. Auntie and I knew Granddad was being treated badly, but it's not like he could complain. They probably weren't moving him, wiping him down, or changing his diaper as often as they should, and he might have bed sores or atrophied muscles by now, maybe a weakened heart. Neither of us went to check on him, nor did we dare tell Granny, in case she picked a fight with those fierce nurses. Besides, living among the gossips of Southern Courtyard, could she really not know? Like us, she was probably only feigning ignorance. Knowledge would have meant confrontation, because her reputation for taking no nonsense wouldn't have allowed her to let this slide. She was old now, and didn't have as much energy for scrapping, especially over something so trivial. It made no difference to her whether Granddad lived a few years more or less. The whole family made a tacit agreement not to mention Room 317. Maybe we were just waiting for news of his death.

This news never came. In the fall of 1995, I went back to the room. I'd just had an argument with Granny—I was almost fourteen, and frustrated that I still had to share a room with Auntie. I'd asked her to move some of the boxes from the living room so Auntie could sleep out there with her. Granny refused—the boxes weren't going anywhere, and she couldn't afford another bed. Auntie, meanwhile, was sulking at what she thought was my rejection of her.

In a temper, I decided to run away from home. The next day was Saturday, and I set out first thing in the morning with my rucksack. At the long-distance bus station, I stared at the unfamiliar names on the signs, watching the buses disappear one by one in clouds of dust. Noon arrived, and I still hadn't mustered enough interest in any distant place. I felt more and more fearful, and a voice mingled with hunger and exhaustion urged me to go home—but it felt shameful to retreat so soon. It only counted as running away if you stayed out at least one night. Where could I go? Granddad's face floated into my mind, like a bodhisattva materializing.

It was evening by the time I got to the third floor and walked to the room at the far end. The door to 317 was ajar, and in the light spilling across the floor I thought I saw a woman's silhouette. I looked inside and there actually *was* a woman there, giving Granddad a sponge bath. She lifted his sweater and gently wiped his chest and belly with a damp cloth, then turned him over to do his back. When the sweater had been carefully smoothed back into place, she raised him a little so she could pull his loose white thermal trousers down to his ankles. Grabbing the towel that had been draped at the foot of the bed, she ran it over his calves. As her hands, through the towel, slid along his shins, I noticed his legs quiver, even though they'd been motionless all these years. She fetched the flask from the window sill and crouched down on the other side of the bed. A cloud of steam rose into the air—she must have poured the hot water into a basin to rinse the towel. The splashing and her being momentarily out of sight made me anxious. Eventually, she stood again and spread the hot towel, which the twilight dyed scarlet in its haze of vapor. She folded it into a rectangle and passed it from hand to hand until it had cooled down enough, then ran it over his groin and inner thighs. Lifting his limp penis, she tenderly wiped it, her damp fingers stroking its purple-brown surface and hungry folds of skin. Slowly, she set it down into its thicket of white fur. I was breathing so fast I thought I might drown. My heart was beating somewhere outside my body. She got a tube of ointment from under his pillow and rubbed it into his bum, then held him up till it had dried.

I'd seen women wiping Granddad before, but these had been nurses doing a rushed, sloppy job. This was different—unimaginably patient, as if she wished she could go even more slowly, to prolong the task. Although she faced the door, she was too absorbed to notice me. Nothing in the world mattered more to her than cleaning Granddad.

When she was done, she returned the flask to the sill and pushed the window open. Only then did I realize it had been shut, probably to prevent Granddad catching a chill while he was damp. Leaning against the sill, she got a pack of cigarettes from her trouser pocket and lit one. A pigeon took off and she turned her head to watch it soar.

As she smoked, I made myself calm down and studied her carefully. She looked about Auntie's age, though her baby face seemed more suited to a younger woman—her dull eyes, slack jowls, and drooping lips seemed tragically out of place. Her hair was pulled back into a messy ponytail, leaving long strands dangling from behind her ears down to her shoulders. She wore a baggy indigo denim shirt, its sleeves rolled up unevenly.

She wasn't wearing a white coat and didn't look like a nurse. Besides, I'd never seen any of the nurses in this building behaving so tenderly. Who was she? A good-hearted volunteer? Someone from the church? I didn't really want to know. Better to remain in the scene I'd just witnessed, recalling each of her movements and how they made me feel.

I left when she put out the cigarette—that might have meant she was ready to go. Bumping into her would have meant explaining that the person in the bed was my granddad, and she might stop coming if she knew he still had family who visited. So I had to leave, if I ever wanted to see her again. I didn't go far, just to the fruit stand by the entrance, where I hid and waited for her to appear. She walked slowly to the bus stop across the road. The number 11 bus came and took her away. More people came along, and someone took her spot. I waited some more before heading home. Would I see her again? The uncertainty tormented me. I was almost home before I remembered why I'd gone to 317 in the first place—to run away from home, because I'd wanted my own room. But that wasn't important anymore. My mind was on higher things, and these annoyances now seemed minuscule.

She showed up at four every afternoon, and stayed about half an hour. After giving Granddad his sponge bath, she also tube-fed him, and changed his clothes and diaper— everything the nurses ought to have done. I watched her from the doorway, then lurked by the fruit stand till the number 11 pulled away. After two weeks of this, I got there a little early and ran into her in the corridor, on her way to fetch hot water. Flustered, I blurted out that the man in the bed was my grandfather. She said, Cheng Shouyi is doing very well, you can go. I'd like to stay, I said, I haven't seen him in a while. She said, Weren't you just here yesterday? I was silent. Give me a hand, kid, she said. Go get some hot water. I took the flask from her and said, My name is Cheng Gong. She nodded but when I got back with the hot water, she said, Put it over there, kid. I hustled to pour the water and hand her the towel, scared she'd tell me to go away.

Standing this much closer when she cleaned Granddad, I felt my heart throb with warmth. I said, A bad person did this—my granddad was a sharpshooter in the Liberation Army, and he'd have dealt with anyone coming for him openly. She ignored me, and I wasn't sure if she'd heard. Before leaving, she said, Don't let anyone know I was here. I nodded, Sure, good deeds should be anonymous.

I saw her every afternoon after that. After a while, I started skipping study hall and brought my homework to Room 317. I treasured the moments after she was done, when she would linger by the window for a while, and I would stand beside her. I had a lot I could have said to her, but silence was fine too. Sometimes she would produce an apple and peel it with her little knife, thumb on the back of the blade, the skin coming off almost transparent, round after round, a single unbroken strip. Her eyes never left her hand, enjoying this process. Then she'd slice it in two and offer me half. Is it sweet? she always asked, as if she couldn't taste it herself. It's sweet, I would say. I've loved apples since then.

As I walked her to the bus stop one evening, I couldn't resist asking where she lived. Far away, she said. I asked if anyone was waiting for her to have dinner, and she shook her head. Before I could ask any more, her bus arrived. She was wearing a woolen coat with orange and green checks that day, a beautiful garment, but from behind she looked sad and lonely.

In early spring the following year, Granddad had a high fever that resisted medication. His body twitched, his face turned purple, and there was white foam on his lips. The woman said, I'll stay with him tonight—this is just a hiccup and he'll be better soon, don't tell your family. I agreed—I hadn't planned to tell Granny or Auntie anyway. I didn't want them coming to Room 317 or going to see the director and demanding Granddad get moved to the new block, where there were too many nurses for the woman to intervene. Besides, I somehow trusted her to save Grand-dad, even though all she was doing was pressing ice cubes to his face and alcohol rubs over his body. When his temperature spiked, she cooled him every half hour all night long. I stayed very late, and skipped all my afternoon classes. Not only did I fetch her hot water, I also brought her food, including an apple from the fruit stand. It took a week for the fever to go down. Now Granddad had been miraculously healed, she fell ill and stayed away for two days. For two long afternoons, I paced the room, realizing I didn't even know her phone number. If she'd vanished, I had no way of tracking her down. When she showed up on the third day, my eyes dampened and I almost ran over to hug her. Instead, I shook her icy hand. She pulled away and said, Quick, go get some water before the line starts forming by the dispenser.

At the end of March, the university announced that your grandfather had been made a medical fellow. The happy news was plastered all over the campus noticeboard, along with a photo of your grandfather staring sternly ahead with pursed lips. I stuck a piece of gum on his forehead. The university held a grand ceremony for him. The middle school got half a day off so the students could attend. Everyone went except me—I got to Room 317 early and waited for her. When she showed up, she said, It's quiet here today, I went to get a new tube from the nurses but the office was locked up. I told her everyone was in the science auditorium because a professor—I refused to say his name—had been made a fellow. Oh, she said, absorbed in arranging Grand-dad's blanket. Then she paused and asked, That professor, what's his name? Li Jisheng, I said. She stood there absolutely motionless. After a while she said, A fellow, that's good.

She didn't say a word for the rest of the afternoon, and though she carried out her usual tasks, she seemed distracted. When I came back from fetching hot water, she'd finished feeding him, but the tube was still in his nose. She was staring at him, as if she'd forgotten the next step. She poured too much water into the basin, and though I tried to warn her, she scalded herself reaching in to test it. When I tried to help, she shoved me away.

Afterwards, she leaned wearily against the sill, but didn't light a cigarette as usual. She was staring at something in the distance through the window, and when I asked what, she said, Is the ceremony over? There are a lot of people walking around. I looked towards the campus, but the science auditorium wasn't visible, just a clump of grayish buildings melted together by dusk. Normally she'd be waiting at the bus stop by now. Her eyes remained fixed on that spot and her shoulders shook. I thought she was about to burst into tears.

She only stepped away and put on her coat when it had gotten completely dark. At the door, she turned and said, Could you do me a favor, kid? I immediately nodded. She paused for a while before saying, Go to Li Jisheng, tell him Wang Luhan wants to see him. Tell him to come here tomorrow or the day after. I'll be here all afternoon.

After she'd gone, I went to the grove and sat for a while. Overhead the tree canopies were like dark clouds with chunks bitten out of them by the wind, suspended in the night sky. I felt as if a blindfold was gently slipping from my eyes. Who was she and why was she here? I'd been avoiding these questions since I first saw her. I was supposed to have a keen nose for secrets—how come I'd never sniffed out the suspicion on her? I'd turned off my sense of smell. Answers to these questions might destroy a lot of things. I had to protect my feelings for her, to keep them from harm. I learned that from you. Your departure made me grow up a lot.

Secrets become secrets and get hidden away because they have the capacity for destruction. That's what drew us to them, two kids who loved digging up secrets. It's hard to say what it was that suppressed our childhood creativity, but we couldn't create, only destroy. Or maybe it's because in this country, destruction is always seen as the highest form of creation. It felt exciting to light the fuse of a secret and blast a hole in the world. Such mysterious joy in the instant of explosion. I was hooked, and even if the thing lay buried close by, between the two of us, I would still detonate it. A moment's pleasure, like taking revenge. Then I'd find myself standing in a shattered ruin. Your removal from my life might have seemed like chance, but I knew it was because of me, because I hadn't taken sufficient care of our friendship.

You once asked me, in the undergrowth behind the library, what a secret smelled like, and I said sweet, like a melon split open by ripeness.

On this spring evening, however, I thought I detected the true aroma of secrets: ancient and perilous, reminding me of lava and meteorites. Not sweet at all. My first impulse was to tell you, then I understood that would never be possible again.

The next day, I went to your grandfather's office in the new admin block, on the same floor as the school directors. He was there, but his doorway was crammed with people and cameras—two TV stations, one interviewing him, the other shooting a documentary called *A Day in the Life of a Fellow*. I left still holding my note—*Come tomorrow afternoon to Room 317 in the long-term patients block, Wang Luhan wants to see you.*

In the end, I had to go to his apartment—but what if your grandmother answered the door? Though Wang Luhan hadn't said so, I'd sensed this message needed to be kept secret. I perched on the rear rack of a bicycle parked across the road, idly ringing its bell. Finally, he showed up on his battered old bike. I followed him up the stairs, thrust the note into his hand, and fled. He probably hadn't had time to see who I was, and I didn't manage to catch a glimpse of his expression.

It was gloomy the next day—the dawn fog didn't dispel till afternoon, when it was already getting dark. The sky was the gray of a pigeon's wings, as if it had been painted for camouflage. Looking out from the third-story window, the steel-colored buildings looked large and flat, like a poorly executed sketch. Luhan and I had planned to air out Granddad's bedding, but this wasn't the weather for it. The heating hadn't been turned off for the season yet, and the gusts of warm air made me drowsy. We opened the door and windows a crack to let some of the heat escape. Luhan worked in silence. She was wearing a moss-green sweater I'd never seen before, which emitted crackles of static electricity when her arms brushed her torso.

A gust of wind swept into the room through the window, making the door creak. I jumped to my feet and Luhan swung around. We stared at the door, waiting for it to be pushed open.

But no one was there. He didn't come that day, or the next, or the next, or the next.

After a week of fog, we finally had a sunny day. Luhan said we should take advantage of the good weather to wash the sheets. It was as if we were back to a week ago, and she seemed just as focused, even a little frantic, once again treating these tasks as if nothing else in the world mattered. I followed her to the window, feeling a sort of happiness bloom in my heart. All my suspicions of her had gone like the dark clouds, and I hoped they'd never come back. I was suddenly very afraid Granddad would die, because he was why we got to hang out. If he wasn't around, we wouldn't be connected any longer, and would have no reason to meet. I lifted Granddad's bum in the air so Luhan could pull the sheet out from under him. His pupils gleamed in his swollen eyes, and a very faint smile appeared at the corners of his mouth. I hadn't looked closely at him for a long time, but he'd always been able to find ways of getting my attention and making me notice his existence. I understood now that this sealed body had unthinkable power locked up inside. There'd always been at least one member of our family who didn't want Granddad to die. First my dad, so he could extract ever more compensation from the hospital, then Granny, so she could get herself a bigger house, then Auntie, so she could keep her job. And now me, so I could keep seeing Wang Luhan. He seemed able to attract these things we wanted, and in order to get them, we'd have to sincerely pray for his continued survival. I had no idea if our prayers worked, but he looked healthier than any of us, as if he might go on forever, a living fossil.

The year passed quickly, and it was Christmas before I knew it. For a couple of years now, this imported holiday had been gaining traction with kids. Christmas cards, snow globes, white baubles adorned with red hats. Some of my classmates bought thirty or more cards, wrote identical messages in all of them, and handed them out like playing cards. Dabin was one of them, even though more than twenty of his thirty-odd recipients had never really spoken to him before. He liked giving gifts and pleasing people; no matter the outcome, he was satisfied. One Saturday before Christmas, he went shopping for gifts at Dongmen Market and dragged me along. The market was packed. People were grabbing greeting cards by the dozen—turns out the world was full of kids as generous as Dabin. Amid this chaos, Dabin opened a pop-up card that played a carol. Standing behind him, my attention was caught by another stall's glittering display. I picked up a leaf-shaped lavender barrette, its veins studded with gemstones that of course I now know were just plastic, but to a kid's eye they looked like shiny jewels. I held Luhan's face in my mind, then turned to a rack of earrings. Passing over the oversized loops and dangly ones, my eye lighted on a pair of pearl studs the size of my small fingernail, perfectly round with a milky sheen.

I hesitated between these two options. Luhan probably

needed a hair clip more. What if she didn't want earrings? I recalled the dried-out holes in her ears, which seemed to reveal her despair. Maybe wearing these would make her happier. I wasn't sure but couldn't resist the strong urge to see them on her. I paid for them, and the stallholder put them into a pink cellophane envelope. Dabin was still going through the Christmas cards, opening them one by one to make sure their batteries worked. I felt sad for him—he was taking such care, yet there wasn't anyone he truly wanted to give something to.

I put the earrings in my trouser pocket, but the next morning, my trousers were gone.

"Oh, I washed them," said Auntie, raising her eyebrows. She wasn't usually this diligent. I knew she always checked pockets, and asked her about the earrings.

"Earrings? What earrings?" She blinked. "Oh right, they're on the window sill."

I went over and found the pink envelope, the pearl studs still inside. Auntie followed me. "Who are those for?"

"A girl in my class. It's her birthday." I clutched the envelope tightly.

"Anyone I know?" She tickled my armpit.

"No. A new transfer student."

"You know what, they remind me of your mom. Have I told you about the time she used some of her own money to buy some government bonds? There was a lucky draw, and she got third prize: a pair of earrings. Clip-ons, so she didn't need to pierce her ears. She was so afraid of losing them, she never actually wore them."

I put the little envelope deep in my schoolbag and zipped it shut.

"Does this girl have pierced ears? She's a bit young for that—don't her parents mind?" Auntie said, smiling. I shouldered my bag and walked away.

The earrings were a mistake—because they were obviously a gift for an older woman, and especially because they made Auntie think of my mom. It had been years since Mom had departed our lives, but Auntie couldn't let go of this one-sided rivalry. She was loyal to her emotions. Later, she told me she hadn't slept a wink that night. Those earrings were so like my mom's, who else could I have been giving them to? Unable to imagine there might be another adult woman in my life, one she didn't know, she'd come to the conclusion that I must have secretly stayed in touch with my mom. This theory expanded through that long night of tossing and turning, and by dawn, Auntie was convinced that Mom must be back in town, that she was meeting me regularly, and that she might soon be taking me away.

On Christmas Eve, Luhan and I said "See you tomorrow" at the bus stop, puffs of white breath coming from our mouths. I thrust the pink envelope into her hands, turned, and ran away—smack bang into a middle-aged man. Before he could recover, I was far in the distance.

When I saw Luhan the next day, her hair was down over her ears as usual. I wished I'd bought her the hair clip too—that way at least one ear would have been exposed. I helped her wipe Granddad down, and as she stood, her hair shifted to reveal a bare earlobe. She must have noticed my disappointment, but didn't offer an explanation. Quick, go get the hot water, she said, and on your way back, stop by the nurses' station and tell them the window latch is broken. They won't care, I said. Anyway there's wire holding it shut, isn't there? She nodded and walked over to the window, prodding at the wire looped round the faulty latch. The north wind is turning tonight, she said. There might be a storm. She was pinching the backs of her hands. These tics I'd once found endearing now enraged me. I grabbed the flask and stormed out.

I was still angry as I stood in line for hot water. Not about the earrings, but the way she had no regard for me. She didn't see anything I did. Despairing, I almost didn't go back to the room. It didn't matter whether or not I was there. I imagined her alone, working away every afternoon like a piece of machinery. Withered hands extending from her flappy sleeves, brushing dust off the bedside table, picking up the flask and slowly walking downstairs. Leaning against the window sill, producing a wrinkly apple and peeling off its snakelike skin. Without me there, who would tell her the apple was sweet? It didn't matter—she couldn't taste the sweetness herself anyway. I could see her unwinding the wire from around the latch each time she opened the window, and securing it in place again, loop after loop, like it was her own hair. The white plastic coating flaking off the wire, exposing its metal insides. Eventually, it would get replaced. In the evening, she'd walk out with her hands in her coat pockets, cross the road to the bus stop, and hop on a number 11 bus. She lived in the cracks of this world, and no one noticed her existence except me. I had a strong sense that she was all alone. No family, no friends. I might have been her only connection in the world. You wouldn't understand the deadly attraction of that word: *only*. Back when I thought my mom was mine only, she actually belonged to Dad, and then on those sunny afternoons, to Uncle Candy. I thought you were mine only, but you wouldn't stop talking about your father and about fucking Siberia and Moscow. In the end, you followed him to Beijing. Auntie almost left me for Tang. All of you had other people you cared about, and I felt defeated by these rivals. I hate competing, hate the panic of losing. Luhan was different. She didn't care about me, but she didn't care about anyone else either. No one was going to take her away. I felt safe placing my heart with her.

By the time I came back with the hot water, I was no longer angry. I'd fix the latch the next day, I decided.

I brought a toolbox from home the next day, and after school I went straight to the hardware store. All the latches looked similar, and I hadn't thought to bring the old one with me to compare. I got a couple in different sizes, which clanked in my pocket as I ran.

I got to the third floor and found the door ajar. Shadows flickered in the light of the doorway, and yelling was coming from inside, a familiar partridge squawk among the jumbled voices. I shivered, steadied my nerves, and walked in.

Auntie and Granny had their backs to me, facing the window, where Luhan was standing.

"Stop pretending, Wang Luhan, I know it's you," said Granny.

"What are you up to, sneaking in here?" Auntie was so worked up she sounded like a different person.

Luhan's lips remained firmly sealed.

"What are you plotting?" Auntie walked over and shoved her.

"I suppose you're angry that the old man is still alive? You think your father was wronged, and you won't be happy till you've killed my husband? Let me tell you, if you did such a thing, no revenge would be enough—not even if your whole family was wiped out," shrieked Granny.

Auntie shoved Luhan again. "Who sent you here?"

Luhan staggered and steadied herself against the sill with both hands.

"God sent me." She was looking ahead, her gaze fixed beyond them.

Auntie and Granny exchanged glances.

"God brought me here for a chance of redemption."

"You want redemption? Then do what your dad did, and hang yourself," screamed Granny.

Luhan shook her head. "Suicide will only increase our sin."

"You could die a hundred times and that wouldn't be enough." Granny spat at her. "There's something wrong with your brain. Probably inherited from your mom. Get out of here!"

"You can't make me leave. God sent me here to take care of him."

"Don't let us see you here again!" Auntie grabbed Luhan's arm and dragged her towards the door, looking like a fairy-tale monster. Luhan held on to the bed.

"You have no right. God wants me to stay."

"To hell with your god. You just want to feel good about yourself." Granny laughed icily. "I'll never let you feel good. While I'm around, you won't set one foot in this room ever again."

"Why not ask what he wants?" Luhan pointed at Grand-dad. "He knows everything. His soul is still in there. He said he wants me to stay."

"Enough of your nonsense!" Granny caught hold of Luhan's hair while Auntie wrenched her arm. Luhan was still clutching the bed, which rattled as if it might fall apart. Granddad remained placid. Stuck full of tubes, he was like a goldfish in a bowl, living in an invisible container. Could he really see everything that was happening in front of him? I looked at him curiously. His eyes were still swiveling around, and his lips wore an enigmatic smile.

His soul is still in there. Luhan's words made me think of you. You'd said something similar, standing in almost the exact same spot. That's why I made the intercom. It chilled my heart, reminding me of how I'd wanted to rescue my family's honor.

Luhan was like you, I realized, a descendant of my enemy, exuding mystery and menace. You both enchanted me, and I gave myself up to you. Then you broke my dreams apart and made me see how lowly and helpless I really was.

Watching the three women fight filled me abruptly with loathing. Not looking back, I ran down the stairs, the latches still clanking in my pocket. When I got to the entrance, I dropped them in a trash can.

First thing the next morning, Granny marched up to the head nurse and demanded to know who'd given Luhan permission to take care of Granddad. The head nurse was a woman in her forties, known to everyone as Auntie Yun. I'd seen her in the corridors, dressing down nurses much older than herself in a shrill voice. Her face was long and so was her philtrum, which meant she was going to live to at least a hundred years. She didn't look apologetic in the face of Granny's ranting. The nurses didn't enjoy caring for Granddad, she said, but here was Wang Luhan willing to do it, and doing it well, so what was the problem? The hospital didn't have anything against volunteers, and the head nurse didn't care what kind of grudges were involved—the old man was in his bed, and not one hair on his head had been harmed. Granny asked if they could change the lock on the door, but Auntie Yun said no to that too. Why not just bring him home, she added, you can install as many security doors as you like, not a fly will get in. Granny was furious, but that did no good. She stood sentry at Room 317 that afternoon, and when Luhan showed up, Granny chased her away with a broom. She came home to shovel down some dinner, then went back to the hospital, this time bringing a wooden plank with nails hammered into it. Sure enough, Luhan came again, and got attacked once more. Apparently she got a cut on her forehead and bled quite a lot.

Meanwhile, I was stuck at home with Auntie watching over me. Granny had threatened to break my legs if I snuck off to see Luhan again. Auntie sighed and pulled me in for a hug. You've got it wrong, she said. You saw her taking care of your granddad so you think she's a good person—you're too naive. No one does good deeds unless they expect something in return. And you're so good to her ... Auntie looked down, bit her lip, and muttered, You never got me earrings. I pushed her away, ran into the bedroom, and climbed up to the upper bunk.

The following day, Granny brought a locksmith to install a new lock on Room 317. She and Auntie had the only keys.

Then she went to the hospital director and said this so-called volunteer Wang Luhan was actually plotting to murder Granddad, could he please keep her away. In order to get rid of Granny, the director ordered Auntie Yun to assign a different nurse to the room. This new nurse, face like thunder, got the key from Granny, who told her over and over not to give it to anyone else. Still uneasy, she kept coming to the hospital every day. Once, she clocked Luhan pacing near the building, but Luhan walked away quickly when she caught sight of Granny.

Each day I came home right after school, ate dinner early, and went straight to bed. If I couldn't sleep, I lay there listening to music, wearing out all my tapes. I didn't let myself think. If I felt a thought forming, I turned up the volume of my Walkman until my eardrums hurt and my scalp went numb. Many years later, Dabin was going through a period of heartbreak—he'd managed to meet Peixuan while they were both studying in the US, but was still so intimidated by her he simply couldn't bring himself to ask her out— and so I suggested this method to him; he almost deafened himself. After more than a week of this, I woke up with a perfectly blank mind, apart from the single thought: I'll never see Wang Luhan again. Too late to put on my headphones. A year's worth of memories flooded in, seeing her every day, carrying out mundane tasks, every little detail. Her sluggish eyes, devoid of warmth, her stiff, mechanical movements, like a thick layer of winter ice on a lake. It may have been wishful thinking, but I'd felt very close to her, almost breaking through the ice to the warmer currents below. Maybe she was still pacing by the hospital. I had to find her, before she disappeared into the crowd.

I skipped school and hung out at the hospital, but she never showed. I decided to go back at the weekend, but on Saturday morning, before I'd set out, Auntie got a phone call to say Granddad had gone missing.

I hurried over there with Granny and Auntie. The nurse

in charge of Granddad said she'd found the lock jimmied open first thing in the morning, and the patient was gone. Granny was shaking. She grabbed the bed to steady herself, then ran from the room, followed by Auntie. I stayed put. The room looked strange. There'd always been a person in that bed, as far back as I could remember, lying there in all seasons like an item of furniture bolted in place, part of the room. That's why I felt so at home here, connected to this place. Now, that was gone. Room 317 was just another hospital room, unrecognizable. Once again the unspeakable horror of the familiar becoming unfamiliar.

I looked at the bed. The sheets were sticky after not being washed for several days, and I could make out a vaguely human-shaped outline. I tried to imagine how Luhan could have carted away Granddad's substantial physique, but all that came to mind was her look of determination. She'd been guided, summoned, and given permission to do this. Not only was her faith strong, she had courage to match. Nothing could stop her.

In another room somewhere else in the world, she would half-fill a basin with hot water every afternoon, dampen a towel, undo Granddad's clothes, and wipe him down. Her careful hands moving through the steam. I felt a gush of warmth and shed a few tears. I would never see her again.

The hospital spent a lot of time investigating, and the police were involved too. The main question was how Granddad got transported out. There were only two exits, front and rear, and both were locked at nine. The sentry said he hadn't seen anyone suspicious. There was one other route, via the morgue, but that was also locked. Everyone who held a key was questioned, with no results. Another theory was that he'd gone over the exterior wall, which was lower on the north side—but even if this had been an inside job, they'd still have needed a ladder, and there were no markings on the ground. Luhan was the prime suspect, of course, but the last official trace of her dated back to 1993, when she'd signed to acknowledge her husband Li Muyuan's death certificate. The case was never solved, and Wang Luhan was never found.

So Granddad's gone, and Granny died this summer. There's nothing keeping me here any longer. You know the story of Exodus? I want to be Moses—part the Red Sea in two, and walk right out of here.

Li Jiaqi

All the booze is gone, but I'm not sleepy at all. Is it still snowing? The sky's getting brighter, but the light looks different from normal dawn. Maybe it's reflecting off the snow. This grayish light isn't coming from the sun.

In the spring of 2000, I met Yin Zheng—he was the editor at a literary journal where I'd submitted some of my poems. I bought one of his collections, and dog-eared quite a few pages. When I saw he was having a book signing, I skipped my evening class to be there. It was raining, and there weren't many people in the bookstore. Yin Zheng gave a short speech about his understanding of poetry and his worries about the state of the literary environment. He recalled the poetry societies and poetry journals of his college days as belonging to a golden age of literature. I hadn't realized he'd been one of Dad's classmates—he was five years younger than Dad, and looked much more boyish. I'd forgotten that the first intake after they brought back college entrance exams included a wide range of ages, because so many people had had their education interrupted. He didn't mention Dad's name, of course, but every word he uttered seemed to circle around Dad. Afterwards, I brought my book to the front for him to sign. He looked at me and asked which university I was in. I said I was still in high school. You must be very busy with homework, he said. Thank you for coming. He also asked if I wanted to join them for a drink at a nearby bar afterwards, and when I didn't answer right away, he added, You can have juice.

There were seven or eight of us, huddled under umbrellas, heading for the bar. The others were all his students. They ordered beer, so I did too. One of them suggested we all recite a poem. I chose one from Yin Zheng's collection. He said, That poem hasn't received much attention, but I'm very fond of it. He wrote it many years ago for a girl in his class, while he was a visiting a scholar in America. Everyone asked him to say more. The girl was American, he said, and had smoky eyes and many arm tattoos. Thanks to a heroin habit in high school, she'd spent time in rehab, and was only now in college at twenty-four. She still looked like a wreck, and didn't participate much in class, as if she wasn't really present. For some reason, Yin Zheng kept finding his gaze drifting towards her as he taught—she made him feel calm. He wrote this poem while the students were doing a test, and he had a lot of time to observe her. Why is it, he asked, that sometimes dangerous things can make us feel warm, a mystical sensation? He laughed. A male student asked if he'd thought about confessing his feelings for her at the time, and a female student asked if he had a photo of her, they all wanted to take a look. This was the first time I'd heard a man around my father's age talking about his own feelings. Had Dad spoken like this with his students? You ought to give her this poem, I said. Every poem is a letter, and this one belongs to her. He smiled and said, It was a long time ago, and if not for this poem, I'd have forgotten she even existed. I must have looked downcast, because he said, I know young people like you don't want to believe that situations change, but it's inevitable, strong feelings can't last for very long, just like in chemistry, some materials have violent reactions, but those are short-lived and in the end they're transformed into a different substance. I wished I could tell him my dad's feelings weren't like this.

The students kept saying they wanted to go, but Yin Zheng insisted on staying a little longer. He'd had a lot to drink, and his eyes were gleaming. We stayed till the bar closed at three in the morning. It was drizzling. He lived near my school and offered to see me home. There weren't any taxis around so we walked. I held an umbrella but didn't unfurl it. The air was chilly, and each droplet felt like a weak electric jolt as it landed on my face. To my right, Yin Zheng was tall and skinny, and his footsteps were light. When we got to my school and he saw the locked gates, he realized I'd planned to wait here till they were opened at dawn. He said he would wait with me, though the temperature was falling and we were both shivering in our thin clothes. After a while he said, This won't do, come wait at my place.

We went not to his apartment but to his office: two small rooms in a loft, one lined with bookshelves, the other with a desk and a single bed. He poured me some warm water and asked, Will you get into trouble for staying out? Will the teacher call your home? I said I didn't know. He said, You don't seem worried at all, don't your mom and dad care what you get up to? I said it didn't matter, tonight had been all worth it. I'm very happy today, he said, it wasn't easy getting this book published. Not many people read poetry nowadays. He poured me more warm water and said, You should sleep, you have class tomorrow. I said I wasn't sleepy, and asked if he could teach me to write poetry. Sure, he said, bring me whatever you've got and I'll tell you what I think. I repeated, I believe each poem is a letter you write someone, to say what you otherwise couldn't say. Without a *you* in mind, I wouldn't be able to write anything. He asked who I was writing to, and I said my father. He laughed and said, I thought you were going to say a boy in class you liked. I said I found boys my age childish. He looked at me and said, Growing up too soon isn't always a good thing. I shrugged and said I didn't care.

The sky was brightening, and sunlight came through the little round window, illuminating the dust that slowly rose and fell through the air. The room smelled thickly of old books, reminding me of visits to the library as a kid, Dad taking me to borrow the bound *Children's Literature*. Whenever Dad came into my mind, the memory would keep expanding until it had taken up the entire space. The light and scent of this room made me think he ought to be among us. My father's name is Li Muyuan, I said, you might know him. Yin Zheng looked at me, startled. Of course, he muttered. Were you close? I asked. Yes, he said. We were classmates in college, then we chose the same research area and stayed on at that school after graduation, in the same teaching and research office. He stood to get more water, then turned back to say, He'd be thrilled if he knew you were writing poetry.

I asked many questions: What was Dad like at college? Did you often get together to read poems? I was pleased to hear he respected Dad's talent and thought he was a very fine poet. Then he said, Tell me how you get on with your mom. I said, She was supposed to marry this guy when I was eleven, but I ran away to Beijing so they had to postpone the wedding, then the guy got cold feet. Now my mom and I live with my aunt in a crowded little house and I try not to go home too often. He said, Now I understand why you've grown up so quickly.

There was more light in the sky now, and my eyelids were growing heavy. He said, Why don't you lie down, I'll wake you when it's time to go. I tried to hang on, but I couldn't keep my eyes open and dropped off as soon as I was horizontal. After some chaotic dreams, I woke to find a blanket over me. He was in a nearby chair, reading. I sat up tentatively. Backlit by the sun, his face looked like a bottomless well. Time for school, he said gently.

Before I left, he handed me a plastic bag containing some sliced bread and a couple of books. Breakfast, he said, this is all I have here. I looked at the books: foreign anthologies of poetry, old ones with library markings on the spine. Don't lose those, he said, they're out of print.

On the weekend, I photocopied both books, and went back to the loft to return them. He'd said he was usually there in the afternoons, which I'd taken to mean I was welcome to visit. Sure enough, there he was, writing a letter to a friend. There was a pile of manuscript paper on the desk. It was a cold day, and he wore a gray sweater-vest. His shirt sleeves were rolled up, revealing a luxuriant growth of hair on his forearms. He seemed delighted to see me, and produced a large bag of snacks from a desk drawer, as if he'd been expecting me to turn up. I showed him some of the poems I'd written, and he actually remembered the two I'd submitted to him before. He said, You ought to come to the next recital and share these with the group. My new poems showed improvement, he said, and asked why I hadn't sent him any more. Keep writing, he insisted, don't stop.

I stayed till dusk. He got a phone call and said to me, I'm meeting my wife for dinner, why don't you join us? I expect your dorm doesn't feed you on weekends. Along the way, he told me his wife Meng Jing had been a dancer until a leg injury forced her to stop, so I shouldn't mention dancing in front of her.

Meng Jing was already at the restaurant and didn't seem surprised to see me, so I guess Yin Zheng must have told her I was coming. For all I knew, he'd told her everything, including that I'd spent the night at his. She didn't seem to mind, though. Maybe this was nothing to them. She kept her eyes fixed on me as I walked over, and when I'd sat down, she said, You slouch, you ought to pay more attention to your posture, sitting up straight will make you look more confident. I replied that I didn't lack confidence, but what I actually wanted to say was, What's it matter, it's not like I want to be a dancer. We were in a dimly lit Western restaurant. White candles burned on the tables, and the silverware gleamed. I ordered a Caesar salad and grilled cod. A waiter came by and poured wine into our glasses, and Yin Zheng suggested we toast to a beautiful weekend. They ate out almost every weekend, he said, and Meng Jing always chose excellent restaurants. I'd never tasted wine before, and found it sour.

It was strange sitting with them. I felt a sense of déjà vu, as if I were with my father and Wang Luhan. Wanting something to happen too much turns it into a recollection of an event that never was. In this false memory, when I went to Beijing in 1993 they brought me to the famous Maxin's restaurant, then we visited the Shichahai lakes and the Forbidden City, and had a fantastic time, taking lots of pictures. By the time I came out of my reverie, Meng Jing had pushed her plate away, having only eaten a tiny bit of her steak before declaring she was full. Was it more elegant to have an appetite as small as hers? I was starving, though, and wished I could have gobbled down her leftovers as well. Languorously, she watched me eat, then suddenly asked, How old were you when your father died? Eleven, I replied. Car accident? she asked. Yes, I said, He was drunk and collided with a truck. She said, Some people think it was suicide, what do you think? I stared blankly at her. Meng Jing! Yin Zheng roared. She kept her eyes fixed on me, waiting for my response. No, I said. You don't think he killed himself? she said. Mm, I don't think so either. Your dad always wanted to come out on top ... Meng Jing! said Yin Zheng, Please drop the subject. Then he summoned the waiter and said we should order dessert.

I stood up and said I was going to the restroom. Instead, I walked out of the main door. Outside, I burst into tears. I couldn't stop crying. I went into a nearby convenience store to buy cigarettes. The shopkeeper scrutinized me the way you would an adrift young woman. I walked back with a cigarette in my mouth, fumbling with my lighter yet somehow unable to make it work. I was almost back at the restaurant when I collided with Yin Zheng. I looked at him for a moment, then buried my head in his chest. I looked everywhere for you, he said, gently stroking my back. In that moment, whether from loneliness or some other reason, I wanted very much to win this man's love. To steal him away, I should say. The three of us, sitting in that dingy restaurant, brought me back to the warzone of when I was eleven. I'd wanted to steal my dad's love back from Wang Luhan, but death put a stop to all that. Maybe now that interrupted game of chess could resume.

When Yin Zheng first met Meng Jing, she was a dazzling dancer with hordes of suitors after her, and he was just one among many. He waited many years till she finally agreed to marry him, but even after that, he still felt like just another suitor who had to keep trying to please her. In order to fund the lifestyle she wanted, Yin Zheng was forced to constantly travel abroad to give lectures, and serve as a consultant for cultural agencies he despised. He told me all this another afternoon, looking tormented. He always had to accompany her to various parties, he said, getting drunk with a bunch of people he didn't know, dancing in crowded rooms. She thought that would bring him inspiration. Ridiculous. Then Yin Zheng asked me, Do you know an American author called Fitzgerald? I shook my head. He said, Meng Jing is like Fitzgerald's wife, she has an urge to destroy her husband.

I asked what happened to Fitzgerald in the end, and Yin Zheng said he drank himself to death. I thought of my father and felt sad. Yin Zheng said, I asked my sister if I could use these rooms of hers, so I could have a space of my own. Am I disturbing you by being here? I asked. Not at all, he said. You're welcome anytime.

I started visiting every Saturday afternoon, and then we'd go for dinner, without Meng Jing. I didn't ask how he'd explained this to her, but she never called again. We often talked about her, though. He had no one else to complain to—to the outside world they had to play the part of the perfect couple. I asked if he'd thought of leaving her, but he said she wouldn't be able to go on living without him. Anyway, he said, at my age, I don't have the energy to fall in love again, or rather, I'm unable to, it's something you lose as you get older. I said, I think I've already lost it. He laughed. Silly girl, he said, how old are you again? I liked when he called me silly girl; it felt tender. In a poem he wrote around that time, he called me "my most special friend." I didn't copy it down because I could easily memorize poems then, and thought I'd never forget it. Now, though, I can only remember the opening lines. It probably wasn't his best work, but the main thing was that he was writing again—he hadn't managed a single word for over a year before that. Jokingly, he said I was his muse. Some afternoons, he sat at his desk while I lounged on the bed and read, eventually dropping off. As I drowsed, I'd be aware of the scratching of his pen on paper, of his cup leaving and returning to the desk. These sounds protected me, they made me feel safe. Then I'd wake up and find the room full of pale blue light—impossible to say if it was twilight or dawn. If only it were dawn, I'd think, so I wouldn't have to go back and spend a long night alone.

Every Saturday felt like a holiday. The rest of the time, I studied hard, as I'd promised him. I want to get into your school, then you can be my professor, I said. He said, No, you ought to go to a better university. This went on till the winter, and just like that the first year of the millennium was almost over. New Year's Eve wasn't a Saturday, but there were no classes and I didn't feel like going to a party, so I went to the loft. I found Yin Zheng getting ready to go out—Meng Jing's friends were having a gathering. I stood at the doorway and watched him clearing the teacups from his desk, putting on his jacket. You could not go, I said. He said, I promised, I have to. He patted me on the shoulder but I didn't move. Could you come back here after your party? I asked. It depends, he said. I'll be waiting here, I said immediately, It doesn't matter how late you are. He sighed and said, Fine, but if I'm not back by the time your dorm locks their gates, don't keep waiting, okay?

But I waited long past that time. I didn't know if he would come back, but I didn't want to be anywhere else. When he finally showed up, I was dozing on the stairs. I felt a hand on my head, warmth cascading down me from my scalp, then he helped me up and kissed me on the forehead. Silly girl, he said softly. I wept. He led me inside, poured me some warm water, and produced some fruits and a piece of cake he'd bought along the way.

It was almost midnight, and fireworks kept shooting up into the sky. We stood at the window watching them. Could you kiss me again? I said. Call it a New Year present. He hesitated, then bent to kiss me. In the glow from outside, the kiss was red, then green, then white, blazing in different directions, shattering into tiny stars. Sparkling, then vanishing. We broke apart and went back to the window. I said, I want you to want me. In silence, he went over to his desk. Is that okay? I said. Come here, he said, sit down. I shook my head and remained where I was. I must look like a giant joke, I thought, but my dignity was nothing in the face of the vast desire inside me. I asked, Is it because I'm your old schoolmate's daughter? No, he said, it's because you're still a child, and this is foolish talk. I'm eighteen, I said. But you're still a child, he said. He led me to the bed and pressed on my shoulder to make me sit.

Jiaqi, he said in a rasping voice, You're so innocent and pure, it makes me feel guilty. Of course I like you, of course I do, you're adorable, but what can I give you? I'm starting to get old, I'm only going to become more distracted and dull.

Sometimes when I argue with Meng Jing, I realize I'm relishing the fight. For a long time now, I've had no creativity to speak of, and my poems stink of decay. I know what those young poets think, they think, Ha, this old guy's past it, but he's not aware, and so he keeps scribbling away, how ludicrous. Really, your dad might have died young, but that's no reason to be sad—that way, he'll always be a fighter.

He looked at his hands, as if wondering if they still grasped anything. After a while, he looked up and said, Jiaqi, you're very like him, you're a fighter too. But I hope you'll take care of yourself. Don't damage your weapons, and don't get hurt. Though getting hurt leads to growth, so maybe that's good too. I said, You mean like now? Exactly, he said, looking over my shoulder at the wall. He mumbled, I've hurt you, I know I have.

My last memory of that evening is the stark, clear light of dawn seeping into the room, like the smoke from a bonfire that had grown cold, still smelling of burning leaves. For a second, I imagined him dying in this room many years from now, laid out on the bed behind me, sunken eyes, slightly parted lips, one hand on his chest, reaching for the thing he called his heart.

I didn't visit him again after that. Summer arrived, and with it the rainy season. I began waking up earlier and earlier, and realized I could hear the dawn chorus even through a storm. The birds seemed to be somewhere else, not in the rain. I sat up in bed and read Fitzgerald. My favorite was *Tender Is the Night*.

The day after I got my university acceptance letter, I went with some classmates to Qingdao, and we had a barbecue on the beach. I stuck a bamboo skewer into a pigeon's scrawny carcass, rapt at the rupturing sound of taut flesh being pierced. A stereo blasted Coldplay and everyone got up to dance, pretending they were on drugs. My classmates knew where they were going, I thought, and knew what sorts of people they would grow up to be. That was the greatest difference between us.

I went swimming alone that evening. The sky was getting dark, and a strong wind was rising. The few people in the water were making their way back to shore, while I headed out to sea. There was nothing out there, I knew, but I wanted to see for myself. Just like a few years ago, when my dad took me to the park and insisted on reaching the other side of the lake. Waves pushed me farther and farther out, but I struggled back on course. The water was so cold I could feel my bones creak, and my legs grew numb. My movements slowed. I tried closing my eyes and sinking into my breathing, which I could feel was getting ragged. Night descended over the ocean and the stars winked out. I waited for a bigger wave to engulf me, for saltwater to pour down my throat. My fear vanished, my consciousness faded.

From somewhere I couldn't see, a ship's horn sounded, like a plaintive voice in my ear, like a summons. It went on a long time, getting closer, a lifeline flung at me from a great height. I thrashed my way to the surface and caught hold of it. Swimming in circles, I realized I had no idea which way the shore was. Swinging my arms as hard as I could, I propelled myself through the water. My strength was ebbing, and I was losing sensation. I might shut down at any moment, but still I kept going. When I finally found the beach, my body felt like it was falling apart. I lay motionless on the sand.

That September, I left for Beijing. The city had expanded since my last trip there, and the roads were wider than before. Despite the changes, it still felt familiar. My father's departure had solidified my connection with this place. I'm back at last, I said to myself. Even after eighteen years in Jinan, Beijing still felt more like my hometown.

A classmate from high school became Yin Zheng's student and would often bring me news about him. In our third year of college, she told me Yin Zheng had gotten close to a girl in his class. The girl's mother had come to the school and caused such a ruckus, everyone in the department knew what had happened. Yin Zheng didn't show up the following semester, and the rumor was that he'd been transferred out. Was the girl pretty? The most vulgar question, and still I asked it. So-so, said my classmate. He was infatuated with her.

I pretty much stopped going to class after that, just sat in my dorm room and listened to music, tears seeping from my eyes. I'd never loathed myself so much as now. I didn't deserve love, no one would ever be infatuated with me. One night, I got all the poems I'd written over the last two years, which I'd been storing at the bottom of my suitcase. There was a vacant piece of land behind my dorm building. There, I lit a match and threw one page after another into the flames. It crossed my mind that I should hold on to the ones I'd written for my father, but I could no longer remember which ones those were. Yin Zheng and my dad had merged into a single person, to whom I'd written all these verses. I threw them all into the fire, watching the papers curl and the words wither. They seemed to float in the air for a second before they vanished. Then I noticed someone standing on the other side of the flames. When they'd died down, he said to me, You know, you're not supposed to light fires here. I said nothing, just walked away.

That guy was Tang Hui. He started asking me out on movie dates after that, and to be honest, his interest in me was a salve for my wounded dignity. When I'd regained my senses, I realized I ought to explain the situation to him, so I told him what had happened with Yin Zheng, and said he should forget about me. Silly girl, said Tang Hui, that wasn't love. He pressed my hand to his chest. This is love, he said, can you feel it? You might not feel anything for me right now, but you will one day.

But I didn't, not until the moment Tang Hui left me. That evening, I stood in the doorway watching him pack, which reminded me of Dad leaving us, of the devastation he left behind. I heard a cracking noise, and understood I was bidding part of myself farewell.

When I stopped seeing Xie Tiancheng, Tang Hui said to me, Now that you've sorted out what happened with your father, I hope you'll stop getting entangled with these people from the past. Please let this be the last time, please respect me. Perhaps in his heart, no longer optimistic, he knew this wouldn't be the last time, but he can't have imagined the next time would be with Yin Zheng. In his words, I'd gone in a big circle, and ended up at my starting point.

It happened at something called "Parting and Reuniting," the final event of Poetry Week last summer. The pictures of the two special guests were on the poster. I stood by the bookstore, staring at his face. The dark, slightly bulging eyes. The self-mocking smile. He'd gotten older. Maybe I only went in order to verify that. I felt suddenly sad, as if I was the one who'd abandoned him. My resentment disappeared in an instant, leaving only tenderness. I went into the bookstore and sat in the back row. I'll just see him, I said to myself.

He was animated all through the talk, often interrupting the other guest. He had many opinions to share, and wouldn't let go of the microphone. Then his eyes passed over the audience and suddenly halted. He kept talking for a moment, but quickly wrapped up and was mostly silent after that, staring at the floor. His answers to the audience's questions were also sparse. Realizing that something was up, the emcee ended the event early. While everyone surged to the front to get their books signed, I picked up my bag and headed for the door. Jiaqi, someone called from behind me. I took a few more steps, stopped, and turned back. He was smiling at me. Jiaqi, we meet again. He held out his new collection. On the title page, he'd written my name and signed it with the date.

He brought me to the "Night of Poetry" he was attending

that evening. We stood at a high table near the back of the room. I could see the field outside through the plate glass window. There'd been a wedding or something that afternoon, and they hadn't taken down the floral arches. A couple of children were running between them in the dusk light. People kept stopping by to say hi to Yin Zheng. Between, we stood in silence, just looking at each other. Finally Yin Zheng said, You might not believe me, but I had a feeling you were in Beijing. Every time I'm here, I hope to bump into you. Are you well, Jiaqi? How time flies. I still think of you as the little girl in school uniform.

A man came by and said he had a couple of people to introduce. Yin Zheng left with him, but doubled back to say, Don't go anywhere, okay? He waited till I'd nodded before going.

The room got crowded. A guy who looked like a college student kept staring at me, until finally he came over and asked nervously, Are you a poet too? I shook my head, and he went off. I had to go outside for some air. It was dark, and the sprinklers had come on, leaving the grass glittering. Workers were dismantling the arches, removing the roses first, leaving bare metal frames. At this moment, Tang Hui would be at home, planning our trip to Kyoto next month. But what did those beautiful streets and temples have to do with me? I would soon forget them, but I'd never forget this evening. Even if I hadn't spoken to Yin Zheng, I'd still remember it. I stood there, smelling the damp grass, the fallen roses. Clouds roiled through the summer night. The same sorrow I'd felt aged eighteen descended on me, like a benefaction. I understood it was only at these moments, when my emotions were awakened, that I truly felt alive. All those long, empty hours, waiting for moments such as these. Like a beam of light rescuing me from the shadows.

Yin Zheng came out and stood next to me. We stared out at the field. Beijing is lovely in summer, he said with feeling, though I always feel like I can't wait to leave this city, I can't stand it here. Why? I asked. It's too big, he said, and too noisy. More than a decade ago, I thought of transferring to a university here, but in the end I didn't. He looked at his watch. Jiaqi, shall we go? If you're not in a hurry to get home, shall we find somewhere to sit? He suggested the open-air bar at his hotel, which was nearby. We walked through the empty streets of the embassy quarter. Tall parasol trees stood on either side of the road, and the light from the streetlamps was soft as it mingled with the moonlight. Are you still writing poems? he asked. No, I said. Oh, me neither, he said. Because you're writing a memoir? I asked. He looked at me, startled. How did you know? Oh right, I mentioned it at the event. I'm getting old, writing even a little exhausts me. I'd hoped to finish it this year, but it looks like next is more likely. I asked, What are you writing about? He said, My childhood, the Cultural Revolution, college days, everything up to now, very long-winded, maybe no one will want to read it, but it's important to me. He looked at me meaningfully. I'll send you a copy, he said. We reached a crossing and waited for the lights to change. He turned to look at me and said, I remember the night I first met you; we sat outside your school. It had just rained, and the air was so cold—it must have been fall. It had actually been spring, but I didn't correct him. Perhaps he'd imagined an autumn night, and that had solidified in his memory.

The bar was packed—we grabbed the only free table. Yin Zheng looked at his watch and said, I need to make a phone call. He stood at the counter, holding the receiver, smiling. I downed a few mouthfuls of white wine and sent Tang Hui a text: Ran into a friend, home late, don't wait up. After a few minutes, he replied: Ok. Yin Zheng returned and we clinked glasses. He said, That was my daughter on the phone, she needs to hear my voice before she'll go to bed. I must have looked startled. He said, A few years ago, Meng Jing changed her mind and decided she wanted a kid, after all. It took a few rounds of IVF, but we did it. A girl? I said.

Yes, he said. She's five now. That's good, I said, Meng Jing can teach her to dance. He nodded. She's a good mother, he said, I hadn't expected that.

Wind rustled the bamboo that was growing against the nearby wall. He said, Jiaqi, do you still blame me? I looked at him. Huh? He said, Never mind. I poured more wine. Slow down, he said. When he realized I wasn't going to listen, he started drinking quickly too. I didn't mean to hurt you, he said, you know I worry too much. I nodded and kept drinking. He ordered another bottle. The waiter topped up our glasses. Watching him leave, I muttered, I don't know that, do you worry with other girls too? He looked at me and a strange smile slowly appeared on his face. Finally, I had attacked him, and asked the question that had been stuck in my throat. Its power was undiminished, and as I spoke the words, they hurt me again. My self-esteem was shattered. I waited for him to say anything, to save me. But he was silent, watching the bamboo, drinking.

After a long time, just as I'd thought the evening would end in silence, Yin Zheng sat up very straight and said, Jiaqi, there's something I should have told you: I was never your father's friend—we were more like rivals. When we put the poetry society together, we were both in line to be its leader. We were young and competitive, and neither of us would give way. He had his supporters and I had mine. Finally, I got tired of fighting, and stepped aside. Your father had his own ideas that he insisted everyone should abide by. For him, poetry had become something like power, a sort of religion.

Yin Zheng took a deep breath and said, I shouldn't say these things about your father, I know you respect him a lot. I did too, that's why I was so disappointed. I was sad when he stopped writing poetry, not just because I'd lost a worthy opponent, but also because I could imagine how painful that must have been for someone as ambitious as him. No one knows what happened. But, after all, talent is given by the gods, and can be taken back at any moment. Not that your dad would ever have admitted this. He claimed he'd stopped writing because he found it meaningless. He put his energy into teaching and scholarship, and I have to admit he was talented in these areas too. Then he published a scholarly book that didn't get the attention he thought it deserved, and lost an opportunity to be a visiting scholar in America. In despair, he started helping the department head with admin, in the hopes of being appointed his deputy. He had some radical ideas, and got into a fight with the head over those, which killed his chances of being promoted. Soon after that, he quit. Just like that, this outstanding personality vanished from sight. We later heard he'd struck it big doing business in Beijing—I wasn't surprised at all, I truly believed he'd succeed in anything he turned his hand to. Then the car accident ... For a long time, I couldn't believe this had happened. When he left Jinan, I'd thought our conflict wasn't over, and that we'd meet some day to resume it. Then I ran into you and thought, ah, this is how it's going to be. I didn't mean to deceive you, I just didn't want to show you something so ugly.

I said, So you thought it was too cruel to make me choose between the two of you, that only one of you could be a good person? He shook his head. No, the cruel thing is neither of us were good—there are no good people in the world. He took my cigarettes and lit one for himself.

The bar was closing, and the other customers were leaving. The outside lights went out. Yin Zheng stared at the candle on our table. He said quietly, I wrote a letter reporting your dad for his actions. One of his students told me the sorts of things your dad had said to them, and I replied, don't repeat that to anyone else, you'll get Professor Li in trouble. If I hadn't said anything myself, the whole thing would have gone away. Then one afternoon a month later, I was alone in the office preparing the next week's classes. I was tired, so I made myself a cup of tea. Dark clouds were racing across the sky—it was about to rain. The air pressed down on me. I reached into my drawer for some paper, uncapped my fountain pen, and wrote the letter without pausing. I didn't read it over afterwards, just put it in an envelope, walked downstairs, and dropped it into the department head's mailbox. A colleague walked past and I said hello. Back in the office, I ripped up the bottom sheets of paper that had the imprint of my words and stuffed the pieces in my pocket. Then I sat and finished my tea. It was still warm. The rain began, spattering against the window. Sweat was beading on my forehead, but I felt very calm, as if this had been an ordinary moment of exertion. This calm followed me afterwards, and even your dad's resignation didn't break it. I ran into him as he was gathering his things for the last time. We exchanged nods of greeting and I said, *The Compendium of Contemporary Chinese Fiction* will be out next year, shall I mail you a copy? Sure, he said, and closed the door behind him. It had been a few years since we'd actually spoken, and though we'd both been in meetings about this anthology we'd been editing together, we had managed to ignore each other. The compendium came out a year later, and I asked a colleague to pass him a set. Then we got the news about his car accident, and some people said he'd done it deliberately. I sat alone on the balcony for a very long time that day, smoking one cigarette after another. Finally, I convinced myself that a person's fate is decided mainly by his own character, and doesn't have much to do with other people. This kept me going until I met you. The first time I saw you, I thought there was something tragic about you that I was connected to. I've had complicated feelings about you: fondness, pity, guilt. When you looked at me with those too-mature eyes, my heart clenched, as if you could see right through me. That wasn't pleasant, but I couldn't resist you. I told myself you needed me—I would lift you out of the nihilism you'd sunk into. But when we were actually together, I felt I was the one being rescued—

the thought made me ashamed. That last night, your innocence hurt me. I couldn't do it, not just because of my family, or because you were still a child, but because our relationship would have started with deception. Please forgive me for not telling you this before. Perhaps you would have suffered less if I had, but then again, perhaps you'd have become disillusioned with the world instead.

He paused and shook his head. Still in a soft voice, he said, Maybe this is all excuses, maybe I just wasn't ready to deal with the past. Can you forgive me, Jiaqi?

I wiped the tears from my face and said, Are you ready to deal with it now?

He said, I've written about your father in my memoir, and said I was behind the anonymous letter. It wasn't an emotional confession, I just wanted to look objectively at who I was back then, including all the mistakes I made. Everyone's soul has dirty, ugly portions mixed in with the kind and good. There's no way to cut them out, all we can do is acknowledge them. I'm writing this book for myself, and if it has any value, it's as a way of dealing with my sins. For that, I thank you, Jiaqi. I'd never have written it if I hadn't met you. The motivation came to me in those dark days after you vanished from my life. This may be the most complicated thing about being human: acknowledging our mistakes doesn't mean drawing a line under them; as long as we're still drawing breath, we'll keep facing new tests, and we'll have moments of weakness.

He wrapped his arms around me, pressing my face to his chest. He was swaying, the delayed effect of alcohol or something else. His heartbeat thudded against my eardrum, then grew quieter. It was very still. The air was warm and damp. Weariness came over me, as if I'd finally stopped after walking a very long way. For a while, I thought I was asleep. I opened my eyes and looked up at him. I was certain he'd been crying. I kissed him on the lips and he kissed me back. Then I pulled back and he withdrew his arms to his sides. It wasn't alcohol, I now knew, the slow-acting substance was just time. After a moment, we looked at each other again. The sky was beginning to turn white, and birdsong came from high above us. My voice sounded like another me talking to another him, as time rushed past us. All these years, I'd wanted to find out exactly what kind of person my father was, but the more I found out, the blurrier he got. Each time I got closer, it was another farewell.

When we left the bar, the streets were silent and seemed wider than before. Sunlight gleamed on the road where it had been sprayed with water, a grayish light. When we parted, he said to me, This might have been the most special night of my life. Goodbye, Jiaqi.

Tang Hui was sound asleep when I got home. I sat by the bed a long time, waiting for him to wake up. Eventually, I dozed off, and woke to rumbling thunder—it had started to rain. Tang Hui had his back to me, and was emptying his clothes from the wardrobe. I looked at the alarm clock: it was one. Next to the clock were my bag and Yin Zheng's poetry collection.

I walked over to Tang Hui. "I'm sorry. Nothing happened."

"I didn't go through your things," he said. "Your bag fell over. But it doesn't matter. I'm going." He opened a drawer and grabbed his sweaters. A packet of mothballs rolled out and landed at his feet. Its scent had faded, lost in our mundane days, but we hadn't got rid of it. Now he picked it up and put it in the trash.

"You said you'd never leave me," I muttered.

"Yes, I'm going back on my word. While I still can. Or is it too late? I can't tell."

"I always knew you would walk out on me."

"I believe you when you say nothing happened last night, but at the same time, a lot of things must have happened. You always see the darker side of life, so what's happening now can't come as a surprise."

He closed his suitcase and set it by the wall. "Are you going to tell me you found a new clue about your father's past, so you had to meet up with someone from long ago?"

"It's not like that. Last night was the end."

"That's the only way you can feel alive, am I right? The rest of the time, you're a walking corpse."

"Please stop. It's all over, Tang Hui."

"Do you know what I think of your life, Jiaqi? You insist on occupying a history that doesn't belong to you. It's a form of escape, because you can't deal with your actual life. You don't know why you exist, so you hide in your father's era. You feed on that generation's scars. Like a vulture. You pick up scraps of his life, and piece them into a love story featuring him and Wang Luhan. A shame it's all imaginary, Jiaqi. Do you even know what love is?"

I stood motionless. Cold air seemed to rise from my feet.

"I just don't understand." He shook his head, picked up his umbrella and suitcase, and walked out. The window rattled as he slammed the door, then silence resumed.

Some time after this, Peixuan came back to China and I moved in with her. Grandpa began to reappear in our conversations, and also in our silences. Then Peixuan left, while I stayed on in the apartment another two months. Mom kept phoning and urging me to go back to the white mansion. Her repeated pleas merged into a single summons that grew clearer and clearer. I realized my journey of retracing Dad's steps was nearing its end, and decided to come back here to see Grandpa.

Was Yin Zheng right? Does confessing and pointing out sin purify the soul? I don't know. Still, it's a ray of hope, and I hope Grandpa will see the light before he departs. But that's his business, and no one can force him to do it, or do it for him. Which means I'm only here as a witness. All I can do is wait.

Seeing you yesterday, I suddenly understood that the destination of this journey wasn't Grandpa, but being reunited with you. A lot of things will end here, but this is also a beginning. Our connection won't be severed once Grandpa is gone. It will always be there, tight as ever. And after today, it will be completely in our hands.

The Morning After

The sky is bright and the wind has stopped rattling the window. Gray light fills the room. On the table are two empty wine bottles and two glasses. Li Jiaqi goes to the window and looks out.

"The snow's not so heavy now," she says.

"I should go," says Cheng Gong, but he does not move.

Jiaqi looks into the distance. "I think I can see Dead Man's Tower."

"There was a fire a couple of years ago. It got burned down."

"There aren't any trees around there, how did the fire start?"

"Not sure. Kids setting off fireworks, I think."

Cheng Gong goes to the window.

"Kids like it there," says Jiaqi.

"All the bones were burned to ashes. Maybe that's what they wanted—the dead people, I mean. To not leave any traces in this world."

"Mm."

They look out the window. Snow covers the jagged rocks of Central Gardens, the winding pathways, patiently wrapping everything in the world, softening its angles.

Jiaqi turns to Cheng Gong. "Your spirit intercom. What happened to it?"

"Can't remember. I think it's in one of the boxes on our balcony. Why?"

"Wanted to have a look," she said. "Maybe it still works."

Cheng Gong shrugs. "It never worked."

"I remember once we were playing house, and when I sang a song, your granddad blinked. I thought I could use the spirit intercom to sing to him ..."

The man in the bed stirs. As Jiaqi and Cheng Gong go over, he opens his eyes.

"Everyone's here," he mumbles.

Jiaqi looks at Cheng Gong. "Maybe you should fetch the pastor."

"The pastor died two years ago." Cheng Gong looks out the window, frowning, trying to bring something into focus. His hand sinks into his pocket. "I'm going out," he says. "Cigarette."

Jiaqi watches him go, then turns back to her grandfather, Li Jisheng.

"The nail. Do you remember the nail?" she asks.

The man in the bed looks at her. An enormous force seems to be pulling him into a world behind him, a world whose gates will soon be shut forever. She strokes his forehead gently.

"Do you feel guilty?"

He stares at her, though his gaze passes right through her to some cavernous space.

"Turn off the light, it's too bright," he says.

Jiaqi goes over to the wall and puts her hand on the switch, but doesn't press it. The light is already off. In the gloom, she hears the man sigh. She goes back towards the bed, but pauses in the middle of the room. She listens. Silence here, silence outside. The walls vanish, the room is limitless. Jiaqi kneels and buries her face in his side. Through the blanket, her temples sense the shape of his hand. Jutting bones, which might conceal strength that hasn't yet ebbed away.

Jiaqi stands. On the TV is a village dirt road, a dog standing by a field. Subtitle: *In 1921, Li Jisheng was born to a farming family in this village. His mother had been widowed three months before this. All the villagers knew about her was her name, Liang.* The dog turns to glance at the camera then sprints away. A black-and-white shot of scattered village houses, which could still be in 1921. They'll dub this with a baby crying, Jiaqi thinks. It's so quiet in here. She hears another sigh, or maybe that's the wind shaking the curtains.

She walks out and sees Cheng Gong standing in the corridor, an unlit cigarette in his hand.

"It's all over," she says.

Cheng Gong lights his cigarette, saying nothing.

"I'll phone Peixuan later. She should still come back," says Jiaqi.

"Yes, I'm sure the funeral will be a big production." Cheng Gong stares at the flame in his hand.

"Hang on, I need to close the windows."

She comes back out, and shuts the door behind her. They go down the stairs. At the ground floor, Cheng Gong pauses and looks around the empty hall. "The social dance we saw that time—that was here?"

"Yes."

"The music teacher liked sitting by the east window. The overhead light made her look like she was in a Rembrandt painting. She must have known, that's why she always chose that seat."

"You boys all thought she was beautiful."

"And the girls?"

"We thought she was so-so."

"She got esophageal cancer later. I tried to see her while she was dying, but she didn't want any visitors."

"She didn't want to say goodbye in those circumstances."

"Now I feel that every time I saw her in the dance hall, under that light, it was a sort of goodbye."

"It's all over," Jiaqi says. "Did I already say that?"

"Yes."

They reach the front door. Jiaqi reaches for the umbrella leaning against the wall.

"You don't need to walk me out," says Cheng Gong.

"I could do with some fresh air, I've been indoors too long."

The snow is ankle-deep. Ahead of them is a blur of white.

"I was thinking, you could actually stay at the white mansion for a while," says Jiaqi. "No one will know you're here."

"What about you? Will you stay too?"

"I don't know. Maybe I'll go when I've dealt with everything."

"Where to?"

"The south." She smiles. "Somewhere warm, where I won't have to think of anything."

They keep walking till they reach the crossroads.

"Let's toss for it." Jiaqi pulls a coin from her pocket and hands it to him. "Heads you go to the train station, tails you stay in the white mansion with me. I'll bring you food. I've learned how to make egg fried rice."

"Can I have noodles?"

"No, I don't like noodles."

"Zhajiang noodles. Learn how to make them. It's really easy."

"Deal? Flip the coin, then."

Cheng Gong runs his finger over the coin and sends it spinning into the air. It lands in the snow without making a sound. They stare at each other. When they look down, the falling snow has completely covered the coin. He and Jiaqi stand there, listening to distant noises: a car engine starting, a dog barking, children shrieking with laughter. Sounds of early morning. Cheng Gong smells the aroma of frying meat. Thick sweet sauce bubbling in a wok. Wait, then wait a moment longer. Scoop it from the wok, mix with shredded cucumber, ladle it into a pure white bowl.

END.

JEREMY TIANG has translated over twenty books from Chinese, including novels by Shuang Xuetao, Lo Yi-Chin, Yan Ge, Yeng Pway Ngon, Chan Ho-Kei, and Geling Yan. His novel *State of Emergency* won the Singapore Literature Prize in 2018. He also writes and translates plays. Originally from Singapore, he now lives in New York City.

Book Club Discussion Guides are available on our website

On the Design

As book design is an integral part of the reading experience, we would like to acknowledge the work of those who shaped the form in which the story is housed.

Tessa van der Waals (Netherlands) is responsible for the cover design, cover typography, and art direction of all World Editions books. She works in the internationally renowned tradition of Dutch Design. Her bright and powerful visual aesthetic maintains a harmony between image and typography and captures the unique atmosphere of each book. She works closely with internationally celebrated photographers, artists, and letter designers. Her work has frequently been awarded prizes for Best Dutch Book Design.

The title is in Virtuose by Changki Han from Seoul. The letters grow thicker towards the bottom, narrowing the negative space and making them more like cocoons. They are stacked to form the shape of a water tower and to evoke the traditional orientation of Chinese script. The font of the author's name is Colonel Serial by SoftMaker from Nürnberg. The image is of marbled paper. The shapes are determined by the chemical reactions of the marbling process, not the artist, much like the individuals in *Cocoon* are subject to the whims of state power.

The cover has been edited by lithographer Bert van der Horst of BFC Graphics (Netherlands).

Suzan Beijer (Netherlands) is responsible for the typography and careful interior book design of all World Editions titles.

The text on the inside covers and the press quotes are set in Circular, designed by Laurenz Brunner (Switzerland) and published by Swiss type foundry Lineto.

All World Editions books are set in the typeface Dolly, specifically designed for book typography. Dolly creates a warm page image perfect for an enjoyable reading experience. This typeface is designed by Underware, a European collective formed by Bas Jacobs (Netherlands), Akiem Helmling (Germany), and Sami Kortemäki (Finland). Underware are also the creators of the World Editions logo, which meets the design requirement that 'a strong shape can always be drawn with a toe in the sand.'